rehabilitation

First Printing May, 2009
Second Printing October, 2009
room6 productions & Illegal Dog Press
Copyedited by Kimber Randall
© Timothy James Brearton, 2009
ISBN# 978-0-578-03487-4

For Jessica

BOOK ONE

REHABILITATION

I'm in Long Island City, Queens. I'm sort of back where I started. At least, I'm close.

It's hard to do this. Not hard because it's emotional (well, that's dicey too, okay) or because it's tough to remember (some spots are gone, yeah, and some are fogged right up like a drunken Christmas holiday), but it's difficult because of the drugs that are in my system. It's hard for my mind not to wander. I'm going to have to stop and start quite a bit in order to write this little epistle here. I'm going to have to jump around some, and grab what I can from my memory, and try to make sense of it.

She wanted to know what I saw happening. She wasn't satisfied when I told her "I see tanks, I see war." She wondered about the people that didn't have ailments, that didn't come for therapy. Were they going to be forced into it anyway? How do you force an entire country into something like that? I saw the people lined up, you know, with congenital heart failure, with type two diabetes, with heroin addictions, and they were all there to get cured. To get rewired. But she wanted to know about the healthy ones, about what *they* would do. If they would revolt. And yeah, I thought, they would revolt.

But then I thought something else.

I thought: there won't *be* anybody who doesn't show up. Not really. Maybe one in a thousand. Which, yeah, becomes about, I dunno, 600,000 people – I'm not so great with math. How do you organize 600,000 people all over the continent? You don't. They would just be there in the margins. If they babbled about the whole thing too much, tugged on too many sleeves, *wham*, a fucking bat to the head. And why wouldn't you? Why wouldn't someone just shut them up? A neighbor, glasses perched on the bridge of his nose, looks up from getting the morning paper across the lawn at the diffident who stands there saying, "You've been poisoned. You've been manipulated." Day after day, what are you going to do? That car salesman or accountant or press junket videographer living in Connecticut is going to do what anyone given enough time would do – they're going to take care of it. That dissenting neighbor is the new infidel, after all.

And people want it so bad, I would tell her, if I could talk to her now. We want to go back. To the womb, to the unconscious, to a place where someone else takes care of everything. We're like actors. We're just loosey-goosey from head to toe if you tell us what to do, happy as clams. But if you don't, we're lost, most of us, rigid. We need to know which drum we're supposed to be banging. We need to know which bandwagon we're on. Is the majority conservative this week, or are we really swinging for the trees on this one? Everyone wants to be an individual, I know. It starts with standing out in the school play in the second grade. You're *Mowgli* in *The Jungle Book*. See? I'm wandering. But what we want even worse? Security. It's not even that we want it, or think we do – we *crave* it.

So, that's what I would tell her, if I wasn't here, hooked up to all these tubes, these machines, if I hadn't been given these drugs. They poke and friggin prod me, man. And soon… well, that'll be "it" for this kid. A long way from where I started, but close to home. All the way to Costa Rica, all the way to the Northern Kingdom, and back again. Back home. Very near to you, old pal. This is where I'm going to die.

THE CITY

My name is Jack Aiello. But that's not my real name. It's enough for now. You can even call me X if you want to. X is an appropriate title for me. There are many exes in my life – ex girlfriends, ex jobs, ex friends, and especially, ex bars. Ex addictions.

I am also an X because I am, in some sense, *persona non grata.* I don't even exist. Not wholly, not really. Much of me is product. Government product, private sector product, one or the other, I don't know, but I'm going to find out. It is also appropriate to call me X, because X marks the spot. While I am not a fixed spot on the map, not a marker at the end of a dotted line where the treasure is buried, the artifact entombed, though I am valuable, I am also moving. I am a moving target. Currently I am moving south, on a Honda Shadow 850 motorcycle, a loaner, if you will, with a maroon tank and some rusted chrome. I am on Route 4, a smaller route, a no-trucks-allowed kind of route, staying away from the main arteries as best as I can. I am in Vermont, the Green Mountain State. Of course, even the smaller routes will be doomed to surveillance soon, as will everything. The Man is headed that way, and there seems to be no stopping him. Personal freedom is history. I only hope I can get to see my daughter in time, before anything else happens, before they try and take me back.
*

I also have gone by the name Jack Landi. I was thinking about this name as I roared over the hilly Route 4 on the way to see my daughter. I was thinking about this name, as I think about all the names I have had, because each one represents a time period in my life that is distinct, that stands out for me like a chapter in a book. When I was Jack Landi I was wrestling with an addiction to cocaine, but primarily it was my relationship with alcohol that was the most troubling at the time; if I wasn't drinking I wasn't doing cocaine, so you can see the situation there. I was practicing what has been called "moderation management" in those days. Saying that I was "practicing" it though is really giving myself too much credit, inferring that I have some sort of willpower where really I seem to have a big problem with willpower – my willpower seemed to have a mind of its own, driving me to do things that I probably shouldn't have been doing (I think of stomping on George Klembeck's head, bottle of vodka in my hand) and not working with the things I needed it to be working with. My willpower was a lot like a motorcycle, like the very two-wheeler I was piloting down the winding Vermont back route to see my daughter, and, conjunctively, Katherine Glaston. When I had somewhere to go that wasn't a great destination, a place to go that was going to take me away from the people that loved me and the things I needed to be cherishing and not taking for granted, that bike ran like a top. But if I needed to get to some place good, some place to heal, to sit, to be in the moment, to be in the universe and not running from it, to, really, let's be honest, to face God, that goddamn engine wouldn't even turn over. Or, it would, and I'd get going for a little while and it would sputter to a stop.

When I was Jack Landi my metaphorical two-wheeler was doing that start and stop, jerking occasionally to life and then invariably quitting on me. I was in Costa Rica then, and I was working with the Brandis brothers (who'd stayed back in Brooklyn), and it was my first big job for them. A billionaire by the name of Calvin Blair had been kidnapped. He was a billionaire because he was involved in gambling – internet gambling had made him the tycoon he was – and the Brandis brothers had one of their fingers in his honey and it was hurting them that he had been kidnapped. Not so much the computer tactics, in Latin America, not so much identity theft, just the hacking into the physical space of the rich mark and the theft of his very person.

But wait a second. I can't start telling you the story here. That wouldn't be fair. Things don't always work chronologically, do you know what I mean? They may have happened that way, but they don't make *sense* that way. Where this really started, where it makes sense, is in the city. What they call the "Queen City." For real. Here's the deal:

I always knew I'd be that guy chewing the hell out of the red straw, sipping on a watered-down Coke, knee bouncing like a jackhammer. I always knew it, kind of like how you know you're going to kick off someday. It's there, right on the back porch in your brain, but you don't want to switch the light on it; you don't want to see the full form of the figure standing in the dusk. I always knew I'd be that guy, eyes darting around, nervous, agitated, chewing on that red straw that I would flatten out and then rotate so the width could be mashed down next (repeat process if desired). And I desired. I always knew it would be me, I just didn't know it would be here, now.

I had first gone to work for the Brandis brothers, Lincoln and Lucius, when I was sixteen. They'd sort of been like uncles to me. When their nephew Philip turned up missing in Burlington, Vermont, they sent me to find him, to bring him back. I didn't really know Phil, only as the nephew. I never expected to hear he was dead in a place like Burlington. Not here. Not when kids were being tied to chairs and starved in Bed-Stuy. Not when cops were getting shot by other cops at White Castles in the Bronx. No way. Half that shit was what drove me to drink in the first place. Burlington was supposed to be nice. Nice and friendly and gay. I wasn't gay, but I figured that a town full of gays couldn't be all that rough. Lots of festivals and singing and stuff. Like San Gennaro, but with different kinds of meat. I'm kidding. Hey. If you were in the situation I was in now, as I write this, you'd be goofballing it too. Blowing off a little steam. You would be, for real.

I knew I wanted to get sober for the first time when I saw this friend of mine do it. We'll call him "Marcel Moresco." Back then I didn't even know I had a problem. I got bored, sure. But depressed? No way. I went out and partied like a rock star until four a.m. but I could be up in front of a jury the next day testifying how good my life was going; how everything was shaping up just right. Marcel Moresco was a clerk at an electronics store, but he moonlighted as web designer back when nobody knew what web-designing was, including me. That was his nook.

Marcel was at a bar one night, called *Nice Guy Eddie's,* on Houston Street in Manhattan. I remember looking over and seeing him sit there, being pretty low-key, and he was drinking seltzer. Seltzer with a lime in it. I had kinda known, at the time, that Marcel had quit drinking or something, but I hadn't found out until later that he had gone away and did rehab and all of that. He'd really put it out there. Marcel had been thirty-two when he sipped on seltzer-with-lime that night in New York. I was thirty-two now, and there I was, at one of those round, high-top tables with three "friends," drinking the kind of bar-tap Coca-Cola that has that smoky, rusty aftertaste, my right knee jackhammering, the sound *taptaptaptaptaptaptaptap* as a buckle on my boot struck the chrome legs of the high stool repeatedly. By now the poor squashed straw looked more like a mangled twist-tie. Your eyeballs would probably disappear into your head if you tried to suck some soda through it.

Daniel, the guy to my right, was a real sweetheart. He wasn't a "Danny," or a "Dan," and no way was he a "Dan-o" (I had known all three of those types during my "former life", each version of the name a skin-tight suit that the guy fit into, the connotations were so accurate), this guy was a "Daniel." Soft spoken, polite, effeminate, well-dressed, Daniel *was* Burlington. Burlington was the new Chelsea and Daniel was its poster-boy. He had on those black, rectangular glasses. Do you know what I mean? I mean, I know that the metrosexuals can wear them now, but it was the gay guys that really pioneered that look, if you asked me. Bully for them. The square glasses, the high-n-tight messy hairdo (Daniel's hair was black – blacker than mine) and that coat that came down to the backs of his knees, one of those tan coats that looked like it was inside out so you could see the fluffy seams. Daniel had his own company called *Wildcat* and it was all about saving the planet and preserving the local ecosystem. (I'd seen the Winooski River by then, and on a good day it was only maybe slightly less polluted looking than the East River or the Hudson. I half expected to see a body come to the surface and bob and twirl along in the brown water when I'd pass over it, with its matted dreadlocks, worn, crushed-cork sandals and all.) Daniel worked out of his home. He didn't get out much so he was kind of pale and skinny. Plus, Burlington was always overcast with an ashen slate of cloud cover. Daniel was a nice enough guy though. He was my new roommate.

On Daniel's right, across from me, was Peter. Peter had a big beard and played the congas, or the congos, or the djambe, whatever the fuck those African drum-things were. He smoked pot and drank a lot and was in a couple of different bands. He represented the second Burlington contingent. So did Josh, sitting next to him. Josh had a trimmed beard and drank a little less. He was calmer than Peter who got really fucking going and wouldn't shut up or stop performing for you when he was drunk. If I was drinking still his antics probably would have been a riot. Sober, he just seemed drunk and lost.

The missing contingent in our little group, after Daniel the gay save-the-earth type and Peter and Josh, the jug-band disciples, was the college student. Burlington had a huge college, UVM, and that college spilled down from the hill and cascaded into the cafés and bars that ran along the paving stones of Church Street. The college was kind of like the mansion on the hill that presides ominously over the quivering, helpless small town whose residents are all dependent on the dweller of that mansion in some way; the college students were the impish lords of the town. They were the embodiment of their parents' money that the pizza-throwers and club-owners wordlessly, expressionlessly pocketed to send home and help more Italians and Mexicans and Peruvians and Ukrainians hump their way out of despondency and into the good life here in the green mountain, brown river state. I knew one of those Ukrainians, actually. Vince Horbachefsky. His family was down in Brighton Beach and he'd come up here, all of eighteen and standing six-foot-three, to sling some dope and try and get laid by the meek, crunchie college girls that he sniffed after. That was until one of them fended off the big Russkie by kicking him in the balls so hard he passed out. She'd had two college boyfriends take him and dump him in the woods along the Winooski River. They didn't know that Vince was a diabetic and when he came to, already sugar deficient and slipping into shock, he was disoriented and couldn't find his way out. His works for his diabetes were in his backpack which the frat boys had tossed into the woods along with his lunky frame (God how they must have struggled.) He never found his works and died of seizure. I can see him in my mind, his body flopping around in the snow-crusted leaves like an electrocuted fish.

I was about to finish my Coke and head to the bar for another one, wondering how much longer I could hold out before the Drink seized me and I would break down, toss a twenty onto the bar and start ordering shots of *Patrón*, when the guy I was looking for came into the place. His name was Terry Hackford, and word was he'd been friends with Phil Brandis, and he had taught at UVM. He was my lead. I wasn't going to confront him or talk to him or anything like that (without the booze I was far too chickenshit for any hipshot, gunslinger action like such.) No. I was just going to slink around. Watch him. Maybe follow him home later. With no booze in me at night I had lots of time to fill.

I walked self-consciously over to the bar and the bartender was there. My heart did a gallop in my chest. Daniel had brought over the first round so I hadn't seen her – I couldn't have known. She was beautiful. My tongue dried out and swelled up in my head. I set my glass down, my eyes flicking away from hers and I eked out, "Coke, please." Wordlessly she placed my glass in the sink, took another one down from the rack above her head and filled it with ice. I pretended to watch Terry as she did this, but my interest in him had been completely eclipsed. Suddenly I didn't give a shit about Phil Brandis or his supposed death or this supposed acquaintance of his, Terry Hackford. In that terrible moment, I just wanted to know if I could ever, *would* ever get laid again now that I didn't have the bottle to imbue me with that *Casanova* spirit.

Two days later and I woke up with what felt like a scorching hangover in a grassy field overlooking Lake Champlain. My body ached like I'd been beaten by a baseball team, but I realized as I sat up, squinting in the overcast haze, that I hadn't. My chest and lungs ached from the two packs of cigarettes I'd inhaled the night before (one pack leading up to my relapse and one following) and my head ached because I was dehydrated and toxic.

The demons were with me again. They didn't hop around on the grass and hiss and spit like you'd think demons would. They were in my brain. Demons would get into my brain and monkey around in there and cause me to think all kinds of horrible shit when I had a scorching hangover. They would get in and infect my thoughts, my hearing, my vision. People's eyes would glow and enrapture me with horrible knowing guilt when I had a scorcher. The whole world would know that I was wrong, that I had done wrong.

Daniel would be wondering where I was. He was like that. It was like living with a woman. He wanted the place neat, okay, sure. And he claimed he didn't care about where I went or what I did, but there was that look he'd get on his face when I'd show up late or fall out on a promise to be there for dinner, to have some of his homemade *miso* soup followed by the sharktail dish he'd found on some Asian cooking website. It was like living with a woman again, yeah. But it was alright. I'd told David that I was a recovering addict, and he'd nodded and looked at me sympathetically with tacit understanding. I honestly think it's why he gave me the room. I think he wanted to help me.

I sat up in the field, palm pressed to my temple. On the bike path went a rollerblader (not hot) followed by two chicks on mountain bikes. The chick in tandem looked over at me. She had a purple bike helmet on. I tried a smile on for her and she quickly looked away. As my smile faded I realized that I had disappeared from reality once again. And I realized that I never should have had any kind of conversation like the one I'd had with Terry Hackford in the bar that night with Daniel and Peter and Josh. I just couldn't help it. I wouldn't have, really, if it hadn't been for him. If he hadn't actually shone up at the bar right when I was sitting there, then things wouldn't have gone like they had. I'd be up right now after doing yoga with Daniel and eating egg whites and hummus. I most certainly wouldn't have been here, lying in this dog-shit-ridden patch of grass along the lip of Lake Champlain.

I wanted to kill Terry Hackford for that.

"How ya doin?" I had asked Terry.

"What's up."

That's how any conversation begins, if it's going to begin, between two white dudes that want to be forgotten by the world in a place like Burlington.

I bobbed my head and looked away. I looked at the greens and browns of the liquor bottles on the three-tiered shelf behind the hot bartender. The bottles were backlit by fluorescents and they glowed and shimmered. My head bobbed and swiveled 180 degrees in the other direction. Then, on a string, it swiveled back. I couldn't stop myself. Buzzless, I hadn't the courage to talk to the vixen bartender, but I could talk to this guy. Maybe it was because I was angry. Still, I was tactful. Thank the god of Sobriety for that.

I asked, "You teach at the college here?"

Terry was watching the bartender pour his draft a little further down from us, where the taps were. He looked at me sideways. "No," he said.

"Cool," I said. He was lying, or there was something more. He was bobbing his head. I was bobbing mine. Behind me I heard Peter going off about something, trying to be a riot again.

"I like this town," I said. I sipped my Coke. My whole body was vibrating. Was this what adrenaline felt like? Back then, I didn't really know.

"Oh yeah?" He looked back to the bartender as she flushed some of the head off of his beer and finished filling it. She started walking toward us. I thought she looked like a supermodel and shrank back from her.

"Yeah," I said. I was losing him. She placed the pint in front of him. "Four-fifty," she said, and I marveled at the way her jaw and her lips worked in concert. *God damned.* But I was over those women. I needed a normal girl. One who would treat me right. One who would make me eggs in the morning. A family.

He paid her and my mind fluttered. I said: "I have a friend that used to live here."

Terry smiled at the bartender. It was a good smile. Direct eye contact. The kind of smile that could get a guy laid. He was of average height, square-faced with a reddish brown bushy crewcut and stubbled jaw. I wondered how much he'd had to drink before walking in. I wondered if he was one of these guys that didn't need any booze to be suave with chicks.

She made his change and he left her a deliberate skimpy tip. He left her the coins. *Oooh,* I thought, *good.* Then he looked at me. He stood there against the bar and sized me up. My hypersensitive sober mind could feel his judgment rape me up and down like some red laser-sensor. His eyes cast a disinterested, dismissive look my way, half-lidded as he took the first sip of his beer. My dry mouth started to water.

"You have a friend that used to live here?" He swallowed the sip. Some foam from the head stuck to his upper lip and he licked it off with the tip of his tongue. Even his tongue was masculine. I wasn't sure if he was going to say anything else or disappear into the crowd. Then he said: "Who?"

I swallowed saliva. I lifted my eyes from his drink. I felt a calm come over me, and I had no idea where it came from. "Vince Horbachefsky," I said.

I don't know what I expected. Maybe for him to pull out his six-gun and try to blaze me down. Maybe for him to take a step my way and bare some knuckles. But he did neither. He took another sip, looked into the room and said, "Don't know him."

But I knew he was lying about this too.

I had been dodging the cops for years in Brooklyn. I'd just get back from another night and as I'd stick my keys in the door a cruiser would be lit up on the street behind me, barreling along to catch another law-breaker. I'd cross myself and push the door open.

Terry Hackford never had any fear of the law. He was probably from the suburbs.

"It's a long, hard road that leads out of hell and up to heaven," Terry said. He leaned over to his buddy, Rupert, on his left. "Izzat how it goes?" Rupert shrugged.

"Anyway," Terry went on, "I think Hell and Heaven are states of consciousness. You know? They might exist after life, and they might exist before life, but they exist in life too. Probably they exist in life more. We probably extend them – what's the word? – project them into this afterlife, or whatever. But I think they're here. I think they're states of mind."

I was nodding. I'd heard this type of talk before. It was usually the type of talk a guy like Terry got into around his second pint of the local, microbrewed ale. I imagined he had a t-shirt somewhere rumpled in his closet with the brand name of the beer on it. I wasn't interested in the talk. Not just because of what was happening now, but because it made me uncomfortable. You had to have some device with you to talk about these types of things. Either you had to have a pint in front of you or a lectern to stand at and a string of letters after you name. Philosophers and scientists and religious types talked about this sort of thing like they were solving a puzzle. Like life was a game removed from them and they could review and study. I didn't feel that way. I just felt empty, with nothing to say. The only thing I might have been thinking was whether or not Terry Hackford had it in him to kill somebody.

That, and I was thinking: Why am I still in a goddamned bar? It seemed to be the only place to conduct the social business. It was where the people congregated. Where else was there? Every other venue was fleeting. You couldn't really talk in a supermarket (not that I'd ever wanted to) or at the bank, or on the street, not at any length anyway. What did people do? Where did they go? The gym? Did they talk at the gym? On hikes or long walks? What did they do at home, with the television blaring, or music pumping out of the speakers? There was only the goddamned bar. I looked around and inventoried the patrons there with us. They were the typical cross-section. College students, musicians, dreadheaded skaters, guys with black-framed glasses on, girls with white button-down tops on. There were two guys sitting in a booth along the back wall, young guys, dressed in suits, looking like a couple of dot-comers from years past, but otherwise it was all the standards.

Did someone like Terry have it in him to kill a guy? Why did I think so? Terry was only a name the Brandis brothers had given me; making my spite of him into a conviction of murder – was that what I was doing? Still – could he have been the one that sent Vince Horbachefsky off to whatever might be this 'state of consciousness,' like heaven or hell? All I knew was that he kept looking at me, and he kept looking at the Coke I was drinking. He would look from his pint to his buddy Rupert's pint and then to my Coke glass with darting eyes, and then he would look at me briefly. He didn't like it. I could tell. It made him uncomfortable that I wasn't drinking.

"So you said you had a friend used to live in town?" Terry slugged from his pint after he asked me and looked around the room, appearing disinterested in any answer to the question he'd asked.

I swallowed. The Coke was making me thirsty. "Yeah," I said.

"He split?" Terry looked like he was considering another pint.

"Sort of," I said. This was my big moment. "He's dead."

Terry didn't flinch. "Oh yeah? Sorry."

"Sorry, dude," said Rupert. Rupert was drinking slower than Terry. He was a big guy and he sat with a hunch, tucked into the round table, his big shoulders rounded in. He had black hair and a scraggly black goatee. Everything about him was scraggly. He was what my dear, late gramma would've called a "slouch."

"Thanks," I said. I took the red straw out of my glass and began to chew on it, deciding to play cool as best I could. "I didn't know him that well, really. But still…" I looked at Rupert's face. He was eyeing the glossy table top. "You don't expect people to die like he did in a place like Burlington."

"Oh yeah," Terry said, looking over at the bartender, "we have homicides here."

Homicides? Did he just say homicides? My heart started to thump again. My mouth felt even drier. I wondered if I had those little white curds at the corners, like marathon runners get I would see crossing the Brooklyn Bridge. I licked my lips. "How did you know it's a homicide?"

Terry looked at me. It was a sharp look. I couldn't tell, right away, if it was a look of indignation or a look of guilt. "I remember Vince," he said, "now that you mentioned his death. One of those things. He had diabetes, or something." He stood up. "Rupert?" "I'm good," said Rupert. Terry looked at me again and his eyes slid down to my soda. "Another, umm – what was your name? Sorry."

I gave him the alias again and said no thank you. Now I just wanted to leave. But I felt like I'd gotten under the lip of the rug just a little bit. As much as I wanted to get out of there I wanted to pull that rug back some more. I had to.

Terry was already over at the bar. A second bartender, a short brunette cutie that I hadn't seen yet, beamed at him. Terry was a dick, I decided. And a pompous dick at that. I knew women tended to eat that up, as much as they might profess the opposite. It was true, it was true. It was hard to get close to a pompous dick, and women were drawn to that. They might tell you up and down that they wanted someone sincere, someone who they could be close with and trust, but Terry was the real lady killer. He kept them interested. He kept them in pursuit, and that's what they wanted. The longer the pursuit the bigger they thought the pay off would be. It didn't matter that there would be no pay off. There would always just be Terry being a pompous dick. I suddenly found myself wondering why I cared so much, and realized I didn't want to think about the answer.

Instead, in that moment, oddly, I found myself thinking about Daniel. Word was going around that Daniel had gotten drunk a few times and fooled around with girls. There was a clandestine, loosely gathered group of people I'd come across that were placing bets on whether or not he would eventually consummate one these drunken, moonlight excursions. I felt a little protective of Daniel, and didn't like the talk and the gambling at his expense, but I'd be lying if I didn't admit I wanted my roommate to take a solid hit for the team.

Terry was back. I thought he was going to make a remark about my not drinking, as his mouth was open as he sat down. Before he could say anything, though, there was a loud crash and I looked up to see the cute little brunette bartender leaping over the bar.

Daniel came in one morning, bleary-eyed and acting hungover. This was unusual for Daniel. Daniel was a homebody. Like I said, he worked from home. Not only did he work from home but he cooked from home and he watched movies at home and he usually had his dates at home. I had met one of his dates not long ago, a chunky kid named Arnold who looked like he had been on the streets for a while, like Daniel had found him there. Daniel had that Mother Theresa thing going on. He was trying to save the planet, or at least the planet's environment, trying to get people to sustain the population, to sustain their businesses, to sustain peaceful relations, all of that sort of thing.

From what I was told, Daniel was different from the typical homosexual. I didn't know what the typical homosexual was. I had known a few in my Brooklyn days, more in my East Village days, and they were eclectic. Some were junkies and just sucked dick to get rock. I don't know if that made them gay or just desperate. Some were flamboyant, some were promiscuous, some dressed just like you and me and you wouldn't really suspect anything until that twinkle came into their eye after a couple of vodka tonics and you felt like they were looking at your stomach from time to time, or their eyes wandered up to your hair. When I left, anyway, it was especially tough to sort out or define the whole gay culture thing. That new title was floating around, "metrosexual" and a lot guys I knew would shop at *Dolce & Gabbana* and gesture kind of girly but they were still supposedly into chicks. I mean, none of it makes any sense to me anyway. Just because a guy puts mousse in his hair certainly doesn't mean he's gay. I knew guys in Benson Hurst that caked-up their hair with goop every morning before going out and breaking open other guy's chins with baseball bats.

Anyway, Daniel was supposed to be unusual because he wasn't all about looks, like gay guys are touted to be. Apparently his ex-boyfriend, his partner for five years, was an ex-model, but none of Daniel's dates after that were, I can tell you. There was just no pinning down what Daniel's "type" was. And then there were the rumors that he was getting drunk and picking up women.

"Late night?" I asked. I was in my boxers on the couch reading *Seven Days* and smoking. I had been smoking a lot lately. Though Daniel didn't smoke he never seemed to mind it. He told me that everyone in his family smoked and he was used to it. He told me that his mother used to scrub the walls because of how yellow they had gotten in his nice but modest Vergennes family homestead.

He scowled at me and said, "Did any one call for me?"

"Where's your cell phone?"

He waved a hand in dismissal at me and headed for the bathroom.

So was she good? I didn't have the heart to ask. Suddenly he popped back in the living room and stood looking at me. He'd been wearing a tie the night before, I remember, but it wasn't on him now. His shirt was untucked and his usually steel-reinforced hair was sticking out in weird places. His hangover, if he had one, seemed to vanish and his mouth opened. He put his hands on his hips and looked at me.

"Is that a black *eye*?"

My fingers went to my eye right away and probed gingerly around. "Yeah," I said.

He sat down on the ottoman, crossing his legs. "What happened?"

That was Daniel. If there was any sign of crisis or need he forgot all about himself and got right into it. He was a good guy, Daniel. It was a shame what they were doing to him, and how I never got to thank him for all his kindness.

I proceeded to tell him the story.

*

The cute brunette bartender had hopped over the bar and into the midst of four jug-band disciples having a heated argument. *Aren't these guys supposed to be a peaceful people*? I wondered. I also wondered how it had slipped my attention that there had been some altercation brimming. Normally I was keen to these kinds of things, as was supposed to be my "vocation," but this instance had slipped right by me. I must have been too wrapped up in the Terry Hackford thing.

The jug band disciples were arguing, two-on-two, and the brunette bartender stepped in between them, outstretching her arms. Her arms made me think of the containment bars we used in packing trucks when I was doing that kind of work – a steel bar with notches on it that you spread so that it pressed against the walls of a cargo van or truck, holding the contents in place. She looked strong like that.

The guys were swiping at each other over her head. Then one of them connected a blow and it all broke loose. The bartender was crushed in between the two teams and Terry Hackford – Mr. Pompous Dick Superman – rushed over. Soon it was an all out bar brawl, the likes of which I had never seen, even in my so-called raucous youth.

I happened to glimpse two other guys, the guys I had seen before, sitting in one of the shadowed booths along the far wall, watching and smoking. They were sliding off the bench seats now, looking like they were going to get out of the place. Suddenly I was off my bar stool and walking quickly after them – I felt their guilt in the scuffle somehow was implied, but I didn't know why. Maybe it was the black suits they were wearing. They'd

looked like corporate guys, and much out of place for this Irish pub.
"Whisperers," my gramma would've called them.

I got a couple of steps and was punched by an unseen adversary.
What am I calling him an "adversary" for? He was a douchebag. My nose
stung and my eyes were filled up with tears so that everything looked like it
was behind some watery prism. Rupert helped me to my feet. I was looking
at his face and trying to blink and focus on it when he spun away and said
"No!" I turned to look in that direction and that was when I saw a fist, and
Terry Hackford driving it, coming straight at my head.

The next thing I knew I was on the ground, looking up at Rupert, he
of the Terry Hackford disciples, who was saying something to me. His
voice was lost in the shouting going on. I tried then zero in on what they
were saying, the dudes that'd started all the bloody knuckles and busted
teeth and torn shirts, and I heard:

"You're a liberal fuckin' pansy! You know *exactly* what it said in the
contract! Once you make a commitment, you stay the course!"

"…government *by* the people, *for* the people! We were *totally* within
our rights as a company…"

Here I'd had it in my mind that these types of guys, the ones fighting,
they were *hippies*, man, they were supposed to be about peace and love.
And they were bashing the shit out of each other and arguing about
capitalism.

The two men in the suits were gone.

*

"Were there police?" Daniel was leaning towards me now, his eyes wide, his own previous night forgotten to him.

"Yeah," I said. "Cops came."

He sat back. "Wow. And…did you give a statement?"

"I told them what I was doing there and what I had seen, yeah."

"Did you, uhm, did you tell them who you were?"

"Yes. And no."

"Did you tell them about the guys in the suits?"

"No. No, I didn't say anything about them."

Daniel seemed to consider this. He looked at me and I could tell he was thinking about whether or not to say something. Whatever it was he swallowed down because he said, "I thought you New York boys were supposed to be tough." He raised an eyebrow.

"Anyone can get sucker punched," I said in my defense.

He cocked his head. "I thought a sucker punch was when somebody came up behind you."

"Go take your shower, Daniel. You smell like pussy."

He surprised me by throwing his head back and cackling. I'd thought I would have struck a chord there, but Daniel stood up and walked out of the room, his cackle tapering off into giggles. I heard the squeak of the tub knobs and the shower come pattering down. Steam soon rolled out of the room. Daniel took his showers *hot*.

"I know Terry Hackford, by the way," he called out to me.

I sat up a little. "Really? How?"

"We used to date," he said, and I heard the bathroom door close as I just about fell off of the couch.

Part of my cover was to get a job, blend in. So later that week I was pounding the pavement, looking for employment. My employers, the Brandis Brothers, had given me one big wad of dough upon sending me off, telling me it would be too conspicuous for them to send money once I was there.

I wanted to find something that was different than the day job I'd had at home – I wanted to reinvent myself. I hadn't had a drink since the morning I'd woken up on the banks of Lake Champlain, now five days down the river, and my head was fuzzy. I had heard from various recovering addicts that there was supposed to be a lucidity, a clarity that came from getting off of whatever junk you were on, but all I felt was hazy. I couldn't seem to sort my thoughts out, and that wasn't very, you know, conducive to making sense of the things that were going on. So I had a nice, convenient little comfort about why I had gone and gotten stinking drunk again; to sort things out. Ain't it grand, the mind of justification.

I found myself in front of the City Market. I'd been in there once – overpriced health food and overbearing hippie staff. There was a sign on the bulletin board for landscaping work. I thought about it. Why landscaping? I suppose the compulsion was because I would be out of doors, and it would be physical labor and it might help me focus my mind, those endorphins spilling down into me and all. And I was hesitant because I had seen some of these besmeared, darkly tanned landscaper-types stumbling home at seven o'clock in the evening as I sat on Daniel's porch. One guy, in fact, I had already seen three times, just like clockwork. At seven p.m., there he would be, side winding his way down the sidewalk, shoulders hunched, lost in the alcohol fog. *Poor Bastard*, I had thought, like I had been sober for 10 years. But it was the kind of job, I knew, that a lot of guys just got shitfaced after, because it was dead-end, and they knew it. I'd had a job like that, loading trucks; the day job. But I'd had another gig too. Yeah, I mean, well, yeah.

In truth, I was a spy for 10 years. I was a spy and I loaded trucks from a shipping facility near my apartment in Prospect Heights. The spy thing is not as exotic as it sounds – not all spies are Tom Cruise in *Mission Impossible* or anything like that. The stuff I did was usually pretty low-key. I would wear little disguises and watch out for people selling fake watches and shit like that. I didn't work for the police, exactly, but it was still involved with the law, let's just say.

The very next day was raining and I spent it indoors, watching movies on HBO and smoking cigarettes. Once or twice I smoked them on the balcony and I would see a jogger or two running along old North Winooski Avenue. I would be standing there with my hooded sweatshirt on, squinting into the rain and smoking and there would run by this girl, one flight below, with spandex holding in her prematurely flopping thighs. *It takes all kinds to make the world go 'round*, I thought, realizing I wasn't the first to have thought it and, unshaven and with a mild case of diarrhea, would go back inside to watch another movie or two and continue smoking in there. I'd stand looking at my face in the bathroom mirror a lot, too. I have dark brown hair and olive skin and green eyes. My nose is crooked; it bends to the left. Well, to me the left, to you the right.

Around the third or fourth flick the day thickened with gloom and I started to get restless and weary. It's an unnerving combination, the gloom and the restlessness, if you've ever had it, and I'm sure you have. So I went into my black zip-up *Filofax* and started checking my notes about Vince Horbachefsky, Phil Brandis, about Terry Hackford. I didn't last long and the notes made little to no sense to me. Some of them had been made while drunk that night, a torrent of them really, the majority, your Honor, had been penciled in, and while they were partially illegible, they read more lucid and sanely than the ones I had taken while sober. It was as if, while drunk, I wrote to myself considerately and thoroughly, probably thinking that I would need help to remember, when the daytime me, helpless and immured in hangover, would need that extra, kindly, guiding hand by which to make sense of the goings on. Notes written while sober were terse and cryptic. It was as though in this case I gave myself too much credit; I was too cocky or I thought I was being clever and codifying my notes somehow, or that it was the way of the world, to shorthand things like this, to make notes that were clever and staccato and encoded with arrogant beat journalism. So I stuffed them all back in the *Filofax* and zipped up the thing and told myself that I was taking the day off. It wasn't time for the real world job to start yet anyway. That wouldn't be until after the weekend, but still I felt it lurking there, a junkyard dog on the other side of the fence grinning at me, and soon that fence's gate was going to slide open…

"Resting up, champ?" Daniel would periodically walk by with one beverage or another – I think he was drinking Red Bull and Sprite – and make a comment. He wasn't doing it to get at me or to make me feel bad for laying there, he was just irritable and picking at things in general, just trying to be sassy, as if being sassy would keep at bay the tumult of his quandary over the sexes. I hadn't said anything to him about it other than the crack at him smelling like pussy. I didn't want to. Yes, I didn't want to rock the boat because Daniel was sort of my caregiver, my nurturer who'd taken me in like a stray dog, but I also didn't want to say anything because there was a time I had been ridiculed for some closet behavior – not the sexual kind, or drug-related or anything, but I was an in-the-closet painter for about two years, right smack in the middle of my twenties when I must have been having that sort of evil crisis, and when some of the guys loading truck with me got wind of it I never heard the end of it. It was like being called gay, the way the truck boys had fun with it, calling me *Rembrandt* and *Venus de Milo* without knowing what the fuck they were talking about but getting my goat just the same. I was sensitive.

"Yeah," I said, "resting up for the next round."

"For the next round," he said, and scuffed into the front room in his pajamas. The front room was his office. The place was a three bedroom, but the front room, the room with the only real light in the place, was his office. There were two gaping windows overlooking North Winooski Ave., and French doors that separated it from the living room. The floors were hardwood in there. The curtains at the windows were thin and white and rustled in the cool breezes. It often made me homesick for Brooklyn, that

room. For someone I didn't like to think about anymore. And it smelled of
a certain incense and candles in there that, though my Italian gramma had
never lit a stick of incense in her life and had only lit candles at church,
reminded me of her place on 7th in Park Slope, and of her warmth.

Daniel left the French doors open today and I was mindful of the
volume as Sharon Stone crossed her legs in the movie I was watching,
tossing an eyeful of her beav at the sweating cops in front of her, riding their
chairs backwards like they were cowboys.

They were protesting the war on Church Street. People were handing out
fliers and parroting, "Stop the war; get our troops home." It occurred to me
briefly that the two suits guys at the bar the other night could've been
recruiters, but then, raconteurs like them always wore their full military
dress to show off how snappy and elite the whole thing was, not dark
business suits like imitation mobsters.

"Stop the war; get our troops home," said a woman with a tight hair
bun that looked painful. "Take our paper," she looked at me and I kept
walking. "Opposition to the war is just more conflict," I said, my father
coming out in me. There were always books by *Krishnamurti* lying about
our apartment growing up, books on Buddhism and such, defaming violence
and suggesting that even if you were to be slaughtered, non-violence meant
total discursion, total abstinence. The woman with the tight hair threatening

to peel back her forehead bristled and said, *"excuse me?"* And as I passed
her I thought, *well, there you go, bitch.*

I wasn't for or against the war, or any war. People sometimes told me
in life you had to choose sides, but I always thought that choosing sides was
the source of most problems. Anyway, I was just trying to stay sober, which
was choosing a side, I guessed, and instead of getting easier, each day
seemed to get a little bit harder.

It was only noon and four p.m. – the itch zone, I called it, or "period
of appetence," Daniel once said – was a ways off. If I could just get through
the evening without cracking I'd be starting a new job as a landscaper the
next morning. The storm had passed over. There drew slivers of a yellow
sky in the east and it looked like it was going to be a hot one within 24
hours. I was walking along the paving stones of Church street, passing these
protesters with their fliers when I saw Peter, the bearded drum-beater from
the bar, coming out of one of the restaurants – a health food joint, one where
they made smoothies with "boosts" and all of that, you know, spirulina, and
wheat grass and all of the rest of the "homemade cures" – and he was taking
off his apron, lighting up a cigarette.

At first I felt myself trying to avoid him. I thought of ducking into a
store or something, but that was the old me, the guy who was always on the
paranoid lookout for someone to expose him – to expose him for his closet
art tendencies, for busting crooks like the ones he consorted with, or expose
him to a girl he nailed in one cloudy drunken, puffing, all-promises haze.
Awkwardness. Hungover days were always a minefield of potentially
awkward, threatening moments. It was no way to live. Plus, I had to talk to
him – he was the best thing I had going to get me closer to Phil Brandis
since Terry Hackford had…fuck. You know. So I made eye contact with

the wild-animal-eyed Peter who was already looking at me and I walked over. There were white plastic chairs scattered about so we took to a pair of them.

Peter seemed genuinely happy to see me, and I had no idea why. "Hey," he said, "what's up, man? I'm genuinely happy to see you." He shook my hand. There was no grip to it, but it was all right. It was Burlington.

"You too," I said, and we sat. "You on lunch break?" I was chewing on my red straw; rotating, chewing; rotating, chewing.

He scowled and looked in at the place he'd just come out of – *Soulshine.* "Nah," he said, "lunchtime is too busy for breaks. We take breaks later in the afternoon, when it slows down." He looked down at his lap where he was balling up his white, red-streaked apron. "They just fired me."

I blinked, I paused in mid-chomp. "They fired you? Why?"

"Ohhh," he said, "lot of reasons."

"Like?"

"Ohhh, I show up late. And I got a couple of drinks wrong. Here and there."

I looked at him, looked at his eyes. "You stoned?"

"A little, yeah."

"Drunk?"

"A little, yeah."

"Uh-huh." I leaned back after examining his eyes and catching a wiff of his B.O. I don't know why, but I felt a bit big-brotherly about the whole thing. I don't have any siblings, so I don't know how that whole thing works. Still, there it was. And, you know, I put Peter at about mid-twenties.

Thing about the twenties is that – and probably you've heard this, it's nothing holy-shit coming from me – the thing about the twenties is that the first half is great. You know, you're rising toward the Promised Land. I scratched the inside of my cheek with the red straw and thought about it. Seriously, you are on your fucking horse and you are riding toward that distant land (that always remains distant) and people are cheering you on. Somewhere in the middle of that ride the people start to disappear and the terrain gets rough and lonely and, well, you can figure out the rest. Something descends, anyway, something changes and suddenly no one is interested and you are alone. It was like the New York Marathon. Crowd there in the beginning, crowd there in the end, just you and the hot pavement for the stretch of it. Peter seemed like he was getting there, to that stretch, and I felt for him. I only wished I could tell him that it got better.

"So what are you gonna do?"

He shrugged and looked around. He squinted to the east, where the sun was breaking even faster, the clouds blanching and peeling away. "I dunno. Get a new job." I had the hunch that Peter was couch surfing and didn't have a place of his own. I wondered why Daniel hadn't taken him in – or, for that matter, if he hadn't already at one time or another. Peter was a stand-up kid, once you got past the beard and the dreadlocks and the smell. "How are you doin'?" he said. "You find anything? Daniel said you were looking for work."

I wasn't happy – kneejerk reaction, instilled from days past, you see- that Daniel had said anything to anyone about me, but I smiled anyway and told Peter I had found some work landscaping and told him where the ad was that I saw and that he should check it out.

"Yeah," he said, nodding, "yeah," but he seemed noncommittal. He just kept nodding, and grinding away at his apron. Peter didn't strike me as the nervous sort, even at the prospect of being unemployed, so I asked him, just on a lark, "You got something else in mind?"

He squinted to the east again. I kept my eyes on him. "Nah," he said, still looking that way, and shrugged. Then his gaze returned to me and it looked like his face had just remembered who he was talking to. Not being arrogant, I'm just saying; when I first walked up Peter acted like he was being visited by the Living Christ (which he resembled in his own way, a bit, as did a few of his kind here in the Queen City) and whatever had stolen his prostrations away was there in that moment. But before he could speak someone came out of the *Soulshine* place and gave us a dirty look. It was a girl, perhaps thirty, my age, and she put her hands on her hips and generally looked sour and uppity. "Peter," she said, "please. This is a business."

"What?" He threw out his hands and looked at her in a familiar way. "I can't just sit here?"

"Peter." She looked at me right after she said his name again and gave me something of an eye. I liked to think she was checking me out, a little bit, but she probably thought lowly of me given my company, the bitch.

"Want me to buy something?" Peter was getting agitated. He was fumbling and pushing into his jeans pocket like he had just done a line of coke. He produced some crumbled single dollars, which looked rather greasy. "Here," he said, "here, I'll buy something. Here, take it out of my severance pay, okay? Take it. Get me a fucking banana-strawberry enema, okay? Here." He tossed the sad crumpled ones at her but they were stolen down street by the breeze. I found myself stifling a smile and ground the straw with my molars.

"Peter, that's it. I'm going to call the cops then."

I stood up. "That won't be necessary." I turned to him. "Peter, come on. Let's go, man." He looked at me, saw something in my eyes, I guess, and got up. He nearly snarled at her as we walked away, and he kicked over one of the white plastic chairs.

"That's damaged property, Peter!" She called. "We'll have to withhold your last paycheck!"

He turned and opened his mouth but I caught him by the shoulders. I spun him back round before he could yell back at her. I smiled at him and after a minute a big grin broke out on his face and we were walking hurriedly down the street. "This isn't the wild west," I said. He nodded and looked back but we kept walking and he was still grinning and so was I. B.O. wafted from him with the momentum but it was alright, I'd smelled worse. "A banana-strawberry enema," I said. I laughed. "You should have said 'with a two-finger boost.' Now that would have been funny." He howled at that and we were nearly running. I'd found my first cronie in my new life. Maybe Daniel's altruism was rubbing off on me, maybe I was just getting lonely, maybe I really did care about getting a little closer to Phil Brandis. It all felt good anyway, so good that we went right over to Peter's friend's house and proceeded to get stinking drunk.

I woke up early the following morning with another scorching hangover and the onset of severe paranoia. Where was I? Why did I come to Burlington? Who were these people? Were they even people – did they really have

names, or was it all just an illusion? Was there some reason I was here –
some sort of mission? Already the hallucinations of detoxification were
settling in, as were the cloaks of denial. I was still a little drunk, so the
worst was yet to come. I decided to take advantage of the lingering
analgesic effects of the drink and phone in to the landscaping firm I was
already 15 minutes late showing up for. It was 7:15 in the morning and I lay
there concocting my story.

    Of course, the night before, after I'd gulleted down the first two
rounds of drink to push hastily past the tremendous guilt that I was, indeed,
relapsing and drinking, I felt like I would still be getting up to work without
incident. *No problem*, the drink assured me, *this is nothing. This is a little
bit of fun. You owe it to yourself. You have been good. This is just a little
parting gift. You'll be fine.* And I listened to the voice and I drank and I
drank and I drank some more.

    Peter's friend's house was a waystation for all sorts of musicians and
party girls and deadbeats and poets and people saving the world one bong hit
at a time. After those first couple of drinks that I sucked down as a
wallflower, and my guilty eyes spent their purpose mainly fixed on my
shoes, I started to become my old, rambunctious, charming and drunk self,
shaking hands and leaning in to make introductions and witty remarks over
the blaring music, cutting jokes and perpetrating carefully crafted and wily
antics for all to enjoy. I rose to star status in a matter of hours, in a matter of
a few drinks, and at the crescendo of the evening was crooning along with
Peter as he banged on his guitar, marveling at what a voice I had and what
harmony Peter and I had together, soaking up the adulation of the poets and
deadbeats and earth-savers as they nodded along with great mops of hair and
sloshing beverages, thinking to myself that this was the way it was supposed

to be, this was how people were supposed to behave, this was *life*. I could have painted, had there been canvas.

Somewhere at the end of the evening I thought I saw the two men in suits, off in a far corner. I tried to walk across the room to them but I tripped. There I'd blacked out and awakened the next morning on one of the downstairs couches. (That couch, to me, had been wonderfully charming the night before, a real thrifty grab, a real old-school number with striped upholstery and orange stuffing puking out of the seams. Even the dog hair had been perfectly quaint, a sign of real life, of real people, of real organic stuff that makes up life – the stinking lot and mess of it – all okay to me in my inebriation, all really magical and soulful and fine and *real*. The next morning the couch, stained and lumpy and old and covered with those white-tipped, coarse dog hairs that were all over me, which I hastily scraped off, was a disgusting pile, a testament to those who stooped to sub-standard living, an infestation of germs and bad smells and allergens.) I wondered if I'd only dreamed of the two men in suits.

Seeing and hearing and deducing that there was no one else yet up besides me (I suspected a human being under a lump of covers on the ratty recliner across from the couch) I rolled off of the couch and set out to find the phone, which, if I remembered (I think we had called for a pizza the night before) was in the kitchen. It was.

"Champlain Landscape, this is Belinda."

"Hi," I said, and felt that my voice sounded level, "is Tom there?"

"No, Tom is not here. Tom is on site. Can I take a message?"

I told her my name and told her that I had just been hired and that I was supposed to work that morning. Alas, I told her, as I had just moved here I had a crisis back at my old home and needed to return for the day –

would there be a way to keep the job? Then I pulled my trump card – I had another healthy, able-bodied male that would be willing to start with me ("oh yeah, fucking great! I'm in! I love the outdoors!" Peter had spit out when I mentioned the prospect to him over our sixth *Double-Bag Ale* the night before) – would that be something Tom was interested in?

"I don't know," said Belinda, "he might be. We have some new contracts and as you know Tom has been advertising for help. Would you like me to ring his cell phone? If you give me your number I could have him call you right back."

"Oh no, no, that's okay," I told her, "I don't want to interrupt him while he's at work. I mean, it would be great if you called him, to tell him how sorry I am about this unforeseen turn of events, but it's not necessary to have him call me back."

"Okay. That's fine. Thank you." She hung up and left me unsure, left me paranoid that Tom was going to bellow into his cell phone at her and that I wasn't going to have a job after all. I would say that I didn't care, and, sober, I wouldn't have, but with a good guilt-ridden hang over like that, any of the slightest misdeeds on my part felt mountainous in their retribution. I would pay for this; I was bad, I was wrong, I was a liar. I needed to stop drinking once and for all. All of that jazz.

I skulked out of the apartment and I skulked home, avoiding the main streets and trying not to be noticed by anybody. My plan was to get back to my apartment with Daniel, slip into my bedroom and remain there for 24 hours. It was like quitting junk, it was like quitting any narcotic, and I would have to seclude myself and wait it out. That was my plan, anyway, back when I still thought I was the one calling the shots.

When I saw Terry Hackford along the street it didn't occur to me, not then, how it all was being orchestrated by something larger than ourselves.

A higher power, you might say.

Terry was all apologies; he was a different guy all together, outside of the bar. "Dude, I'm so sorry I hit you. I didn't even know it was you. I thought it was one of those crunchies, man. I was just going to lay one of them out in the fracas, you know? Get away with a good crack to one of their greasy heads. You okay? Man, you went down. You okay now? You look…"

He was talking like he had been up all night doing lines. But, of course, he didn't seem to be strung-out in a bad way. Terry was one of those guys I hated – could drink all night and stay up and do lines and get fucking *housed* and then hit on the cappuccino girl at Starbucks the next morning with the aplomb of a millionaire bachelor.

I was looking all around and at the ground and at the passerby in the park we were in. I could feel my blood rushing up my neck – my nerves were kicking in fierce, my capacity was maxing out and I was having an anxiety attack. I needed to run. I needed to get away from Terry. What was worse is that he looked at me in this kind of oddly compassionate way.

"You alright? Rough night last night, *amigo*? You need to sit down."

I need to go, I wanted to say, but instead found myself sitting down on a bench with Terry Hackford. I fixed my eyes on a legless vet playing chess with a blonde kid and tried to quiet my racing mind, tried not to be so hyperaware of everything. Terry settled in, put his arms out on the back of the bench and seemed generally at peace, if not a little concerned for me.

"Yeah, some hangovers can be bad. Like, it fucks with your head. You see and think things that aren't real."

It was surprising to hear this coming from a guy like Terry, and I couldn't help responding. "But what's real? How do we define what's real? If I think it, if I feel it, then isn't it real?"

"Yes," said Terry, leaning forward, putting his hands between his legs, "I think reality is what's collective. I think it's the truth we strive for – stability, contentment and so on. I think reality is how you see these things around you right now, people driving their cars, going to the bank, talking to each other on the street."

"But those people are all at different mindsets. They are all going through their own version of it."

"Yes," he said, "but they're working at it. You know? It's all about your conscience. If your conscience is clean, then you're going to be okay. And sometimes you've gotta work to make your conscience clean."

I couldn't resist. I looked him in the eye for a moment, but got that ripping sensation, that intensity of his soul, or another person's soul, and I had to look back at the chess game. Still, I managed to say, "And how's your conscience, Terry?"

"Clean as a whistle," he said, without missing a beat, and I noticed that there was no condescension in it, there was no reproach. He just meant it. Or, he was a hell of an actor. Terry, I thought, like so many others, was capable of controlling his mind. Maybe he'd been in the military. Maybe he'd learned how to "train the mind," while mine was still something I considered a cross between a wild animal and a madman at the controls, someone other than me. He may have done all kinds of reprehensible things, and still be doing them, but somehow he told himself that it was alright. I rued it. I rued him. Still, part of me was marveling at these uncharted waters I was sailing along in with my new confidant Terry Hackford. "Clean as a bird," he said, and pulled a medallion of some saint or another out of his shirt, and kissed it. "Oh," was all I said.

"So," he said, "you gotta do whatever it is that makes you feel clean. Some people can get away with being dirty, but only for so long before it gets them."

"I got a job," I said. "No priest, though."

He ignored the comment, or hadn't heard it. "Oh yeah? Doing what?"

"Landscape crew."

"Which outfit?"

"*Champlain Landscapes*, something like that."

Terry nodded. I looked at some squashed gum beneath the bench we sat on, then back at the chess game with the no-legs veteran and the blonde kid.

"You don't think you could be dirty and just are blessed with the ability to tell yourself that you're clean?" The blonde kid make a move. The vet stroked his jaw and contemplated the board.

Terry laughed. "Blessed? I don't know if that would be a blessing or a curse," he said.

"What about Vince Horbachefsky?" No sooner had I decided to ask the question than it was already halfway out my overworking mouth.

Terry looked at me, some of his amicability gone, and something passed in the shadows within him, I was sure of it.

Terry was the name the Brandis brothers had given me. Terry
Hackford. They'd heard about the death of Vince Horbachefsky, and when
Phil, their nephew, went missing, they'd linked the two, perhaps, and given
me Terry's name. They hadn't said why, and I hadn't asked. You had to
know the Brothers. But, then, you wouldn't really want to.

"I told you what I knew about him. Had diabetes. Died. Unfortunate,
thing. You got something else on your mind?"

"Phil Brandis," I said. We were into it; so be it. Let the anxiety work
for me. Let the panic earn its keep.

Again I was sure I saw something pass through Terry, this time at the
mention of Phil's name. Some internal switches flicking on in there, some
recognition Terry tried to shield. He turned from me then and watched the
chess game. "You ought to back away from this," he said. "I don't think
you know the stakes. Sorry about the other night, the shiner." And with that
Terry Hackford got up and walked away. I thought of going after him, but I
didn't. He would have to wait.

I sat there for a few minutes watching the crippled war veteran finally
give up with queen to the blonde kid, whose face was oval and calm. I
realized that I was learning to socialize all over again. When you drink
regularly, your social encounters are with an altered state of mind. Small-
talking in the post office or along the street corner is something you
developed. Persistent altered states atrophied the ability. Not that it was this
great thing to do, small talk – it was unavoidable. Better to be prepared.

Two days later, as scheduled, I rejoined the land of the living for the
second to last time. I would have one more slip, and a bad one at that, but I
felt good. I was walking the walk. Terry was right that night in the bar,

though he got the quote wrong. The quote is: "Long is the way and hard, that out of hell leads up to light."

I left the park, and went back to Daniel's for one final day of something we all might call normalcy, thinking about this idea of collective reality.

I was given a rake and a trash barrel and was expected to provide my own gloves. I had Peter with me – he'd actually made it; he'd shown up on time and everything and, to my amazement, he had bathed.

Our first job was in a cemetery. The cemetery, Stender Hill, was visible from Pearl Street, abutting McIntyre street on the south end and North Winooski on the east. On that side the grounds bordered residential homes, and I immediately found myself wondering how anyone could live with their backyard as a cemetery.

There were three of us: me, Peter, and an older guy named Les. Les had a small, wiry body, reminding me of the actor Billy Bob Thornton. He had big, horsy teeth, the color of pearls, that must've been veneers or falsies because he chain-smoked worse than I did. Les didn't say much. For a few minutes after we'd arrived and Peter and I had introduced ourselves to Les, a pick-up with *Champlain Landscapes* on the door rolled up. It was a little rattletrap Toyota pick-up and the woman driving was rather large. The small truck dipped to the driver's side under her weight. It pulled up to the curb and when the big woman got out, the shocks squealed and the pick-up

righted itself with a bob, making me think of a floatie-doughnut in the pool
after an obese occupant slid off for a dip. This was Belinda.

Champlain Landscapes was a true-to-form Mom 'n Pop operation,
with Tom as the pop and Belinda as the mom. I hadn't met Tom in person –
I'd been hired by phone – but I imagined him to be as skinny as Les, maybe
even more so, once I caught sight of his wife, Belinda. My gramma had
read a book to me as a child called *Socks for Supper*. The couple in the book
was very poor and had a sad little scraggle of a Christmas tree. They often
had to eat their socks for supper. What was more, the woman looked no
worse for it – she was a big plop of a thing. The husband was quite thin –
apparently any leftover sock went to the wife. I never ended up meeting
Tom at all, just his large, new age wifey. Looking back, I now know that
this one day on the job was the gateway, this small business man I never met
and his large, squishy wife the gatekeepers to the new world that I would
come to call real.

Belinda had a belt saddled around her girth that, upon first glance, I
thought was ammunition. As she hoisted the tools out of the truck bed and
tossed them to our feet, I reconsidered and thought they were cleaning
products. "Magnets," Belinda said, observing where my eyes had fallen.
Belinda also sold magnets. She lauded the power of magnetism and sold
them on the side. She was convinced she was going to be a millionaire and
that everything was in the power of positive thinking. The Law of
Attraction. *The Secret.* She told me later that day, that if you *wanted it*, you
had to *envision it*. You had to believe it and it would stream right out of the
universe to you. She was into *The Secret* before the secret was out, before
the "Law of Attraction" blanketed the world, an oversimplified candy for

new-agers who were desperate to be smart about something when likely they were born to privilege.

In the meantime, Belinda explained, magnets helped to assuage a bad back (like hers) or could enliven you with energy, calm your anxiety, help you think straight, ease muscle pain, even prevent disease. She walked around with that funny little belt on, the Velcro straps holding cigarette-pack-sized magnets around her shadowed waist like she was a comic-variety superhero. I liked Belinda. I wondered if those musicians who'd been in the bar brawl the few nights before could've benefited from a couple of magnets.

That first part of the day she was relatively close-mouthed and all business. She curtly introduced herself and threw down our implements. She explained that there was a large plot that needed maintaining in the center of the cemetery and she would come back to get us at lunchtime, and we were expected to be finished by then. "Moss and lichens on the headstone," she said, "I want that scraped off. The bushes pruned, the plot raked and the grass standing straight up. Get rid of any debris from the trees; toss it in the burn barrel. Don't throw any sticks or anything on the other plots." I thought to ask her about the regular caretaker, if there was one, but kept my mouth closed. The day was grey and I had sunglasses on. I chewed on a fresh red straw, instructed not to smoke. Peter watched and listened to Belinda with his mouth slightly opened. Les said nothing and looked around at the cars passing by, the sky, the sidewalk. The air smelled like spring blossoms, car exhaust and wet leaves – that fruity-rot smell. I could hear distant voices of people – locals, mostly tourists – marshaling down toward Church Street, a few blocks away.

We went to work raking the site. Les was the senior landscaper and delegated to us once Belinda left. She'd pulled him off another job – Tom's orders – to kind of train us and get us going. I scraped moss and lichen from the headstones, Peter raked the leaves and Les went about the pruning. The plot was a large one – six stones in all. The family had two names, Milton and Renault. The stones were a mess and I wondered how in the hell I was going to get them all shining by noon.

"Where you from, Les?" Peter asked. Peter was very amiable.

"Milton," said Les, and I glanced at the headstone I was cleaning with a small yellow wire brush. I said nothing.

"Oh yeah?"

"Yuh."

Peter asked him about it, and it turned out that Les had been a dairy farmer for years. He'd lost the farm (he didn't say why) and was now landscaping. I wondered what he made an hour. I found myself asking Les, "So you've lived in Vermont all your life?"

Les stopped pruning and looked at me. His eyes were small and he squinted even though the day was overcast. "Mostly," he said, and went back to pruning. I asked him, "You ever heard of a guy named Vince Horbachefsky?" He kept pruning. His back was to me. "Heard about him, yeah." I didn't say anything. I scraped. "College kid with the diabetes," said Les after a few moments. "Found in the woods."

"Yeah," I said. "What about Phil Brandis? Ever heard that name?"

To my surprise, Les said, "think so, ayuh."

"Really," I said. "What do you know about him?"

"Went missing like the other fella. Had something to do with that commune group."

I glanced at Peter. He was busy raking with his head down, his back in to it. I didn't know if he was listening or not. "What group would that be?"

Les was clipping away and then he stopped. He reached into the bush and yanked on something. A second later and he was flittering orange-colored dead brush to the ground. "Whaddoo they call that?" He considered it, looking at the orange-colored detritus. "A *movement*," he said.

"A movement." I considered this. "Like a spiritual movement?"

"I had a movement this morning," said Peter. He was listening after all.

"New Age. Generic food, or something. Junk." Les was pruning again, standing back now and then to examine his artistry.

"You mean genetically engineered food?"

"I think I heard about them," said Peter. He paused and leaned on his rake. "They have a commune, right. But they're not, like, hippies." Peter was unaware of the irony. He pronounced "hippies," like he might be saying "they're not communists"; he clearly did not associate himself with such a clan – hippies. "They're very organized," he continued, "and they dress up and go out and sort of invade the public. Very organized, clean cut. I think they have some sort of a business. They–"

"Let's get to work," said Les. He was looking at Peter. Peter went back to raking, saying "yeah," and putting his back into it again.

My mind was jogging. This was key information. I felt good.

When noon came around we weren't finished. Belinda took Les aside and talked with him seriously while Peter and I stood a few yards away, waiting. Then we all piled into the truck – Les opting to hop in the back – and Belinda took us off to the next job site, cleaning up a park where the city had been working on the sewer line. The smell of sewage still hung in the air. Nothing was said about us not completing our first task on time, we just went right into the next, with Les moving away from us and not saying another word for the rest of the day. The last thing I remember from that day were the maintenance crews on site of the sewage mishap standing around in their orange vests and talking about "brown trout" and "white mice."

I was awake all of that night. Luckily in the morning it was Friday and I only had to work through the day until the weekend arrived. As soon as Saturday morning rolled around Peter borrowed his friend Josh's car and the two of us drove north to where Peter was sure the commune was located. Such was the end of my job cover – two days of landscaping.

     We arrived in a town called Eden (that's its real name). The place was a ghost town. No one on the streets, vacant storefronts, blinking yellows. Peter, though, was a real scout – his nose took us right to the local bar.

     "This is where they're at," Pete said, and I could only assume he meant those among the living in Eden, Vermont. He got out of the car and shut the door behind him. Seeing that I hadn't moved, Pete opened the door back up and leaned in. "You coming?"

     I looked at Pete, then I looked across the street at the bar. A red *Labatt's* sign flickered in a dirty picture window. The window reflected the street, the car, me in it, Pete obscured behind the car where he stood in the gutter. There was no seeing in the window, but I knew what waited in there.

"Go ahead," I told him. "I'm going to sit and go over my notes."

I had no notes; I'd gotten finally frustrated enough to give them up too. Pete bounded across the street, his dreads bobbing, his loose clothes flapping in a summer breeze. *My representative,* I thought. I tried convince myself that I was, really, going through notes anyway, in my head. Allowing for Pete to do some of the grunt work so I could think. Reflect. That it had nothing to do with the fact that if I walked into that bar I was going to walk out drunk.

Sometime later I awoke from a doze. I banged out of the car and crossed the street. I could tell by the long bands of parking meter shadows that the day had lengthened. When I got to the door I realized I wasn't breathing; I'd held in my breath. I exhaled and opened the door.

The place was sundusted in the front and cavelike in the back. An enormous bar ran the length of the wall to my left, stocked with every liquor imaginable. To the right were four booths, and, in the back gloom, a pool table, more booths, and a couple of round tables that listed one way or another like they belonged on a pirate ship. The bartender was a woman in her forties or fifties, thin, her skin taut and wrinkled, her bony elbows poking out from rolled up flannel sleeves. I nodded to her as I entered and she eyeballed me with the mixture of disdain and resignation a small town bartender has for tourists.

Two old coots were curled into the bar, talking. Whom Peter had referred to as "they". Both the men looked over as I walked toward the back, unabashedly giving me the same eyeballs as the bartender, only not with contempt, but with a sort of cynical amusement, possibly with certain scenarios passing through their minds that I was not privy to, but most likely involving my ridicule some how, or perhaps not so malignantly, my dissimulation of their weathered ways.

I saw right away that there were three figures in the back and I imagined one of them to be Peter. Though smoking was disallowed in Vermont bars and restaurants, I could see the lenticular drift of it under the pool table light and scented it in the air, along with the odor of spilled, spoiled beer and the tincture of various liquor poisons. As I drew closer I could sort out that Peter was not among the three figures. One of them rose from a round table and cracked into the balls on the pool table's green felt, a riveting sound that was very loud in the quiet bar. Another of the three walked to a battered jukebox and began plugging in quarters. As I reached their area, not seeing Peter and unsure how to proceed, *Sweet Home Alabama* began to blare. "Turn that down, Rusty!" The bartender was shouting over to the man standing at the jukebox. *Rusty*, I thought.

The three figures were three men, looking each about the same age and socioeconomic status as the two tucked into the bar. At the end of the back room was a hallway that led to the bathrooms. The door banged open no sooner than I had figured this and another woman came out, surly, spindly, and smoking a cigarette. She was watching the floor as she walked but her eyes rolled up to me and her fingers went self-consciously to her cigarette. "Woops," I said, just a whisper, and stepped to the side so that she could pass. She said nothing. I stood there, like an idiot, looking into that back hallway. Then I decided to go into the men's bathroom.

"Bathroom's for paying customers," the bartender called to me. I walked back to the bar.

The bottles on the shelves behind her, towel draped on her shoulder, vibrated and chattered like the F train was running below, like an earthquake. They clinked and clattered, the bottles, and I saw the *Stoli*, and the *Sweet Vermouth*, and the jar of olives, and they all jittered and rotated and clinked like axle rods in an alley. It wasn't an earthquake, though, and it wasn't the F train. It was the jukebox. I snapped out of it. "Turn that shit down!" The lady bartender stomped her foot when she yelled out the command and flipped the towel off of her shoulder and slapped the bar with it. Then she looked at me and said, "yeah?"

I ordered a Coke, feeling the eyes of the two men at the bar, the three at the jukebox, the lone woman with the long cigarette, all crawling over me, and I began to sweat. I paid the bartender, cursing Peter in my mind. "There ya go, lady," I said. I started to get angry. I took my Coke, sipped, and walked to the rear of the bar again. I entered the men's bathroom. No Peter. I started to grow more angry still. I set my Coke on the sink. Where the hell had he gone? I heard a toilet flush behind me in one of two stalls. Peter popped out, his face flushed. He winced when he saw me and said, "Oh, dude. Sorry. Hadda drop a deuce." I hated the euphemism. I had never been impressed by it. I was no longer impressed with Peter. "You've been in here way too long," I said. It was an uncomfortable scene, there in the grimy bathroom. "I know, I know," he said. He turned and went back into the stall. He reappeared with a glass in his hand. It smelled like Jack Daniels. "How many of those have you had?" Peter shrugged. "Three?" He gulped it down in front of me.

I knocked the glass from his hand and it shattered against the graffiti-scrawled wall, its contents smattering. Peter's eyes widened, his head jutting out, his lips pursed from drinking and his hand still in the air. He maintained this position for what seemed to be a long time, and then recoiled from me.

I couldn't stop myself. I grabbed Peter by his shirt with one hand and his dreads in the other. I saw the old violence in my mind. I saw that kid, George Klembeck – remember him? – getting the piss stomped out of him with Ryan and Victor at my side. There was no mirror in the bathroom, but for some reason I wanted one, I wanted to show Pete his own face. I wanted to see mine behind it, snarling. Instead I hotwalked him to the door, spun him around, and shoved him up against it.

"Hey," he was saying, "hey, hey, ow, ow." Up against the door he said, "I was taking a shit, man. I had a *movement*."

I let my grip loosen. I felt my heart pounding, rattling my chest. I thought of the rattling bottles.

"Hey," he said, "I was doing what you wanted. I was asking around. I hadda buy a drink man – the lady said I had to if I wanted to use the bathroom."

I let go of Peter, and my hands flopped to my sides. I looked down at his sandaled feet. I nodded, then, the sort of big nods you see people do, up and down bobbing, their whole shoulders and head, and I said, "I know, I know."

I stopped bob-nodding and looked back up a Peter. His head was turned away from me a little, his eyes locked-on, unsure. I brought my hands up and he flinched. For some reason that sickened me, and I thought I might throw up. The stink in the bathroom was not helping. I had the rusty taste of the soda in my mouth. I turned away from Peter and went to the sink and ran the tap. I suddenly needed water in the worst way. I splashed a couple of cupped-hands-full into my mouth and when I turned around again, Peter seemed a little more at ease. "So you get anything?" I asked.

Peter nodded his head. "Yeah," he said. He licked his lips. "Yeah, I got somethin'."

I left the Coke on the sink and we left.

One of the old coots in the bar had told Peter that he knew of the commune before Peter had needed to drop-trou. We headed southeast out of Eden. The commune was supposedly somewhere on the fringes of the Green River Reservation and so we started looking around – by that I mean we took a right turn off of the state route which cut through Eden and soon found ourselves at a dead end. We'd passed a couple of ramshackle homes but nothing else. There was no sign indicating the reservation. We could go back to the state route and drive further north and then turn right again, Peter suggested. We could just walk around, Peter suggested. We could go back to the bar and ask for more specific directions, Peter suggested. He banged out of the Subaru and took a piss on some honeysuckle. I stepped out after him, and gazed at the end of the road.

"We keep goin' in," I said.

The road didn't really end; it became wagon wheel ruts, maybe a logging road. The Subaru might make it – but it might not. It could bottom out and Peter didn't want to risk it. *Another couple of Jack Daniels, maybe,* I thought, and knew that I was jealous of his altered state. We had brought

some camping gear. I had never been camping before, and now here I was
in the remote wilderness of the Green Mountain State. I told myself it would
be a good idea. Afternoon was tumbling into evening and I figured we
should hit the logging trail before I got too edgy.

"Josh won't mind if we keep his car overnight?"

"He's all wrapped up in this Aspen girl," Peter said over his shoulder,
still leaking, legs straddled.

"Oh," I said. "She's from Aspen?"

"No," he said, shaking off, "her name is Aspen."

I looked at the logging trail ruts. They went on for a while and then
bended out of sight, maybe an eighth or so of a mile away. "Does he always
date girls named after cities?" Peter looked at me, puzzled. Then
enlightenment dawned on his face. "Oh," he said, "no. His last girlfriend
was named Susan."

That was Peter; I forgave him.

We rustled up the camping gear and headed into the woods.

I don't know what I expected a commune to be like. I had heard about
communes, of course. When I thought of a commune I thought of
dreadlocked, beard-wearing, unwashed hippies growing vegetables. I
thought of shanty shacks and fires going and some central advocate wrapped
in a sundress with a wreath of hibiscus around her neck and a tiara atop a
nest of sunbleached hair, decreeing orders she read from a scroll. I also

thought of the David Koresh-type commune. I pictured a cult of people bowing and chanting. I had heard of the Oneida community, the one formed by John Noyes in the mid-1880s. Noyes was eventually lynched for sexual relations with a young girl, though part of the commune's policy was freedom from sexual exclusivity. I had heard they now manufactured silverware. Jim Jones had dipped his pen in the communal ink at Jonestown, everybody knew that. I envisioned people carting pails of water from a babbling brook or people dressed in black robes carrying staffs and murmuring some obscure creed, brainwashed by their demented leader. I also figured that communes couldn't be infinitely sustainable. It wasn't within human nature to be content. Humans were about progress, about seeking, about power upheavals. Change was inherent in man, and in the culture of man. Man's culture was always in flux. There was no way a commune could remain unchangeable – something always happened that dismantled it, usually something from within.

I was thinking about this sort of thing – about entropy, I guess you call it (you were always the smart one, old pal), as we made camp. Peter showed me how to pitch the tent. I had some experience lighting fires, but of a different kind. Peter was a real woodsman-pro at it. By the time the sun had dropped behind a ragged row of evergreens we had a fire going, the tent erected, our sleeping bags unfurled, and we were settling in. It was eight p.m. and the air was developing a twilight summer chill. The fire crackled and I could smell the burning pine – a pleasant and comforting aroma, better even than peanuts at a hot dog stand. Around us was silence and the shadowmasks of the forest.

Peter was rubbing his head. His eyes were heavy and bloodshot and I figured he must be coming down from his drinks back at the bar in Eden. I

was about to say something to him about this when we heard a snap in the
trees near us, and then a flash of light.

The light bobbed at us in the dark perimeter of our campsite. The fire
rendered the night surrounding us darker – the sky above was still a
thickened blue, hazy along the jagged line of treetops. In that inky blackness
backdropping the fire, the oval light floated and seemed to come at us and a
disembodied voice boomed, "You two can't camp here."

The light bounced toward us and a figure stepped into the firelight. It
was a man bearing a moustache and wearing official looking fatigues. There
was a patch on his left breast reading "FPR". On his hip there was a gun.

"We didn't know," I said.

"Yeah, we didn't know," said Peter, "sorry."

I checked my watch. It was 8:15 p.m. The figure swung his flashlight
over to examine me as I did so. "You need reservations to camp," he said,
"this isn't even a park campsite."

"Where are the park campsites?" Peter asked.

The man jerked the flashlight over to him. Peter flinched in the glare.
"Not here," said the man. The man seemed to scrutinize Peter. He looked
around the campsite, probing with his flashlight. It felt like a hand groping
us over. "I'm gonna have to ask you to pack up and leave."

"Sir," said Peter, "we're not from here. Are homes are a long way
away."

"Well," the man said, unsympathetic, "there's a motel back in Eden.
Or in Lowell. I suggest you go there."

My mind started working. I felt suddenly courageous. Maybe it was
because I'd resisted the temptation to drink back in the Eden bar. "Sir," I
addressed him, "we're looking for something."

The flashlight beam came back upon me, crawling over me. "What?"

"We're looking for a commune."

"A commune? There is no commune on the reservation. There is a reservoir here, there are public campgrounds, but there is no *commune*." I couldn't see much of the man's face with the light trained on me, but I put him at about my age. He seemed older, with the authoritarian garb and the gun, but I didn't think he was. I thought I could smell liquor, but it might have been Peter. "Are you with...?" I didn't know how to finish.

"I'm with the Vermont Forest, Parks and Recreation Department. Now pack up and get going."

"We hiked in about three miles," said Peter. He seemed to be psychically with me. I silently praised him for it. "How are we going to get back to our car with all this gear in the dark? I mean, will you lead us out?"

The FPR guy seemed to consider this. The fire popped and crackled between us and him. With his flashlight lowered I could see the shadows thrown by the fire on top of his cheekbones, the slope of his forehead. "You drove in in the white Subaru?" Peter and I exchanged a look. "Yessir," Peter said.

"That's not three miles from here. More like a mile, maybe a little more. You'll be fine."

"Sir," said Peter, but I already knew we'd reached the end. The FPR guy stepped toward the fire. "Look, pack up your gear, walk out of here. Do it or I'll have to make you do it."

I saw the gun plainly on his belt, and I saw his radio. I wondered if he was out here alone. I looked over at Peter. *Enough. Let's hit the road.* Peter seemed to understand. "Okay, okay," he said, his hands up, palms out. "Very sorry for the trouble," I said, and started rolling up my sleeping bag.

Peter did the same. The FPR guy stood watching us for a little while until
we were breaking down the tent. I wondered why he didn't have a vehicle.
Was he just wandering around out here in the woods? Was there another
road nearby? As the tent collapsed I heard him say, "Next time make a
reservation and camp in designated camping areas."

Once he had walked away and disappeared beyond the throw of the
firelight, his voice floated towards us. "Don't let me catch you back here."
Then there was rustling and cracking as he ventured back into the woods.
My eyes found Peter's. *Shhh. Wait a little bit.* Again, Peter understood.
We folded the tent in silence – a rather consuming task in and of itself.
When enough time passed I said, "You know, I guess I'm a city boy, but
isn't he worried about the fire?"

"Exactly," said Peter.

"And is there, whaddyacallit, a ranger station around here
somewhere?" I said.

"It's like he just came out of nowhere," Peter agreed. We listened in
the stillness for the sound of truck engine, a four-wheeler, anything –
something we might have missed before with our chatter and ruckus. There
was nothing. I was once more impressed with Peter – it was official, I had
deputized Peter, He of the Jug Band – and he looked at me and said, "Do we
follow him?"

I looked beyond the fire, back at Peter, and nodded. "Yeah," I said.

*

The FPR guy had about a five minute start on us, but I was confident that we'd be able to track him – don't ask me why; maybe it was because when I needed something enough, a drink, a gram, I'd always been able to find it. I had to need what I was after. It made for a shitty snoop, I'm sure.

We had one flashlight of our own but Peter and I weren't going to use it. It was still faintly light and we could see enough to make our way along. We'd put the fire out and hidden our gear in the bushes around the small clearing we'd made a campsite of. Now we only had the clothes on our back, a flashlight and cigarettes. We had no food with us. Neither of us owned a cell phone.

We headed in the direction the man had left in and scanned desperately for sign of him – his flashlight – and listened for any crack or snap or brush of his movement. After what might have been an hour slogging along in the tangle of underbrush, dead branches that pawed and scratched at us it had become completely dark. I felt a hand on my shoulder and could smell Peter's ripening B.O. I wondered if Daniel would be worried about where I was. I wondered if he was getting drunk and unclasping the bra of a young UVM student. I wondered if we were being watched.

"I think we're lost," said Peter.

We continued on. When my watch read 3:12 a.m. we were both so exhausted we opted for sleep. The night had grown colder and we put our backs together for warmth. Once I finally fell asleep I dreamed about a group of black-robed disciples in a great field, chanting and worshiping at the altar of an enormous wooden bear. I saw Terry Hackford's face partially hidden underneath a black hood. I saw Phil Brandis, disrobed, being carried toward the bear-idol. Little naked children ran around leaping beneath him. Finally I saw the man in the FPR fatigues sitting in the driver's seat of Josh's white Subaru and peering out into the night, his face still flickering with the shadows of our campfire. And he was drinking.

THE COUNTRY

I should tell you a couple of quick things, some you know, some I never told
you.

I was born in Fort Greene, when the neighborhood was still relatively
rough-edged, and throughout my youth I witnessed the gentrification of my
home, the "whitification" of my neighborhood, and the recession of crime
and poverty. I'm white – that is, I'm of Irish descent and Italian descent; my
father so dark people could have called him black if it wasn't for his wavy
hair. My mother was very fine and fair. Her hair was auburn, almost red,
but not quite. I have an early memory of my mother when we lived in a
third floor walk-up efficiency apartment. We had to share a shower with
three other apartments on the floor. In the memory she is sitting by the
window and I am either in her arms or looking at her – in truth it feels like
both, like I am cradled in her arms but I am also standing there, watching
her, maybe watching her and myself at the same time. I don't know why I
remember it this way, I just do. She is there and I am there and she is
rocking me in the chair and looking out of the window and humming a tune.
Then she was singing the tune, she just sort of broke out into it, and I was
stunned at the quality of her voice. I don't know how I could have known
that my mother had a great singing voice – probably every kid thinks their
mother croons like Nina Simone – but I just knew it, and she did. She is
singing and staring out the window and rocking with me and I remember

thinking that I wanted to be just like her – I wanted to be detached, like she was, I wanted to just be able to sit and rock in a chair and gaze out the window despite the fact that the summer temperature was climbing up over one hundred, and we weren't allowed an air conditioner in the apartment because utilities were included with the rent. How could she be so aloof? How could she be so – for lack of a batter term, considering – *cool*? I really liked that. I remember really liking that. I remember noticing how my mother could always turn a bright face on no matter who she was talking to or what she was going through at home, with my father, with her family, with anything. She was like an actress – more, she was like a secret agent. She could conceal anything. She could walk up to someone with a hatchet sticking into her forehead and say what a nice day it was and have them commenting on the weather with her; they'd forget completely that she had a hatchet stuck into her. She could make you see, she could make you *un*see, and I remember that first day it dawned on me, there in the rocking chair, like any other kid's memory from the cotton fields on down: *My mother can do anything*.

I saw my father frequently, but it was in fast motion; my father moved very quickly. Everything he did was done with great speed and dexterity, always with this intent scowl on his dark, fisted face. My mother was a slow-mover. I today, am a slow-mover. I inherited my mother's sloth gene. I do just about everything slowly, yet at the same time I have the nerves of my father, the high-strung gadabout, it's just that it's stuck down deep inside. There's an itch I can never scratch, an amount I can never achieve. I suppose this is why I abused alcohol the way I did – I was always trying to "get there," you know? Even though I looked like I was taking my ponderous time about it inside I was racing red hot and thirsty to get there and to drink it down and to solve it and to fix it and go and go and go.

Loading trucks is great for this kind of personal proclivity. Only they said I moved a little too slow. I could keep the pace, when reminded, but the good part was that I was anesthetized. The work totally numbed my mind because all I was thinking about was loading that truck. Well, it's not all that I was thinking about, but everything else at least receded to a background din instead of chattering in the foreground, crowding me in and clattering away.

My dad was around plenty, moving quickly, lithely. He was tall and took great strides and would have looked clumsy or brutish standing still, like he had the potential to be clumsy, but he was dexterous and he was light. There was a light touch to everything, there was a kind of grace about the tall, dark-skinned man, and that is my dark secret. My dark father is my dark secret and it is this: he was an artist.

My mother was something of an artist too, but my mother didn't do too much about it. She didn't seem to care. She sang and she made our little apartment on Willoughby look very nice and quaint and from time to time I think I caught her sketching things, but that was about all. My father was an artist about everything. Everything he did, I now understand, was art. I think there's a quote – "everything the artist shits is art" – and that was my father. He was a plumber and he was an electrician and he worked in our building and other buildings as the maintenance man of sorts, working by reference for property managers and landlords, and my father would take iron and copper and make sculptures and he would use scrap plywood and luan and use it as canvas and make oblique images that were dark like he was and he would sometimes do specialty work like tiling – and my father was never satisfied. There were other jobs he took, moonlighting that he never told me about, maybe even never told my mother. I heard my father reading poetry to my mother on more than one occasion from my bedroom, and I saw him once through the crack in my door where I spied in on them and his chest was out like he was having trouble breathing, his head tucked back into his neck and his cheeks were red – really they were a kind of purple, the blood rushing up under that perpetually tanned skin – and he was reciting a poem to her while she held her head down, her hands between her legs in a light cotton dress that was white and had some red flowers and vines of sorts on it, all very faint, and her auburn hair was tamed up behind her in a clip and I could see her lips and there was a smile on them as he read.

That my father was an artist is just the beginning of the secret, because at around age thirteen or fourteen I found myself gravitating towards the artsy things in school, looking forward to studio art class in my eighth grade year.

"School is a waste of your mind," my father told me that year. He was drinking, and my father never drank though my mother said once or twice that he had the "characteristics" of a drinker whether he was boozing or not. "It's a waste of your mind, putting all of that nonsense in there," he told me. "The only thing that you need to do is discover everything for yourself, and to be honest about it, and to portray it honestly. That's what the world wants anyway – not that you want the world, *fuck* the world – but that's what they want. Everybody is walking around looking for something new and something honest and they wonder why it's so hard to get to because we keep teaching ourselves the same shit year after year after year. There's no memory. It's stale." He spat then, in the stairwell where he sat

and I stood, and the spit was red, and it wasn't because what he was drinking
was red. He looked at me when I looked up from the red spit, and then he
looked *into* me with his black eyes (they were so dark brown they just
looked like huge pupils to me) and then he came back out of me and
softened and said "do what you want, my *bubbala*, is the point anyway," and
he looked at the bottle he was drinking from and set it down beside him and
looked into me one more time and said "do what your heart tells you, and
your heart is always the kindest voice, your heart is always the voice
pointing you in the right direction," and the he stiffened, and swiped his
mouth with his sleeve and stood, he was so tall, and I felt small in front of
him though I knew I was almost a man then, and he said: "All the rest of it,
school, no school, rightwing, leftwing, it's all a big fucking waste of time."
He started up the stairs and I could smell my mother's cooking – yellow rice
and fish, cumin and curry wafting into the stairwell. "All most people do in
this life is waste their time – they date, they socialize, they watch sports and
bleed their fucking dreams." It was the most I had ever heard my father
swear. He banged in the apartment and when I followed a few moments
later he was asleep in one of the three rooms – their bedroom – and my
mother was humming a tune.

My secret was that I was becoming an artist like my father, and there
was nothing I could do about it. My mother knew it, but she just served me
up my dinner with a smile and her humming. And her humming became
singing again after we finished eating.

*

When dawn filtered down through the trees we awoke and stood up,
stretching out the aches of a brief, troubled sleep. My eyes were itchy and
heavy. Everything was wet. My pants were soaked.

"Did it rain?"

Peter shook his head. "No, it's just dew."

I was shivering. It felt colder now than it had been the night before.
My mouth was dry and my stomach rolled and growled. In a home, in an
apartment, you get up, you make your coffee or your eggs, you watch the
news, read the paper, take a shower, get dressed, brush your teeth, comb
your hair – it can take an hour, just to sort your shit out before the day
begins. In the woods, I realized, all you did was stand up. The day was
there. Peter looked over at me. His eyeballs were wrapped in red twine.
"What do you want to do?"

"Let's find this place," I said.

We started walking back in the way we thought we'd been going the
night before. After an hour or so we hadn't found anything but more woods.
There were songbirds chirping away in the trees and the drone of crickets
still buzzing from the night – or maybe what I was hearing were frogs.
Whether I was confusing the two or not, their noise was familiar, though I
couldn't place from when or where. I tried to avoid the wet leaves for as
long as possible but eventually gave up. My sleeves were sodden and
dripping. My ass was cold and wet. I started to get irritable. Peter just
looked tired, spaced out. "Where the fuck is this place, if it even exists?" I
asked. "Where the fuck are *we*? What the hell do we think we're doing?"

Peter just looked at me and seemed to decide for himself that they were rhetorical questions.

We continued slogging through the heavy, wet leaves. I stopped to piss – I couldn't imagine how I was producing urine. I had nothing with me to drink. My stomach felt hollow, like it had been swabbed out with a big piece of cotton. For some reason I found myself thinking of witches. I had been susceptible to witches in my younger days. You may not think witches exist, but they do. People roll their eyes and act all superior and smug when you tell them something like this.

For instance, Somebody once told me on a job that they thought Jackson Pollock's art was bullshit. They gave me the same simpleminded rhetoric that it was just paint splashed on a canvas; it wasn't art. I tried to explain that Pollock wasn't someone who just painted on weekends and tried to shortcut the process by paint-splattering; he'd arrived there after intense study, painful introspection, both disciplined and manic bursts of creative activity, the anguish of a tortured soul; he was a true artist. I tried to explain that Pollock had *arrived* there at the paint splattering – he was seeking the formless, or, at least, allowing the painting to be its absolute self. What resulted was this direct, emotional explosion – the paint was only the medium, but the medium was completely itself. People just didn't get it. Like direct cinema – just holding the camera there and allowing something to happen, something to be captured. It was so easy for people to discredit this type of art – if it didn't seem like someone was doing some lowest common denominator standard of "hard work," it wasn't anything. The problem was that there were a lot of poseurs out there who DID try and shortcut and not learn the forms – but Pollock had been really studying before his breakthrough.

I said all of this to the guy driving the truck at the time and he had just stopped listening to me. I hated people that thought they were right about shit like that. They were the same people that would grin smugly when you tried to explain collective consciousness, or that witches and vampires were real. They thought of a witch on a broom. They thought of a vampire with fangs, drinking blood. Those were just caricatures of the real thing. Then I realized, as I batted away the drooping, wet branches with ebbing concern for my lack of dryness, that I had done the same thing. When I thought of communes I'd thought of the stereotype, the caricature. I was completely ill-prepared for what I saw when Peter and I stumbled across it.

We had been headed toward another clearing, one that we thought might be *the* clearing, but it had spread wider and deeper. The instant we'd stepped from the cover of forest we were greeted by a young woman. I saw that she had a cell phone attached to her hip. She held up her hands, as if in surrender. As she did, some distant part of me knew that I would be a sucker all over again, that I was still in denial about a great many things. Putting down the drink was just one step among many.

"Who are you?" She was beautiful; brown haired, sparklingly brown-eyed and wearing cute-girl Gap-type clothing. She wasn't unwashed or unkempt looking – she looked prepared for the day like she'd spent an hour or more drinking coffee and showering.

"We're lost," Peter said.

"Well where did you come from?"

"We were camping," I told her. Our eyes met. She had a symmetrical face – she could have stepped out of a catalogue. Her eyes betrayed mischief, power, an otherworldly knowing. She was a witch, but I was

instantly in denial of it. I hadn't been laid in months. It probably stank on
me more virulently than Peter's acrid B.O.

"You can't camp out here," she said.

"I know – a man came and told us to get out. We said that it was dark
and we'd have trouble, but he just left us to it. We walked and got lost.
What's your name?" The words poured from me like I had been drinking
my own coffee that morning – only I hadn't been. I was sleep-deprived,
hungry and excited. The woods had an energy.

"Well he shouldn't have done that," she said. "Who was he?"

"He didn't give us a name."

Peter was looking over her shoulder. "What have you got going on
here?"

"You guys can't be here," she said.

"Why?" Our eyes danced together. I felt good.

"Because this is private property."

"Private? I thought this was a reservation. State land." I enjoyed
challenging her. This was my way. Idiot that I was, I was flirting, trying to
be charmingly difficult. She squashed it.

"You're *off* the reservation."

"Off?" I suddenly remembered the map with great clarity. My senses
were running optimally. I thought I should get only four hours of sleep more
often. Forget about food, too. "If we went off the reservation we would
have crossed route 14 – we would have crossed the Black River."

She looked me up and down. "Black river is behind me, to the east.
So is route 14. This is an outpost. It is separate from the reservation. If you
know so much, why are you telling me that you're lost?"

I didn't know how to respond. I felt instantly stupid and belittled. I recognized the pattern and decided to put a stop to it.

"There's a lot of woods out here, lady. Now, listen, we came out here looking for a commune. *Your* commune, I'd imagine. Unless you've got something to hide, why don't you take us there? We're not going anywhere else until we see it." It felt like cold, pure air rushing out of my lungs.

Her hand went to her cell phone, like she was a gunfighter in the Old West. "Are you a reporter?"

"Maybe *si* maybe *no*," I told her. I wanted to speak Spanish to her. I wanted to tell her: *Nunca he visto los ojos tan bonitas como los tuyos.*

Peter said, "And we're hungry."

She plucked the cell phone from her belt and dialed. Her brown eyes wandered back and forth between the two of us as she put it to her ear. Peter looked at me and smiled.

"Cam? I've got those two guys here with me." Back and forth, went her eyes, me to Peter, Peter to me, as she listened to the voice on the other end. "Okay. Uh-huh. Okay. Bye." She snapped the phone shut and replaced it. "Well?" I raised my eyebrows.

She pulled a gun from behind her back and pointed it at us. "Cam says you have to go."

I'd had a gun pulled on me a few times. It doesn't get a whole hell of a lot easier, but Peter, apparently, never had any such experience at all. He started backpedaling, flailing his way into the woods where he promptly fell over. I stood my ground. Things had become surreal; instead of feeling the clarity and acute senses from the sleep-deprivation, I now felt like I was in a dream. It was too absurd to be happening. "You gonna shoot?"

"If you don't start hightailing it out of here, yes, I will shoot you."

"Hightailing? Who says that? What's your name?"

"That's none of your business."

"You ever shot anyone before?"

"Get out of here."

"I don't think you have." Truth was, I kinda did.

"Listen, who the fuck're you? What, did you come from New York or something and so now you think you're all tough? This is a .38 special pointed right at you, and I'm someone who's going to use it on you if you don't turn the fuck around, join your hippie friend and get going. This isn't what you're looking for out here, okay? You're not going to find peace, serenity and a better way of life." She looked at Peter. "You fucking tree-hugging wood hicks are the reason that things are so fucked up now anyway. Now get going."

I stood still, my heart thrumming like a V-8. "No," I said.

She pulled back the hammer with her thumb and straightened her arm. "Go," she said, "last chance."

"Hey hey hey!" The voice came from my right. I looked over, cold sweat upon me, and saw our old friend the FPR guy stepping into the clearing. His hand was on his own gun. I whipped my head back to the girl.

"Get out of here, Mike!"

The FPR guy, Mike, kept walking along the edge of the woods toward us. "Hey hey hey! Maya! What're you doing?" *Maya.* Her other hand went back to her cell phone and I watched as she struggled to unhitch it from her belt. Seeing my opportunity, still awash in surrealism and gnawing hunger, I rushed her. I was mindful of the gun first and foremost and dislodged it from her grip. "Peter!" I yelled. We fell to the ground, me on top of her. She squirmed and kicked beneath me. The gun was only a foot away. She groped for it. The grass was wet and was soaking her, turning her khaki paints a dark olive. I could feel the moisture all around me. I could smell the fragrant, fertile earth. Mike, the FPR guy, was running toward us. I could see in my peripheral vision that his gun was out, wagging stiffly in front of him. Peter came up behind the two of us as we wrestled. He grabbed up Maya's gun. I looked up at him as he did this and Maya's fingers got into my mouth. She yanked. A second later there was a shot and I saw Peter go sprawling. I glanced in Mike's direction. He parted the puff of gunsmoke with his grimacing face as he ran through it. "You idiot," Maya breathed beneath me. I rolled off of her and away from her. I scrambled over to Peter. He was shot between the shoulder and chest. I thought of his subclavian, ripped through by the bullet. I saw blood in the grass beside him. He was still breathing. The gun, Maya's gun, was in his grip.

Behind me, Maya stood. "Mike!" Mike was still coming at us, only yards away. I grabbed the firearm from Peter. I had held handguns before; I had a buddy in Bed-Stuy who sold them, for one. The SIG P239 was always my favorite. This felt like something from a civil war reenactment. It felt almost brittle. I got to my knees and swung it round at Mike. Something was terribly wrong.

Maya was between us, arms spread, palms out, like a woman between two brawling, pigheaded men at a bar. Her head whipped to me and her eyes were wide. "It's not–" she said, and then Mike was knocking her down. He just bulled right into her, sending her sprawling with a real jolt. A WHAM and then she was spinning, falling. Down for a second time. He was upon me and I pulled the trigger.

There was a pitiful "click" as the hammer came down and nothing else. Me and my big ego, thinking I knew guns, thinking since I had guns aimed at me before that I was some sort of fucking expert. *It's not real*, was what Maya was going to say.

He knocked it out of my hand anyway, Mike, and he pressed the muzzle of his own, very *real* gun, to my forehead, pressing me back. I leaned back on my knees, my sore quads stretching painfully, my hands plunging into the wet earth behind me. I heard Peter gasping for air behind me and I looked up at Mike's face. The sun that was just peeking over the trees lit him up along one side and his eyeball glinted. *He's crazy*, I thought, and then my head exploded and there was a dreamless black that followed.

There was a clattering, jangling, and I thought Daniel was coming in, drunk again, fumbling with his keys, and I thought of bottles, all aligned on their shelves in formation.

As I came around, a feeling washed over me that was both terrifying and terribly disappointing – I had been drinking again myself. My head was pregnant with it – throbbing, kicking, like I was to bear wild foals; they would emerge in a frenzy from my eyes, flailing and neighing and me screaming, their hooves still smoking from hell. Goddammit, I had slipped up again – and so soon. Man, I was saving that last slip up for something good, for something really worth it. Like, the next time I was about to get laid, maybe, I'd be knee deep in a big, classy bottle of wine. Or maybe even

– and you can't tell anybody about this, old pal – but maybe the day I had my paintings in a show, you know, a grand opening and all of that. A Gallery, I guess they call it (though "gallery" always made me think of a long hallway with red and pink lingerie draped over the pearly white busts of dead presidents and rockefellerians, don't ask me why.) Hungover, again, dammit, and once more going to have to hit the restart button, recharge in solitude, ford the paranoia, the humiliation, the withdrawal. Maybe Daniel had brought something home with him – a bottle, something light, like a couple of wine coolers I could just wind down with…

Daniel was still fumbling with the keys, the old drunk queen, and when he pushed into the apartment, his shoulder mashed into the oak, ramming with all of his hundred-thirty-five pound might, the door opened with the squeal and groan of a giant, steel thing, a thing of metal and locks and bars-

I opened my eyes. I saw things sideways. I saw a stainless steel sink. I saw something limping toward me, something like a mummy, and behind it some kind of bear. I sat up and my head went from mute throbs to stabbing pains above my left eye and temple. I cried out and leaned forward, taking my head in my hands, looking between my legs. I heard the screech of the door sliding closed, the clank of it latching shut. The sounds pierced my thoughts. I couldn't make sense of anything – I was in jail?

Someone sat down near me. The light, even bouncing off the floor, was excruciating, digging into my skull like a bird pecking away. Under my butt was more stainless steel – a bench. The other person with me had sat down a few feet to my left.

"Julianne?" I didn't dare look over – I didn't dare move my head any more, but kept it cradled in my palms.

"He's still in the hospital," said a woman's voice. *Maya.* Not
Julianne. Maya. "You should have listened to me. You should have gone
when I told you to. None of this would have happened. What did you think
you were doing, anyway? What did you expect to find? A bunch of
ragdolls dancing around a bonfire? Guys like you, you get one little whiff of
a bigger world outside of your brick and mortar and you think it's all about
being a vegan and chanting along to some eastern religion. Wake up, little
susie."

Her voice reverberated softly. I squinted and blinked and tried to look
up. It felt like there was a manhole cover on the top of my head, weighing it
down and a drill boring into my left temple. I kept my head as still as I
could. "Where are we?"

"We're in county, Brooklyn. Orleans county jail."

"In Eden?"

"No," she laughed, "not in Eden."

"Where?"

"We're in Newport. About four miles from the border."

My thoughts were jumbled. "What border?" I thought of Nicaragua.
Of riding horseback.

She laughed again, but it was cut short, and I thought I heard her suck
wind, like she was in some sort of pain too. I tried to remember.

"Where do you think you are? The Canadian border, ace. We were in
Orleans County. Now we're at the Sheriff's Department – county
headquarters."

"...how...?"

"How do you think? Mike called us in."

"But...he's a real...?"

"He's a conservation officer, yes. He says he's one of the Naturalists, but they don't know that. Or, it doesn't matter to them. I think he doesn't give a shit either way." She made a scoffing sound like *pfff* and shifted – I thought she might be resting on her side now. I could only see shapes to my left. I didn't dare roll my eyes that way. I alternated keeping them shut and looking at the square of concrete between my feet. "They're idiots. They still believe in neo-Darwinism. Natural selection. I mean, if you still believe in Darwin you've got no understanding of biochemistry. They think we're fucking creationists." She laughed until she started coughing. When she resumed her voice was grave. "On the molecular level, we're all machines. We all should have the same rights, the same respect. Everyone is equal – it's in the fucking Constitution." She paused. "That's a pun."

"I have no idea what you're talking about," I said. My head was a mess of pain. There was no pinpointing where the hurt was coming from anymore, it was everywhere. I wondered if I could get anything. I wondered if I'd even been given anything so far. Had I been to the hospital? What had happened to me? I thought back…I remembered the smell of the wet grass – I saw vividly blades of the iridescent green stuff plastered all over Maya's arms as we wrestled in the ground. Droplets of dew as big as snow globes. Then I saw her being hit, spun like a quarterback sacked, Peter's blood there, beside him, and then Mike, the goddamn FPR guy, bearing down on me. He'd had a gun…he'd…

"You got pistol-whipped, I'll give you that. Otherwise you are pretty fucking dumb for a reporter. Aren't you guys supposed to do research?"

"I'm not a reporter."

"Then what are you? P.I.?"

I thought about telling her – crazily – telling her, in that moment, because I felt vulnerable, I felt scared, really scared for the first time. I could just blow my cover, breakdown into tears and lay my head in her lap. I would tell her all about it. Tell her about Lincoln and Lucius. Tell her about the woman. The baby. The drinking. All of it. She would understand. She would stroke my hair and console me, sooth me, lullaby me. It would all be better. I just needed to let it all out. Get rid of it. Be done with this terrible business, this thing starting to feel like a wild goose chase. But if I did, well, then they'd probably come looking for me. There'd be no Coca-Cola at the bar, no razzing Daniel about his transforming sexuality, no romps with Peter in the woods, no raking up cemetery plots. It would all be over. Instead, I said, "you know Phil Brandis?"

A moment passed and she said nothing. My heart did a somersault. "I'm a friend of his," I said.

"Oh yeah?"

That's two of them, I thought. *Both Terry Hackford and this Maya girl – both of them know something.* I pressed my palms against my temple and the raging pain subsided a little. "Mike *pistol whipped* me?"

"Yeah, or whatever you call it. He hit you over the head with his gun."

"And he made the call to the cops? He was the one that had us arrested?"

"Well, you think I did? You think I'm in here now just to keep up face? I don't think so, Brooklyn. I don't think so." She stood up and I heard her scuffing around the cell. I wondered if my gramma would think Maya was a *slouch* too. I didn't think she was. I thought she was bored, maybe. Whoever, or whatever she worked for, was a part of, they didn't give her enough power. She was bitter. She felt she could do more. Something. Something. She was hungry – I could smell it on her. It reminded me-

"Is Peter going to be alright?"

"I don't know," she said, "he was in critical condition."

"And nothing is going to happen to this Mike guy?"

"Well, Mike said you were trespassers. He'd already asked you to clear the land, to head off down to Elmore – somewhere where there was registered camping. You didn't." I heard her stop walking. I wanted to look up at her, but I still didn't risk it. Not with the chance of fiery tines spearing into my eyeballs.

But then I did look. The pain was terrible. I saw that pain register on Maya's face. If she had been being coy, it vanished. I thought I saw her countenance real concern in that moment – I could have been wrong, but I didn't think so.

"You look really bad," she said. She walked over to me. "Here, put your head back down. Hold on." I did as she told, dropping my head between my shoulders and reapplying pressure to my temples with the heels of my palms. I heard a ripping sound and then running water from the bluish brushed-steel sink. When she returned she applied a cool bit of cloth to my head. It felt good. It felt really good. I felt like sucking on it. "Thanks," I said. She took my right hand and put it to the cloth. "Hold," she said.

We stayed there like that for a little while, she sitting next to me, me on my back, the torn fabric she held on my head already starting to lose its cool and absorb my heat.

Then she spoke again. "Who is Julianne?"

"What?"

"When you first woke up, you thought I was someone named Julianne."

"Oh," I said.

"I don't even know your name," she said.

I gave her one and said, "You said Mike was a Naturalist. What do you mean? In terms of conservation and all of that?"

She stood up again, and I had to grab the cloth from slipping from my head. I held it there a second longer, then balled it up. "Listen," Maya said, "you don't want to be a part of any of this."

"What if I already am? I'm in jail. My friend has been shot because I brought him along. My brain feels like it's bleeding and I can't even get a fucking baby aspirin. Okay? I think I'm in."

She was quiet, considering this. "I'll just have to show you," she said.

My heart started up again, beating fast. *Tachycardia*, I thought, but dismissed it. I had hypochondriac tendencies I was sure I inherited from my melancholic father. Dad's legacy: painting and paranoia. "And how are we going to get out of here?"

"We're charged with criminal trespassing. A misdemeanor. Arraignment was held without us since we were all three incapacitated. Bail is 1500 a piece. I've got someone on the way here now. I'll have him put up your bail too. We'll go make sure your friend Peter is alright and then we'll go get you some baby aspirin. Okay?" She stood. "Guard!" She yelled. "Phone call!"

I wanted to ask: *why were* you *incapacitated?* But I didn't. Instead I asked, "How do you know where I'm from?"

She turned from the bars and looked back at me, at once icy and vulnerable. "Just a guess," she said.

I loved her.

Our savior was a clean-cut square-jawed young man in a casual suit, his eyes hidden by wrap-around black sunglasses. I instantly had it out for him for two reasons – one, he was a guy, and Maya acted very familiar with him; I suspected they were involved, or maybe had been, anyway. Two, he looked just like one of the guys sitting in the booth at the pub that week before when the fight had broken out and Terry Hackford had belted me in the nose. Only this guy had a tattoo snaking up out of his black v-neck and just over the collar of his leather jacket. I put Cameron at about my age, maybe a year older. Maya was just a young thing, twenty-four, twenty-five at most – a dangerous age for a beautiful girl. Both of them were fit as a fiddle.

I stewed in the back seat as we careened along the broken streets in his Toyota *Yaris* while Maya talked with him – most of their conversation was lost in the wind since both windows were rolled down. Maya's umber-colored hair flew over the headrest in a wild fray, like she was underwater. Like the tentacles of a jellyfish.

We made it to the hospital which was in Newport Center, about three miles away. I didn't have my watch with me – it hadn't been returned with my baggie of personal affects. I suspected, of course, Mike had a new watch on his wrist. That thing had been a present from dear old gram, my dad's

mom, still living in her rent-controlled apartment in Park Slope. I vowed
that I would find Mike and take it back if I had to rip off his entire left arm.
It didn't matter to me that he probably outweighed me by thirty pounds. I'd
get to him, and I'd get the watch.

The driver, our rescuer – he had introduced himself only as Cameron
– pulled into one of the spots and told us he'd stay in the car while we went
to go in and check on Peter. Suddenly I was no longer interested in Peter. I
felt badly about what had happened, of course, I felt terrible, but I had been
completely shanghaied by this new development – by Maya and Cameron
springing me, and her incredibly enticing promise to "show me" what it is I
was after. I was rooted to the backseat. The sun was beating in through the
car roof and things were getting hot. Maya got out and then ducked her head
back in, looking at me. "Well?" I had to go see Peter.

After we had checked in at the desk and were headed to the elevator I
asked her, "So, you and Cameron…?"

"What?" We stepped in and she hit the button for the third floor. It
was the top floor. The hospital in Newport Center was no Mount Sinai. The
elevator jolted and started up slowly.

"Are you two together?"

She laughed. It was a completely ambiguous thing. It could've
meant, "Are you joking? Of course not." It could've meant, "Are you
jealous? You obviously want a piece of this ass, don't you?" It could've
meant, "Yes, we are, oh what a story." It could've meant anything. Maya,
in any case, went straight for the throat. "Why do you ask?"

"Just curious." The pain in my head had mercifully subsided. We'd
stopped immediately after leaving the county jail and Maya had gotten me
some drugs. Advil, not aspirin. I dug it.

"Just curious," she echoed. The elevator bounced onto the third floor and the doors opened. "He's down this way," she said.

"Yeah, I heard the receptionist." It was bitter and sarcastic. Maya looked at me and grinned. "Your head is feeling better," she said. We walked to room 33, where Peter was sitting up, a wide white bandage around his chest, pulled taut against his slender breadth. No severed subclavian artery. He was watching something on a small white TV at the end of a mechanical arm. He smiled when he saw us. "My first gunshot wound," he said, "wait until I tell the band." That was Peter.

"See," Maya said as we got back into the hot Toyota, "everything is going to be just fine."

"What about Mike," I said. "What are we going to do about him?"

Cameron spoke into the rearview mirror, his eyes hidden by the liquid black of the shades.

"What are we going to do? Nothing. Mike's not our concern. Mike doesn't bother us. You brought the trouble."

I looked at Maya but the back of her head was to me. Her arm was propped up on the door and she was gazing out the window as we headed south along route 14. He was right. I had brought them the trouble – whoever they were, whatever they were about. I was starting to put it together. Mike, and maybe some of his ilk, they weren't just necessarily conservation officers, but they were these "Naturalists," a vague term that in this case had something to do with Darwinism, according to Maya's rant in the holding cell, if I could make heads or tails of it. They were a group, and Maya and Cameron were a group. They were feuding groups, but they had to occupy the same area and live in harmony. That was how I summed it up with what I knew at the moment. I thought of apologizing to Cameron and then thought again of the phone call, the one Maya had made back in the clearing. "Well, that may be true, but I think I have Mike to thank for my life." Cameron watched me in the mirror and I could sense Maya's ears perk up. "Oh yeah?" "Yeah," I said, "I seem to remember a phone call Maya made – who'd you call Maya? Cam, right? Yeah, you called Cam, hung up and pointed the gun at us." I had them. Maya had been going to execute us.

"Yeah," Maya said, turning halfway around. She looked at Cameron when she said it. "The *fake* gun." Cameron smiled. I hated them both. I was an idiot. I had completely forgotten. In the midst of it all, with my head pounding so hard I couldn't think straight, I had forgotten, jumbled things up. I slunk back down in the seat, hoping that if I didn't speak for another 15 minutes, or however long it would take to get where we were going, they'd forget that I was there.

Cameron's arms were wrapped with ropy muscles that bulged as he dragged a chain over a private dirt road. I watched through the window along with Maya, who twirled her hair and seemed off in her own world. Who were they? What was down this road? What the hell was I getting into? It all seemed harmless enough; fake guns and trespassing charges and Toyota hybrids. Not the sort of alchemy that opened strange doors to the occult. Peter had been shot, yes, he had, but we were in Vermont. For all I knew people got shot in the woods everyday. Phil Brandis was missing, after all, Lucius and Lincoln's nephew, and I was to track him down. If there was something going on, if there was any truth to the reasons I was here, these two were now my tour guides. And what had I expected? Only children and kooks believed in fire and brimstone. This was real life – this was a series of oddities. Guys dressed in urban chic with rolled-up sleeves dragging chains across dirt roads and wrapping them around tenpenny nails. Young witches in their primes dreaming up new spells to seduce and manipulate men with. I knew I was contradicting myself – thinking about witches and séances but not unconcerned of any real threat, but, like I said, my head had been bashed in. I was doing the best I could.

Cameron returned to the car and we got going. I was starting to get excited. My mouth got ahead of my brain. "Where are we going?"

His eyes still concealed by the large black sunglasses, Cameron looked at me in the rearview mirror. "We're going home."

"Do you know Terry Hackford?"

Again, the masked eyes groped me – I felt it. "No."

"He was asking about Phil Brandis," Maya said casually. She had the window rolled down and her elbow propped up on the door. The cool spring air blew in, scented with the pine and cedar forest.

"Phil was someone we hired for certain functions," Cameron explained, almost too quickly, I thought. Then: *Functions*? Was this a corporation or a commune? "And I'm glad you brought him up," said Cameron.

"Oh?"

"Because he was a city boy like you. And I'm going to tell you the same thing I told Phil." Maya glanced over at Cameron and then looked back out the open window. I watched her as Cameron talked. "What you are about to see is not for the public. You are stepping out of the public and you are becoming part of something private. We revere and need our privacy – it is vital to us for the time being. So, in taking this step, you are giving up some of your rights."

"Which are?" I watched Maya examine her fingernails.

"Which is your right to talk about this to anyone else."

"Oh," I said, suppressing the urge to roll my eyes. I thought of Maya naked, instead, and what she might taste like in the neck, along the thigh. "Is that why Phil Brandis is dead? He talked and you had him whacked?" I grinned, despite myself. Maya looked at Cameron again – I hated the way she watched him, like he was a leader she was taken with, marveling at, in awe of, taking cues from. I imagined her lying on his bare chest, adoringly stroking his arms and shoulders, looking up at him with groupie adulation. I dismissed it, for my own fantasy's sake. Besides, Maya was clearly too individual, too powerful for that. I'd felt it.

"No," said Cameron, "we didn't have him *whacked*." He smiled a big, handsome-jack smile, revealing rows of perfect teeth and he glanced at me again through those thick sunglasses.

"Well, then let me ask you this – if this world of yours is so secret – why bring me here?"

Cameron and Maya exchanged looks. I was getting irritated with their silent *parler*. "Because," Cameron said shifting a little in his seat, "you're the relentless type. You have been asking about Phil since you arrived in

Burlington. You made your way up to Eden and it was clear you didn't intend to leave until satisfying your curiosity. Well, it's more than that, I know." Cameron reached up and removed his sunglasses. His eyes were a ridiculous blue, glacial. "I know why you're here."

"I see," I said. But I was a little nervous. I waited for him to say, *because you're a drunk – you took this job as a chance to get out of your life and sober up.* I didn't want Maya to hear that, but, of course, Cameron didn't know it.

His mouth was open to speak, but I got there before him. "Well let's just say you do and leave it at that." I saw his mouth close and jaw clench. Maya was looking askance at him, her hair tousled. I realized, maybe, that I was thinking about protecting her as much as myself. It was the beginning of something. And I owed for past deeds.

The rest of the ride was nerve wracking. The road, for one, was less hospitable and had us each jostling about, holding on to the *Yaris*'s frame to keep from ramming our bones into things. Cameron reminded me of a prep-school kid from Connecticut who went punk somewhere in his mid-twenties. I could see him in the early days sitting around a round oak table puffing on a pipe, saying "old chap" to his comrades while they wagered their inheritance on poker games and drank blood-colored brandy. Sure, he didn't have a sweater around his neck now, he wasn't wearing an Oxford business shirt or boat shoes. Cameron was the turn-of-the-century hipster with a

Diesel leather jacket on (I'd seen the patch,) Merrill shoes, designer
sunglasses, the whole nine. What killed me, though, what absolutely burned
me up was how such a rich snotpunk could have affiliation with my
employers. The Brandis brothers were as hard as they came – and where
they came from there had been no tea time or trust funds. I hadn't always
been their biggest fan, no – still wasn't – but I was loyal, and I did have
some lofty ideas about Lincoln – he held a place in my heart that was both
filled with anger and pride at the same time. This denigrated that, this
ridiculous connection. Cameron was obviously determined not to humor me
with any more information and let me stew in the questions and confusion –
I was sure he was deriving pleasure from it.

Maya remained a mystery, not saying anything at all, only twirling her
hair, watching the woods roll past and bobbing along with us. I silently
blamed my father's romanticism for how I felt about her and willed my
mother's deadpan to take over. I only heard my mother singing, albeit
distantly, as though far away in a twilit field, a charcoal sketch alone.

Then we were there. The dirt road had petered out to nothing but a
couple of ruts through fragrant onion grass and then the ruts led us into a
clearing where other vehicles – all a pretty penny, upon first assessment of
them – were parked neatly around the perimeter. Cars were something I
hadn't expected. This looked more like a graduation party in the woods I
had once attended. A friend had graduated from SUNY Purchase and his
gang had celebrated somewhere in the neighboring farm country – there had
been rows of rich-kid-cars, just like these, and guys puking into the bushes
and sticking their hands in the bonfire to impress the bisexual girls.

Cameron shut the car off and we got out. I wondered how far we'd
driven in from the main road – two miles? Three? I kicked myself for not

noting the odometer. I had been too busy ogling and fantasizing about Maya naked and hungry, her mouth open as she crawled toward me on all fours.

The sun was beating down and heating up the day. I felt warmth radiating up from the grass – the evaporating dew ran up my legs and back. The whole place was alive with the sounds of what I again thought were crickets – but weren't. Maya told me later they were cicadas – bugs in the trees. I thought, for some reason, that she was lying to me – that they were frogs after all, like I'd thought the morning before. We walked out of the clearing to a path that wound back into the forest. Cameron led the way and Maya trailed behind me. I wanted to talk to her but my thoughts were a mess. I had no game. It wasn't the right time, anyway, I rationalized. There were bigger things at stake.

"We're here," Cameron said. It had been a brief walk. He was stopped in front of me. I walked up behind him and stepped to his left. I looked. I stood and looked. When Maya walked up on my left hand side, I barely even noticed.

"What do you think?" asked Maya.

I gaped. The place was alive with activity – thrumming with it. There were generators. There were Quonset huts and houses – real houses, single-storied houses with curtains in the windows and wood-shingle sidings. There was one large building that looked like army barracks. There were paths winding through the village; fieldstone patios adorned the front doors of the six or seven houses. There were even mailboxes in front of those houses, replete with double-digit numbers on them. And everywhere, everywhere, were greenhouses. I looked again at the generators, gleaming in the sun, the size of small cars. "How come we didn't hear the generators?" I whispered the question to myself.

Maya leaned over and whispered back, "Because they're *quiet*." She loped off down the gentle slope toward the village.

Cameron, who had donned his sunglasses once more, looked over at me with a drawn face. "Welcome to Utopia," he said with a matter-of-fact tone. He held out his hand. In mild shock, I shook it. "I am Dr. Madison," he said. He nodded toward Maya. "And that is Dr. Burns." He read the question on my face. "We're biochemists." Maya continued away from us, toward the village, jogging now.

I started down with Dr. Cameron Madison, following his lead. For some reason I thought of Mike again, the FPR guy. I thought of Peter, lying in the hospital back in Newport Center, and for the first time since I'd arrived here, if only because I realized how far out of my element I had finally come, I began to feel completely alone.

Now that Cameron was here – excuse me, *Dr. Madison* – he was affable, talkative, relaxed. He had been stonefaced and irritable when I'd met him hours before, now he strutted like a young professor might parade along the winding walkways of his University, hands behind his back, chest outthrust, nostrils flared on the scent of roses in bloom. He seemed pleased to answer questions – I wondered how long it had been since there was any outsider here, anyone to impress, to teach. Deeper than that curiosity, of course, was my concern for not knowing how *I* had really come to be allowed here – if I

were to believe them it was because I was tenacious, really, but there had to
be more…

"Biochemistry is the new science. It's not about quantum physics.
Quantum physics is the philosopher's science – the condition of all possible
states, electrons once in contact with each other still able to communicate no
matter the space and time separating them, the field, the great curtain, all of
that – that's the philosopher's science. Dust in the wind. You can't do
anything with it. There is no function, no tangibility. But biochemistry –
that's digging in the soil, that's the real, physical stuff. Biochemistry is
about the nuts and bolts of life, the tiniest machines – the molecules of
chemistry that make up the cells that make up the organs that make up the
systems that make up the organism. Biochemistry is *it*. What witch doctors
have been at one time or another, humorists, the doctor that made house calls
with his black bag in the little house on the prairie days – that's the
biochemist today."

"You make it sound like you chose this profession because it was
hip."

"No, I chose it because it was the most relevant." If I had offended
him he showed no sign of it. He did, however, stop walking and turn to face
me. He even took me by the shoulders. I felt like looking around to see
where the TV cameras were hidden, who he was mugging for, but he wasn't
of course. He, and probably like all the others, now émigrés, just…didn't
get out much. They only had other heady, nerdy, neurotic scientists to
socialize with. I found myself wondering if there was a bar somewhere here
in the commune or if everyone just kept to their private stash. "You know,
most people don't know how to make a difference, or they simply don't
care. Kids growing up want to be a cop or a fireman or an actor or pop icon.

Maybe they achieve it. Others fall into things – they take over daddy's business, start working construction one day and never leave, that sort of thing. All I ever knew as a kid was that the human race – *life* – was mutable. Nothing *had* to be this way. Not the symbols, not the illusions, not the structures – none of it *had* to be this way."

"Ah," I said, feeling a rush of braininess, "but how did it *come* to be this way."

He shook his head, his eyelids fluttered. "I don't care. That's Maya. She's the one set on debunking Darwin. Look, the point is, I knew that life could be changed. Not by marches, not by politicians, certainly not by wars. I knew that life could be changed *on the molecular level*." His eyes were wide and he was gripping my shoulders tight. I remembered the title of a book I had read and loved as a kid – *Mad Scientists*. It was about a group of brainy, precocious adolescents running experiments out in the woods. Cameron suddenly looked embarrassed. Or, rather, I thought, maybe a little dissatisfied with himself. He stood up straight, brushing off my shoulders. "Sorry," he said.

"It's okay. You're passionate. My father was like that."

"He was," said Cameron. It wasn't a question, but a statement of fact.

I felt anger, or something like it, replacing the timidity that had come over me upon entering the commune. Maybe it was that high-strung wistfulness of my father, that red-faced passion pacing the cage of my mother's malingering ways. This had gone on long enough.

"What? How did you know my father, Cameron? Tell me."

"I was a student of his."

"He was an artist," I said immediately. The words felt clunky on my tongue, like plastic squares I was spitting out. Still, I had never told anyone

that and felt oddly comfortable telling Dr. Cameron Madison, like it fit
somehow, telling him. "But," he said, "he wasn't a teacher."

"Maybe he didn't teach you," said Cameron, "but he taught me." It
was a gutsy thing to say, I thought, but maybe Cameron Madison wasn't
afraid of me. That brought up my inferiority complex, making me feel
shamed, but I pushed it away, as I had been learning to do in sober times, by
remembering he would have no reason to fear me in a place he controlled. I
was the outsider, the one dependent on good graces. Still, Cameron had also
said he knew my employers, émigrés, you might say, in their own right, like
he was here in his new home. Even so, it might not be a reason to fear me.
He could know something I didn't, and I hated that. I was about to say
something when I thought of my father once telling me that when confronted
with authority, give a person the idea that they are superior. *You* then will be
the one in control of the situation. It was one of the only things my father
had taught me, aside from that day in the stairwell.

Cameron was watching me think, I suddenly realized. I wondered if
he could see my cells moving around beneath my skin, and he was thinking
about manipulating them. Maybe he was onto a way to stop apoptosis, to
unearth the spring of eternal youth. "He taught an art class," Cameron told
me, instead. "It was an evening class I took as an elective, but it ended up
changing the way I thought about a lot of things."

"You went to Pratt?"

"For two years, as an undergrad."

So I had learned what my father did, at least one thing, in his furtive
moonlighting.

"I know he kept it from you. He told me."

"You're from Brooklyn?"

"Sort of," said Cameron, and now he started looking around. His eyes came back to mine. Suddenly he broke into a wide grin and spoke significantly louder than he had just been. "It's fantastic," said Cameron. He seemed genuinely pleased, despite the sudden histrionics. "An artist like your father would love what we are doing here," Cameron said, and then he looked around again, like somebody might be watching.

"And what *are* we doing here?" I sensed vulnerability in him then, and I enjoyed it. I wanted to eat it.

Cameron turned on a different smile. More of a smile his face seemed familiar with. He waved his hand at the greenhouse nearest us. "Come on," he said. We approached. Though the sun was climbing and the day was warming the heat emanating from the greenhouse was palpable from twenty feet away. The thirty-something Doctor with the blue-black hair and shades on his head led the way. Maya had disappeared on me. I briefly looked around before entering the greenhouse. Once inside, I could barely breathe. The humidity was wonderfully stifling and the aromas filled my nose, my throat, my whole being. Feeling a little nasal, sweat beads rolling down my tight neck, I looked at Cameron, who was beaming, hands on hips. "You're horticulturalists?" I found it hard to believe that all of their secrecy and cryptology was about something as un-scatological as gardening. The sprinklers came on, spraying the rows of exuberant greens, yellows, siennas, ochres, purples and meringues with a fine mist. I saw something swinging in the spray down the row to my right that looked like an incredibly red tomato. "No," Cameron said, "we're food engineers." I thought of Les, the gardener, saying *generic food* and *New Age*. My mouth started to water.

*

"We're going to change the way people eat," Cameron said, walking quickly. I admired his enthusiasm, but wasn't this already happening? This was nothing new and nothing secret, genetically engineered food – or, bioengineered food if you will – "and by changing the way they eat we're going to increase the life expectancy by thirty, forty years, we're going to wipe out obesity, we're going to eradicate urban sickness, and, ultimately, the kicker."

"What's the kicker?"

"C.I.C.R.," Cameron explained. "Corporate Implanted Consumer Reflex."

"And that is?"

"That is every private corporation who stands to make money off of you by manipulating what you think, what you want, what you feel you need."

I thought of the Brandis brothers, but I pushed the thought away.

Cameron said, "Just about everything you desire has been manipulated. Your needs and desires are sculpted in just about every form. It's not just billboards, it's developmental psychologists working with toy companies to increase the 'nag factor' in children. It's the manufactured idea of what's beautiful, what's powerful. It's how you buy, it's how you vote."

I thought of the war protesters on Church Street. I thought of *Halliburton* and *Philip Morris* and anti-tobacco campaigns.

"And you're going to change that with food?"

Cameron only grinned on one side of his mouth. We turned a corner and started walking towards one of the small, suburbia-meets-*Gentle Ben* houses. I kept looking around for other people – Maya, mostly – but had seen no one else so far. I kept wanting to ask Cameron about how many were here – I had so many questions for him, but he had more to tell, it seemed, than I had time to ask about. He was excited, clearly, but not just because I was here. There was something else going on. They were close to something...something was close to them...I didn't know – what I did know was there was an electricity in the air, a certain edgy poise in the stillness of this modern oasis.

"Did you know that pharmaceutical innovation is on the decline? It's true. Do you play the stock market? Invest in your nearest biotech company. I always knew it. When I was a kid it was all in the role-playing games." I swallowed. This guy played games like *Shadowrun*? I would have figured at 15 he was playing piano at Carnegie Hall, working on his second doctorate and courting yet another thirty-something bombshell mistress, even in spite of what I knew of him as being, at one time, an ordinary undergrad at Pratt. Me as a teen, I was still peeing in my pants when I got laughing too hard, hiding my paintings in the alley between our building and the next and still jerking off to the JC Penney catalogue. "It's a terrible cycle. Two years ago *Zocor*, *Ambien,* and *Zoloft* all expired. Generics are aggressively trying to make up for the dearth in the industry, but there's no innovation. So jobs are lost. You know what it means? People are waking up. They get their prescription filled, sure, and they come back for maybe one refill, two tops, but people that are supposed to take meds for a longer time usually don't. In fact mostly they don't. See, people want a pill because it's a quick fix. A pill you gotta take everyday for six months to a year or more, that's no quick fix. That's tantamount to working out for these lazy slobs." He had keys out and was fumbling with the lock. Why was the door locked? Why did he have such contempt for these people he loved so dearly and wanted to save? "Drugs are the new Greeks," he said, looking halfway over his shoulder at me. "Do you know there's a program out there called 'Epocrates'?" I shook my head. I hadn't heard. "How wild is that?" Wild. The doctor burst in the front door after getting the right key in.

The place smelled stale inside, like an old closet. It smelled like a theater does, if you've ever been backstage where the props are and where people change their tights. I had been a few times with my dad who painted and built sets here and there. I didn't like that smell. This place kind of smelled like it now. It was the odor of fakeness and bodies. "Pfizer is down. Johnson & Johnson down. Bristol-Myers down." He stopped and stood there, breathing on the heavy side. Then he snapped out of it. "Welcome," and he lifted his arms up at his sides. I looked around closely at my surroundings. Nothing was personalized. There were no pictures of Cameron sunbathing with a bikini-clad Maya off the coast of St. Barts, like I'd half expected there to be. The only pictures were generic, the finishing touches on a generic place. There was a framed still-life over one set of shelves filled with books bearing no titles on the spines. There was a ceramic jar on an end table, one like my gramma used to keep, filled with mints. Only I expected to find this one filled with nothing, and did, lifting the ball-knobbed top of it.

Truth was, I was starving, and all I could think about was that giant, ripe, red tomato, even though I didn't care much for tomatoes ordinarily and stuck mostly to fried food. The kind you could get – chicken and fries – on the corner of Willoughby and Atlantic Avenue, that was my bag.

"This your place?" Cameron nodded. "Home sweet home. Got everything. Except septic. But there is running water. We have a tiny waste-water treatment facility and we recycle most of the water. We have electric. We have heat."

I frowned. "I would suspect that you people would be burning vegetable oil and standing under solar panels. Doesn't look too lived-in in here, anyway."

Cameron's face darkened. I suddenly realized that in this strange little house – like one of those houses at Disneyland that's supposed to be lived in by magical little creatures but is just an old-armpit-smelling prop. I was with a strange man I had only met hours ago, out here in the middle of nowhere, caught up in something I had only the foggiest clue about. I needed to be careful. I needed staying power.

"*You people*? See, that's the problem. You're all used to sitcoms where there's a neat solution for everything in a half an hour. Look, man," he lowered and shook his head. He seemed displeased with me and it made me think he had held a better opinion of me until just now. Now I was like all the rest. "Look," he said, "just because you hear about alternative power doesn't mean it's the answer. People think hydrogen fuel cells are the answer to our prayers. You get hydrogen through electrolysis, which you need electricity for, which you need coal or oil to generate. The oil crisis is just a symptom. The problem isn't even that we're dependent on cars. It's that we've grown dependent on a kind of spoiled, overindulged *lifestyle.* None of this kneejerk green-earth bullshit does anything except engender another industry."

"Sorry," I said, but what I meant was that I was sorry he thought less of me now. Damned be that inferiority complex. "Isn't that how things are done? Through industry? So what if the green movement makes some people rich. There's no way it will get done otherw–"

"It's industry that got us here in the first place!" Cameron's face was red. The tattoo popping up from under his collar seemed to darken a shade, even to stretch higher, like a knife nearing his neck, a needle about to plunge in. His eyes glared at me. Then, suddenly, like a flipped switch, he relaxed. "Sorry," he said, "long day. Let me show you where you can clean up." He walked towards some stairs and I followed. His head was lowered and he had a hand pressed to his temple. His shoulders hunched. He appeared to have a whopper of a headache. The air around me continued to smell like I was in someone's attic, where no one had been for weeks, months, maybe years.

It was like I was somewhere that didn't exist.

I showered and the water had a sulfuric smell to it. My skin was dry and itchy afterwards. I wondered how Maya's skin was so vibrant and smooth if she cleaned herself with the same water. Maybe it was a miracle of biochemistry.

Cameron was slightly shorter and stockier than I was, but I fit into a pair of his blue jeans that came up a little high around my ankles. The shirt I borrowed, on the other hand, was loose fitting. I felt like a thinner, gawkier version of Cameron and found myself wondering again about what sort of facilities, if any, these brainy science-types had for libations. Surely they must have occasion to drink like the rest of the world?

As I walked down the stairs, buttoning up the shirt, I thought I heard something coming from outside. An animal, maybe. It sounded wounded. I could have sworn, if I had my bearings straight, which was questionable, that it had come from the direction of the barracks I'd seen. I dismissed it; we were in the woods, after all.

There was nothing to drink in his fridge. There was really nothing at all in his fridge but a couple of condiments and what looked like it once was a cake. Cameron found me standing there and asked "hungry?" I nodded vigorously. "It's been a while." He smiled, "well, you've come to the right place." Cameron was definitely dynamic. One minute antagonizing henchman, the next a mad doctor, and the next an exuberant host. He could have been an actor or a politician. "Let's go get something."

We wound our way through the village to one of the Quonset huts, a large silvery dome. Still no one else was in sight, but Cameron continued to surveil, as if expecting somebody. The hut we entered served as food storage and was chilly inside. Cameron admitted the use of Freon in the air conditioning system and told me "Global warming is not our biggest concern. It's like the gas-powered vehicle – another symptom of the illness." I had a salad, some kind of soy-based sandwich and soymilk to drink. He explained about the engineered nutrients, about the rearranged nucleotides in the food, but I only listened with half an ear, gobbling up the meal. I thought to ask about animal food but I didn't. It didn't seem in line with Cameron's unorthodox attitude to be vegetarian, or vegan, but I decided not to broach the subject. Not now anyway. Instead I asked him about where the funding came from.

"Grants," he said quickly, "We have excellent grant writers." He took a sip of Vitamin water he had in a bottle, seeming to ponder something. "And we have a couple of independent investors who choose to remain anonymous," he said, and he smiled. I didn't like the smile.

"Not part of Big Agribusiness, I would think."

"I can't say," Cameron told me.

We were soon back outside, strolling. He had yet to tell me what he had in mind for me, or what the day would entail. At the moment we seemed to be waiting for something, but he wouldn't say what. I had more time now to formulate questions. One in particular was nagging at me; my eyes were continuously drawn back to the structure. "What's in the barracks?"

Cameron glanced in that direction. It was a very quick look, and then his gelid eyes were scanning the sky. "Equipment," was all he said.

Ten minutes later the sky was filled with the thudding of a helicopter. For some reason, I didn't like the sound of it. The trees to the south were swirling and then the chopper appeared above their tops, already low, colored with a yellow stripe down its green bodypaint. "Stay right here," said Cameron, and he jogged out to an area where there were no buildings, half the size of a football field and, ducking as he ran, leaving me to stand there.

The helicopter touched down like two feet getting out of bed. Drop, drop. The blades continued to spin and the door opened. It was a small helicopter, one of those…gyrocopters, maybe, but just a little bigger. The wind blew my loose clothing; the shirt and pants flapped around my body. I caught movement to my right and saw Maya standing there, her hair whipping around her head. She shielded her eyes from the lashings with one hand, making a visor over her brow.

A man stepped out of the helicopter in a black suit wearing sunglasses that were the wrap-around kind, like the type Cameron had been wearing earlier in the day. He looked left to right, stopping on us, Maya and I. I thought he looked familiar, like someone I'd seen on television, or in the news, maybe, but not quite – you know what it's like; it felt like déjà vu. He seemed to look right at me, even though I couldn't see his eyes. Cameron then took the man by the arm and the two of them, bent over, jogged away as the copter climbed up into the sky again. Cameron and the man in the suit ran in the other direction from me and I walked over to where Maya was standing.

As the thudding faded back to the south again I neared her. "Who was that?"

"One of the investors," Maya said.

I saw Cameron and the man in the suit disappear into the barracks. "Who else is here? There were a lot of cars back there." She looked at me. "They're working." Then, abruptly, "Come on, I'll take you home."

"What?" It didn't make any sense. Cameron had acted like I was the new guest of honor. Until this new guy showed up, of course. That had to be it. I pointed. "Is it because of this guy just got here?"

"Don't worry about it." She flashed me an award-winning smile, a smile filled with perfectly white teeth and two slightly pronounced canines. She held out her hand. "Come on, handsome."

You can imagine I didn't let the door hit me in the ass on the way out. Within twenty minutes we were back at the *Yaris*, and then winding our way through the country roads back to Burlington. I had a head full of questions but I couldn't formulate one of them. All I could think about was Maya, and if she was planning on staying the night, and how I might get her clothes off if I wasn't drinking. Still, I figured I would be alright. I just had no idea what I was in for. One way or the other. She smiled at me as we sped along, the trees rushing past in a blur, and in her smile I heard that strange, wounded sound, somewhat animal, somewhat human, but I pushed it away and smiled back at her.

I should tell you something else now.

The summer before I moved to Vermont I spent two weeks in the state, seeing about an old friend.

There was a guy I loaded truck with, named – you got it, Marcel Moresco – who also worked as a long haul trucker. Some of the boys just called him "Guy." Anyway, as a long-hauler he was prone to diners, roadside cafes and, then, when they appeared briefly, the so called cybercafés. He'd gotten into the internet and chat rooms and things of this nature, esoteric things to us Brooklyn bums who still lived pretty much in our neighborhood like it was still the 1970s and we had to piss in the street and beat on people and be territorial in order to survive. Marcel brought his laptop down onto his stoop one night and as we sat around drinking Chivas and beers he took me on a cyberspace tour. Set me up an email right then and there. Showed me how to "Google." I had long thought the whole thing was for yuppies, but Marcel showed me otherwise. I ended up tracking down an old girlfriend. *The* old girlfriend.

The old girlfriend was Katherine Glaston, the girl who I happily handed my virginity. Katherine was beautiful in a will-o'-the-wisp kind of way, with long sixties-style feathered brown hair, emerald eyes and a killer ass. I was still a teenager and she was into her late twenties when it happened. I fell in love and would've died for her. That's how some guys lose their virginity. I've known a lot of guys in my days, working the trucks and bumming around with the drunks and druggies and womanizers of the lower-to-middle class Brooklyn nests, and for most of them losing their virginity was a chauvinist's conquest – the girl a tool to be used and discarded. Some of the guys were stand-up about it, sort of Catholic, sticking with the girl for years or more. I know that Jimmy McKenzie married the girl he bed for the first time, both of them taking each other's virginity. Yuri Pete (his last name was really Petrovsky, or something, but Yuri Pete sounded like "you repeat" so we stuck with it) – he spent four years with the fifteen-year-old he stunned into sexual maturity, but then Yuri started getting really into Biggie Smalls, joined up with a hip-hop crew and got into bitches and chronic and bourbon and all of that. Eddie Wiesz was a guy that was your white, Jewish rapper kid, who used to pal around with Yuri, and when he saw what Yuri was doing he started this hip-hop group of his own, whose mission was to find as many virgins as possible and untie the apron strings. You see how it goes. *There's room in the choir for all God's children*, my gramma would say, and then refer to the neighbor's kid as a "slouch."

No, I was the guy who fell dumbly, star-spangled in love. I was drunk, of course, the night it happened. It was late for a guy – I was one of

the last few virgins I knew of, and I didn't have a religion to justify it, or a
debilitating disease like Louis Jackson, who had MS and played basketball
like he was a blade of grass bending in the wind, poor kid. No, I was a
virgin and hitting the booze already and quite snookered when it came to
that first time with Katherine, but I was with it enough to know that I loved
her instantly, fully, stupidly. We lasted about four months and then she left
town for the west, someplace in New Mexico, and I heard that years later
she'd returned east and was up in Vermont, a place I thought of as trees and
gay hillbillies, like most of Brooklyn does (except for those kids from
Vermont living in Brooklyn to chase the dream, invariably and sadly falling
into the same rhythm as everyone else of their tribe in a changing New York,
gentrified scene: they get dogs and square-rimmed glasses and vintage
clothes and all race to have the best, sleekest, newest technological toys,
dreams forgotten while managing an *Olive Garden*.) I forgot about
Katherine after that, but when Marcel sat there sipping *Chivas* with his
laptop open in the sweat brick summer night and said, "look up anyone you
want," Katherine Glaston was the first person that popped into my mind.

How was the old gal? Was she doing well? Was she still as viciously
attractive? Ultimately, would she have sex with me again; did I still have
rights to her? Though, as I pawed over these questions I had no real
intention of seeking her out if I found anything. I was too paranoid about
everything. I had made nothing of myself. I was a guy who loaded trucks,
moonlighted as a cheap spy and painted lurid, sexual paintings in secret. I
was mirroring my father to a tee. And I hadn't had a girlfriend in months
and hadn't been laid (not officially, anyway) in as long. This old gal
Katherine would see me and smell it on me and I'd be rejected all over
again. But a funny thing happened that night – when I did find her, old

Marcel, with the enormous belly and sprouts of hair coming out of a mole on his thick neck; Marcel, who was perpetually tucked into himself, like a massive turtle; Marcel, who was a real sweetheart but could become a really mean drunk with a punch that was like hydraulic piston coming at you, greased and ferocious, a square block of steel on the end – Marcel would have these moments of Zen-like wisdom. When I finally found Katherine and got her address up on the screen, I sat there biting my nails and told Marcel that the internet was a cool thing, thanks, but I ain't never gonna go seek this girl out. Marcel looked at me with those very dark brown eyes, rolled over my way, bits of blood bramble in them, and said, "You think you're some kind of loser?" I don't know. Maybe that doesn't make sense to anyone else, but what Marcel said that triggered me into action.

Thing was, it was Marcel I secretly called from Daniel's cell phone the night that Maya was over and I felt pressured to drink in order to perform. Marcel was actually down on that same stoop when I rang him, he told me (good ole "Guy") and I mentioned my dilemma. I told him that I felt like drinking. Marcel was silent for a second, just a second or two, and then he said, "So what's stopping you?" My mouth opened to respond, but, of course, there was no response to give. Again the first domino was knocked over and down they all went. It would seem a rhetorical question, and it was, in a way, but it wasn't. It was literal too. It got me thinking about how far I'd come and all that I had gained since I'd gotten off of the sauce and so my answer was right there. Everything was stopping me; everything that was good. I thanked Marcel and lied and said I'd be down soon to see him and all the boys and hung up. Maya came out of the bathroom, snicking her own cell phone closed. She'd had a secret call too, maybe.

"Nice place," she said.

"Thanks." Daniel wasn't home. He had three cell phones and no landline, so one phone was always at the apartment, the one I'd just used. "My roommate's the decorator." She sat down on the couch next to me and I felt my blood heat up and crawl into my face. "I've ah…I've got a problem with drinking," I told her.

"I know," she said.

"You know?"

"Yes."

"How?"

"I'm a doctor."

"What, did all my tiny little parts give me away?" I winced as soon as I said it.

Maya smiled and I felt something like relief. Maybe the worst was over. What I'd been dreading was over. Just a moment. Just that terrible, abysmal moment was over, the moment that had been trapped and throbbing in the perpetual future, the plastic-encased future, sitting there, pulsating like a red button. The button was pressed. All that had come out of it was a little hiss of air pressure releasing. My heart thumped against my ribcage. I leaned over to kiss her.

"Woah, woah, tiger." She pulled back. "What're you doing?"

The heat was back and I felt my adrenaline come threading its way into my blood and nerves, keying me up, making me feel like vomiting. "Oh," I said. "Sorry." She laughed. "It's okay." She then sat back, sort of plopped back onto the couch, slapped her hands on her jeaned thighs and looked up at the ceiling, sighing. I was going to scream or cry. "I just can't get involved with you." Zing! The blood subsided and my heart returned to a regular rhythm, still fast, but even keel. She liked me after all – she had thought about it, she had thought about this – she was conflicted otherwise. I didn't care what the conflict was – it was enough that she felt it. It was good, good. So good. I was a yo-yo.

"Why not?" I asked. This was almost as good as if we were going at it right now. Maybe even better. There was a drama here, a mystery. Or, maybe, she was just toying with me. "Because," she said, "of what's going on."

"What's going on? You mean with the commune?"

She looked from the ceiling to me. "I mean with everything. With everything that we're doing. You're... I couldn't."

"Is it because of Cameron? Dr. Madison?" I pronounced the second name mockingly and instantly regretted it. She shot me a look. "No," she said, "it has nothing to do with him. Well, with our work, yes."

"What does growing vegetables have to do with seeing someone?"

She laughed then, and her laugh filled me up like the fauna in the greenhouse, warming me with love and lust and infatuation. She was spellbinding. I watched her lips intently as she spoke. She wore no lipstick but her mouth was a perfect shade of red. Like she sucked blood occasionally. "You're handsome," she said, her tone as though this was the first it had occurred to her, and cocked her head to the side. My approval-crazed mind slurped it up like spilled vodka. I fed on it. "Oh yeah?" "Yeah," she affirmed. Then she looked thoughtful. "So what do we do if you can't drink?"

"You can drink all you want," I told her, emboldened, and I winked.

"Oh?"

"Sure."

"Alright then. Let's go find some action."

We stood and I just had to ask her. I looked her quickly up and down, taking her in. Five foot 7. Slender, athletic, feminine. Her jeans and her white top and her leather jacket. "Maya." She looked at me directly. I asked her, "What're you doing here?"

"You mean what am I doing here if I didn't come here to have sex with you?"

"No. Yeah."

That laugh again. "Field research," she said, and held out her hand. "Let's go into the field."

We patrolled the night. Soon we were sitting at one of the round-tops in the Irish pub. I started drinking my Cokes and getting hyper, chattering away about Peter, about nothing. Maya was a good listener, but it was tuned in to the surroundings. She kept one eye scanning the place as she listened to me, smiling, making eye contact. I soon grew self-conscious of my blabbering as I started sugar-crashing from all of the Cokes. I asked her about herself, about her field, and started to feel depressed.

"Bio-chemistry is the baby of science," she told me, "only about forty years old. It was born when proteins were first found and identified."

"Proteins," I said, "the building blocks of life." It made me feel worse to say it, but I did, trying to be a good host like always.

"Exactly. Proteins are built by amino-acid chains – there are 22 amino acids – but yes, essentially, proteins are the machines." She looked around the barroom and I wondered if she thought we were being eavesdropped. I wondered if the cute brunette bartender noticed me with this smashing chick.

"So you don't believe in evolution? I recall when we first met you waving a gun in my face and saying something about Darwin being full of shit."

She smiled. "A *fake* gun," she said. Then she grew serious, academic again. "Darwin and evolution are not inseparable. Yes, I believe in evolution, but not in Darwinian dogmatism." She leaned forward. "You know, people are pretty simple. Life is full of business. You wash the car, do the laundry, go to work, pay the bills – by and large you watch a lot of TV and read a lot of fiction. You tell someone that it's a warm summer because cars are heating up the atmosphere and pretty soon you've got the Global Warming parade. People don't care about the details."

"They want a cause."

"Exactly. Exactly." She seemed genuinely pleased. I reveled in it, and felt a little better. Like celebrating with a drink, almost. I had regressed to the state of a 17-year-old virgin. "They want a *cause*. Not data. People shy away from data. It's boring. Moreover, people are generally intuitive. And that's good – that's good. One of my favorite quotes is from Freud – 'Everywhere I go I find a poet has been there before me.' I think I got that right. What we do in science is generally elucidate the ethereal, abstract of the artist's thinking, of the poetic, intuitive feeling. It's all there. I mean, what proteins do, we do. Proteins work in groups. We work in groups. Proteins have a mission, a purpose – so do we. When proteins bond with chemicals – proteins that are enzymes – they fit them like pieces of a puzzle, just like we fit together, just like we catalyze one another. What's microcosmic is mirrored in the macrocosmic, and vice-versa. So we find that painters and poets and writers are like scientists and doctors and researchers – they're just working in different fields."

"So, if that's how you see it, why do what you do?"

"Because it burns me up that people go around with the 'Darwin fish' on their car bumpers." She raised an eyebrow. "People are simple. All you have to do is give them a little bit of information, be persuasive, and they're content to have that cause, though nobody knows, really. They've got to pick one side or the other, this group or that group. When you get down to the very microscopic level, you start to see the secrets." She winked and leaned back. "People go the other way – they go out. Hitler tried to rule the world. The U.S. tries to police everybody – I know that is a platitude and it's probably mostly to do with the last oil reserves, but I'm not military-minded, or nation or empire-minded. What I'm saying is, that is dubious control. Dubious and very dangerous. It will never work. Historically, it never has. The real control," and she leaned in once more, "is found in the little things, at the biochemical level. You control that, and everything else falls into place." Her eyes snapped off to lock on something over my shoulder.

I said, "And bioengineering food is going to control the public?" I knew it was a stupid question but it fell out of my mouth like a hapless poop. Maya wasn't listening anyway. I looked over my left shoulder, feeling like – intuitively – I already knew what I was going to see.

I watched as two young men in black suits slipped from a booth – the same booth, I was almost certain, they had been sitting in the night Terry

Hackford bashed me in the nose. They slipped out, looking sideways at
Maya, and then headed for the door. I turned back. I suddenly remembered
who and where I was and slipped off of my chair and grabbed Maya by the
arm. "Come on," I said, "we're going to follow them."

I saw her smile approvingly at me out of the corner of my eye as she
grabbed up her jacket.

"Our field specimen cometh," she said.

It had started raining. The wipers of the Yaris whicked back and forth,
sluicing off the water. My window was cracked and I could smell the oils
slicking over the streets. Maya was driving again; her insistence.

The two suits were a couple of cars in front of us, driving a Dodge
Neon. For all of this cloak and dagger shit, we didn't have the right wheels.
We were going along Pearl Street, headed toward Winooski, when the Neon
made a quick right. "They're headed for the campus," Maya said. She made
the turn and I thought I heard the tires give a little squeal. As we
straightened out and surged forward Maya said, "So what was the problem
with drinking?"

I took a breath. Nobody had asked me about that yet. Daniel had
taken on that attitude where the problem is quietly understood and not
dragged out of the closet for autopsy. Sometimes that attitude was a bit
worse than the "interventioning" types. Marcel knew about me going on the
wagon, but he was the only one from the neighborhood who did. Maya was

the first outsider I'd told, besides those who suspected, obviously, like Terry Hackford and Rupert, Peter, and Josh. Oh God, Peter was still up in that friggin' hospital. Happy-stoned-go-along and stinking Peter, who had just been into it for the adventure. I made a mental note to thank him somehow. Maybe a nice can of Right Guard. "Well," I said, searching for the right words. How did I play this? Was I discrete and tight-lipped about it? Did I say what I felt? Did I even know what I felt? "One drink always became drunk. Thing is with booze is it kicks you out of your body and then the next day your soul is looking to get back, but your body's all sick and closed out. So your soul is hovering around, naked, exposed, floating there protean and vulnerable and you have to face all of these illusions and symbols and make industrious sense of them." I took a breath.

"Colorful."

"Yeah," I said out the window, "that's me." I had just sounded like a complete jackass.

"So you believe in a soul?" The Neon was only one car ahead of us now. I wondered how much Maya knew about tailing somebody – from her driving so far she was pretty green. If these guys were the suspicious, watch-your-ass types, they had made us. They had looked right at us as we left, besides. There had been almost foreknowledge in that look, perhaps even an agenda – they'd known, or even hoped that we'd follow them. It was all conjecture. I was holding on for the ride, feeling like I'd just blown my wad with the alcohol thing, feeling like an idiot.

"A soul. I don't know," I said. Better to take the middle road now.

We reached Williston Road. The light was red and we pulled up behind the Minivan that separated us from the suits in the Neon. I could see the passenger side – just an oblong shadow of a head – and then the light turned. We both made left turns. I asked, "do you?"

She sighed. We could have been in the back of a cab speeding over the Brooklyn Bridge for a casual night in the city, the way her demeanor was. "It's hard to believe in something like a soul when you see all these tiny little parts to everything. Kind of takes the mystery away. But, you know," and she spun the wheel left and we jostled over the first speedbump unto the UVM campus, "just because you can see the parts doesn't mean there isn't something going on. I'd be just as bad as Darwin fanatics if I leapt to any conclusions. It's just…"

The Neon fed itself into a parking space. Maya kept going, past the parking lot. I opened my mouth but she finished her thought. "…it's just that people treat everything so mutually *exclusively*. You have to be one way or the other. If you eschew Darwin then you are said to espouse Creationism. If you say 'there is no God,' and you mean that there is no guy in a white robe up on high, then you've got to be an atheist. It's ridiculous. Who said God was in a white robe? Maybe it's teal." She laughed lightly. "But, well, you've just got to think bigger. Most people are just pissed off, is what it is. Gays are pissed off that they don't fit into Christianity, so they hate it. Conservatives don't have to be anti-abortion, either. I'm conservative – fiscally, really – and I'm pro-choice. You know, all of these things don't have to be married to each other. You just have to have a little vision. But, like I said…"

"People are simple." I chose not to add anything about abortion. Somewhere along the way, I had learned. A little.

"People are simple," she agreed, smiling. There was another parking lot on the backside of the gymnasium and she took it.

"You're a conservative?" I smiled too. We were on a date. A date that involved a short, run-of-the-mill car chase. A little surveillance. "I don't know," she said, "am I?"

She obviously knew where the two men were headed – and it was into the gym. She popped the trunk of the Yaris. For a minute I thought she was going to pull a shotgun from there. It was a flashlight she produced instead. "You got a cell phone?"

"No. Why?"

"A reporter without a cell phone," she said.

"I'm not a–" but she was tapping at her phone. "I know," she said. "There – silent mode." She put the phone away. Then we were trotting over to the gymnasium, winding through the parking lot, both of us hunched over and I was reminded of the helicopter, the commune, the strange, surreal world I had been in just that morning.

A muffled roar went up from inside the gymnasium – the sound of a crowd excited. For some reason, maybe it was the flashlight, I had expected we'd be going in to a darkened, empty building. There were, of course, too many cars in the parking lot for that to make sense. I was failing miserably as a detective. And I seemed to be getting miles away from finding out about Phil Brandis. At least I was sober. I raised my eyebrows and looked at Maya questioningly as we jogged to a side door. "Basketball," she said. "UVM's got a great team."

"Oh," I said. I was about as sporty as I was self-assured. Maya knew her way around. There was a side door we took that lead into a maintenance room with assorted tools and an ATV parked in the small bay. Through another door and we were in the gymnasium. The roar blasted into me as we snuck in, and the smell of bodies, sweet candy and spoiled beer commingled

in the dusty muck under the bleachers. I followed her to a slot in between
sections of the seats and she immediately stood upright and started casually
sauntering into the public view.

   The players' shoes squeaked and a whistle blew. The crowd rippled
with excitement. Most of the seats were filled. We started up, excusing
ourselves and brushing past the legs and arms of engrossed fans. After a
minute or so Maya found a spot and we sat down. Her eyes were vigorously
scanning all around us – there were no bleachers across the court from us,
but the sections abutted the hardwood, shining floor for a good 270 degrees.
The crowd surged as the whistle blew again. I watched Maya's eyes. She
was no longer searching the crowd but watching the game intently. I kept
looking at her sideways. She wasn't just watching the game, she was
watching one player in particular. I felt the rat teeth of jealousy go to work
on my stomach. Girls had often told me how sexy basketball was and I'd
always been a shit player, tall enough though I was. I nabbed her attention,
grabbing at the flashlight. She winced and pulled back. Then she relaxed.
"I don't think you'll need that in here," I shouted. "I didn't bring it for the
light," she answered. "I brought it in case I needed to hit somebody."

   I swallowed. Not very good security in this place, letting a girl like
Maya in. I leaned over to her, smelling her as I did. Her perfume was a
triumph amid the gym/stadium smell of sweat and fried food. "Have you
seen them?"

   She didn't take her eyes off of the court. "Come on, super sleuth.
You can do better."

   Suddenly I wanted to get up and leave. Fuck this bitch. It was a
quick, electric feeling and it passed, as nimble as a fish, and I was in love

again. Where were they? Then I felt it – it was almost a burning sensation in my shoulder blades. I turned slowly around.

The two suits were at the top of the bleachers in back of us. Both of them were looking at me, one guy sipping a soda through a straw. He raised a hand and twiddled his fingers.

"What the hell is going on?" I whispered through clenched teeth, feeling absurd. I should have been used to this, what with all the slinking around I'd done to expose the Ukrainians selling illicit imports, wearing wigs informing on the Italians who did more than chop vegetables in the kitchen of *Mamma Mia's*.

Maya ignored me. On the court, the player I was sure she was watching launched into the air. The ball spun through space, came down and swished through the net. The crowd went crazy. People stood up, including Maya, clapping wildly. I turned around again. The guy sipping the soda titled his head and shrugged at me. He grinned and started clapping. The other guy didn't look so happy. Were they cops? Feds? Something else? I was starting to get antsy. Too much time on the outside. I was getting treated like an asshole. Maya was toying with me. Why, I didn't know. At this point, I didn't care. I stood up and started making my way down from the bleachers. When I got to the bottom I turned to look back. Maya was right behind me.

"Come on," she said, "I've got something to show you."

Alright, I thought, *one last time.*

She smiled, as if she were reading my thoughts. I stepped aside so she could pass and lead the way once more. There was more action behind me on the court and the fans erupted once more. The sound was deafening – a bunch of fucking robots. Herd animals. Simple folk, looking for a cause.

Maya lead, and I followed. I hated that yet another woman was leading me, and that I was following, but I let it happen. I let it all happen.

As we ran across the spongy campus lawn in the dark I began to feel intensely irritated. I realized I hadn't had a cigarette in what must have been hours and I stopped and lit one up. Again, I thought, to hell with this, to hell with Maya.

A few yards ahead of me she stopped. She was a shifting shape in the dark – we had trotted out beyond the throw of the walkway lights. "*Come on.*"

"Who were those guys?" I spoke as if we were two students standing around in the light of day discussing a class. I was consciously flaunting our cover. I didn't care. I was getting pissed. Maya walked over to me, lighting her own cigarette. "I thought they were with you," I said, "I mean, I thought they were the commune people when I first saw them."

"The commune people," she said, not quite whispering. "That's funny. You ever see *The Da Vinci Code?* Or read the book?"

"I saw it, yeah."

"What did you think?"

I was at the end of my rope with Maya and her questions and her cleverness. "Maya, whatever you have to show me, show it to me now. Otherwise, fuck off. I'm sick of this."

I could see the glint of her teeth as she smiled in the dark. "Wow. Okay, okay. Just tell me, come on, I'm curious – what did you think?"

"It was a good movie."

"Come on…"

"Okay, Maya, I thought 'who cares.' Nothing 'proves' to me whether something is divine or not. People throw around the word 'divine.' 'From God.' Okay, I don't see it that way. I have a much broader definition for things like divinity and miracles. So, you know what, while everyone was hemming and hawing about it I was like 'so what? So what if Jesus married Mary Magdalene?' I'm not saying that he did or didn't – I wasn't there. But who cares? Jesus is still cool, man. I still dig Jesus."

Maya blew smoke into the air above her head. "You can't be this naïve."

"Look," I said again, walking forward, forcing her to take several steps backward, "I know there's a huge difference. I know the whole idea of Christianity is based on the divinity of Jesus Christ. I know the idea of Jesus marrying a woman is a huge, huge deal, a huge threat to a religion – kind of like discovering irreducibly complex molecular system is a real caveat to Darwinism, right?" I saw her eyes widen and was satisfied. "First of all, I went to seminary school, and then onto theology school. Okay? My gramma is a devout Catholic; I was practically raised by her. Second, I'm not naïve. Don't ever call me that again. And three, you're the one that said people were simple. It doesn't matter to *me* what Jesus did – I don't judge him. But I know it's a huge upsetting topic to a lot of people, okay? Now, *who are those guys?*"

I was breathing heavily. My eyes had opened and I could make out more of Maya's face. She was beautiful, but there'd better be a point to all of this.

"They're Christians," she said. "They work for Terry Hackford."

Maya seemed to be able to get anywhere she wanted to – and she knew how to get there. We were standing in a laboratory together, the light of the hallway throwing our shadows across the pale green tile creating stretched-out, ghoulish versions of ourselves.

"What are we doing here?" I whispered. It was fairly clear to me – as it had been since Cameron's "tour" of the village, his erratic behavior, and the arrival of the man from the helicopter, that the biochemists at Utopia were not really engineering food. Or, if they were, that was just a cover. Just for show. Whatever they were really up to eluded me for now; I wasn't even sure I really wanted to know. But, of course, that was my job; I had to know. Maya shut the door behind us and turned to me.

"How are you so familiar with this place?"

"I did grad work here."

"Uh-huh," I said, and took a leap, "so that's how you know Terry."

She nodded, but didn't look surprised. She licked her lips. "He was one of my professors, before he got canned for talking God."

"I knew it," I said. I took a step back and leaned against a smooth, tiled wall. I dropped my head. "Maya. Why are we here?"

"For this," she said. She pressed her body up against mine and kissed me. Her lips were bituminous and hungry. I felt the soft press of her breasts against my chest. She put her hand against the small of my back and pushed me into her. My body instantly responded. Amazing to me, though, to this day, is what I did next. I pulled away. I pulled away and stepped back from her and looked directly into her eyes. I didn't know what had come over me. I thought of Daniel. But that wasn't it, not quite. "No," I said. "Stop." She just looked back at me, unblinking. "This is what you brought me here to 'show' me?" I waited for her response. Instead of acting dejected or hurt, Maya was as coy and mysterious as the moment I had met her – a truly self-possessed witch. She sauntered backward, a light smile on those lips, and then spun around. She walked through the high desks with the sinks in them, winding her way to the back of the room and she walked through another door there. I stood, rooted to my spot, still a bit in shock at my own behavior. Maya stuck her head back into the lab room. "Come here," she said.

I walked through the lab. The connecting room was more casual – there was a desk, some chairs, like you might find in a living room or lounge, and a long table against one wall with the more prototypical plastic classroom chairs pushed into it. Maya had seated herself at the desk on the other end of the room and was swiveling back and forth in the chair there. She looked like the hot substitute – only the hot substitute I found more dangerous than intriguing. Maybe sobriety was a good thing after all. I seemed to be learning.

I stood in the doorway and shrugged my shoulders and held my palms out. "What the hell am I looking at?" Maya only grinned at me. It was then that I heard the footsteps behind me. I spun around on the balls of my feet and saw the two men from the bleachers – and before that, the Irish pub – bearing down on me. With a surge of adrenaline, like a cornered animal I tried to get out of the room and squeeze past them. I almost made it, crashing into the two men with my shoulder, but as one of them went down he caught me around the shin and I toppled forward. A second later there was a tremendous weight on my back as the other one, I imagined, leapt up on top of me and pinned me there.

"Easy! Easy!" I heard Maya say. I heard her footsteps coming around the desk she had been sitting at. "Get him up." The weight lifted off me and I was yanked to a standing position. The men had my arms behind my back – my shoulder was painfully wrenched beyond its normal range of motion and I cried out. A hand was clamped over my mouth. "I said *easy* guys – you're supposed to be good God-fearing Christians, not Mafia. Go easy on the guy." Maya appeared in front of me, looking both masterful and concerned. I tried to gouge her brain with my eyes. She only blinked with her long lashes and looked me up and down. "Are you hurt?" I didn't respond. "Will you cry out again if they release you?" Again I didn't offer any gesture. I could feel my heart pounding. I could feel the adrenaline, cortisol, epinephrine coursing through me. Suddenly I lurched forward toward Maya and broke the hold my captors had on me. As soon as I was free I spun around. I felt inhuman – I was enraged. I nailed the one suit with a right hook and his head whipped back and he stumbled away. With the countermotion I caught the other suit in the head, along the temple, with my elbow. He staggered back and the two of them entangled and fell over backward, through the doorway into the next room. I charged after them, leaping through the air, coming down on them, completely clueless as to what I was going to do once I had pounced on them. As soon as I did, however, Maya was on my back. "Stop it! Stop it! Please!" My hands were all over the two of them – I think I was searching for a gun. Luckily – for all of us – I didn't find one. I found something, something square and bulky and was about to extract it when Maya's arm slipped around my neck. Then I heard "Hey!" and saw a flash of light. I turned around – I swear a growl escaped me – and saw a campus security guard – must've been 20 years-old if he was a day – standing in the doorway to the lab, poking his flashlight in on us. I sprung up and started toward him. Maya yelled after me again. The security guard's eyes widened and he disappeared from the doorway. I stopped short of following him – some sensibility was still within my power. I stood there, chest heaving, and felt an explosion in my lower back, right where Maya had touched me and pulled me close minutes – maybe only seconds – before. What happened next was one of the worse feelings I have ever experienced. It was like a seizure. Every muscle in my body strained. My testicles turned to burning coals. My back arched and I was looking up at the ceiling – I'm pretty sure I was on my tip toes, my arms straight behind me, pointing down, like I was poised for flight. My whole body vibrated; my teeth chattered, my vision blurred, I didn't breathe. My intestines, my lungs, everything squishy in me felt like it was burning. *I'll be damned*, I thought. And then I blacked out.

*

Maya shut the door behind us and turned to me. "For this," she said. She pressed her body up against mine and kissed me. Her lips were bituminous and hungry. I felt the soft press of her breasts against my chest. She put her hand against the small of my back and pushed me into her – I was instantly hot and enthused, suddenly insatiable. I felt a surge of aggression unlike any other I had up to then, coupled with a lust that I was incapable of containing, it spilled from my every pore and I drank her in with my mouth.

She seemed equally enthused, excited. There was something in the back deep of my mind that whispered *this is what she wants* but I ignored it. I was sweating. I yanked her pants down over her hips, and heard them tear. I felt her smile through our continuous kiss. I didn't bother to pull her underwear – it was a thong – down along with the pants, but simply ripped them from her, and her small buttocks jiggled. She stepped out of the slacks now pooled at her feet, her sex exposed, and thrust her hips at me, wrapping her legs around my butt and lower back. I spun her – us – from the door and planted her on one of the tables with the sinks and she undid my pants and I removed them and stepped from them.

I felt like I could barely see, like I was going blind. Things were blurry, even Maya's face right in front of mine was blurred and running, like a painting sprayed with turpentine, bleeding. Still I didn't stop, couldn't stop. The instant I was inside of Maya my mind exploded in white light and all was gone of the lab, and it was years ago, years before I'd ever arrived in Burlington, and I was in the garden with Katherine Glaston behind her two story Victorian house, and then we were in her Queen-sized bed with the white linen canopy, her curtains had been white linen too, and that's what I

was seeing now, the sun streaming in, the white iridescence, somehow
Katherine's eyes iridescent, and I turned and looked into her face and it was
Maya.

I came to in the back of the Yaris and I lifted my head to see Maya's eyes
looking back at me from the rearview mirror, then back to the road. We
were in the middle of nowhere. On either side of me were the men in suits.
The Christians, I was to believe. Terry Hackford Christians. Custom-jobs.

"Welcome back," one of them said. Maya was driving. Her eyes
flicked to the rearview mirror. "Hello raging bull," she said, though I
detected no humor in her, nor any indication that we had had sex together in
a UVM school laboratory, her ripped panties on the marble floor.

"Where are we going?"

Neither of them answered me. I glared at the one to the right of me.
It was my good side.

"Who are you?"

"I'm Watson and this is Crick," said the other suit, talking behind my
turned head.

I felt like spitting; my mouth tasted like rust. I wondered if I was
bleeding. My voice sounded thick. "That's funny," I said, "The DNA
guys."

"They'll do as our names," said 'Watson', on my left. My head hurt
all over again. Just when I'd thought the pain had completely subsided from

getting pistol-whipped the first time, I get pistol-whipped again. There would be no third time. Whoever tried cracking me in the skull or the face – or anywhere else for that matter – the third time, I was going to rip out his throat with my teeth.

I was starting to see spots. Little Tinkerbells dancing. I tried to calm down and breathe deeply like Daniel had told me about his yoga. I looked into the rearview mirror again. "Who was the guy in the helicopter?" This time Maya kept her eyes on the dark road; I didn't expect an answer.

"I can't tell you right now – you wouldn't be safe," she said.

"Safe? This is safe? Thanks, but I'll go it alone. What is he – Christian Coalition?"

I felt a jab in my ribs and cried out. That was it. I started to struggle, to fight with Watson and Crick. "Hey!" Maya shouted and pulled the car off of the road. Crick, I think, tried to hit me in the head. I ducked it just in time and brought my head right back at him, smashing his nose. The doors flew open and I was dragged to the edges of a vast cornfield, blood all over the front of me, blood on the nice button-down shirt I'd borrowed from Daniel's closet for Maya's and my "date." Crick had blood oozing from his nose, getting into his mouth. "I hear we're overproducing corn," said Watson. "Yeah," said the Crick, sounding like he had a bad cold, "corn syrup is in everything now." "Hear that?" Crick was speaking down at me. "You'll be in some kid's orange marmalade."

"Kind of like Soylent Green," said the other. I was on my back, the two of them dragging me, arm for arm. I started to kick with my feet like I was riding a paddleboat upstream. I yanked with my arms. Out of the corner of my eye I saw the moonlight flash across the black cylinder of the Taser.

I felt it coming out of me. I yelled at them. "Hey come on," I yelled, "you guys are *Christians*!"

The commotion stopped. Watson and Crick stopped coming for me, the Taser in Crick's hand lowering to his side. Maya stood in between them Her eyes were very white in the night, like they were bioluminescent. Crick squatted beside me, the Taser in his one hand, my forearm gripped in the other. "You ever heard of Sanhedrin, dumbshit? He sold Jesus to the authorities for thirty pieces of silver." He brought the Taser towards my neck.

"Not a good business move," said Watson.

"Wait!" It was all I could think to say. It was all anybody ever said.

I closed my eyes. I saw Maya, her long body there against the door to the lab, the room dark, a lock of hair in her face, that lascivious grin. I saw her in the field, the clearing where Peter and I had first met her. Gun in her hand, fake or not. Getting cracked in the head by Mike. I could smell the edge of cornfield nearby, the fertile, wet soil, the slice of moon in the sky, I saw it, and I took a breath, and I ripped my arm free of Crick, grabbed *his* arm and jerked him so the he fell over me and crashed into Watson's legs. Then I was up, somehow I snaked out from under Crick's akimbo legs, and I was on top of them, both of them, and I had a fistful of each of their hair and I lifted, I mean I really fucking yanked, and then I rammed both of their faces into the ground. I grabbed up the Taser which lay next to Crick, and I held it up. I had no idea how to use it – I was just going to bash them each to death with it.

Maya cried out and grabbed at my arms, held over my head. I tore free of her and shoved her back, pushing at her hips, knocking her off balance. I raised the Taser again. I brought it down, hard, on Crick's head, who was starting to try and get up. He face-planted back into the dirt. Watson had raised his head and was looking over at me. I smashed his face, I saw a tooth fly from his head. I was ready to keep going.

"Stop it!" Maya screamed. She was really yelling at the top of her lungs. I felt good. I felt like the old me again, stomping some ass on my turf, no longer this luckless, shoe-lace-tied fuckshit who couldn't drink, who couldn't find his own ass with two hands, couldn't talk to women, a useless expatriate limping through life. I'd been pathetic lately. I'd been a chump. I was sick of it. It was time to take it all back. I raised the Taser again.

"Jack!"

I stopped, weapon in midair. Watson and Crick were both throat-deep in the soil in front of me, unmoving.

"That's your real name – Jack. But they call you 0035. That's your batch number. Or, the batch number of what's inside you."

I looked at Maya, sitting there on her duff in the moonlight, mascara smeared, lipstick smudged. Her hair was tangled. Her leather jacket half on and half off of her. My chest heaving, I listened. I couldn't help it.

"Bullshit," I said. "You know who I work for. The Brothers. You know that."

I started laughing. For some reason, just hearing myself made me laugh. I didn't know what was going on with me, but it felt so good, I just kept on laughing, and soon I realized I wasn't going to be able to stop. I bit my fist. I actually did that. I bit it, and I bit the thing so hard I drew blood. My own fist. I was a real mess, only I didn't know it. Not yet.

Maya planted her hands in the moist earth. She swung herself around and slid down the little embankment to me like someone with numb legs, like a mermaid. She was looking at me but then she checked out Watson, closest to her. She felt for his pulse. Then Crick's. In the meantime, I got off of them. I sat back. Both Maya and I were pig-dirty.

She sat back again, apparently satisfied with their vitals – if there were or weren't any, I didn't care, but since she didn't open her cell phone to call for an ambulance, I figured they were still breathing.

Maya looked at me. There was nothing playful or devious in her eyes now. I felt a pang of regret, misplaced though it may have been.

"You're an experiment, Jack." I remained still, just sitting there. The night seemed to sing around me. The wind soughing through the whickering corn husks, the crickets along the road's shoulder. No traffic so far. I wondered when a car might come by, how much time we had, and I realized I was coming down from whatever the hell I'd just gone through. Coming down was familiar enough to recognize. "Listen to me. Listen." She was urgent. She must've sensed me drifting. She knew we didn't have much time. I could see her eyes search the corn for a second, then come right back to mine. She looked like a doctor then, like the real McCoy. "You're a bioengineered subject. Product Number 35. Do you understand me?"

I was hallucinating. I was still unconscious from the Taser and I was hallucinating. Or – no – I was drunk. This was a drunken dream. I knew the terrible nightmares that came with a big drunk, those mid-morning whoppers with demons and apocalyptic tragedies; I was familiar there too.

"Listen," she said again, and I saw her glance at the road behind her, "you're not alone. Okay? There are others."

"Uh-huh," I said. I decided it was time to stand up, so I did. Whatever this was, it was coming to an end. I was ending it. I walked around Watson and Crick and past Maya and up the short embankment to the road. I was going to hop in the next car going by and head back to Burlington. Time for a cocktail, maybe.

Standing on the edge of the road I said, "What am I – I'm a clone?"

Maya huffed, as if offended. "No," she said, "you're not a *clone*." She got up, brushed some dirt from her legs and walked toward me. "Your DNA was not manufactured. Despite what you may read in the tabloids, or what's in the latest techno-thriller movie, nobody can do that yet. Not quite. You are an experiment in the sense that you have been tampered with. Cellularly. Genetically... chromosomally. Your genes. Do you understand?"

I looked down at my waist. "My jeans? Cellularly? I don't own a phone. Remember? Stupid for a reporter."

"Jack," she said. "Stop it."

I spun on her, and I was tempted to take her shirt into my fist and pull her close and scream into her face, but I didn't. I said, "What're you doing, Maya?"

"I had to see. I think there are adverse effects. I think it's inhumane..."

"Adverse effects? You mean like almost killing your fucking boys, there?"

"I'm sorry," she said, and she swiped hair back out of her face and looked past me, down the road. "Just think about it. Okay? They've engineered you. That's why you...that's why you're not drinking right now. Why your gay roommate is sleeping with women. Why number forty-three just put up 32 points on the board for UVM tonight. That's where it started, anyway."

Maya's face seemed bright again, seemed to have its own glow, and not just from the moon. I turned and looked behind me and saw headlights coming our way. When I turned back around, Maya was looking at me, not so much as a doctor now, but something else entirely. She looked older too. Somehow, I thought, she'd suddenly aged. I now thought that her thing, the sexy, jubilant and bad-girl thing, might've been a ruse.

"You're a traitor," I said.

"What?"

"Don't get haughty. You're a traitor. Whether it is mutiny aboard *The Bounty* or betraying the President of the United States, where I come from, there's loyalty."

Maya studied me. Her eyes flicked over my shoulder. I could hear the car now, the tires whirring on the pavement, a thudding sound getting louder, like heavy bass.

"I am," she said, "A traitor. Yes."

We stood like that, looking at each other, the car closing in.

The car whooshed by, barely even seeming to slow. Music thumped behind tinted windows. It was a Honda or Toyota or something, tricked out with baseboard lights, and then it was fading away.

I could feel the panic start to creep. I could sense that if the panic hit, it would be worse than any of the anxiety-ridden hangovers I'd experienced had ever been. I had to believe her. Even for me, my emotions were all over the place. "How old am I? How long since I've been product?"

Maya looked at me with what I thought was relief, though she was still pensive, older looking, no longer the girl from the ride into the commune, or the one tempting me with her hips in the dark UVM lab. But maybe both were still in there, somewhere.

"We took you from the edge of Lake Champlain three weeks ago," she said, "so, you're practically an infant."

"An infant," I said, nodding, curling my mouth down at the corners, looking over at Watson and Crick (Watson was starting to stir.) "Phase one," I said, tasting the words. They tasted charred. I stood there, swaying with the corn.

"Jack," she said, and I looked at her, and in her face was the kind of beauty I'd never seen before, the kind that there was no way to trust. "Come back with me to Utopia. Help me. Your questions will be answered there, I promise."

I said nothing. I started down toward Watson and took his arm and started to try and help get him to his feet. Maya joined me. I continued to smell the corn, the crickets sang in my ears, and I decided to believe that, for just the moment, this was all happening to me as a little boy. I had simply fallen asleep in my mother's arms while she sat in her chair and rocked with me, the white linen curtains blowing in the breeze.

THE CRUCIBLE

The ride back to the commune was something like a nightmare; I still wondered if I was dreaming. Dreams usually blended things together, taking abrupt turns; characters spontaneously became other characters right in the middle of a scene, people that were there one minute were gone the next, locations changed while you were within them. Like my day was going.

Watson and Crick were gone. Maya had convinced me to get into the Yaris and lock the doors as she went and roused them. I had done as I was told – truthfully, I was glad for it. The anger gone, the rage having coursed through my system, I felt weak and tired as I sat there in the passenger seat, watching in the sideview mirror as the two black-suited men got to their feet, their faces bloody and caked with black dirt (Crick pulled a tooth from his mouth.) Had either of them come to the car, smashed the window and tried to get back at me, it could have happened. It could have, easy. I was done.

They didn't. Maya worked her characteristic magic. I watched her gesturing there along side the road, the two men watching her, neither looking over at the car, at me. Even for that I was grateful. Not only had I felt physically weakened, I felt guilt too. I watched her talk to them, her arms waving and the corn waving in rows behind her. Another couple of cars passed. I saw her talking into her cell phone. When she got back in the car, she said that she'd called them a car service; they'd refused an ambulance.

"They don't believe in doctors?" I'd asked her when we were already a couple of miles away.

"No. Not that" It was all she had said. We'd driven the whole rest of the way in silence.

I was beyond tired as we drove slowly through those dark-stained woods. My head ached, my whole body ached – muscles, tendons, bone, you name it. Maya got the flashlight back out of the trunk when we finally came to rest. Part of me hoped that Daniel had called the cops by now, worried sick over me – but another part of me wondered if I even knew who Daniel was. If what Maya was selling me was true, then Daniel couldn't be trusted to do anything on my behalf.

Maybe that was why the so-called Watson and Crick duo were infiltrating. Maybe they believed that this was Man finally having gone too far, and not an issue to legislate or discuss in public forum, but to do away with quietly, the good but oft-dirty work of the Lord. God's little Taser-happy soldiers. But how had they convinced Maya? Or had she gone to them? Was she having some sort of spiritual crisis? Unlikely. Maya didn't seem the type. Though she had softened somewhat (I was still musing about how protective she seemed over me when I was attacked in the lab, and, of course, her intervention along side of the road, but maybe that was no more than an inventor not wanting any harm to come to the invention,) I was regressing back to my first impression of her, that she felt undermined by Cameron and possibly others, and that this was her way, then, of getting back. Watson and Crick could have been Muslims, I thought, and it wouldn't have mattered to her.

We walked slowly through the woods. The path wound and undulated in an unending spool. Occasionally Maya swore softly as she batted away a tree branch. Mosquitoes buzzed around us and the cicadas Maya had long ago identified (or falsely identified) droned in the background, a lush sound, a full-bodied, three-dimensional sound that gave space and depth to the forest, that chilled me with memories. I was thirsty. Thirsty for water, yes, but I wanted to drink like I had never known. I wanted a tall vodka on the rocks, cool and alcoholic, greasy on top like a slick of gasoline behind a motorboat at the dock on a summer day. Yet somehow, strangely, providentially, I found myself thankful to be sober, whether I had been engineered – *reconstituted* felt like the appropriate term – or not. My last thought – or, the last discernable thought out of the mucky state of my mind – before we stepped into the Utopia clearing – was of three women together: Julianne, Maya, and Katherine Glaston. Three. A triumvirate. I knew I was heading towards doom, but I didn't, or couldn't, stop.

We were greeted by half a dozen figures, silhouetted by the lights of the village. I saw that the walkway that snaked through the buildings was now alight with torches. I recognized Cameron's face. He looked at me differently this time, the guise of friendship dropped. I was escorted to a small "house" wordlessly where I was locked into a heavy chair. Anklets were clasped below my chins and snapped into the iron legs of the chair. Handcuffs were secured, one on each wrist, and my hands were pulled around to my sides. A chain, I imagine, was attached, one end on each handcuff. There I sat, dressed casually in the date clothes I had scared-up for my trip to the bar with Maya, back a thousand years ago when my biggest concern had been whether or not I could pull off getting laid.

Two nameless, faceless men had replaced my Watson and Crick. The two men who had accompanied Cameron as I was brought into the small house had gone out the front door. I thought of them as *goombas*, you

know, what my gramma used to call the guys that played blackjack and
listened to loud Creole music below her apartment. "Goombas," she would
say. I think the Americanized form of it is "goons." Maya, meanwhile, had
gone upstairs. I'd given her a look as she went, and her eyes conveyed: *go
with it.* I couldn't hear anything up there now, though I strained to. I did,
though, hear something else. It was that wounded animal sound again, the
one I was sure was coming from the barracks. It was low and pained. There
was a bang, like a screen door slamming shut in a backyard, and then the
howling sound was gone.

There were no lights on in the house; candles flickered in two of the
windows I could see from where I sat. The little house was much like the
one Cameron had brought me to the day before. I was in a small living
room. The chair I was in had been dragged out into the middle of the room.
There was otherwise a couch, a loveseat, two end tables and two lamps.
There was a picture on the wall that I couldn't make out – a painting, an
impressionist painting; it could have been a step-up from the crappy still life
from before, or maybe it was just the shadows and the candlelight.
Something like thunder growled in the distance.

Cameron had his back to me. When the animal sound was in the air
he had been looking – I was sure – in the direction of the barracks. At the
sound of the thunder he cocked his head. His hands were clasped behind his
back, his legs splayed and feet planted shoulder-width apart. He looked like
a soldier, standing like that, and he did an about-face to look at me.

"So Maya told you," he said.

I said, "I'm 'universal soldier.'"

Cameron watched me, saying nothing. He stood at the bottom of the
stairs and across from the front door. Behind him was a dining nook, and

around the corner, on the other side of the stair wall (the stairs were open on the living room side) was the kitchen. There was one more room on the ground level in the back, off of the living room and perhaps the kitchen as well. I thought it might be a study, or an office of some sort. Upstairs I imagined were two bedrooms and a bath. Quaint.

"Did she also tell you that time was running out for you?"

"She didn't mention."

Cameron scowled at me. He seemed to regard me with a kid of low grade antipathy, as if I were a dog he never loved and now had the bothersome duty to put down. "Well," he said, "it is. Once we found out that you're body was not accepting the biotherapy—"

"*Biotherapy?*"

Cameron ignored me "-we knew you were…not working out. Some things, yes – you've managed to stay sober. But your testosterone has been oscillating, your adrenal glands are overproducing, and your mirror neurons don't seem to be functioning."

"I see. No mirror neurons. How will my synapses know if they like their new haircuts?" The bandy was a means of deflecting the reality for me, a way of stoicism, I suppose, a way of escape, more likely; I could barely help the idiot words falling out of my mouth. Perhaps that too, was some other side effect. One could hope.

Cameron turned around and took a step toward the table in the dining nook, a small oval oak table. He worked something together in his hands and then turned back to me, brandishing a syringe. "This isn't…science," he said.

"I don't follow."

"Science is research. Research, study, experimentation. This isn't science," he repeated, nodding toward the syringe. "The drugs, the captivity. The other doctors don't like it. They make *me* do it. I don't mind so much."

"It's not captivity," I said, "I volunteered."

Cameron looked at me. There was a lot going on in his face – I decided he wasn't offended by my statement, but looking past it, if you know what I mean, but I didn't know what, exactly, was over my shoulder. Instead, I had a sudden, vivid image of the Cameron who had picked me up after springing me from jail, the one in the wrap-around black sunglasses, the one who's barbed wire tattoo was poking out of his collar. He took two and a half strides quickly toward me, knelt on one knee and jabbed me. His movements were so quick and precise I barely had time to react. When it was over he stood back on both feet and took steps, more casually, back to the bottom of the stairs. I became instantly hyperaware of every sensation in my body, wondering what he had given me and how it was going to affect me. I thought of asking him, but I didn't. Not yet. He stood there, his back as straight as a board, hands back behind him. If he had replaced the syringe on the table he'd done it so deftly I hadn't noticed.

The room was quiet. Again thunder rippled like a giant sheet of metal, distant. Cameron folded his arms. "So," he said, "you have questions?"

"What did you give me? Sedative?"

"It's a mild psychoactive. To keep you from flipping out."

"I don't think I need it."

"You don't think you're flipping out?"

"Is that a medical term?"

Cameron looked at me. I could see his eyes glistening. They looked like wet balls spinning soundlessly in his skull. "You don't feel…scared, given this new information? Or, maybe you just don't believe it? Rejection is common."

"Did Phil Brandis reject it?"

Cameron smirked. More thunder rolled. It sounded closer. Cameron said nothing. He looked at the stairs, where Maya had disappeared.

"What's in the barracks?"

He slowly turned his head to look at me again. "I told you," he said. "Equipment."

My head was feeling heavy. "Am I 'equipment'?" Cameron said nothing. For a minute I thought he was walking toward me, but then he appeared unmoving. "We're going to have a full work-up done on you in the morning, in our facility here. For now, you're in my custody. You're my problem."

"You thought I was a reporter," I said.

"Maya did," Cameron quipped back. "She didn't know. I called and told her while she was at your place last night."

"But what about Watson and Crick?" I said. My words yawed out and twisted away from me. I could barely work my lips.

"Watson and Crick? What are you talking about?"

"Sounds like a storm is coming," said Maya, appearing at the top of the stairs. She started down and her body trailed her, like she was smudging paint along the stairwell along side of her as she descended. "Coming from Burlington – taking its sweet time, building force." She reached the bottom of the stairs, looking at Cameron. Then she turned and looked at me. Her eyes were alive and electric. She spun in my vision; while she stood still,

she twisted round and round. Marigold light unfurled toward me in satiny
vines. Shimmering motes, clusters of small stars – electrons maybe, glinting
pearls of wisdom – drifted along the serpentine white pathways towards me.
She moved in slow-motion, left to right across my field of vision as she
floated toward the door. Her hair pealed out in brown curls of buoyant
smoke behind her. I was filled with a feeling, an assurance, a carefully
gilded notion: Maya was on my side. I couldn't say anything to Cameron
that might betray that. I'd fucked up. Just like with Julianne. I blinked. My
mouth opened and this time the words that tumbled out came slow and
syrupy.

"How…do I…stay…alive?"

Behind Maya, Cameron's face was impossible to read in the flaring
candlelight. Where Maya's had been jubilant, his was a grey statue's. With
her back to him, facing me, Maya brought a hand up in front of her,
abdomen level, and then the other. She then interlaced her fingers together,
and raised and dropped her hands, interlocked like that, just once. I didn't
know what it meant. *Cage? Gate?* Her eyes were wet-looking, like
Cameron's, but I hoped I was seeing the onset of tears, of real emotion, and
not some hallucination. She blinked and turned. I watched Cameron's eyes,
black as licorice now, follow her to the door. "I'll be in the lab," she said,
looking down at the doorknob in her grip. She opened the door, exited like a
curl of smoke, and the door snicked shut. The thunder grumbled again,
closer still.

Cameron was watching me. His black, spinning eyes fixed on mine,
he reached into his pocket and pulled out a phone of some kind. Distantly I
wondered how they got coverage out here. I felt giddy again. I started to
giggle a little. Unfazed, Cameron put the phone to his ear. I hadn't seen

him dial anything, only heard a *beep-beep*, like he was using a Nextel or walkie-talkie. "Okay," he said into it. There were immediately shouts outside the house, and I heard a scream – Maya's scream. I tried to protest but I couldn't move or talk. The stone slab of Cameron's face seemed to be sliding off from his skull, slipping down, down. He walked toward me. "Women," I heard him say. I tried to speak again. I struggled to push the air out, to form the words.

"Ha...I...aye...ive."

Cameron was now right there on top of me. His face was a haunted mask of flame and shadows. I suddenly saw him in the driver's seat of Josh's white Subaru, staring out into a rainstorm that had yet to arrive. "Shhh," he said, and I saw that he was right next to me, felt as he placed a hand on my shoulder, "Shhh thirty-five, shhh. It's okay now, boy. Daddy's here."

Daddy's here. Everything had become a painting, and the candles had become licking flames, the heat melting the paint. I tried to look up and my head lolled to the side. Cameron leaned down to accommodate me. Great thunder crashed and light was everywhere for a moment. Cameron's face was in front of mine. His eyes were those wet, oily-black globes, spinning, spinning. There were no irises, just the million colors of the dark, as you lay in bed as a child, looking up at the ceiling. The eyes spun, like marbles on a desktop, and his face melted, his voice boomed. "Shhhh," he said, like the torrential downpour of the storm finally come.

*

I was in bed with Katherine. It was not a fantasy. It was not a dream. It was 12 years after I had first met her, after our four months together – the four months that changed my life. She was 37 now, as gorgeous as the day I had met her, her high cheekbones flushed, her brown hair naturally oiled, fanned out on the pillow, and I watched her sleep, the white comforter pulled up to her neck and it was raining outside. I laid there in bed awake for hours, listening to the rain, naked, sex drying on my skin, like it had when I was 17, lightly drunk, a bit fearful of the next morning, but otherwise happy.

By dawn I would slip from the bed and disappear from Katherine, vowing to myself as I wandered the Vermont roads south that I was going to get sober as the rain soaked my clothes, drenched me and purified me.

I was wet. That much was certain. I was waking up, but I still felt dreamy. The drug, whatever it had been, had not entirely worn off. I opened my eyes. In front of me were the barracks. I was back in Utopia.

Two men were holding me up by the armpits. My feet were dragging but as I came to I stiffened and dug my heels in to try and stop them. A figure appeared in front of me that I thought was Cameron but wasn't. The figure looked rubbery to me, walking like a man crossing through the quicksilver floating over a sunbaked road. He unlocked the huge doors to the barracks. They swung open with a creaking sound. The rain pummeled the ground all around us. I could smell the wet earth. I could smell the mud; it smelled like freshly opened reams of paper in the loading dock office, and sulfur.

Maya, I thought, and remembered the scream. The doors were opened in front of me and I was ushered inside.

There was a row of sodium vapor lights hanging down from a track high above, reaching to the back of the barracks. The rain drummed the corrugated steel roof, incredibly loud. On either side of the room were rows of what looked like stainless steel refrigerators, the kind that I imagined a big farm would use to store hunks of beef. There were four doors on the right, four doors on the left. The rows ended three-quarters of the way into the barracks where the room then opened up. There were several banquet tables, the fold-up kind, placed end-to-end to create one long table. There were unnamable pieces of equipment sitting on the floor, things that looked terrible and torturous – gangling robotic arms on one, tank tracks on another, then a set of school desks, some chairs, a blackboard – like a school for machines. I could only see just so much of it and I was, I figured, still heavily drugged.

The two goons on either side of me dragged me along the path between the meat lockers, if that was what they were. "Stop! Please!" someone yelled, and I realized it was me. The guy who had opened the barracks, walking in front of me, turned around. His face was small and tight, his eyes little black points. He cocked his head and looked at me queerly. Then he turned to one side and with a big set of jangling keys went to work on opening one of the refrigerator/meat locker doors, the second to the last on the right side. I struggled with the two men. Whatever Cameron had given me had diminished my strength considerably more than it already had been. I was like a little kid trying to escape two men who had taken him off the playground swings while his mother was chatting with a friend, looking off in another direction.

"Let me go!" Yes, we say such things when we are held under duress. We are reduced to things like "stop!", "wait!" and "let me go!" when we are in such situations, when strange men are about to shove us inside sealed meatlockers after we've just been informed that we were a genetically altered life form that has become a liability. You'd like to think a person came up with something more colorful, more severe when they are faced with such a situation, but I am here to tell you that we don't. We just start yelling out like we are five years old. We start thinking about everything we've taken for granted, and then our mothers, and we start to long for it all terribly.

The man with the beady eyes opened the door to one of the cubes with a grimace and a grunt. He nodded to the goons and they threw me in. I caught the edges of the doorway and held on, willing all of my remaining strength to keep me there. I felt a glance of pain between my shoulder blades and then I was toppling to the floor, and the door was swinging shut behind me.

For a horrible moment I was suspended in total darkness. Then, as the door suctioned shut behind me and I heard the thick latch snick into the doorjamb and a lock turn, a light flipped on above me, a single bulb encased in metal, like a dog muzzle. I looked around. There was nothing in the small space with me. It was perfectly empty. I was in a cell, about 12 feet long by 7 feet wide. I stood up and went to the door and started to pound on it. Then, I lost it. I was screaming hysterically and pounding. I stopped after a minute or so and tried to rally my senses. I felt along the walls. A pliable off-white material lined the steel. There were circular rivets, like buttons, pinning the panels of material against the wall. I tried to pry one loose by couldn't even slip a fingernail underneath the head of it. The place was sealed as tight as a drum. I sat down, my heart racing.

I heard noises once I had stilled. I could hear my heart beating in my ears. I could hear the rain pounding the roof – very muffled now, very faint. More than a sound, actually, it was a vibration I felt. There was a hissing sound coming from above me and I looked up. I had noticed the light in the ceiling, but hadn't registered anything else. Now I saw it – there was a vent about two feet from the light fixture. The hissing was coming from there. I swallowed, and I felt an obstruction in my throat, like a lump. I stood and lifted my hand to the vent. I was an inch shy of six feet and the ceiling was about nine feet, so I couldn't reach it, exactly, but I could feel what was coming out of it. Heat. Hot air. Maybe something poisonous. I didn't know. I instantly felt panic thrumming through me. Were they trying to kill me? Were they gassing me? I sniffed the air. I couldn't detect any odor. I thought back to moments ago as I was brought into the barracks. I scanned my visual memory – had I seen ductwork of some kind? Tubes going into the tops of the meat lockers, the cubes? I didn't know. The lockers were too tall – I wouldn't have been able to see over the top of them. I had been dazed by the hanging lights, the lights with shades that reminded me of rice-pickers somewhere in Asia, wearing those big sun hats. There must've been, though. Even if it wasn't gas, it had to be pumping in air – these lockers were hermetic. The panic coursed through my body now, full tap, and I started to sweat. I dropped into an Indian-style sitting position and started to rock back and forth, putting my hands to my face. I whimpered then, I mewled and I whimpered and I mourned my life. I still didn't know what to believe, but even if what these sons of bitches had told me was true, and I was some kind of experiment, some sick joke, I still mourned my life. I still wanted to go on. I wanted to see people again. I wanted to see the world again. I wanted to stay sober, to never drink, to make something of my life, to contribute something. I wanted to save the world in my own way, however I could, I wanted to add that loving fuckin' touch. I wanted to open myself up. I wanted to just let go of whatever had been stopping me, whatever had been holding me back. I wanted to live.

I prayed then, the only prayer I knew.

"Our Father," I said, my words sounding small and sucked away by the padded walls, masked in the hiss of whatever was slipping into my cell through that vent above me, "Who Art in Heaven..."

I thought of Maya – I saw her face float clearly in front of me. Maya. The girl I thought was a witch. Not a bad witch, but a witch nonetheless. She was just a girl, just as vulnerable, just as scared as the rest of us. She had been trying to do the right thing. Whatever she had seen in her involvement with this madness she had felt immoral, or irreligious, or unethical – something, anything, enough of something that she had sought outside help. I saw her standing there in the field, the way I had met her just days before – days that felt like months. Did I have a job, or something, doing landscaping? Did I live with a gay environmentalist? Was I a guy from Brooklyn, living in a new city away from my home, trying to start over? Had I just been kidding myself? What was all of this for? The hissing continued above me. I felt the sweat now rolling down my cheeks, though it could have been rain, or tears.

"...hallowed be Thy name."

I was terrified, but the old familiar prayer gave me some sort of consolation. Cameron, anyway, had said that they were going to do work on me in the morning, whatever that meant. It meant, at least, that they weren't trying to kill me in here. Then why was it getting so damned hot? Was it – or was I still hallucinating? Could a man like Cameron even be taken at his word?

"Thy kingdom come, Thy will be done...uhm...Thy will be done..."

Who was I? Was I what they said I was? How was it possible? Was my recovery from crime and alcohol addiction a recent forgery? But they had only gotten to me recently – I had been already going on my own steam. Were they watching now, waiting until the moment these mad doctors took the final needle to me, or worse? I felt pinned in the middle of a triangle, a butterfly penned up by its wings. I dropped my chin to my chest and looked myself over, rolling my eyes, the sweat coursing down in salty rills. I looked at my arms – the same arms I had always had, just longer, just hairier. I looked at my hands. I often contemplated my hands when I was painting. I wondered if they were "artist's hands," like my mother said my father had. It was me – it was me. This was my body. I was a creature of this world no matter what anyone said. I had a right to live. *People are simple*, Maya said. Yes, simple. Simple little children.

The heat swelled around me and I started to feel claustrophobic. The panic filled me like an ink, leadening my veins. I began coughing and felt my head swim. "...on Earth as it is in Heaven," I guess-remembered, wondering how I could end my life, and then something happened that made me jump.

There was a scratching sound to my left, smothered by the lining of the cell, but sharp enough beneath. Something was on the other side of that wall. I recoiled from the noise, then sat staring at the buttoned white. The scratching was in a sweeping motion. There was something on the other side of my cell, definitely. In memory I heard the wailing, howling sound that I had heard on two occasions here in Utopia.

Slowly, moisture dripping freely now from my scalp, down my forehead, along my temples, off my brows, I pushed myself over to the wall by my palms, dragging myself along the stainless steel floor. The scratching went back and forth, back and forth, sweeping the other side of the wall. I raised my hand up slowly, and I pressed it to the vinyl.

Thud thud thud. Again I recoiled. It was an instinct. I forced myself back, I laid my palm on the wall. It felt warm. Whatever, whoever was over there on the other side might be baking like I was. *Thud thud thud. Swisshh. Swisshh.* I held my hand there against the wall. Then I lifted it and brought it down once, hard, on the heel. *Whap.*

The noise from the other side instantly ceased. I held my breath. I heard the hissing from the vent. I felt the thrumming of the rain outside, the rush of my blood, the pounding of my heart. The silence rang in my ears. My hand hovered in space. I was about to hit the wall again when-

Thud. Then nothing.

I hit twice.

The report came back: *Thud thud.*

Déjà vu seized me. I'd been here before, like this. Trapped. Someone in the cell beside me.

I struck the wall three times – *whap whap whap* – and the response was immediate. *Thud thud thud.* I lost control then, getting to my feet and battering the wall. I was yelling as I did it – "Help! Help! Help!" – and when I returned to my senses I heard nothing. I slumped back down against the wall, terrified all over again and crying freely, sweat and tears commingling, coursing down my face, my chest, beneath my shirt in warm rivers. I was going to dehydrate soon – I'd have nothing left. I was reminded of the woods, of being thirsty and yet having the ability – the *need* – to pee like a racehorse. I felt another scream rise up in my chest, an animal, guttural scream, but I swallowed it down. I waited. Had I scared it off? Or him off? Or her off? I waited and watched the light bulb and listened to the hissing duct and grew hotter still. I removed my shirt – well, Daniel's shirt – a custom tee, probably from Urban Outfitters or some such yuppie trap. It was soaked through entirely with rain and sweat and tears. I tossed it into the far corner where it lay like a crushed white cat.

Thud.

I twisted and hit the wall once more, lighter this time, ridiculously trying to convey comfort. This was the thing: when you are in a dire situation it is very helpful to have someone more hysterical or more vulnerable than you are. It makes you feel more together.

There was silence on the other side once more. I lifted my hand again but my arm felt heavy. I dropped it to my side. I could feel the heat now, a living thing, filling up the room and gathering around me. It must've been a hundred degrees. What was the purpose of this? Were they trying to cook me to death? "Impurities," I said to the balled-up shirt lying in the corner of the cell. "They're trying to sweat out my impurities." I leaned into the wall, feeling the slight give of the padding, feeling it take the shape of my shoulders and skull. I watched my stomach rise and fall.

I sat like that for a long time – I don't know how long. I must've passed out. When I came around again I noticed that I was sitting in a puddle. My head felt thick and heavy. This was no attempt at wringing out

my impurities – they were just killing me – and somehow, improbably, I had
pissed myself. I was a deviant, a rogue, a liability, and they were
humiliating me, torturing me, exterminating me, making me pee my
goddamn pants.

As I lay there against the wall, imagining that my companion in the
next cell was doing the same, his or her back to mine, I felt that I was
smiling. I had another secret, you see, I had a secret that they hadn't gotten
from me, that I had held on to, that I had buried away in my heart.

With this smile on my lips I lost consciousness for the second and last
time in this hotbox, this crucible. It was one of the most horrible ways to die
I could think of – alone, burning up inside, dehydrated, going insane with
the terrible heat, but I was smiling.

Dream memory. I was back in Brooklyn. It had been almost a month since
I had had my reunion with Katherine Glaston, and though I was drinking
steadily and heavily again, I still had the plan in motion to quit – like I said, I
had been scheming on how and where I was going to get sober for about a
year by the time I got to Burlington.

I was loading the truck with Ricky Loquesto and Ryan Amatto when
the foreman came out onto the loading dock and told me that I had a phone
call. He said it was a woman, but that she hadn't given her name. I
followed him to the office, undoing my lifting belt. He opened the door.
His name was Chuck Goldfine, and he made a disapproving face that said,

there you go, maestro. I nodded and walked in, letting him shut the door behind me. The office was small and smelled like mint gum, stale cigarettes and old paperwork. There were shelves on three sides, but not really shelves; they were those slap-together, do-it-yourself-kit-shelves, just slots, really, stacked ten to a column, leaning this way and that so that the whole set of them was corkscrewy, puffed with papers pink and yellow and white. The desk had a windblown look of its own. It had that mud-smell, but without the rotten eggs. The fourth wall of the office was a window with the blinds drawn but the slats halfway open. I watched Goldfine walk away toward the truck, looking unsure what to do with himself now outside of the office. Ricky was handing Ryan cargo and he looked over at Goldfine, and then he looked into the office where I stood.

The phone on Goldfine's desk had three lines. The first one was pulsing red. I stood there, watching the red telltale flash on and off for a moment, and then pushed the button and picked up the handset from its cradle.

"Hello?"

"Jack? Jesus, I didn't think your guy was going to give you the message."

"Yeah. Sorry."

"You know who this is?"

"Of course I know who this is."

I could hear Katherine sigh. Then I heard scraping and rustling sounds as she jostled the phone about. "You're probably wondering why I'm calling."

My head, at the time, was hazy from hangover. I was high-strung, hyperaware and slightly paranoid – the usual hangover breakfast. My heart started to beat faster – that's the way things go when it comes to stuff like this. Do you know what I mean? If it's happened to you then you'll know what I'm saying – what shook out next was the sort of thing that you know is going to happen before it does. I'm not talking ESP, or anything, but maybe ESP is just a matter of being sensitive to and recognizing the minutia of tiny, impacting clues.

"I don't know," I said. It's what we say when we are thinking of things too big to fit out our mouths.

She sighed. "Hhhaaaaa." Then I heard her inhale. "This is…hhhaaaaa. This is hard. I wasn't even going to call you. You know?"

"Katherine, what is it?" But I knew, of course.

"I'm pregnant."

Man, that gets you right in the gut. And in the chest. And in the brain. It's a triple-zinger. Your life flashes before your eyes. It's funny – every single question is there, like they were all reporters waiting on the other side of the door – they are fat, persistent, sweaty reporters, the door is bulging, and the key to open it is the phrase "I'm pregnant" and then they all come barreling in with their camera and their microphones and their coffee breath asking you every conceivable question. Only most of the questions are not even decipherable since there are so many so fast. You get the general sense that your ability to be a father is called into question, the fact that you drink heavily is on trial, your selfish, self-absorbed nature is highly suspect, and what the hell you feel one way or the other about the mother and what you are going to do about it – morally and realistically – its all there in the gabbing, nagging questions of your own personal reporters. And somewhere, deep down, you know it means you will have to die. Not just in the biological sense, but in the egotistical. Innate within you is the knowledge that you will die to yourself, and then be resurrected in new form as a father. For real.

"Jack?"

"Yeah."

"Well?"

And this, you see, this is where things get a bit controversial. You know, because you always hear about how it's the woman's body, the woman's decision. That's bullshit. That's right, that's what I said; I'm here to tell you it is utter bullshit. Sure, at the end of the day, unless you were to physically restrain her from going to the clinic you couldn't stop her from having an abortion, and short of dragging her there and paying off doctors to do it against her will you sure as shit couldn't force her, but, let me tell you, the woman will take her cues from you. And you, huh, lemme tell you, you have only two ways of responding. You want to have it or you don't. And here's the thing. There is only one way to say you want to have it – by saying you want to have it. Anything else is a *no*. If you say, "Honey, I'll support you either way," then you've just left her all alone. There is no playing this one passive. Not knowing this at the time, I said, "well what?"

"Hhhhaaaa. Jack." She was quiet. I watched Ryan and Ricky finish up the load and pull the door down on the truck. Ryan latched it and Ricky went around to the driver's side. It was a diesel Mack, a 17 footer, a nice, mid-sized truck, a nice hydraulic lift in the back for loading. "Jack," Katherine said, "what do you think?"

"I can't think."

"Yeah, okay, I'll give you that. I've had a couple days."

"When did you find out?"

"Couple days ago, Jack."

"Right."

"I was so freaked out I took four of those EPT tests just to be sure."

"And you're sure?"

"Yes, Jack, I'm sure."

"Been to the doctor?"

"I've been to the doctor."

I didn't have anything else. The denial part goes pretty quick. "So," I said, fingering a stack of papers on Goldfine's desk and feeling like I was in somebody else's body, in somebody else's life, "what do you want to do?"

"I don't know. What do you think?"

"I don't know. I mean, do you...do we..."

"Do we have a life together? I don't think so. I'm pretty set in my ways, Jack. You're still too young for me."

"So..."

"Jack, I've...well, the third time is not the charm in this case. I don't want to do...that...again. But that doesn't mean..."

"What would you want me to do?"

"Nothing, Jack. I don't want anything from you."

"Then why are you telling me?" I could feel the heat creeping up my neck. "You want me to go around knowing that I have a child in the world that I don't see, that I don't have any effect on? That doesn't know me?"

"Jack, calm down. You can always come and visit."

"Who would I be? Uncle Jack?"

"I would tell her. Or him. They would know."

"No," I said, and now my hand was a fist on the desk. I watched the truck pull away. Goldfine stood there with his own fists on the ridge of his hips. Soon he would be coming back into his office. "I think you should have the abortion. I'll pay for it. It isn't right to just have a kid raised by one parent, not knowing the other."

"But it's right to have an abortion?"

"You said…I mean you've had two."

"Jack, is this about you feeling rejected? Is this–"

I hung up. Goldfine was walking back toward the office. I was walking out through the door as he got there, and I brushed past him. Goldfine said nothing, but I thought he knew, I figured the whole world now knew; I stank of it, and I stank of what I'd just said.

Nine months later I got another call, this time at my little apartment. I had only installed the phone a month or two earlier, at the behest of Chuck Goldfine's successor, Banjul Banajab. Banjul wanted things run tightly and smoothly at the dock and I just *had* to have a phone. "If no celphun, den jew must hab a lannline." I submitted.

It was Katherine again, telling me that whether I wanted to hear it or not she had given birth to a healthy, eight-pound baby girl. Katherine had given the offspring a name of her choosing. I thought it sounded just fine.

That following month I spent a considerable amount of time introspecting, even for me. I had stopped going out for months. I would do my drinking at home, alone, where I could control it, relatively, where there weren't temptations to keep drinking, like a chance at getting laid, the roomer of an X party somewhere in DUMBO, or just the call of the night in

general, the endless stimulation and distraction. I had been home alone at
night for months, ignoring the phone and letting the machine get it (if I was
going to get a phone, I told Banjul he would have to spring for me to get a
machine so I could screen my calls and he said "fuck you" with that
adorable Indian accent of his.) I chain-smoked and drank mostly beer.
Occasionally I would slip and hit the vodka, but usually I would be content
with the beer and television and be anesthetized by midnight. I was like a
toy winding down. Inside me somewhere I'd known that Katherine would
choose to go through to term. I had been just waiting for the call, gearing up
for it.

    After a couple days, I went to Lincoln Brandis, Phil's uncle, and told
him about my situation, omitting anything about Katherine and the baby,
only explaining that I needed to dry out, I needed to 'rehabilitate'.

    "I'm glad you came to me, *kleinnes*" Lincoln said.

    Lincoln had once been a boxer – 1st Army, Fort Dix, Oxford
University, Dublin University, Paris University, East Africa (Kenya) and the
New York Athletic Club. A stroke at the relatively young age of 60 had
enfeebled Lincoln and now he seemed only happy to serve as a kind of
butler to his brother, Lucius. It was Lucius who arranged things for me to go
to Vermont, but it was Lincoln who loved his nephew Phil; I didn't think
Lucius was capable of such an emotion (and the only women I'd ever seen
him with were very high paid escorts, usually Polish. Lincoln I had never
seen take a woman, but I'd heard that he'd left a great love behind
somewhere in Europe in the late forties.)

    Lincoln and I made a deal.

    Thinking of myself as something of a ranked amateur spy, what with
all my stings on the fake-wallet-salesman, jewelry forgers and petty

launderers, I headed north to the green trees, grey sky, and hand-holding-in-a-circle state of Vermont. The plan was to snoop around about Phil after I had made the scene a little, get what I could, hopefully enough to satisfy the Brandis brothers, furtively contact Lincoln's man in Plattsburgh on the side (also funneling money to me, albeit paltry and very, very on the QT) and then get into a real job, a real life, and alternately investigate and spend my time getting sober. I wanted to see Katherine, to see my daughter, who lived a few hours away from Burlington, in Bondville, yes. I would like to tell you, old pal, that the plan always included seeing them right away. I want you to be proud of me. But we're never better in procrastinating than putting off those things which scare us the most, are we? It's a lousy defense, I know. In the end, it took something – a pretty big bat to the head – to get me going in that direction. To stop letting the machine pick up the calls, if you know what I mean.

Before I left I decided the whole thing was only going to work if I had one last hurrah (of course, you know, ha fucking ha, of course), so I got shitfaced with Guy, Ricky, Ryan and Victor the night before and detoxed on the bus the whole way up north the next day. I hadn't the foggiest clue, preview, or premonition about what sort of insanity I was headed into, without any thought in the world that I was going to die there.

As my body shut down, as I lay there against the wall of my cell, dying either of the heat or noxious fumes – gas – coming in from the vents I thought of my daughter, who I had never seen, who I would never see, not in this life, I wondered about one thing more than any other; I wondered if she would be a painter.

I was not entirely conscious as I wondered this – I was drifting in the abstract, unencumbered from my body, getting lighter by the second. There was no pain, there was only a feeling of longing, an aching feeling I had ever experienced; remorse, pervading my every thought and feeling, a terrible yearning that I needed to remain alive, to see my daughter, to fix my wasted life. It was the yearning that held me there, suspended, unwilling to go forward into the beyond. And it was in the pain and longing and the heat of submission that I heard another sound from somewhere near my body. It was the sound of the door to the meat locker opening.

When I felt hands on me, lifting me up, and heard something like words, like a person speaking to me, my eyes were closed. As I came slowly back into my body I realized I was being dragged out of the cell. With this realization came a surge of strength – I was revived by the idea of not being a captive any longer, and I reached out just in time to grab the doorway to the locker and hold on. First I had held there so I wouldn't be thrown in, now I was holding on for dear life not to be taken out. As much as I wanted to live I was going to do so on my terms.

"It's okay," I heard someone say, and I pulled my eyelids back.

I saw something then that brought me back around full-swing into consciousness as I groped and grappled with my captor in the doorway. I saw three letters: FPR.

I looked up and there was Mike. Mike the FPR guy was pulling me out of the cell. The rain was drilling the roof above him. The storm was here, fully. I couldn't have been out of it that long. I called for all of my strength to stand up with Mike's help. I tried to speak but all that came out was mush.

"Quiet," said Mike. I could smell alcohol on him. He was unshaven and I could smell his perspiration. Inside the barracks it was very humid. "Come on," he said, leading me toward the back and away.

I heard a noise as I stumbled along side of him: *Thud thud thud.*

I found my ability to speak again, but thickly. "Wait. We have to get somebody."

"There's nobody else here," Mike said. "Only you."

"No – somebody in the locker next to me."

Mike spoke in an impatient whisper, tugging on my arm to keep me going – going toward those inexplicable machines beyond the two rows of meat lockers. "You're hallucinating," he said, "They've been baking you like a cookie in there for almost three hours. Plus they gave you a type of diethylamide, so you might as well be tripping."

"FPR guy," I said, because that's what I had come to think of him, "I'm telling you there is someone else in there. I've heard him before."

"No, there isn't. Come on, *now.*"

I wasn't budging. "Where did you get the keys?" I asked. Mike looked down at the keys hooked to his belt. He looked back up at me. His mouth opened. I hit him then, hard as I could, which wasn't exactly going to knock it out of Fenway. Still, you might think it odd to hit someone in the nose who has just saved your life, but, like Mike had said, I was virtually tripping balls. As Mike stumbled back I ripped the keys from his belt loop – ripping the loop right off of his pants. It yanked Mike's hips forward and he toppled right over onto his back. I heard his head hit the hard floor with a sickening thump.

I was at the other meat locker, the one on the right of mine, a second later, fumbling with the keys. There seemed to be about forty of them on the chain. *Thud thud thud.* It was as though the locker's captive knew what I was doing. *Thud thud thud thud thud.* "I'm *trying*," I growled. I kept failing with each new key. I was losing track of which keys I had already tried. Behind me, Mike moaned on the floor.

The air thundered outside. The rain sounded like pebbles on the sheetmetal roof. I went through one key, and then another, and then another. I was sure I had tried some keys more than once, maybe three times and had left other out. I started over, focusing on remembering the look and shape of each key I tried in the handle's lock. *Thud thud thud thud thud.* I swore under my breath. What was I doing? I was free – I should have been fleeing the place with Mike right now. But to where? What was Mike's plan? What was his role in all of this? I trusted nothing. No one. Only this phantom person on the other side of this cubicle door, a prisoner like me.

Thud thud thud thud thud. Another key no good. My hands were shaking. I was ridiculously dehydrated. My body was shivering all over now as it adjusted to the drastic change in air temperature. Mike was moving behind me. I glanced over my shoulder and saw him start to sit up, saw something dripping off the back of his head.

A key slipped into the lock then. I pushed it all the way in and turned, my other hand grasping the handle. I glanced at Mike again. His eyes were open, his hand up, shielding an imaginary blow, palm facing out to me. The other hand had gone to his nose. It might not've been the full hydraulic whammo, but I'd popped him in the right spot. I started to open the door. "Don't…" said Mike, but it was too late. I no sooner got the door an inch or

two open when something inside it hit it with such force that the door swung
into me and knocked me sprawling. I landed right next to Mike.

"Oh shit," Mike said in a nasal voice. "Now you've done it."

Once the door swung open, knocking me down, nothing else occurred for a
minute. Under the din of the rain drumming the roof I could hear raspy,
labored breathing. Someone was standing there, on the other side of that
meat locker door. I could see feet – the door hung a few inches from the
ground – feet there on the other side, and it looked like shoes, like black
shoes. I glanced over at Mike. The back of his head was indeed leaking
blood. His head must've cracked when he'd hit the floor. Why had I been
so violent? I vaguely remembered Maya telling me something about it, the
aggression...hadn't she? Mike looked shocked and in terrible pain. I was
unable to move myself, paralyzed by the blow and the show of it all. For a
moment I thought of a panther, pushing open the door with the breadth of its
trapezoidal skull, but of course it wasn't that. Instead I saw the fingers wrap
around the edge of the door – pale, puffy fingers, large and hairless and
round and pink, and I broke into motion, backpedaling with my feet slipping
on the concrete, my legs almost totally numb. I was no longer friends with
whoever had been in the cell next to me. I was going to run. *That* was the
same as it was before – the running; *jo vamo*.

"Don't..." breathed Mike, sensing my departure, desperately losing
blood from the smashed back of his skull. But I had no choice. I had to get

out of here. I had to live. I could trust no one but myself to get me through.
I scrambled back on my feet, scrabbling with my hands, about to flip myself
over. The door swung shut and I closed my eyes, rolled over and sprang up.
I started to run, and then I did it; I looked back.

What stood there in between the rows of meat lockers, standing over
the fallen, bleeding FPR guy, chest heaving, was something I will never
forget, no matter what they told me afterwards. I had never seen anything
like it and I know I've never seen anything like it since.

I screamed, I screamed just like I was a little boy and I was terrified
by something so deep and limbic that only my soul could recognize it and, of
course, never be able to articulate it. I screamed and I turned back around
through my scream and thrust myself forward into the sprint again. I ran
right into the arms of Dr. Cameron Madison.

I awoke back in the chamber, the meat locker, the hotbox. Cameron was
leaning down, trying to get me to my feet. "Come on," he was saying
gently, "come on, now."

I shook free of him and toppled back to the floor, limp as my sopping
wet shirt, still there in the corner. My lips were quivering. I twisted my
head back around to look at Cameron, who was leaning down and groping
for me.

"Water," I choked. I had no idea how profound my request was.

"Yes, water," he said, "now you can have water."

I wondered what kind of doctors these people were. Where was my IV? How had they gone and left me to dehydrate like this? I felt like a wrung-out sponge. I felt like I had a terrible, pinching and punching hangover. My heart fluttered in my chest. Cameron struggled to get me to my feet. I looked down and saw that my shoes had been removed, replaced by a kind of white, generic sneaker with Velcro straps. My clothes had been replaced with a plain cotton jumpsuit, no pockets, buckles or straps.

"Don't," I practically sobbed, "don't leave me back in here."

"Back?" Cameron asked, as we shuffled for the meat locker door.

"Yeah," I said, and stepped down onto the concrete floor outside of my padded cell, "I got out. Mike got me out. He needs a doctor. He's bleeding."

"Mike? You mean our old buddy, wood hick Mike?"

I screamed again then, remembering it all suddenly, and I twisted away from the locker next to mine, recoiling in terror. "That baby!" I screamed. "Where is that baby!?"

Cameron grappled with me, kept me from bolting. He was a strong man. He yanked me away from my cell, from the cell next to mine, and toward the back. I turned, my mouth working, the scream tapering into mewling, and I looked up and saw her. Maya was standing there, dressed in a white coat, next to three others in white coats and two men in black fatigues. She smiled at me, and the smile looked like pity.

"Maya," I said, as Cameron pulled me along toward them, "You're alive."

Maya laughed. It wasn't a sweet laugh, nor was it entirely sardonic. One of the doctors – if he was that – next to her smiled and looked down at his feet. The other two doctors were another man and a woman with bright red hair. "Oh no," Maya said, "I'm okay, Jack. I'm okay."

I shuffled past her, Cameron's grip firm, my eyes locked on hers as I passed. She looked away from me, her eyes flicking somewhere else, and I knew she was covering something up. Cameron brought me into the large space in the barracks and delivered me into a black, cushioned swivel chair. He bent and looked at me. "Okay?" I nodded, feeling like I was four again. "Water," I said. "Yes," he said, "of course." I saw the doctors exchanged glances with one another. Then Cameron looked at one of the men in black fatigues. "Private Hackford, would you go get Mr. Aiello a glass of water?"

My body went rigid. I tried to rise but Cameron held me by my forearms. He pinned me. "Hackford? Terry Hackford?" Cameron shook his head. "John, I believe." He looked up at the soldier. "Is it John?"

"Yes sir, doctor," I heard from behind me.

"Now sit still," said Cameron. "Okay?"

I looked around behind me, nodding at Cameron but desperate to get a look at the soldier named Hackford. I only saw his back, and the rifle slung over his shoulder, as he left the barracks for some water. I turned back around as the doctors shuffled past. In front of me was the long desk that had been there before. The chairs were lined up on the other side of it. There were no machines anywhere to be seen. I looked up at the ceiling, thought it was the sound that told me the rain had stopped. The storm was passed.

They all took their seats, Cameron last, sitting in the middle, flanked by Maya on his right and the man who had smiled on his left. The other man and woman doctors took their seats at the end of the table. I kept staring at Maya.

"You said 'okay,'" I told them quietly, "and then I heard shots."

Cameron nodded. I thought he was trying to conceal a smile. "I said 'okay,' yes, and then you heard thunder."

"No," I said, "that wasn't it."

"We gave you something quite powerful," he told me, his direct, blue eyes piercing into me, "It's understandable you had some mild hallucinations."

"Mild?"

"What else did you see?" Maya asked. Cameron turned his head to look at her. It was only a half-turn, a brief glance and then he was studying me again.

"You tried to gas me. Or heat me up. It was over a hundred degrees in there." I looked directly at Cameron's smug face. "You tried to kill me."

"You had a fever," said Cameron.

"I saw it coming in through the *vent*!" My voice echoed in the room.

"Calm down, please," said the doctor who had smiled.

"Fuck you," I said, "who are *you*?" I held my hands out in front of me, shaking my head. "No, don't tell me. You're doctor Peter. Right? I pointed to the other man, the one next to Maya at the end of the table. "And you're doctor Daniel, right? How much are you going to tell me I imagined? Last week? The past year? Costa Rica? The fucking jungle cat that *tore her apart?!*" Now I pointed at Maya, my chest heaving, trying to regain control. "*She* told me that I was a product…that I was some sort of a…a project of yours. Didn't you?" Maya just looked at me, her eyes veiled and unreadable.

"This is Doctor Pembrose and this is Doctor Miles," Cameron said of the two men. Then he looked down at the woman with the boiling red hair. "And that is Dr. Moritz."

"Uh-huh," I said. I folded my arms over my chest. I think I was trying to hold in my thumping heart. The door banged open behind me and I jumped. I spun around, my adrenaline surging. The soldier, Hackford, was coming back in with a bottle of water. He clopped toward me and I watched him all the while. His eyes were set straight ahead, fixed on nothing. At the last minute they dropped into mine as he stopped in front of me. They were grey eyes. Likewise unreadable. "There you go, sir."

I said nothing and greedily unscrewed the top. I guzzled the whole thing and then turned back around. The doctors were quietly consulting one another. Cameron looked at me. "Better?"

This was nerve wracking, being on trial like this, but somehow I was handling it. It was the emotion. The anger. The anger kept me from spiraling off into…places I had been before. Bad places. So I held it close. I dropped the bottle carelessly beside me to show them I meant business. None of them seemed to notice.

"You mentioned a baby," said the redheaded doctor, Dr. Moritz. The other doctors glanced at her, except Maya, who kept her eyes fixed kindly on me. *I'll be in the lab*, she'd said, after tunneling into me with those dark browns, telling me to keep her defection in confidence. *Okay*, Cameron had said, and then there were shots.

"What baby did you mean?"

I looked at the five doctors. I looked at the soldiers, the guards. Hackford and Ramirez, read their pocket patches, standing in their Desert Storm-looking fatigues, still as statues on opposite sides of me. I remembered the grey slate of Cameron's face sliding off of his skull. My anger slid from me as well, and I dropped my head into my hands. I didn't cry, but I felt, finally, completely lost, helpless, alone.

"It was a big…child," I said. "Like a baby." It sounded insane. I was beginning to doubt myself. Doubt all of it. I hated these people for that.

"A big baby?" I could hear the mockery in Moritz's tone. The anger wanted to well up in me again, but it had no place left to go, nothing more to feed on. I was tapped out. I kept my head down, watching the ground. At the same time, something stirred. The water had made me feel a little better, I thought. I felt strength returning.

"Yes," I said. "The thing in the cell next to me…fucking weirdest… scariest thing I've ever seen."

It had been. The pudgy, round fingers had come around the edge of the door and swung it shut. As I had ran I had turned back and I saw it. The thing had a face like an infant. It had been sweet and innocent and shiningly smooth, but at the same time it was hideous. The lips were pulled back in a snarl, white, spaced-out teeth exposed. The eyes were crinkled with mendacity, hate and insanity. It must've been standing over six and a half feet tall there, towering over Mike, a hulking thing. It had been wearing clownish, colorful striped pants, only the pants were smeared with dried blood and what could have been feces. The white, taut shirt was stained as well, ripped in a few places. It stood awkwardly, bent and hunched, one leg shorter than the other, one arm shorter than its pair, the hair on its head wild and malformed, longer in some spots than in others, one eye wild and leaping out of its skull, the other more diminished and beady. The pink tongue had come out, delicate like a baby's would be, curved in a u-shape, and it had screamed at me, a sound both high-pitched like an infant's and low and guttural like a bear's might be, not a panther but a towering, slobbering grizzly about to maul and gore, rabid with hunger. It had started for me in that instant, this hulking, deformed thing. The rain was hammering the roof above us, Mike was writhing and bleeding from the back of his skull through his blood-matted brown hair, and it had shuffled forward toward me, one huge baby hand held out, puffed and wrinkled, and in its round, enormous face I had found torture.

I didn't tell them all of this. I couldn't. I wasn't afraid they would think I was crazy. I simply didn't want to recount the whole thing for them; I only gave them a rough idea. Something told me that it was the best way to go. They were probing me; they were trying to learn something and I didn't want to give them the satisfaction.

"Sounds terrible," said the redheaded doctor. Moritz.

"But I assure you," Cameron picked up, "that it was only a hallucination. You have been safe inside the defib chamber this whole time. Privates Hackford and Ramirez were on guard entirely. You were never in any danger. Your door was never even locked – did you try to open it? We're not sadists here. We had you under video surveillance the whole time."

I lifted my head up. "Cameras? Where?"

"In the vent, Jack. Did you look into the vent? No, probably not. You thought deadly gas was coming from in there."

I watched them, waiting for them all to break up into laughter at my lunacy, my childishness, but they didn't. Maybe that was worse. I hadn't looked into the vent, no. "Can I have my shirt back? It's not mine. It belongs to my roommate and I'd like to return it. You may know him. You're trying to rearrange his sexuality, or something. Aren't you?"

"That's amusing," Cameron said, but I saw the doctors looking at each other furtively. Cameron looked to the side of me. "Private Hackford? The man's shirt, please."

"Yes sir, doctor." I heard the soldier walk back and open the meat locker door. I faced them all, looking from one to the next, now officially at the end of my road. "What am I doing here? Who are you and what are you doing with me?"

Cameron sat back and looked to the other doctors. I heard Private Hackford walking back with my shirt. He stopped on my right hand side and held it out in front of me. It looked dry.

I grabbed his rifle then, yanking the strap over his shoulder, standing up as I did so, and tilting back my head. When I brought it forward I caught Private Hackford in the chin with my forehead and he went stumbling backward. The strap of the gun was caught around his utility belt and I pulled as he fell, taking his legs out from under him so that he fell back squarely on his back and head. I heard a nasty crunching sound as he hit, but I was already swinging around on the other soldier and firing. He had his gun down, I'll grant him that, but he must've been daydreaming a little because I got a round off first, catching him in the leg. I immediately ran to him, crossing the room in front of the panel of good doctors and I kicked his rifle away. I ran next to where it had slid from my kick and threw it over my shoulder. I spun back around, training the gun on ole Ramirez. He howled in pain and shock, clutching his leg with both hands, his face a mask of pain.

Dr. Miles was standing and looked like he wanted to run over. He eyed me. "Sit down," I said, calmly.

"He'll bleed to death. You hit him in his pulmonary."

"Sounds painful," I said, "Let him bleed." The others were watching Hackford. Maya was up and walking behind her seated colleagues. I pointed the gun at her. "Sit."

"Jack," she said, "let me just have a look at him." She meant Hackford. For some reason, maybe it was because it was Maya, maybe it was because of the name Hackford, I said nothing. I followed her with the gun as she walked around the table, over to where my chair was and knelt next to the fallen soldier. I heard him moan.

"He's got severe head trauma," she said, "cranial fracture." She looked at me. "He's barely alive."

"Whoops," I said.

"We've got to get him to the medical facility."

"No," I said.

"Jack…"

I looked at Maya. Everything was gone. Those had been my last few emotions, the last few scraps of my so called personality, there, in the chair. "My name is 0035," I told Maya. "Now fucking sit down."

Maya kept her eyes locked with mine. "No, Jack. I've got to get him out of here." She started to lift him. "Somebody help me." Moritz and Pembrose stood. I fired and hit Maya in the shoulder. She went toppling back, her mouth a wide "O" in surprise, her eyes shocked. I swung the gun around on the other two Doctors. "Soon, I said, "there won't be anybody left to go to the medical facility. So. Sit down. Let's finish our meeting."

Maya coughed and sputtered on the floor next to Hackford. Hackford wasn't moving much. The other soldier was still making noise; gritted-teeth moaning. He'd probably realized that he was a soldier and he was supposed to be tough. "Jack," Maya gasped, "Jack, you shot me."

"Quiet please, everyone," I said. I felt like smoking, but I doubted any of the good doctors were carrying. I longed for my red straw. "Anybody got a smoke?" Both Miles and Moritz produced packs of cigarettes. Pembrose was apparently fumbling around for his. I laughed. "No matter what you guys got going on here, nobody can escape Big Tobacco, right?"

"Jack…"

"Maya, shut *up*." I walked over and selected my cigarette from Moritz. She held out a lighter and flicked it on. I took it from her and walked away, lighting my cigarette in my own safe space. It was a *Tempo* – pretty shitty for a cigarette, but given the circumstances it was a Cuban cigar.

I dragged, exhaled, looked at the cigarette and then at Cameron. I raised my eyebrows. Time for answers. Time at last.

"You came to us," Cameron said to me. "You were desperate. You found out about us and sought our help. We experimented on you – we changed your very DNA, much in the way the nucleotides of reproductive cells inform a mutation for evolutionary purposes, we evolved you into a better, more fit being – one without the charming addiction to alcohol, anxiety and depression. But there were problems. Alcohol addiction doesn't come from any single inherited gene. There area a cluster of genes we know to be primary contributors – and it is a grey area – this spills over into that along

the edges, that spills into this – you get the picture. But we mapped your
genes and demarcated the ones that seemed most specifically correlative to
alcohol abuse. We did this, we worked on you, and you did, indeed, stop
drinking. But there were consequences. Other areas, emotions, seemed to
try to compensate for the engineered dearth. Your lust. Your aggression.
We began a parallel hormone therapy to the gene therapy to try and diminish
the aggression, a sort of anti-steroid that makes you feel the need to urinate
frequently. Other qualities were diminished as well, nuances of your
personality. You may derive from this that you have to take the good with
the bad, that in order to have gifts, of a sort, you must have balancing out
faults. But that is a myth. That is hogwash in the ilk of intelligent design, or
a Creator, or a meaning to all of this. In reality, we are just in the fledgling
stages. In time we will be able to more effectively isolate and reorient
problematic genes."

I stood motionless. Suddenly I remembered the soldier shot in the leg
and turned around. He was lying there on his side, unmoving. The pool of
blood around him was dark red and shining under the sodium vapor lights,
reflecting the barracks ceiling. I turned back to Cameron, playing into it for
the time being. "Then why did you wipe my memory of it – of the meetings
I had with you, the experimentation – the whole thing? If you're just
learning – what, were you embarrassed? Tried to cover it up?"

Cameron laughed. "No, we weren't embarrassed. You signed a
contract agreeing that knowledge of our relationship, and all it entailed,
would be muted. The purpose is simply for sake of our privacy – we're not
shaman or witchdoctors – we don't want the villagers lined up around the
block with their sick children in their arms. We're not saviors – not yet. We
need to preserve our anonymity while we work. And also, and more

importantly for the work itself, it was important you had no knowledge of what was done. The body, you see, made up of cells, is a learning machine. Everything you do and feel is taken in by the cells of your body. Addiction is on a cellular level. Smaller: it's biochemical. The more you do something, think something, say something, the more you crave the repetition, the reinforcement of that behavior. If you were walking around thinking of what had been done to you, you would naturally challenge that and the receptors of your cells that were dying off, deprived of the peptides they craved, would become alerted to the skepticism. It is quiet possible that your body would try to override what had been done to it and revert back to the old behavior."

"But how is that possible if you changed my DNA? Wouldn't the cells all follow suit?"

"DNA is a set of instructions. DNA is not the Gestapo. Your hypothalamus is more or less your epicenter for change, dictator to the legions of cells in your body. Though the actions of your hypothalamus are somewhat predicated on your genetic make-up, your hypothalamus has vetoing power, if you will. Think of it like checks and balances."

"I thought you didn't believe in balance."

"I never said that. I said I didn't believe in meaning." Cameron coughed and looked bored. "Nothing cogent, anyway." He looked at me directly, and then his eyes dropped down to the gun. "Now, are you going to shoot us all with that or are we going to handle this in a civilized manner?"

"What about the basketball player? What did you do to him?"

"What do you think? He wanted to play better. He's only five-foot-eleven, about your height, he's white, he's one of the older boys on the team."

"You made him a better athlete?"

"He had a bad heart. We fixed that."

"By altering his DNA?"

"No."

"So you're practicing heart surgery too?"

"It's more complicated than that. But enough. I think it's time you gave me that gun."

"Bullshit."

"Bullshit?" Cameron folded his hands in front of him.

"I'll tell you what," I said, "I'll make you a deal." I felt like I was equipped with some mental GPS. I was headed in a direction before I knew I'd chosen one. "I can go with you, right now, and we can take care of this whole thing. You'll fix what has gone wrong with me, get me back up to speed, and then wipe my memory of the whole thing." I smiled, "I can even start drinking again, if I want to. You can put me right back the way I was. I'll even be painting again in no time – or didn't you think I'd noticed that receded as one of my habits as well?"

"Or?" Cameron asked. I glanced at Maya. She was sitting up, cradling Hackford's head in her lap. It looked like she was crying. Her white doctor's coat was covered in blood. To my left it seemed that Private Ramirez had died. He was no longer moving, no longer moaning through his clenched teeth. Both Moritz and Pembrose looked morose. Miles seemed unfazed, but he had one of those inscrutable faces.

"Or," I said, "I continue with this charade. I run away from here now, like I've done in the past, carbine slung over my shoulder. I believe in all of these paranoid fantasies about man-made people, giant babies and Maya being kept under duress by you, and run from this and run from the everything and never be the same again, maybe never have a good life."

Cameron was watching me, squinting a little. Maya was maybe dying.

In the end, I did what I did for my daughter. This was that moment, old pal. It was the idea that I could have a chance to be with my daughter, to see her and be some sort of presence in her life. If I had left then, at that moment, in those circumstances, I would never get to see her. I would be a fugitive, possibly a murderer. So, I'd already chosen, in a way. We do that a lot, I think. We make a decision right at the onset and then like to fool ourselves into believing we're deliberating, that we even have options.

I gave Cameron the rifles and Maya started crying louder. Moritz and Pembrose rushed to her and Hackford as Miles scrambled over to the fallen Ramirez. Cameron snapped open his cell phone, still watching me, and called in for more help to escort the doctor and two soldiers out, saying that there had been an "accident." He had the facility prepped for my arrival and within minutes I was strapped onto a gurney, propped up and looking around at all sorts of tubes and gadgets and Cameron with a white mask on.

He placed a cup over my face, strapping it around behind my ears and the last thing he said to me was, "don't worry, it's not poisonous," and under his mask I was sure he was smiling.

"Tell Julianne I'm sorry," I said, meaning Maya, and everything went black. Cameron, my gramma would say, was a "man of his word."

I woke up with the feeling of a scorching hangover in the grassy field overlooking Lake Champlain. My body ached like I'd been beaten by a baseball team, but I realized as I sat up, squinting in the overcast haze, that I hadn't.

The demons were with me again. They didn't hop around on the grass and hiss and spit like you'd like think demons would. They were in my brain. Demons would get into my brains and monkey around in there and cause me to think all kinds of horrible shit when I had a scorching hangover. They would get in and infect my thoughts, my hearing, my vision. People's eyes would glow and enrapture me with horrible knowing guilt when I had a scorcher. The whole world would know that I was wrong, that I had done wrong.

Daniel would be wondering where I was. He was like that. It was like living with a woman. He wanted the place tidy, okay, sure. And he claimed he didn't care about where I went or what I did, but there was that look he'd get on his face when I'd show up late or fall out on a promise to be there for dinner, to have some of his homemade chicken soup followed by the chicken dish he'd found on some Martha Stewart cooking website. But it was all good. I'd told Daniel that I was a recovering addict, and he'd nodded and looked at me sympathetically and understandingly. I honestly think it's why he gave me the room. I think he wanted to help me. He'd even pointed out to me an ad in the paper for a group looking for people just like me, people with nothing to lose. Paid work to get asked questions and take tests or something.

I sat up, palm pressed to my temple. On the bike path went a rollerblader (pretty hot) followed by two chicks on mountain bikes. The chick in tandem looked over at me. She had a bright red bike helmet on. I tried a smile on for her and she quickly looked away. As my smile faded I realized that I recognized her, and then I realized where from.

Something came back to me. I watched as the bikers rode away down the path. The one with the red helmet with the red hair tufting out from underneath it I was sure to be a woman doctor named Moritz. I didn't know why I thought that, it just seemed to fit, it just came out of nowhere. I got to my feet.

Daniel would be wondering where the hell I was. I wondered just what he'd been up to – if he'd been hitting for the home team again or if he'd been back to his old self. I wondered if there was any kind of truth, any kind at all that Daniel had been fiddled with, that they had gotten in there and experimented on him; tried to make a gay man straight, and it all came tumbling back. I stood there on dog-shit-ridden patch of grass and remembered it all. Maya, Cameron, bioengineering, a flashlight in the dark, whickering husks of corn, a padded cell. It was like remembering a dream, remembering something the way a dream comes back, all at once, backwards and forwards, a jumble.

As I walked away and sorted it out, I also wondered about Phil Brandis. I was going to have to call Lincoln and Lucius and tell them I'd hit a dead end. Then maybe I could be done.

"Oh shit," I said to the open air, suddenly realizing that Peter was still in the hospital in Newport Center and that Josh would be expecting his car back. I started jogging, this 32 year-old guy in ragged, dirty clothes, feeling hungover but not. I was thinking about Daniel and about Phil and about Peter, and I was thinking about Maya, and if I would ever see her again. I was thinking that I was done drinking Coke in the bars – too much caffeine. I was done with bars altogether. *You failed, Cameron. You failed and I won.* My grin stretched over my whole face as I cranked the jog into a run, thinking of these things, but, on top of it all, really, through the heart of it all, I was thinking about one thing and one thing only.

I was going to go see my daughter.

I needed only a few things. I needed transportation. I needed the clothes on my back. And as I ran back to my apartment my hands dug their way into my pockets and found the red straw, which I stuck in my mouth and began to chew.

I'd always known I'd be that guy.

BOOK II

Planter De La Centro

THE WOMEN

Where was I? I remember now. Moving south now, the Honda Shadow
beneath me. A moving target. Jack Aiello. Number 0035. Or, simply, X.

Now I can tell you. I can tell you about Costa Rica, about eight years
before I ever set foot in Vermont, about the origins, really, of how and why I
was there.

I only started to understand it myself as I was headed to see my
daughter. Maybe it was the adrenaline of that experience – and you'll see
what I mean, shortly, about the adrenaline, about the locus coeruleus, and
norepinephrine. Pretty dope, shit, for real. (But, scary as hell when you
don't know what's going on.) It's just that when I was running – no longer
from something, but *towards* something – running to my baby daughter, that
I started to see the genesis of the whole thing, and how I had been involved
in it from the start, and my name back then was Jack Landi.

Driving through the backroads of Vermont, south, towards Bondville,
the smell of cow shit in long, low methane clouds I kept passing through,
that was when I really remembered. Maybe it was the smell – they say smell
and memory are mixed up like immortality and second glasses of wine.
Something was jarred loose and I could turn now and look back and see that
time clearly. Instead of just dreaming it, instead of just holding the door
shut on it while it bled through and into the present, I could see it for what it

was. So I've got to show you how they went together, the road to my daughter, and the descent into hell in Costa Rica eight years before.

I told you about Calvin Blair. He was the kidnapped billionaire who had been working with the Brandis brothers – though at the time I didn't know all of the details, of course.

Blair had made his money in internet gambling, which was a burgeoning industry in those days; he'd gotten in on the ground floor. And then, swipe, he was nabbed. They said in Latin America, in Central America, nobody bothered with identity theft or any of that jazz. They jacked *you*, and they jacked you good and tucked you away somewhere nobody was going to find you.

I was 23 when it happened. As Jack Landi – as in, during that time of my life – I was trying to practice moderation management, have you heard of it? I was traveling for the brothers a lot. It seemed I could go anywhere and be at home – I had yet to realize that I was medicating myself. On one morning, sitting in Café Arroyo, an open-air café, like most of the eateries and cafes and bars in Costa Rica, I had been dry for three days – long enough to get through customs and touch down and settling into the country without any potentially troubling episodes – and I was about to take the first sip of my *café con leche* when the urge to drink hit me ferociously, really knocked me around.

The place didn't serve alcohol, so I had counted myself lucky – no, I had counted myself smart, because part of moderation management, or MM, was to be smart about temptation. It wasn't the same as the AA belief that temptation had to be avoided at all costs, MM just said, essentially, "don't put yourself near a pyramid of champagne if you're looking to have a non-drinking day." Made sense. So I had, sort of unconsciously, sort of consciously, steered clear of the other open-air eateries on my mountain bike as I had come down the mountain from the Brandis's Costa Rican *villa*, and selected a spot with no liquor license. I figured I would be safe.

But the urge to drink had come on me like a fever regardless – literally, I started to sweat – and I could have sworn I caught the smell of beer in the air, wafting in from somewhere nearby. It was early in the morning, and Costa Ricans were largely hard working, routine-oriented people, and fiesta time didn't start until the day's work was done (unless there was a ground breaking ceremony, for instance, and out came the roast pig). What I smelled was likely just in my imagination – sense memory, or something, was what the actors called it. I felt anxious, uncomfortable in my seat. The strong coffee in front of me no longer seemed appealing, no longer seemed like the truth. Coffee represented sanity to me, and now I didn't want it, because now it would make me insane.

"*Perdona, me, senor...esta bien?*"

I looked up. The tall waiter stood blocking the sun, so that it haloed his head, so that his face was featureless. I could barely make out the sketch of a moustache, the glint of black eyes.

"*Si, si,*" I said. I asked him for the bill, paid it, and was about to leave when –

A helicopter was following me. Not then, but in Vermont, on the motorcycle. I had been lost in the memory of Costa Rica and hadn't noticed the distant thudding as early as I could have. It was getting louder, indeed.

I kept the bike on the road despite the jump in my heart rate. I thought of the chopper landing at Utopia, Cameron leaving me there and running over. I felt my skin ripple with gooseflesh and hugged the road with the bike, sinking into it, melting into the heat of the engine. I dialed the throttle back and pushed it up to 60 mph, as much afraid of getting pulled over by ordinary PD as I was of any other pursuers finding me. It was all chainlinked together anyway. The world had become one great big penning fence of policing. Freedom was an illusion. I realized now, as I never had before, that the only freedom we really had was the freedom to complain. The freedom to complain out loud, assemble and complain, complain in print, or, to shut up and not complain at all. Those were our freedoms. It had been building in me like a low-pressure storm all through the years: we had no real privacy. We could be dipped into, tapped into at anytime. Take me, for example, plucked from obscurity and secretively gone to work on like the *Six Million Dollar Man*. Only it would have been cool to have been the *Six Million Dollar Man*, to have those powers and to make that cool noise when I moved. I wasn't. I was still me, still Jack, Jack Aiello, Jack Landi, John Gainesville, and so on; I was still my flesh and my bones and my heart, though I was, cellularly so, in every way, completely different than I had been eight years ago, and that was fine, I liked to regenerate, but I was now tampered with, and different still. Virtually identity-free. *Biotherapy. Gene Therapy.* What the hell was that? How did a biochemist get inside a person and actually change their genes? Their chromosomes? I had flunked chemistry in high school. Cameron had explained quite a bit, but most of it had gone right over my head. I was going to have to pillage Katherine Glaston's library when I got there. And, if I recalled, she had quite an extensive one. But, the helicopter.

I couldn't see it. Inside the helmet, a full helmet with the visor down, I couldn't see. I turned my head and tilted it back as far as I could without losing control of the bike, and still I couldn't see anything. The thudding intensified – it was definitely a chopper, definitely on me, definitely getting closer. I squeezed myself even closer to the Honda Shadow, and I dialed back the throttle a little bit more, edging her up to 65, the curves snaking at me quicker now, the rise and fall of the road starting to feel like the rhythm of horseback at full gallop. I had been on horse before. I had been on a horse in Costa Rica.

I kept craning my neck, trying to see, my heart thundering in my chest like the chopper in the sky, that thudding that choppers do that seems to bend the air, sucking it and displacing it, turning the sky into a pulsing bowl, in out, in out, thud thud, thud thud, now speed it up, now like a dragonfly, now swooping down on me. I felt like I might lose control of my bladder, I felt like I could throw warm scotch down into my gut and then blast a giant, huge fat line off of a glass coffee table before mainlining something very brown and very strong and I felt like my heart was going to explode and that the helicopter was going to land right on me – no, not land on me, squash me, but have the talons of a huge bird snatch me up and carry me away to a nest on a high, scraggly rock mountain on a archipelago out in the middle of an uncharted sea where I would never be heard from again, and never get to see my daughter. What did she look like? Was she talking now?

And I turned and I felt numb now and as I gripped the road with the Shadow, feeling the blood squeezed out from my fingers and thighs, I saw the chopper, I saw it in the corner of my eye, and I nearly screamed.

There it was, flying right along side me now; while still high in the sky, our paths were parallel. It was a white helicopter, not too big, with a blue stripe on it that turned into a big numeral 5 before becoming the stripe again which stretched to the tail. Channel 5 Chopper. Chopper 5. Montpelier's local news. It was the fucking local news helicopter, and soon it banked right, to the south, and flew away from me, probably to cover the erection of a new cell phone tower, or the fire of a motor inn, or ponder the area the suspect was last seen who had shot his father and wore a beard and was suspected of mental illness. Vermont.

I nearly lost the bike as everything in me went limp. I regained control just in time, and a steep curve brought me back around into the mental driver's seat. I had gone limp from relief, but also from crashing. I was a fucking crisis junkie. I was addicted to anxiety.

I was going to need something to keep me calm if it wasn't beer; I was going to maybe need some kind of meds, like it or not, or I was going to become the worst neurotic mess the world had ever seen.

Still, the chopper was gone. It was over. The danger – real or not – was gone.

That's when I saw the lights in the Shadow's sideview mirrors, twirling reds and blues coming up on me fast around the curve I'd just made.

In Costa Rica was one of the women I met that I ended up falling in love with – but you couldn't blame me on this one. No, she wasn't the Latino beauty you're expecting me to talk about, she was an American, she was actually from a place so close to my own home. Such was the manner in which we broke the ice – that we were practically neighbors where we hailed from (though of course the exact whereabouts in I gave her was a fabrication, citing Queens, as much a fakery as my name, Landi) and she was from Pelham, a rich town in Westchester County, the first county north of the Five Boroughs. (Some called it the sixth borough, but those were kids from Yonkers and Mount Vernon and we laughed at them, and were self-righteous and cocky around them the way only us boys could, only smashmouths could, and we were nasty with them, though we made friends, we were nasty because we would always consider them outsiders, as preppy boys, even if Mount Vernon had a worse crime rate than Bed-Stuy, they were Westchester Boys.)

She was in Costa Rica as part of a TOEFL program, teaching English to the Costa Rican kids, living in a very modest kind of hostel the program provided for her, and she was sitting there in the café, somehow sitting right there and I didn't even notice her, and she was sipping on a Corona – the *cerveza* responsible for the odor I'd detected – I was not going insane after all.

"Excuse me. You from the States?" She asked me that question and set the bottle of Corona down on the frosted-glass table, one the little round tops that peppered the patio and its golden liquid winked in the sun at me. I was spilling *colones* onto my own table and they were rolling off and falling and bouncing onto the patio because my hands were shaking. And I hadn't even drank the fucking coffee. I looked over at who was speaking to me, if, that was, I was whom they were speaking to.

"*Perdona me*," the person said, the same person, now in Spanish, "*de donde eres? A Estedes Unidas?*"

"Hi," I said, "yes," I said. She, like the waiter had been, sat between me and the sun. She was mostly a silhouette. Behind her, the *cedro* trees shuffled their big, canvas-papery leaves together as a wind zephyred through. Beyond the trees, sighted in gaps between the thick fronds, the ocean sparkled. The ocean was free in Costa Rica. No one was allowed waterfront property. Here, there was some actual freedom.

The silhouette of the person addressing me, the woman, asking me where I was from, was long and slender. She had shortish hair. I started walking toward the back of the patio, where a wall of smooth stone curved like the rail of a balcony, and which overlooked the jungle, where the howler monkeys were calling, a good fifty foot drop from the café's perimeter here to the floor of the lush forest below. I walked and changed perspective so that the sun moved in the opposite way I did, and she watched me as I made this move, and she probably knew I was doing it to get a better look at her, so I altered my attitude to seem as though I were, instead, casually strolling to the patio wall for a contemplative moment listening to the monkeys and scarlet macaws and spying the Caribbean ocean in twinkling glimpses.

As I walked, I turned my head away from her and looked out along the treetops and said, "and you?"

"I don't believe it," she said, and I realized right away that I liked the sound of her voice; I'm a big voice-man, for some reason. Some guys are leg-men, I'm a voice man. Among other things. Other fetishes. Her voice was soft, feminine and hinted education, linguistic prowess, playfulness, and had a certain tomboy edge that I liked. I had my problems freaking out over shit and could be chickish myself, much as I enjoyed smashing guys in the face from time to time, or breaking the occasional clavicle, so I didn't needed a girly-girl who was all pink-fluffy and shopping and squeaking. I liked a girl who could scrap, if she needed to. It was all in the voice. "I'm from Pelham," she said, "do you know where that is?"

"I think so," I said. I reached the smooth stone wall, the arc of the patio's edge, and spread my hands on the concrete balustrade, imagining in that moment that I wore a Pith helmet, a gold-hemmed cape, and was about to address a phalanx of my troops waiting on the ground below. I really needed to have a drink of that Corona. It mocked me from the corner of my eye. "That's in Westchester, right?" And I had a flashback memory of myself, Victor, Ryan and others all kicking the shit out of these three guys from Yonkers outside of a yuppie bar called *The Alibi*, a kid named George Klembeck among them, trying to tell us to stop, but unable to form the words right after what we'd done to him.

"Yeah," she said, "wow." Then she seemed to get nervous, to clam up a little and maybe think she was acting schoolgirly or something, acting *golly-gee*, and so I turned and said, "that is incredible. What are the odds?" She smiled at me, I could see her now, the sun was highlighting the side of her face and shoulder and tanned arm, and she was beautiful. I smiled back and felt the shakes going away. "How did you get that beer?" I asked.

There was a guy in Costa Rica who went by Wild Dick. His actual name was Ricardo de Cabrea, but he only wanted to be known as Wild Dick. He'd once clubbed a guy with a ball peen hammer who mistakenly called him by his proper surname, de Cabrea, while on the job site. For real. Wild Dick worked construction on the Brandis brothers' home when it was first going up – it was two years before I was there at age of 23 that they had first broken ground. There was a party – the guy who'd incited Wild Dick's rage was the lumber contractor, and after the deal had been sealed with him, he took to the jungle, killed a pig, made a fire, boiled it with yucca and pork fat to make *chicharones*, a kind of extra thick bacon served with yucca and squash and lots of whiskey. In the excitement, the lumber contractor used Wild Dick's heritage name, which Wild Dick didn't like. The guy, smacked in the head with a ball peen hammer, or, really, *crunched* in the head with a ball peen hammer, was in a coma for three weeks. When he reemerged into the walking, talking world, he wasn't walking or talking so good. Wild Dick had done permanent damage to one of the lobes in his brain – the temporal or frontal, I can't remember which – but no action was taken against Dick. The Brothers had the Costa Rican version of workman's comp and the unfortunate lumberer had disability. He never sought legal action against Wild Dick, no no, and Wild Dick went on being wild for a time, but the Brandis brothers reprimanded him. Severely. Wild Dick had many mistresses, and the Brothers knew this. Jimena Lima-Escuerdo was the one woman that had tolerated Dick – she had been around for more than three years – and the one woman he seemed to love. She was precious to Dick. The Brandis Brothers knew this too. They hired a top prostitute, Carlos de Milian de Montalvo, to seduce Jimena and to have sex with her – all which was photographed and then mailed to Dick's small home along the eastern ridge of Zaga Mountain. Wild Dick killed them both, turned away from the Brandis Brothers and was now a rogue.

*

The cop was catching up to me, fast. My eyes dropped to the speedometer. 65 miles an hour. Speeding? Well, doing at least ten over the limit. But had I seen anybody? No. Had I passed a cop, that was, had there been one sitting along side of the road with the radar gun pointing at me? I hadn't seen even a ghost of a cop. Then again, I'd been straining to see the helicopter. I hadn't been exactly paying attention.

I broke out in gooseflesh as I saw the car bearing down on me, vibrating and growing larger in my side mirror.

A thought hit me: *My daughter is almost four years-old and I've never met her.* The paranoia was running in high gear. But there was something else. The anger was coming back, the anger I had felt in the UVM lab with Maya. The anger I had felt towards Cameron. The violence I had envisioned.

I had seen pictures of my daughter. Urged by Marcel to set myself up with that email account while still in Brooklyn, despite the paranoia I harbored then (in some ways greater in those days, but more diffuse; a general apprehension and rebellion cocktail I drank that whispered things to me about One-World, about End-Times, about a military state, and now more acute, more empirical). I did set up the account, wincing every time I logged on, but out of it I coaxed Katherine into sending me pictures of our daughter. Actually, coaxed is inappropriate – Katherine seemed happy to. There she was, my little girl, standing in the lush garden behind Katherine's Vermont home, smiling sweetly and holding what Katherine told me was a Gerbera daisy, at the time our little girl's favorite flower. I'd looked at those photos and, in my vanity, searched for traces of myself in her young face, and found it hard to discern them. She had my eyes, Katherine told me, green eyes, facial expressions like mine were, but in those digital pictures it seemed hard to verify. Scrutinizing my daughter's features for evidence of my legacy, I felt the burning, itching wonder, the question I never got up enough…guff, maybe, to ask Katherine. Who, if anyone, was surrogate-fathering our little girl? Was she calling someone else Daddy?

I pulled over to the side of the road after slowing the bike down gradually, my instincts telling me, of course, to act casual. To act surprised. "What seems to be the trouble, Officer Friendly?" Small stones popped from beneath the Shadow's tires along the dirt-strewn shoulder of Route 4. I could smell the dirt in the air, that alkali smell and taste, and could smell the heat rising off of the blacktop (Route 4 looked as though it had been recently paved, and I was grateful to not have encountered any construction thus far). What was Katherine's policy? Did she tell our daughter about me? Did she tell our little girl that she had a Daddy in New York? Were other men – if any – in her mother's life referred to by their first names? I hoped as much, though I wasn't sure if I had the right or the reason to. I suppose I could make a case for having both. Offspring was offspring, right? And it would have been naïve of me to really take that disclaimer, that idea that maybe Katherine wasn't now, nor had been so far involved with anyone else. The few single mothers I had known back in Brooklyn wasted no time after one rolling stone left their lives in shacking up with another one. How did they do it so fast? I supposed the odds were in their favor.

I put down my kickstand and shut off the Shadow. I knew the drill. Officer Friendly was a woman. I watched the lady cop approach me in the sideview mirror until she was out of my angle of sight, but didn't turn around. She was using her radio, but with my helmet on and the phantom whine of the motorcycle's engine ringing in my ears I couldn't hear what she was saying. Then she was along side of me.

I turned my head to the left and looked over at her, then flipped up my visor. Her right hand was resting on the butt of her gun.

"License and registration," she asked.

Routine, I thought, though I had neither item she'd requested, and began to perform my rehearsed speech for her in my head. First things first, I asked, "did I do something wrong?"

"License, and registration, sir."

"Was I speeding?"

"Doing 62 in a 45, yes. Now let me see your license to operate a motorcycle and the vehicle's registration."

"I don't have them." It just came out of me. My rehearsed speech was still inside my head. I was waiting for its opportunity; in my mind the speech was a paragraph illuminated in black space, red and throbbing. *And the truth shall set you free*, some corner of my mind whispered.

"Step away from the bike, please, sir."

She was mildly attractive, late twenties to mid thirties, her eyes masked by reflective sunglasses. The hair tucked under her policewoman hat was of a yellow, *amarillo*; buttery, streaks of fluorescence. My senses felt heightened. I could feel the blood tumbling through my veins, red and plump and viscous, and the adrenaline, thin, clear, like a gasoline, shooting through the canals of my body. The anger was rising, the lust was rising, the senses strained. It seemed it had to happen in concert this way; whatever was plucking at my hypothalamus gland was not that discerning, hitting spillover regions. And this thought prompted my speech, allowed that pulsing, throbbing need to unleash the truth, or what I knew of as the truth, out. OUT.

"Listen, officer, please," I said, but complying with her, swinging my leg back over the bike, letting go of my grip on the handlebars. "I don't know how to explain this, but please, let me try."

"Step away, sir. Have you been drinking? Are you on anything?"

She was messing with my perfect speech. I had to get it out. HAD to. It was chomping at me, pressing into my brain, a pillow seeking to fit through a keyhole in a locked door, writhing it's way to freedom, forming a protean face and screaming, head tilted and turned up, mouth drawn and terrible, a white amorphism now red and pulsing and monstrous, trying to get out, OUT.

"I've been an unwitting part of a scientific experiment. A group of rogue biochemists, fronting as organic food engineers – making healthier food because the fish are all poisoned and the honey bees are disappearing – you get the idea – I don't know, maybe they were cultivating the food too, I mean, they had a lot of greenhouses and that's a lot of time and effort and trouble to go to in order to just keep up appearances, you know, keep the cover going – but they were doing the other stuff too, they were, they operated – I don't know if you call it operate; is it surgery? See, this is why I've got to get where I'm going – I don't know nearly enough about this stuff, about what's happened to me, about what's *happening* to me, but they operated on me somehow and they either swapped genes of mine via homologous recombination or they tried to repair normal genes through selective reverse mutation – I got at least that much from Cameron, that's his name, Dr. Cameron Madison, but by even telling you this I am putting you in danger, because they let me go, but they didn't really let me go, see, they want to study me, like an animal I'm sure of it, they're following me now, and I have to outrun them, so I can get to my daughter, so they don't catch me doing something, like *kill* you, you know, they could be here any sec–"

And with that I was face down, squashed onto my stomach in the dirt along the shoulder of the road, blowing grains of it from me as my lungs and diaphragm accordioned closed with the cop's knee in my back, right between the shoulder blades, and she was cuffing me, and she was telling me I was under arrest for suspicion of DUI, for not producing a license or registration, for being a general blabbermouth asshole.

My chin in the grit, I looked across the road where a row of black-eyed susans bent in the breeze under an elm tree. I thought of my daughter, picturing her in front of Katherine's garden, standing there with those orange-y Gerbera daisies, the smile on her lips both innocent but somehow wise, somehow even, *otherworldly*, as though we came from some other place, as though we were born not just with sin, but born, in many ways, perfect, with a perfect outlook on life, with purity and spirit, and that life and education and conformity ruined us. I wanted to stop that. I needed to go and protect her. I needed out of this mess. OUT.

Before she had the second cuff latched I rolled the lady cop off the top of me, swinging my arm, bent at the elbow, handcuffs trailing along the wrist, so that I impacted her with my forearm along her shoulder and knocked her further from me. On my knees I made three quick shuffle-steps towards her and went for the gun she was going for too. I was distantly aware – as in I felt like I was seeing a painting of this framed and hung on some wall in eternity – that I was snarling as I bore down on her and her firearm. I wrestled it away from her easily enough – the adrenaline was a waterfall in my body now, a delta, thousands of rivulets bright and clear, though perhaps slightly opaque in places, tainted with the glacial silt of confusion.

I had no mind to use the weapon, on her, or on anyone – at least that part of me was still intact, and remembering too well what my actions along the edges of Utopia had brought me, had brought Peter; what I'd done – or been about to do – to Crick and Watson. I tossed the gun into the bushes beyond the shoulder, and I turned to get back on the Honda Shadow, hearing myself say, as a person would sound through a distorted microphone amid the white noise of a stadium crowd, "I'm not on drugs, I'm not crazy, I'm not even drinking," and I swung my leg over the gas tank and seat until I was fully mounted and turned the key.

The bike roared to life, and dirt and rock fanned up behind me as I shot out and away. I saw out of the corner of my eye and before the world disappeared into the back of my helmet that the lady cop had gotten to her feet – she tossed a glance toward the bushes, perhaps considering going after her service weapon. *Go for it*, I thought. But she didn't, and she remained still, standing there, somehow shocked out of her ingrained police-training, not knowing what to do. I flipped my visor down and gunned the engine, dropping into third gear, a comet of road dust.

I was heading for a bend in the road and about to feel my way into fourth when I looked into the sideview mirror. There I saw, in the thinning dust, the lady cop running to her car, and, behind her, coming up as fast as she had, the red and blue lights of two more police vehicles.

*

Her name was Julianne and she was a beautiful girl, with her dark, shortish
hair and those glossy hazel eyes. The sound of her voice – I couldn't get
over it. I listened to her talk about her experiences teaching English as a
foreign language and asked her questions about how and why she had gotten
into speaking Spanish as a career in the first place (her father spoke it
fluently and attended seminars and taught around the country) and I could
tell that she was a woman who had once not said much at all, who had once
been a very quiet, very internal girl. I could tell this because the Corona
gave me special powers of insight. I could tell this because of the careful
way she spoke, though it would seem natural enough to the casual observer,
there was something extra in it, something still shy and yet sterling – it was
like someone who hadn't swam in years getting back into the water,
someone learning to walk after a coma. Of course that implied an original
time when she had been naturally chatty, and this didn't seem right either.
This was a woman who had learned how to change herself, who had
overcome something – most likely having to do with the parents (didn't it
always) – and was standing on her own two feet, looking to walk the walk
and talk the talk, shielding only what was perishable.

　　　We sat on the patio at the Brandis ranch, her back again to the ocean,
her front facing the home, the siding glass doors to the expansive, clerestory
living room and I watched her and I watched the large *cedro* trees swaying
behind her, as I had watched them outside Café Arroyo where we had just
met. Julianne had a Geo Tracker and I had thrown my mountain bike in and
I'd navigated as she drove us the five or so winding miles from the little

town of *Siquirres* and up the back of Zaga Mountain to the Brandis's Costa Rican home, or, "the ranch", as we referred to it.

I finished my third Corona since our arrival, wiped my mouth with the back of my hand and listened as she finished up her careful dissertation of her past-to-present. I didn't have to look at my watch to know that it was almost noon, the light in the house was dusky as the sun rode over the roof. Though the three beers had set me straight, they had also excited me. I felt like a person who ordinarily didn't have the tolerance to drink for more than ten hours a day, but someone who drinks three drinks and feels a bit wilder and had no need to drink anymore – they've had their limit.

The call would be coming in any moment from home, and the work would finally start. I hated work most of the time. I hated that I was going to have to help out some obscenely rich slob named Calvin Blair whose legacy in life would be his preying on the sick idiocy of chronic gamblers. Probably I felt that way because I had chronic issues of my own; probably I resented Blair for being an entrepreneur, when I was anything but. It seemed at my age then, as far as I could tell, I was a laborer.

"And so…" Julianne said, and smiled the blushing smile of a person who realizes how much they have been talking. Only in Julianne's case that blushing smile had another ghost in it, another face – the one of pride and accomplishment, that this was a big deal to have met someone and been talkative and not so clammed up like she used to, a woman who'd finally started to come into her own.

I stood and I turned for the cooler we'd bought at the store along with the beer. It was the same store Julianne had bought her one beer at she'd had at the café. Café Arroyo didn't have a license to sell liquor, but there was no law to stop anybody from bringing their own party favors and

Julianne always got one for herself on Saturday, even before noon, and brought it in with her. The Friday night before, she explained usually entailed venturing into San Jose to hit the clubs with two young women also in the TOEFL program (one from Great Britain – Dhara – and the other from Austin, Texas – Deirdre) or to stay home, swing in the hammock on her tiny terrace outside of her tiny furnished apartment (three rooms, including bath and kitchen) and drink a bottle of wine while reading Tom Robbins or Russell Banks, two men I had never heard of. Either after the club night or the bottle-of-wine-and-book, the next morning was a Corona at Arroyo. "I'm a pretty routine-oriented person," she'd told me.

Now as I pawed around in the icy water of the cooler for another beer for myself and one more for her I asked her, "So what makes today different? I don't mean to startle you, but you've had more than one beer. Don't tell me you broke routine for me." This was how I got. A couple of beers and full of swagger and charm. Or so I thought. She smiled, though, and then explained the coming Monday was a non-work day, a sort of TOEFL version of a superintendents' day at the school where she had her classes, and so she was allowing herself an extra day of fun.

"So," she said next, after I had sat down, cracked and distributed our drinks, "what about you? Here I've been going on and on..." She looked up at the house looming behind me, at the gable above my head with the parallelogram windows, and she spread her arms and leaned back in her chair a bit and said, "I mean, *this*. What do you do?"

I'd been working for the police as a kind of blue-collar spy, which is how I came to meet the Brandis brothers, fences living in Brooklyn, dirty with everything from drugs to black market kids. And now, some new

fangled thing, some sort of biotechnology I knew nothing about. I'm their
emissary.

I sipped and set the Corona bottle down and said, "Place isn't mine.
Relatives."

"Uh-huh," she said, and leaned forward, propping her arm up on her
knee so that she rested her head in her hand. It was just enough movement
that her scent wafted to me, chased by a drift of the sea air – I smelled
shampoo and saltwater, I smelled her light perfume, something like a Calvin
Klein smell, light as lace and somehow primally stirring. "So, but what do
you *do*?" She looked at me smiling and then her expression changed and
she wiped the hand that had been cupping her hand across her eyes and sat
back saying "Uggh, I'm sorry. That's all people ask. That's all anyone ever
asks at the clubs, all I ever ask."

I shrugged, relieved. "It's a normal question. It's an ice breaker.
Gives people a place to start." I was so agreeable and so fucking smart
when boozing, wasn't I?. "What I do is nothing. Not right now. College
dropout. I'm just looking around – my family seems to think that American
kids, you know, Generation X, whatever, is going to shit. We're lazy and
unfocused and all of that. I tell them, 'wait until the *next* generation – you
ain't seen nothing yet.' Dunno. Just a feeling." I smiled and did my best to
project humility. I had told her a white lie, then a truth, and then blurred it
all with a wet swipe of bullshit.

"Do you speak Spanish?" She asked.

"*Si. Un poquito.*"

"*Un poquito*," she echoed, and I could see that the beer was hitting
her, and not only did she have a past that was about being repressed vocally,
but she had once been repressed – or repressed herself, in other ways too. In

that moment, right in that moment her eyes made the transition. We had just gone through the door – so silent, but so important – and were now in the new world. "Let me teach you something," she said.

"Okay."

"*No puedo vivir otro dia sin ti,*" she said.

"*No puedo…*" I began, "'I can't'…"

"Don't translate it," she said, and she had leaned forward and propped herself up again and the beer bottle swung from her other hand, between her legs, and I looked there, and I traced her body with my eyes, going up, into the horizontal creases her tight, light shirt made along her slender abdomen, over the taut rise of her breasts, dipped into the cup of sweat-glistened flesh between her collar bones, up her smooth, slim neck, out and around her jawline, highlighted in the early sun, up to her cheekbones, then into her light brown eyes, melted by them, causing beads of sweat to pop out at my temples, under my arms, a surge of blood to my genitals, deep into her eyes now, taking her all in, through them and still somehow exclusively only there, in the eyes, in some other place entirely, that place that exists only in the lust of love, that place so intoxicating and alluring and yet somehow devilish and she said, "just say it. Just speak it. There is no translation. It means what it means."

One of the *aricaris* that nested outside of the ranch uttered a shrill squawk and another answered.

"*No puedo vivir otro dia…*" I started, but couldn't finish. The beer dangling between her legs was perspiring too, big mushroom-cap bubbles sliding down towards the bottom of the bottle.

"*…sin ti.*"

"*No puedo vivir otra dia sin ti.*" I finished.

One side of her mouth, lips vital and red, curled up and she blinked her eyes, and they closed and opened slowly, the lashes long, the moment at hand, almost ringing in my ears like bells with what was to come next.

And it was the phone ringing, not the bells, it was the phone, and the trance was broken.

It was Lincoln, not Lucius on the phone, a fact I was usually grateful for. Lincoln, the retired boxer and ex-soldier, was a little easier to deal with than his brother Lucius. Lincoln had gotten a lot of the demons out of him through the course of his life, beating them into the faces of other men, firing them out the end of his Heckler & Koch rifle. While Lincoln had gone to war and traveled the world, Lucius had remained home in Brooklyn. After their Swiss-German parents had died, Lucius had taking on the family business bequeathed to them, working in textiles, moonlighting in everything scatological.

"How are you doing?" Lincoln asked of me. He had yet to suffer the stroke he would three years later, and his speech was clearer than the slurred quality it would eventually acquire. Still, Lincoln spoke slower and with some joviality, where Lucius's words were quick, sharp and devoid of any humor (unless that "humor" was black humor, red sarcasm.) For brothers, they had grown far apart in nature, a tree split in two trunks, each stretching off and away from one another, but still connected at the base, forever, should only lightning strike them apart.

"I'm good, sir, thank you for asking me."

"Sir? That's my father's title." It sounded like, *Zat's my fazza's title.*

"Sorry, sir. Lincoln. Old habit."

"You're too young for old habits."

This was it; this was our usual smalltalk intro. Business would be next.

"You're right," I said to Lincoln. The phone was a heavy, rotary-dial unit with the handset connected to the main body by a short, coiling cord. From where I was in the bright, shining kitchen (a skylight let the high sun drop in and spangle all), I could see out to the patio, but only partly. I could make out one of Julianne's legs, also shining in the sun. I willed her to stay where she was, to not think, to hold the moment. My head was pleasantly buzzed; I could have gone on longer with the good natured small talk, probably have pushed it to far, but, even though Lincoln was the more human of the two brothers, he got down to business. First, the status report.

"Have you seen or heard from Mr. De Cabrea?"

"No, sir. No."

"Did you get the package in town that we sent to you?"

I looked at it sitting on the modest round kitchen table, four chairs surrounding, the same glass top like those in the open-air eatery where I had just been that morning, glinting in the sunlight. The package sat there, a square parcel wrapped in brown paper, taped up with clear packing tape. "Yes, I did."

"Good. Do not open the package until Monday morning, eight a.m."

It was Saturday. I had been in Costa Rica since Thursday, acquired the package in *Siquirres* on Friday. The Brandis brothers did not like sending anything directly to their Costa Rican ranch – they sought to preserve their relative anonymity in the foreign country. They looked to keep hidden.

"Baradez will meet you Monday morning. He is head of security for Calvin Blair. You will meet him at the Blair estate in *Moravia*. Eight a.m. sharp. That's practically noon."

"For you, sir," I laughed, and asked, "are the local police involved?"

Lincoln said nothing for a moment; perhaps two or three seconds lapsed. I could hear in that gap a noise on the line that sounded like the dial-up internet connections that were the most common form of internet at that time. "No," Lincoln then said.

Now it was my turn to be silent. The quiet on my end, however, lasted for than a couple of seconds. My pleasant buzz was suddenly disrupted, like a flock of beached birds suddenly stirred into flight. "Sir," I began, "Lincoln," I said, hoping that Lincoln might guide me some, the ex-soldier who had punished other men for his inner tortures, who had spilled the toxins of his soul out in his blood on the canvas floor of the rings in Fort Dix, in Paris, at the New York Athletic club, a place he took me too once, a place that had smelled of leather and sweat and this other peculiar odor I could not place, an odor Lincoln Brandis had told me was the smell of the fighting soul. "What am I supposed to do here? I mean, what can I possibly do that—"

I saw Julianne's leg disappear at the very moment Lincoln interrupted me to say, "You are there to fulfill a role. You're our ambassador, our family. Wait until Monday to open the package. Tomorrow, meet Baradez. Just be there, just do what comes natural. You'll be alright, *kleinnes*." Lincoln hung up the phone – I heard it clatter before the connection was lost.

Immediately I put the handset back in the cradle and walked quickly back to the patio, grabbing my half-finished Corona up from the island block as I went, realizing I had forgotten it during the conversation with Lincoln.

Julianne appeared in front of me before I could even step out onto the patio. She on the stone slabs, myself standing on the tile floor, the threshold in between us, the sun now beginning to drop from its apex behind her as the day rolled on. I could see from her body language and from her averted eyes what she was now feeling. I denied it, trying to usher us back to five minutes before. "Sorry about that, business. The owners of the place here, checking on it, you know. Listen, we should go to the beach. Do you want to go? We could even walk down, it's a bit of a hike, but we could–"

"Thanks," she said, and her hazel eyes rolled up to mine, and I could just see it, and I was crumbling inside. "I feel like I need to get going. I've had a couple too many of these and I've got papers to grade…"

"You said you had tomorrow off, that today was a freebie, a 'fuck it day.'" I tried to sound charming and not desperate. I imagine I sounded more like the latter. Suddenly I found myself draining the rest of the beer in my hand, unconscious of being right in front of this woman, gulping it down, maybe, as though it were a potion, an elixir I could take in and suddenly become endowed with powers – in this case, of persuasion, or backwards time travel.

"I know," she said, "it's that–"

"Listen," I said, expecting that I was to become more frantic, wide-eyed, but instead my inner workings lined up and shifted gears, as in a row, and I took a step toward her. "I understand. It's an extra day. You've earned it."

I turned and walked over to the refrigerator on the other side of the block island with the cast iron skillets and shining sauce pots hanging above it. The refrigerator was the kind with the vertical freezer on the left, a slimmer bay than the main one to the right. It had the brushed chrome look on the exterior and was ivory white inside. I opened it up. Stocked to the hilt with foodstuffs by the housekeeper, an old man named Ferdinand. He was more the caretaker, I should say, who worked as the gardener, the cleaner, and so forth. I could feel Julianne's presence at my back, heating me up. I pulled a few delectables from the fridge and set them on the wood block.

Julianne started walking over. She no longer carried her beer, but she was looking at the food.

"In the meantime," I said, as planned, "I'm going to eat. I'm starving." The truth was I didn't want to eat at all. I wanted to drink and keep drinking and have sex with Julianne somewhere along in there, preferably while still drinking. As I watched her move across the room toward me, her long-legged strides slow and lissome and yet somehow girlish, her black bangs hanging in her eyes, I felt the nerve-jangling electricity of my developing infatuation beneath the veil the Coronas had helped create. I could see that wild urge now, I could feel that insecurity, and I longed for another drink but had to keep her in this moment.

Julianne stopped at the woodblock on the other side of me. I watched her eyes darting over the food items. They landed on some strawberries, and then she looked up at me. "Rain check," she said, and she leaned across the island and kissed me, once and lightly on the lips, and she walked away, and I realized she already had her pack with her slung over one shoulder, and she showed herself out. Something told me not to move, not to say anything, not even to jump into the chivalrous chicanery of taking her to the door, putting her in her car; we weren't that sophisticated, we were basically still kids, we were drinking at noon on a Sunday, we were ready to jump into bed with one another after only a couple of hours of getting-to-know – at least, I thought we were. I knew I was.

Looking back, I don't know what would have happened had I shown her out to her car, or if I had somehow managed to convince her to stay. It still would have all gone down, for the most part, but maybe not in the same way. Those little things, you know, those little things you do are what stick with you, what you go over time and time again; they fix there in your mind like burrs, clinging for dear life, looking to plant in you and take up root forever, to never let you go.

I pressed the Shadow into the latening day, gripping the road, reaching speeds of eighty, now going on ninety. The lights of the two cop cars blazing after me seemed to be inside my helmet, throbbing reds and blues, inside my skull, flash-strobing their authority, their promise to take my freedom forever.

And yet I realized something. As I edged the needle to ninety, taking the turns in a way that made my stomach roll, I felt pinned to the earth, an unstoppable force, a momentum, a juggernaut. I was afraid, yeah, but what I was afraid of was that I wouldn't get to see my daughter. I realized, as I watched the cop cars recede in my sideview mirror, that I wasn't afraid or paranoid of being "caught" in the way I had been in the past, of being exposed as a fraud, a cheater, a coward. I was losing the fear of not being in control. Because what had I been controlling? My own fucking misery. In Costa Rica, I'd thought I was a big deal. An *emissary*, I'd thought. The truth of it was, I took orders. From Lucius, from Lincoln, and now, from something else.

As I soared along the winding road the cop cars would now disappear in the Shadow's mirror for seconds at a time before they rounded the same bend. I remembered hearing somewhere about cops not being allowed to give chases that went up over a hundred miles an hour, not through residential areas anyway. It was probably bullshit. And we weren't in a residential area. There were farms, here and there, big spreads on either side of me and corn and red barns and brown, sagging, clapboard houses and then there were just trees, hemming the roadway, huddled and fluffing and blurring past.

I decelerated. I downshifted. I squeezed the back brake. Within seconds the cop cars gained on me and came upon me fast, those lights swirling their red and blue, the silhouettes of the drivers leaning forward, hunched, angry.

I stopped right in the middle of the road. A vehicle was coming from the other direction, a minivan, the first car to pass from the other direction since I'd been pulled over by the lady cop. I could see the driver as she passed, a middle-aged woman, pie-eyeing me and the cops who roared to a halt behind me. The first cop car, with a big stalker dual radar gun on the dash, stopped directly behind me and the second passed me and then stopped a few yards ahead of the Shadow. The cop at my rear used the bullhorn.

"Pull over to the shoulder."

The Shadow still idling, I have to admit I did have a sudden urge, a bolt of electric fear pass through me in that moment, to gun the engine and get out of there once more. I even rationalized – in the eternity of that one moment – that I could easily outrun them now that they were stopped. I could get up to speed much quicker than they could, and I would find any one of dozens of dirt roads to turn off onto, even drive into a corn field. I was on a bike, after all, I could go anywhere and do just about anything. This was my last chance.

I wrapped my fingers around the throttle, getting a good grip, my index finger hooked around the rear brake. The door to the cop car in front of me popped open, but the driver stopped swinging it halfway out, and drew it back to a close, though not entirely, leaving it ajar a couple of inches. *He's watching me, he sees my hand*, I thought. Of course he did. I glanced into my sideview mirror. The silhouette in the car behind me wasn't moving. I could make out a hand and a microphone and a coil of wire. The Shadow purred beneath me, ready. I still had a least a half tank of gas – I'd filled up about twenty miles back before I'd been stopped the first time. A half tank would be plenty enough to get me way the hell away from here. I remembered the map – there was a junction coming up in Talcville, and not long after that, one just past Stockbridge. I remembered this clearly because the left turn after Stockbridge onto 107 led to a town called Gaysville. There was actually a town in Vermont called Gaysville. I had wondered what the original settlers were like, and how milking cows may be a different thing for different types of people. There were plenty of places to hide. There were ways to get to my daughter. The Shadow thrummed and my right hand vibrated on the throttle and my left hand could release the clutch in a split second. I'd be off.

I caught a whiff of manure in the air. Over the sound of the three vehicle engines, I could hear the birds chirping. I thought one was a white-throated swallow. Daniel had been something of an ornithologist. He'd made me listened to tapes one night as we sat abstaining from our various addictions and trying to be "good." The smell of manure held beneath it the smell of fresh mown grass. Ah, the country.

I realized I was waiting for the cop behind me to use the loudspeaker again. If he did, I knew I would use it as an excuse. *Don't fucking bully* me *man.* That type of thing. Make it about him. *He* fucked up. He pushed me too hard. I think that had something to do with being passive-aggressive, which Daniel had explained to me one night when we weren't talking about birds. "Overbearing father," he said, "or inherited from your mother. Likely both."

One more time, asshole. Just ask me to pull over one more time.

But he didn't.

I would always be on the run if I ran now. On the run from the Brandis Brothers, on the run from Utopia, on the run from the Law. What kind of life would that be – what kind of relationship would I have with my little daughter?

But what kind would you have behind bars?

And then I, Jack Aiello, or, X really, the big fat nobody, let the clutch out part way and gave the bike some gas.

It was just enough to pull over to the shoulder where I killed the engine and dropped the kickstand. Both cops were out of their vehicles and on top of me by the time I swung my leg over the seat of the Shadow, my belly a pit of stones, my blood and adrenaline thrumming, my senses sharp, alive, everything vivid.

*

I expected Vermont cops, at least rural cops, or Deputies, like these guys,
County cops, to be rotund and slovenly, like you see in the movies. They
weren't. Both men – they looked like they could be brothers – reminding
me of a picture on Lucius's desk of he and Lincoln in their prime, Lincoln in
his brown gloves and shining trunks, Lucius with his cigar and silver suit on,
fedora perched atop his curly Swiss-German hair. These cops were
strapping as well as strapped, one a bit taller than the other but both on the
tall side, both wearing the County Sheriff's Department hats, dressed in
uniforms the color of creamed coffee, and the first one of them spun me
around with such force I thought my teeth and eyes could fly lose from my
skull. He put the cuffs of me and read me my rights while the other deputy
walked around the motorcycle, inspecting it, looking at the license plate and
registration sticker. He pulled the key from the ignition. Neither man asked
me for my license, but the first cop hotwalked me over to his vehicle, the
one that had come up behind me, and told me to lay forward on the trunk.
He proceeded to pat me down.

While the first deputy was groping me, a vehicle coming from the
west, driving up in the same lane the two police cars were in – they'd never
pulled them off to the side of the road – came around the bend and over the
rise and I realized it was the lady cop, though she didn't have her lights
going. The second deputy walked over to her as she pulled up and got out
while the one frisking me found something in my right pants pocket.

It's hard to describe the feeling of being arrested. While cocked, it's
actually something of a good time. It's fun. It beats the same old drudgery
of getting shitfaced until one's pool game goes sour and the ability to talk to

women devolves into a slur. Getting arrested beat the usual business. It was
something exciting at the time, something different to do. My conscience,
though, I could never quite completely drown in booze, try as I might.
There was always some conscientious part of me while I was getting
arrested, the part that knew he'd fucked up, that there were consequences,
that this was not a *good* thing, that this was not going to be so much fun in
the cold, hungover morning. I'd assumed that getting arrested sober was a
horrifying ordeal. I was sure that the tiny point of light that remained the
conscience while boozed-up, that little dot of sunlight while deep in the
ocean of drunk, would expand and become the blinding fire of the sun in
entirety, and that getting arrested would be a horribly invasive, humiliating
thing.

It wasn't. As I watched Deputy Two walk over to Ladycop and talk
to her and point down the road first one way, then the other, and as Deputy
One pulled out the contents of my front right pocket, I knew that how you
felt getting arrested was purely predicated on what you did to get there, and
how you felt about what you did. It was a state-of-mind experience, just
like, I was learning, everything else was. It was the conscience, yes, but in
this case, the conscience was clean; I had *chosen* to stop running. I had
given myself up because…well, do I have to tell you? I had taken a leap of
faith.

Deputy One kept what he had gotten out of my pocket in one hand, I
presumed, while he continued to rummage in the rest of my pockets with his
other hand. "Where is your wallet?" He asked.

"I don't have one, sir." I noticed my voice was level. Calm.

"You don't have a wallet? No ID, no money?"

"Yes sir I have money."

"Where?"

"In my shoe."

"In your shoe."

"Yes sir."

I watched another car approaching from the west, a pick-up truck, rusty and rickety, that came around the bend and over the rise. Ladycop walked away from her car and Deputy Two to do the job she'd just been instructed and began to wave her hands for the truck to slow and then to go around. As she did this, Deputy One, before he went to look in my shoe, tossed away what he'd retrieved from my pants pocket. It hit the ground right on the freshly painted double yellow line. It was my chewed-up red stirring straw.

Deputy Two watched the lady cop for a moment as the pick-up came closer, and must've then decided she'd have things under control, turned his head back towards myself and Deputy One, working to get my shoe off. The smell of manure wafted over again, and grass, and a fermented smell that made me think of an apple orchard nearby, and sitting beneath one of those short, scraggly apple trees and biting into the fruit, and leaning back against the tree.

While I was having this fantasy my right back leg came up and connected perfectly with Deputy One's head, my heel catching him under the chin. Even though his back was to me I knew this had happened because I heard the sound of his jaw snapping shut, his teeth ramming together. He fell back away from me, stunned, and now I turned and saw him for a second in the fetal position, his left arm up over his head to ward off anymore potential blows.

Deputy Two was instantly moving quicker, starting to run, at the same time drawing his firearm, and I found that I had scrambled into the hood to the police vehicle I'd been thrust against, even with my hands cuffed behind my back. I don't know why or how I did what I did and I had planned none of it, but I just launched myself at deputy number two, a man who probably outweighed me by thirty or forty pounds. As I came down on him his weapon came up, but before I was in its line of sight he fired and I heard the bullet punch into the door of the police vehicle. The next instant he and I connected and I thrust my head forward so that it knocked into his and we both toppled to the ground.

He was unconscious. I rolled away and then scuttled to my feet again. I needed to get to Deputy One and get the keys to the handcuffs. At the same time, the pick-up truck was beginning to pass the caravan of cars and Ladycop, I had seen out of the corner of my eye, was starting over to me.

I dropped to my knees next to Deputy One, who was bleeding from the mouth. *Must've clipped his tongue with his teeth*, I thought, and felt this tremendous rush of compassion for him, somewhere beneath the active rage I felt powerless over. I actually felt the urge to ask him if he was okay. He was okay, anyway, because he reached up and grabbed me around my neck. With a good deal of power he sat up and pistoned me back onto my ass, all while cutting off my windpipe and maneuvering me only with that one arm. With his other arm he reached and unholstered his firearm. He pressed the muzzle of it to my temple and he snarled, and his teeth were coated dark red.

I heard Ladycop come trotting up behind me and could sense her weapon drawn as well, trained on me. There really is a feeling you get when someone is looking at you, and there is definitely a feeling you get when a one-eyed extension of them is looking at you. In front of me, behind deputy number one (though at this point I was wondering if they really were deputies, if it was common practice for a deputy to put a gun to an assailant's skull, even if he'd just kicked the officer in the jaw) and on the other side of the double yellow the red pick-up trundled past. I saw myself jumping into the back of it, all three cops knocked out and lying on the hot pavement under the sun, the occasional fly buzzing around them, alighting on their eyelids and noses. Instead I watched, helpless, as the old geezer behind the wheel – somehow reminding me of the (then passed on) caretaker of the Brandis's Costa Rican ranch, Ferdinand. He watched the scene – and made eye contact with me. As he did, his vehicle displaced the air in the road and a current lifted my red straw a little, and then pushed it, rolling, in my direction. It was almost close enough to grab, but I was pinned. With all I had left I jerked my head up and back, connecting with something that flashed bright in my mind. The cop I hit howled and I felt the pressure let up some, just enough to stretch forward and grab my straw. Then the pressure resumed, slamming my face back into the pavement, a gun jabbing me in my neck.

Boy was I in fucking trouble.

After Julianne had left the ranch on her own, I went for another Corona. There were three left from the twelve-pack we'd bought. Julianne had drunk two, I figured, maybe three, tops, so that meant I'd slugged down at least eight of the sunsabitches. I was feeling pretty good, despite the break in continuity between Julianne and me, the disruption in our momentum. I remembered the Brandis brothers had a tape player in the closet off from the kitchen – one of those pantry-type deals with slatted folding doors like those for a linen closet. I passed by the wood block and the towering brushed steel refrigerator and the ceramic countertop with the flower patterns. (The crown molding where the walls and ceiling conjoined had the same pattern – thin green vines, very delicate, encircling the room, leaves and purplish buds here and there, repeating.) I opened the closet doors, folding both sides back and away, and the tape deck was there, the speakers hardwired in through the walls like the rest of electricity, the speakers all through the house. CDs were around then, but the Brandis brothers had yet to upgrade. The sound system was still top notch, a Technix component system, and I grabbed from the shelf below the tape deck *The Allman Brothers Greatest Hits*.

I remember drinking the Corona in that closet, how that somehow it felt to be one of the best moments of my life. In the sun-spangled kitchen light beams slanted every which way, refracting off of the hanging cookware, glaring off of the countertops, the opaque glass dining table, the jewels in the chairbacks surrounding the table, and one such bar of light reaching in and alit my Corona as I tilted it back. Here I was, I thought, putting the Allman Brothers cassette in, a 23 year old man who was in Costa Rica, who was working, basically, as a kind of agent, or spy, special ambassador to the Brandis Brooklyn Empire, and had just had a liquid lunch date with a very attractive (ok, I was smitten with her, the seeds of worship planted but good) American girl, a girl nearly from my neck of the woods, and though she had left abruptly that was actually a good thing – it meant there was something real there, I rationalized, something more than just games. Here I was (I pressed *play*) in Costa Rica (the song "Whipping Post" began) in this gorgeous ranch-house, mansion, whatever the fuck you wanted to call it, totally financed. I had a day to myself before meeting with – what's his name, Barbarez, or something, fuck, I should have written it down (I started dancing to the music and left the closet, leaving the doors folded back) and I had two days before opening that package on the table. Whatever it was, and however badly I wanted to know what was in it, I knew that once I opened it I was going to be committed, somehow, more involved than I was now. Whatever was in there was going to create an inextricability between myself and the Calvin Blair kidnapping, the whole sordid scene down here, but, BUT, I didn't have to worry about that now. Now was good, now was perfect, and as I drained the Corona I danced backwards, swinging my hips, letting my free hand float through the air as Greg Allman sang *me and my goodtime buddies / drinkin' in some crosstown bar* and I was so into it, so into the whole scene, my buzzed, high, sundrenched moment of bliss, that I backed right into the wood block.

The last of the Corona I was drinking slipped down the sides of my jaw in streams and I coughed as some of it caught in my throat, or was inhaled into my lungs as I took in a surprised breath. I turned around to lean on the table to cough more and set down the bottle and catch my breath, but Wild Dick was there, and behind him a man I didn't recognize who was holding onto Julianne, with a gun to her temple, her eyes wide and mascara-streaked, and then Wild Dick hit me in the face and things spilled black, and Julianne's eyes and face melted.

My name was Jack Landi, my name was the Brandis Boy, my name was X. My name was nothing now, as I was in the ether, tumbling in Atman, lost in Costa Rica.

THE RANCH

A major bottled spring water company was being sued for bromate
contamination of their product. This was even before the turn of the century,
turn of the millennium. Chemicals from the plastic seeping into the water.
Packaging, it seemed, was everything. I was thinking about this because I
was thirsty, and because I still had a pretty good buzz on. This was still in
Costa Rica, in the back of Wild Dick's pick-up truck, and I'd been
blindfolded.

It was hot. In Central America, except for the rain season (Brooklyn
summertime) when the temperature had a little more room to fluctuate, there
was little variance in the day. At night it might be in the low seventies, by
noon, the mid to high eighties. Today was hot, and today was near the
beginning of the rain season so temperatures had risen a little higher as, over
the Atlantic, towers of hazy stratocumulus clouds shouldered together like
giants admiring the land they would soon pummel with fat rain. I couldn't
see the clouds now, but I had seen them this morning, had seen them over
the tops of the *cedro* trees and over Julianne's shoulder, out beyond the
mono monkey cries where the light-blue and grey-purple haze of early day
had sat brewing.

Julianne was put in the front of the truck with Wild Dick. I was put in
the back already blindfolded. With me was the second man, a thin man with

a bushy black moustache, the gun he'd once pressed into Julianne's skull now trained on me.

I was in the same blackness I had fallen into when Wild Dick had clocked me. I'd woken back into it, though I had been able to feel the material wrapped around my eyes and knew I had been blindfolded. I heard Wild Dick and the thin man talking in Spanish as they had put Julianne in the front, me in the back. My head hurt a little, but, like I said, the buzz was still there, though fading, and fading in a way that terrified me, because if I wasn't scared now (it was, honestly, hard to be scared of a guy who insisted in being referred to as "Wild Dick," even if he took it to the extent that he'd put that guy in the hospital who refused to follow along), I was going to be scared later. Plus, I was worried about what was going to become of my meeting the next day with Barbarez – no, Baradez, that was it – if I didn't get out of this shit with Wild Dick.

The pick-up bumped and jounced over the dirt road winding down Zaga Mountain. I thought I was sitting on a bench, and that the thin, moustached man was across from me. He looked familiar to me, and I thought of the waiter at Café Arroyo. I slid towards the front and towards the back with each bump, my hands tied behind me.

Along the edge of the road, a trio of *carrablancas* – white-faced monkeys – sat watching us drive past.

*

It was the second time I was sitting in a jail cell in the past two weeks. This county slammer was bigger than the two-stalled Orleans jail, and this time it wasn't some Forest and Parks guy who I'd tousled with, but a Deputy Sheriff whose teeth I'd knocked loose. Seriously, he was going to have to get false molars, or crowns, or something, because of how hard his mouth had snapped closed when I'd kicked him under the chin.

As I sat there, alone in my particular cell, but aware of many others throughout the complex (shouting back and forth between one another, and who, as I saw coming in, occasionally flashed cigarette-pack-sized mirrors), there sat a cop directly across from me. He was another strapping Deputy Sheriff, and he was looking at me over the coffee cup he brought to his lips. He was talking on the phone, murmuring, really, more than talking. I could see from as far away as I was that his eyes were green – they reminded me of a snake's eyes. I thought of the *fer-de-lance*, a Costa Rican snake, one of the most poisonous in the world, one that, if it bit you, rendered you dead from its venom in fifteen minutes.

The cop glared over his coffee and seemed to slurp it extra loud, for my benefit. His lips moved here and there. He was probably talking to another cop, a corrections officer, maybe, about what to do to me tonight. Yeah, they fuckin' hated me here. I'd been handled so roughly I felt like there should have been cameras filming the action for an episode of *Cops*. And how funny that was. If you were on *Cops*, and you were filmed getting your head mashed into the asphalt, with a 200 pound knee in your neck, pinning you in such a way that was smashing your vertebrae, it was all hunky-dory. But if someone hiding in the bushes or filming from their

passing vehicle should happen to get you on video, it was a civil rights /
human rights outrage and would drag on in the courtroom and on TV for
months. This occasion, I'm sure you could guess, was the *Cops* occasion.
Even Rodney King hadn't shattered a cop's teeth like I had, or tackled and
headbutted another. It would be said that their brutal retaliation was
warranted.

I took inventory of myself. I was bleeding from somewhere in the
back of my scalp, my shoulder throbbed and felt hot and out of place
beneath my cotton t-shirt. I had suffered multiple scrapes and abrasions on
my cheeks and forehead and my back was sore from being wrenched around
and stuffed in the car by the second deputy and lady cop, both of them red-
hot with rage at the time.

I would make no friends here. It would be useless to explain to the
cop watching me as he noisily slurped his coffee that it wasn't my fault, that
I hadn't even felt in control of my muscles when my foot had come up like
that and connected with the first deputy's chin. He wouldn't want to hear
that I had actually decided to surrender – cops didn't want to hear that in any
situation, I imagined, because it invalidated their hard work, their pursuit,
their position as the dog chasing the cat. You didn't tell them that you'd
planned to give in anyway. That was no good under any circumstances, and
these were particularly bad circumstances. And it further stood to reason
that it would make *no* sense whatsoever to explain that seeing my red straw
tossed on the pavement had *done something* to me, had triggered some kind
of sense of personal injustice, had made me feel like the Manchurian
Candidate, given a code phrase or a special sign to activate the secret
weaponry that was inside me, that *was* me.

"Side effects" was what they had said. That I was losing control of my anger and lust as a result of side effects from the gene therapy. My adrenal glands were out of control.

The cop across from me coughed loudly and wiped his mouth with the back of a loosely curled fist. He hung up the phone – the old kind, the flesh-colored kind with the bell shaped handset and rotary-dial cradle. He seemed to be telling me that I wasn't allowed to get lost in my thoughts or to consider the past; to try and figure everything out. He leaned forward in his chair, the wooden legs creaking, placing his palms flat on the desk in front of him, his coffee cup set off to the side, and he looked right at me. Yes, body language understood. Do not reflect, do not analyze, do not figure *anything* except for the pain and punishment I would receive, the hatred and bigotry I would endure. Yes indeed: message received, sir. And then he stood up, pushing himself erect with his arms, and he started out and around from behind his desk.

My heart started to beat faster. It had been going strong since I'd gotten here, probably around 90 beats per minute, I don't know, but now that sucker was off and running. I hadn't panicked, I hadn't even really been that scared (in truth immediately following the moment of my takedown I'd experienced a preternatural calm, as though I'd been drugged, and had even wondered if either Deputy Two or Ladycop had stuck me with something) but now the adrenaline was starting to rise again, the heart reaching gallop-speed, and the Deputy Sheriff who'd been watching me over the rim of his mug of coffee while mumbling into the phone was walking toward my cell now, coming right at me, and he reached down and grabbed his keys (attached to some stretch-leash) from his belt.

The jangle of the keys in the hall was somehow a *cold* sound and it elicited comments from other inmates in the row of cells to my left. I imagined the mirrors would be flashing and probing again, revealing the wide eyes of the wrongfully accused. The deputy stepped up to the bars of my cell, to the locking mechanism and inserted the key to my prison.

I did my best not to cringe, not to cower at the back of the cell, to stand my ground in the middle, to look the deputy in the eyes. I did, but then I looked down as he stepped in, not wishing to challenge him, to show humility, even remorse (though it was hard for me to muscle remorse when I felt like I was barely responsible for what I had done, that the culpable ones were the scientists at Utopia, and possibly, even above them, the very government this man worked for, so that it was a vicious feedback loop, a-)

"You've been released."

I almost asked him to repeat it. He'd uttered the sentence in a way Clint Eastwood might have as Dirty Harry – his lips had moved but his jaw hadn't. He didn't let the moment linger and grabbed me by the back of my neck and "urged" me forward and out of the cell. He didn't need to handcuff me again – none of my incarcerators had bothered to get me out of the first set of manacles anyway, and my fingers had since gone numb. I felt that anger flare up, the same bright red flame that had colored my eyes for a split second when my plastic straw went pinwheeling out onto the road just before I lost control of my muscles – my mind – and started attacking. It was wrong, I knew it was wrong; but the hostility I felt was no mere resentment of authority and certainly nothing rooted in an unpatriotic sensibility or disdain for the executive branch, or some heterodoxy up my sleeve, a new manifest or paradigm, it was something deeper, more primal, more limbic.

Where are we going? How did this happen? Whose power has released me? I wasn't going to ask the big cop these questions. I wanted to, but I wasn't going to. I had thought this could potentially happen, yes, but hoped for it I hadn't. For real. I hadn't because I'd been in this situation before where I was in some sort of custody, and in a really bad way, and found it worthless to hope for redemption. And my intuition had already warned me of the darker possibilities of what might be lying in wait for me once "freed."

The cop led me down the hall past his desk, along a corridor of cells where men, all men, gaped or paid no mind at all. At the end of the corridor we started up the mortar stairs with red stripes painted along the edge of each tread and riser conjunction, painted grey otherwise, everything in the place was grey, red striped, offwhite, dead. At the top of the stairs we came to a gate of bars and the cop keyed it and it pushed it open, still with his hands around the back of my neck. The first gate led to another gate and this time we were buzzed through by another deputy on the other side. We proceeded past the deputy who'd buzzed us through, his eyes glinting and locked on me the entire time, looking both feral and humiliated by a terrible sense of injustice – here I was, cop-beater, and I was going free, and they couldn't do a thing to stop it.

The second I had that thought I heard the scrape of chair legs as the cop at the desk shoved his chair back as he stood up. The deputy with the grip on my neck leading me along turned and looked at the angry cop at the desk. I didn't dare turn my head to try and see, but I was sure that the deputy leading me was telling his comrade *No. There's nothing we can do.* And the cop at the desk sat back down – I could here him pulling the chair back in, I could hear the leather cushion squeak under his weight, I could smell the tincture of sweat and starched uniforms.

More officers were in the hallway – two discussing a matter over a clipboard, a man and a woman, looked up and glowered at me. I wondered where the lady cop was from the roadside scene – where any of those three cops were, because I didn't see them here.

To our left now was the main desk and to the right door to the outside world – or door that lead to doors to the outside world. That room, actually, would likely lead into an anteroom where, from behind one-way glass, clerks and cops could interact with visitors to the jail. The cop entrance was somewhere else, most likely.

Along the countertop desk one cop watched me as I proceeded by, but only cursorily and emotionlessly, as if perhaps he had just come on shift – I thought I could even detect a hint of his aftershave. Behind him were other officers sitting at computers, typing away, talking on the phone. I could only see the tops of their heads because the bench-counter was on a raised platform.

Straight ahead was a door with no windows, and the cop leading me again took out his jangling set of keys and opened it.

This room appeared to be a sort of break room, with two green striped couches facing each other over a pale brown coffee table, a TV high in one corner, bolted to the ceiling, a couple of vending machines – a Pepsi and a snack machine, both humming and bright – and a kitchenette area with a refrigerator and sink. I wondered what was going on, why we hadn't stopped at the main desk in order for my process and release. Was I going to see a judge? No arraignment had been held yet, and no one had spoken of it. No one had spoken to me about anything else, for that matter – I figured it'd been eight hours since they'd brought me in – and I hadn't dared to ask. In fact, the only thing that had been said to me directly after "get in there, motherfucker," was "you've been released." I'd been given nothing to eat. I'd taken a piss twice (*parallel hormone therapy*, I'd heard Cameron Madison saying in my head as I'd peed, *a sort of anti-steroid that makes you feel the need to urinate frequently* and I'd wondered what I would've been like without it). I hadn't had any liquids or food since I'd fueled up the Shadow – which felt like days and days before – and I was hungry, tired, aching, and thirsty.

Near the kitchenette at the back of the room was another door. This one required no key. The deputy leading me, silent, opened it. It was a closet, filled with dry goods and cleaning materials – mops, bleach, boxes of urinal cakes (I could tell from the round, pink, smiling mascot on the box) sponges, brillo pads, and a couple of foodstuffs – ramen, saltines, a box of bottled water – and panic seized me. I suddenly felt I understood what was going on. The cop who'd stood up abruptly at the desk back in the hallway – maybe he knew, maybe he didn't know – maybe what had passed between him and the deputy with the grip on my neck was an even more sinister communication than what I'd assumed it was.

They were going to do something to me. Do something bad. Shady. Horrible. I was going to get one of the sponges, soaked with bleach, stuffed into my mouth and then be left in the closet to hallucinate and die a wretched death. Why had there been no one in the lounge, taking a coffee break? The television had even been turned off. Now that I thought about it, it was as though the room had been evacuated so that this gruesome act could be committed with no witnesses, nothing to compromise the beliefs of any of the upstanding civil servants of the county.

We stood in front of the closet for what felt like a long time. I couldn't see my captor's face; I had no idea what was going on there in his eyes, behind his eyes, only what I could fear. And then it happened – still with no water in my body, somehow I managed to pee myself. I felt the hot stream of it run winding down my leg – it chose the right leg, as I sort of "tended" that way, if you know what I mean – and pooled around my shoe there.

"Jesus Christ," said the deputy, and I could see in my peripheral vision that he was shaking his head in disgust. Then, to my surprise, he offered a short laugh. He reached into the closet, leaning in with his grip still on me, and grabbed a roll of paper towels. For the first time, he let go of my neck. He tore the plastic off of the roll and spooled out a couple of perforations worth. He ripped off the sheaves and then bent and said "lift up your foot." I did as he asked, shaking, my whole body shaking now, the questions romping through my brain, nothing making any sense, and he placed the wad under my foot and I stepped onto it, figuring that was the best thing to do. The deputy then replaced the paper towels on one shelf and pulled a bottle of water from the box on another shelf.

I heard the door to the room behind us open and close. I detected footsteps, more than one set, and it sounded like someone seated themselves on one of the couches, as there was a breathy sound, a sound someone might make when they sit down, they take a load off, and the expel some air in doing so.

The deputy then surprised me again as he took his wad of keys, pulled them from his belt on the retractable string, and undid my handcuffs.

"Stay there," he then commanded, and with such blatant disgust and dislike in his voice that it actually made me feel like something or someone truly wretched, even through the kind of relief I was experiencing as I realized I was not going to be stuffed into the closet (though a significant portion of my mind still insisted it was a sad inevitability for me). The deputy then walked away from me and I stood looking into the closet, looking at the smiling urinal-cake-cartoon with the white gloves on the end of his stick arms, and I started to shake even worse.

I heard the refrigerator open and then close behind me. The deputy walked further away and it sounded as though he placed something on the coffee table in between the two couches. I smelled that aftershave I'd smelled in the hallway. Then I heard a voice.

"Thank you, deputy." It was a familiar voice, but I could not immediately place it. I heard a sloshing sound, and a soft thump. It sounded like the bottle of water had been tossed on one of the striped couches. "There you go," said the deputy. There was a moment after I heard the door open again that I could have sworn that the cop just stared across the room at me. I could feel a heat in my back, between my shoulder blades where he must've concentrated his hate and frustration, where pain flared like scalding whips from my tousle with the cops, and above it, a cold band around my neck where his firm grip had just been. Then the door snicked shut. I continued to look into the closet.

"The peeing problem is not getting any better, is it?" The voice was still familiar, still a mystery. "Turn around, Jack." And I did.

*

The first thing I saw as my eyes swept the room was the man standing just inside of the door to the room. He wore a black suit and tie and stood with his hands clasped in front of him, staring straight ahead so that his gaze penetrated the wall to my left. For some reason my eyes then picked out his twin, standing beneath the television set in the corner, wearing the same suit, standing with the same posture. Then I looked in between these two, and into the eyes of Terry Hackford who sat on the couch. In front of him, on the coffee table, was a bottle of spring water.

Terry had on an argyle sweater and wore jeans. His hair was messy and short. He looked more like someone posing for a J. Crew advertisement than someone sitting in between two secret-service looking guys, here in an officer's lounge at a county jail, apparently springing me from what otherwise would have been my garish fate. He looked, now that I thought about it, a bit like Dr. Cameron Madison, my previous rescuer from jail.

My brain hurt. My body didn't seem to want to respond. I stood there immobile for a few seconds. Maybe half a minute. Terry, if anything, seemed to understand. I couldn't believe it was him. Instead of heading right over I found myself mustering what shred of dignity I had left to bend down, wincing at the objection from my lower back as I did. With my spine protesting the eight hours of standing on concrete or sitting/lying on a metal bench in my cell, and from the pummeling I'd taken out on Route 4, I took the wad of paper towel out from under my shoe. I nearly lost my balance and fell over, but regained footing and started to clean up my leg, around my ankle, reaching up under my pants and blotting the urine as far up to my knee as I could. I stood again, the rush of blood to my head making me dizzy so that I saw spots – like confetti twirling in the air around my head, tiny prison mirrors spinning – and blinked them away. There was a trash receptacle in the corner of the kitchenette, the kind you pressed the pedal on and the lid popped up and I threw out the used paper towels. As I stepped and tossed I was dosed with a heavy nostalgia for my gramma who'd had in her Brooklyn flat a very similar trash can (*am I dreaming?*) and suddenly felt I could cry.

"We'll get you some new pants," said Terry, and the indignity of having pissed myself gratefully mellowed the sense of emotion and longing for my departed gramma.

I walked slowly over to Terry, mindful of the man standing to his left and in front of the door leading out of the room, and stopped at the back of the couch. Terry smiled at me. It wasn't a bright, fake smile, it was actually, I felt, a genuine smile, the kind people manage when they are looking at each other in the midst of a crisis or situation they found themselves in, the kind that said, *here we are, and life is happening, and what fools we were to ever think we could have been in control.* Terry swept a hand over the water bottle. "Please," he said, "sit down, Jack."

Still speechless, still shaking, I rounded the couch, glancing once at the man in the corner under the television who was intently watching the refrigerator or perhaps one of the cupboards over my shoulder in the kitchenette. I looked at the other man, standing sentinel at the door. "Where are Watson and Crick?" I asked.

Terry looked at me with some of the good humor draining from his face. "They're taking a little time off, thanks to you."

"Oh," I said, "it's good to get away, isn't it? Where'd they go? Tahiti? Venezuela?"

"How are you feeling, Jack?"

I sat on the couch. I found, despite everything, I could meet Terry's eyes and remain there. After a few seconds his eyes dropped to the bottle of water and he nodded once. Seated, I leaned over and took it, undid the cap and drank. Terry seemed to study me as I did.

The first warm gulp sent bolts of pain through my stomach. I grimaced and pulled the bottle hastily away from my mouth. I looked at it and looked at Terry.

"It'll pass," he said, most likely meaning the cramp my expression had registered. Then, "but it would be worse if it was cold, yeah? Thank God for small favors."

I drank more, and the cramping began to subside. I finished the bottle. The whole thing took about half a minute. As the water spread into me, I realized I did not feel awkward. I did not feel afraid either. I was starting to feel some control again, and with it, ire. My own sense of injustice started to return – maybe it was because I felt somewhat comfortable with a familiar face. Maybe it was just the natural human condition, or my human condition, in that my mood median tended to be somewhere around a perpetual sense of iniquity anyway. Finished with the water I decided to keep the empty bottle in my lap. I placed it, in my two hands, over my wet crotch.

"What're you doing here, Terry?"

He smiled again in that way I had felt was genuine, but was now slowly starting to resent – there was almost pity in it, I thought. His posture was this: seated slightly forward on the edge of the couch cushions, knees shoulder-width apart, his elbows on his thighs, his fingers interlaced in a one-fist grip between the knees. Over his shoulder, the one barred window in the room shone a pale blue day – I could see only sky and the tops of some trees. I wondered why I hadn't noticed the window before. I wondered again if I was dreaming, or hallucinating. Was this all part of something the deputies were doing to me? Some sort of torture? Now Terry broke the gaze between us, lost the smile and lowered his head for a moment to study the shit brown, indoor-outdoor carpeting between his feet. Then he looked back up at me.

"You're wondering how I could pull this off," he said.

"It crossed my mind."

"I'm government-sanctioned."

"I got that too. Religious Right?"

"Not exactly. But, we're interested in your safety."

"Uh-huh," I said. I suddenly wished there was another bottle of water in front of me and even considered getting up and taking another one from the fridge. Best not, I decided, just yet. Baby steps.

"Yes," he said, "we are. Very much so. In fact…"

He dropped his eyes again, and then looked like he was nodding to himself. His eyes came back up. They were hazel eyes, the color of Julianne's. I hadn't noticed before. My senses must've been recalibrating to normal. Then again, I recalled the heightened sensations I'd been having when pulled over after the chase. I'd chalked that up to adrenaline; perhaps this was too.

"Who are your primary agitators, Terry?"

"A corporation," he said.

"I see. Do I know of this corporation? I have a feeling I do."

"Yes," said Terry. "They own you."

And Terry stood up. My eyes stayed on him. Neither of the men in suits – the "goons" – seemed to flinch. Terry walked around behind the couch, glanced out of the window for a moment, and I caught another whiff of aftershave. It hadn't been the desk cop's aftershave I'd smelled, no. Terry must've been right there, somewhere, perhaps waiting in that anteroom. He took the back of the couch in his two hands and massaged it. His eyes returned to mine.

"Do you remember the Exxon Valdez spill?"

"No, who's that?"

"Well, during that time scientists who worked for Exxon invented a bacteria which would eat the oil – really, gobble it right up – and that's how they got rid of the majority of the spill."

Now I wished the empty bottle of water between my legs was no longer a refilled bottle of water, but a bottle of gin. And yet, as I had this thought, something seemed to counteract it, to shove it aside so that I could no longer identify with it, so that it felt like someone else's thought I'd tried to steal.

"Well, the company that the scientists worked for actually patented the bacteria. They owned it. It was the first case of a living thing being patented."

I knew where he was going and I remembered hearing about this very thing. My throat started to close up.

"So, the biochemical technology that is in you right now, that is a part of you, is a patented technology. Therefore, part of *you*, and, but, then, in a real sense, all of you, is owned."

I tried to swallow. My sense of indignation vied with my fear for front-running. Sardonics aside, I said, "the corporation *I'm* familiar with."

"Yes," Terry said, "the Utopia Corporation."

Terry took his hands from the couch back, clapped them together and quickly returned to his first position and said, "My job is to help you, Jack…it has been all along. I'm your friend."

I closed my eyes and wished, more than anything, that I were somewhere else.

When the blackness left me I realized right away where I was: Wild Dick's ranch. I hadn't been here before, and didn't know where it was geographically, but I had heard Wild Dick refer to it before, to really emote about it before, with the big gestures and sweeping of arms and chest thrust out like a proud cock. I knew it was Wild Dick's ranch because of the jaguar. Not the car, the cat.

Wild Dick had spoken to the crew who'd built the Brandis brothers' ranch about the jaguar many times, and as unabashedly as only Wild Dick could. There was no hunting in Costa Rica, and the jaguar in Dick's story was dead. It was stuffed. And there it was, there it was as the thin man with the bushy black moustache prodded me out of the back of the pick-up truck, the jaguar was looking back at me from between the posts of Wild Dick's screened-in porch, its dead, replicated eyes glinting in the midday light.

It was now hot-hot. I jumped from the back of the pick-up, managing to keep my balance after a rollicking, jarring ride that I had judged to have lasted about an hour. I was still bound, my hands tied in front of me with what pricked at my skin like hemp-rope, and maintained my *homo erectus* status despite the handicap. Sweat flung from my hair as I landed, dripped from my nose and from the divot above my upper lip, spilling its saltiness into the seam of my mouth, and dust plumed at my feet in the dirt driveway – an area of dry, blonde dust that could've been a parking lot. Wild Dick's fountain sat in the middle of it all, grey stone, gurgling water like a cylindrical rather than conical volcano.

I could hear other water running – a more powerful flue. I turned and looked behind me where the jungle swallowed the swirling dirt lot, and deduced that the sound was coming from there. A river nearby.

"*Catarata*," said the thin man

"*Bonita*," I said. I had what they called a gisted, or rudimentary understanding of the language. The moment between the thin man and I quickly passed.

I looked through the filthy rear windshield of the pick-ups cab where I could make out two dark blurs of heads. Was Wild Dick talking to Julianne? Threatening her? Coming on to her? Did he have his unit out in front of him now, like a dog's tongue lolling, like a cattail bobbing? What was going on? What we're they doing? I was delirious.

I glanced at the porch again, and took in the estate. There was the jaguar, the stuffed thing standing on all fours, looking at me from the porch, propped next to the rocking chair where Wild Dick likely did his nightly thinking and smoking and drinking – probably more of the latter two. There he would sit with his dead feral cat beside him, the dead beast of the mangrove swamps.

The ranch house, like ranch houses typically are, was long and flat. It was single-storied except for the end to my right, where perhaps the master bedroom was, or any office, some special room of some kind, as the second storey. As I looked down towards that end of the house, and beyond it, to an outpost building that looked like a garage or shop, I caught movement. In between the two buildings and along the edge of the jungle that footed the rear of the building I thought I saw a man move, trying to keep out of sight. It had been a furtive move, dark and quick, but I'd caught it. When the door to the pick-up banged open, I jumped.

I turned and saw Wild Dick getting out, moving very quickly, spinning around in a half circle and tossing something up into the back of the pick-up, something that could've been a parcel, a package a – fuck. Right. It didn't take me very long, and I was briefly proud, given, again, my various handicaps and conditions, that I was still able to think clearly enough, to put two-and-two together. He had the package the Brandis brothers had sent me. The one on the kitchen table. He must've taken it after he'd knocked me out.

Wild Dick had a cigarillo clamped between his gapped-teeth and he was talking around it as the package thumped into the back, and he was barrel-chested with wiry white and black hairs sprouting from his dirty t-shirt.

"This is it," he was saying, "this is it, this is it." He didn't open the package though. (And for some reason, though I couldn't have said why at the time, I was greatly relieved that he didn't, as though the package contained something which, if released at the wrong time, could be disastrous, could be evil when it was meant to be good. Certain things, I thought, and maybe Wild Dick did too, were as fragile in this world as they were powerful, and, taken too soon or too late, revealed prematurely or belatedly, could generate the very opposite of their intended purpose. The road to hell was paved with good intentions.) He left the package there and scuffed around the front of the pick-up, still grumbling and smoke trailing him as he went, rolling over his shoulders and slipstreaming behind him like a tail, and went to let Julianne out into the hot, dwindling day.

She was remarkable as she stood, blindfolded and bound (hands behind her, not in front like mine were) in the dirt lot in front of the Wild Dick ranch. I wasn't surprised by my admiration; I knew that my blood was pumping, my adrenaline, endorphins, the alcohol still active in my system, the surrealism like a wash of milk over my entire body. I wasn't surprised that, though this could be a life-or-death situation, I was looking at Julianne's jawline, her slim nose, her perfect lips, and thinking that the smudges of dirt on her cheek and chin, the tousled, sweaty quality of her hair, and the fact that her eyes were concealed from me somehow made her appear even more beautiful. It was an exotic set of circumstances. But, I knew, I had to get my head into the game or I could get us both killed.

Wild Dick waddled over to me then, the cigarillo rolling from one side of his mouth to the other, and he wasn't really looking at me, he wasn't really making what one would call "eye contact," but sort of looking in my direction, looking at all and none of me, his thoughts somewhere his gaze couldn't follow. Then he seemed to come back from that other place and stopped in front of me and said, "Do you like her? She is beautiful, isn't she?" And he pulled a knife from somewhere beneath the girth of his dirt-

smeared, belly-filled white t-shirt, and held it just in front of my nose. I
thought I recognized the knife – it was one like I had seen fishermen use
along the beaches and once on a trip down the Saba River with Martine, the
white sap from the *cedro* trees spilling into the Saba's brown water. These
fishermen would be using sticks for poles and household string for lines,
sometimes only pieces of bread for bait, but often I saw them with these
fish-gutting knives. I decided to make a mental note of it, simultaneously
growing cold and nauseous in my belly as I wondered what the serrated edge
would do to a person, how it could *rip* a person, and how Wild Dick was
someone quite, I thought, capable of performing the operation with real zest.

    "*Escucheme*," he said, "listen, *pinche guero*, you going to go inside.
Both of you going to go inside. I take you the honeymoon suite – *luna da
miel*," he said, and he looked at the thin man and laughed around his manure
brown cigarillo, exposing those gapped, yet somehow talcum white teeth.
The thin man laughed uproariously and with a high, edgy pitch, and Wild
Dick seemed to shoot him a look that said, *quit kissing my ass, cabron*, and
then looked back at me. His eyes were something of an illusion – I had
heard that it was common for some Latino peoples to have this kind of
trouble with their eyes, it came from a nutrition deficiency in childhood –
Wild Dick had eyes, neither hazel nor brown, nor black, but some sort of
mottled, dirty earth color which had chunks missing from the irises,
crescents removed, so that they appeared like apples with bites taken out.
And the whites were yellowed; they were eyes that were not eyes, no soul
showing through because the windows were opaque and broken. "*Ahora*,"
said Wild Dick, "*lo consigue moviendo*."

    The thin man took steps toward me and Wild Dick turned back around
to retrieve Julianne. I watched her as Wild Dick approached her, she was

standing an unmoving and clearly listening, lucid, thinking. She didn't seem panicked, I thought, but perhaps even a little perturbed. I was more smitten with her by the moment. Wild Dick reached her and said something quietly to her I could not hear and then we all began marching toward the ranch, to be stored in our "honeymoon suite," as Wild Dick had referred to it. As we walked I saw something move again, this time from the south end of the ranch – to my left – as though whomever I had seen cross from the garage to the north end of the building had gone behind the house and walked the length of it to reappear on the other end. Who was back there? The movement I saw was again a dark blur, just a snatch of something in between the building and then the jungle, where it disappeared.

I looked straight ahead and into the porch where the stuffed jaguar stood patiently awaiting us, its plastic eyes fixed on nothing. Something dawned on me then, and before I could ask the question, I saw that Dick was watching the rustle of the giant leaves of the *cedro* trees at the south end of his home and he said, "and if you decide you like to try and leave honeymoon suite ahead of time," he said, "*Tenga cuidero. Tenga cuidero de las panteras.*"

"*Panteras?*" I asked. I was unfamiliar with that particular Spanish word, but I thought I had an idea.

We reached the screen door to the porch, and the thin man opened it with a squeak.

"Panthers," Julianne said, and I looked at the stuffed jaguar, and Wild Dick walked past me with a key in his hand, to open the front door, and lead us inside, and he was laughing again.

*

I watched the barbed wire-topped perimeter fence recede into the distance through the two small, nearly opaque windows of the van. It was like watching an old silent film, where things are kind of tough to make out, and everything looking like a cross between *chiaroscuro* and a Rorschach test.

I was still in my piss-soaked clothing. More clothes I had borrowed from Daniel before leaving Burlington, before stealing the Honda Shadow from the Stop-n-Go. I wondered – why hadn't the police questioned me about the motorcycle? Hadn't it been reported stolen? Of course it had. Perhaps, I thought, that aspect of things had been "taken care of" by Terry. I was sprung, wasn't I? The motorcycle was incidental. It made the most sense.

I hadn't been "processed" by any means upon my release. I'd been bound once again. This time it was not handcuffs. The boys had used the new fangled thing on me, the plastic tie that cinched together and felt totally unbreakable and had brought me out of a side door, exit-only.

They left me in my piss-soaked clothes, I thought, far more angry than humiliated. *And they tied me up again. Captive, again. From one thing to the next. Caught in the trap. Caught in-*

And then, just like that, the interior dialogue shut off. I thought of a computer – the old Dell in Banjul's office in Flatbush, in the loading bay, the day it crashed and the day Banjul nearly had a stroke. The day I got fired, though I swore up and down I had nothing to do with it – I'd flipped the computer on and after a few obligatory warm-up seconds, one sentence had popped up on screen:

Operating system not found.

I'd pressed enter.

Operating system not found.
Operating system not found.

As many times as I'd hit enter, or any key, the phrase repeated, an idiotic litany. The Dell had been fried.

Goon One sat across from me in the van, looking at a spot just over my left shoulder. I fought the urge to spit in his face. Goon Two was driving, and Terry Hackford was in the passenger seat. He turned to me and said, "I need your help, Jack."

I looked at him. Terry looked good. He looked well. Well-fed, well-paid, well taken care of. I wondered who he really was. He'd been the guy in the bar I'd envied, the guy who'd effortlessly glided through high school and college on his good-looks and athletic prowess. The guy who didn't only pledge the best fraternity, but eventually became its figurehead. The guy who, even though he may have degenerated a little bit after the school days were over, and didn't actually end up with the *greatest* job in the world, or the *greatest* house and wife, still did pretty fucking good – and, what was worse, seemed totally satisfied with the mediocrity of it all.

But that wasn't the real Terry Hackford. That was a fantasy I'd put together, a stereotype I'd drawn heavily from in order to feed my own sense of inferiority and patheticness when I'd met him at the Irish pub that night so long ago. Here I'd thought I'd been the one doing the sleuthing, acting undercover, and Terry had out-snooped me. Christ.

Now he claimed he wanted to be my friend. Now he told me he was working for people that claimed to own part of me – or all of me, I guessed, how could I be divvied up? (Insert my grisly half-second thought of a chainsaw removing one of my arms as white labcoats held me down on a brushed steel table in a room too far away for any ears to hear my screams.) Now here he was, this enigma, this asshole, telling me that I needed to *help* him? I swallowed and thought

(*Operating system not found*)

that I would go ahead and play ball with him.

"Oh?" My throat was dry and the word came out in a croak. I cleared my airways with a couple of short grunts and said, "how could I help you?"

Terry smiled at me. It was still that genuine smile – but it might have been the "genuine" smile he practiced in the mirror every morning as he tightened up his tie. It was the I-have-your-best-interests-in-mind smile. The kind car salesmen affixed when they told you about the limited warranty on your new Ford Taurus, sign here please.

I felt something crawling up the back of my neck, something that felt like gooseflesh – I could even feel the hairs at the base of my skull springing to attention, as though electrified.

*Electricity...*I thought.

Biochemical engineering...electricity...bioelectricity...

(Operating system not found)

"I'm glad you asked," said Terry. "I really do want to be friends with you, Jack. I know what you must be thinking – you can't trust me. It's hard to trust people like us, isn't it? Nobody believes anyone actually wants to do any good in the world. They have to have an agenda. They have to be making money."

"Are you turning over your paychecks to Oxfam? To the Vatican?" I asked him. I looked at Goon One, across from me, after I said it, wondering if he'd look back at me. He didn't, but continued burning a hole in that spot just over my shoulder and beside my cheek.

"Could be, could be," said Terry, nodding and looking thoughtful. "We all have masks we wear, it's true. But some of us, some of us Jack, don't even know we're wearing them. Like you. You didn't know what was happening to you, did you? You've worn so many masks, Jack, how could you have possibly recognized one more?"

I was starting to like Terry's tone as little as I liked his smile here in the gloom of the van with the smeared windows. "What exactly do you need my help with, Terry?"

"Well," he said, with a final nod, a commencement nod, "I need you to go back to Utopia."

I laughed. It was a laugh that just fell out of me, that just tumbled from my mouth like a gymnast. I dropped my chin to my chest, chuckled once more, and then lifted my head back up and looked at Terry. "Where..." I started, and then hitched with one last laugh, "where is the sense of community with you people? You're all fucking working around each other, behind each other, above and below. Who's in charge here? Cameron? Maya? You? God?"

"Cameron's a soldier," Terry said immediately, his face darkening. I liked that. I liked to see that and jotted it down on my mental notepad. *Rivalry*, I thought-wrote. "Nothing more. He likes to think he is a visionary, but he's just a soldier." I thought of the two men in fatigues that day in the barracks – one had been called Ramirez, the other Hackford. "He has no idea what's really going on," Terry was saying, "he thinks he's saving the world. Perfecting the human race – going to end disease and suffering. That's not how it works," Terry said, "penitence is how it works."

"Uh-huh," I said. I felt like pushing Hackford back toward the ropes, and I sat up a little straighter. I felt like hurting him. I didn't know exactly why, I just did. "Speaking of soldiers," I said, and I had Terry's sudden attention, "last I knew a soldier with your last name was lying on the ground, his head busted open." Goon One gave me a sharp look, but I didn't care. I wasn't interested in him anymore. I might be in moments to follow, but not just then. Like I said, I was interested in hurting Terry. I smiled and said, "just like the good old days."

"My brother made his own choices" said Terry. "He thought that to serve God was to be a soldier."

"So does half of the Middle East," I said.

Terry turned and faced front, saying no more to me. If I'd wounded him, he carried it well.

"So what *is* the idea, then, Terr? Get rich? You know what they say about rich men getting into heaven and all of that."

"Your psychology skills are on a third-grade level, Jack, and you're ruining our budding friendship."

Okay, the blunted-edge was working somewhat. I was sitting in my own drying, sticking urine; I was allowed a little leeway in my intellectual jousting. Third graders did, after all, have occasion to wet themselves.

"And Maya," I asked, "is she just as naïve? Is she god-fearing, like you?"

"I'm as straight as a fucking arrow, Jack, and you know that. You couldn't trust Cameron, and you knew that too. Maya, well, Maya you probably couldn't pin. Likely you became infatuated with her, many do. She's an illusion."

"That's clever," I said, but Terry had struck home. The driver, Goon Two, made what felt like an unnecessarily hard right. I wondered if he was getting agitated. Though yes-men like him, A-men, sentinels, they weren't supposed to get emotionally involved. Perhaps it had just been a coincidence. Or perhaps I was offending his religious sensibilities as well. I glanced out the small rear windows and saw nothing but trees. Evergreens. I thought I caught an acrid whiff of brakes. "But I can trust *you*?" I said.

"We have to build that," said Terry, seeming to calm, seeming to slip back into his sense of the upper hand.

"Well," I said, and now I did look at Goon One again, and saw that he was looking at me watching me – and then his eyes flicked away, back to their home-spot in the air next to my face, and I felt suddenly powerful and clear inside, like a glacier might feel, knowing that it is unstoppable, that it itself is fate, that it is destiny. "Aren't we putting the cart before the horse? Shouldn't we do a few more trust-building exercises – you know, I could fall back into your arms, maybe, or," I looked at Terry now, I looked into those veiled hazel eyes of his, "or maybe you could have *let me change my piss-soaked clothes, maybe you coulda not tied my hands behind my fucking back*," I said, nearly growling, feeling my muscles tighten, knowing – knowing and feeling the sheer triumph of knowing – that I was beginning to see, that I was beginning to understand not what they did to me, but what it was making of me.

"Jack," he said, and I felt in his voice and glimpsed in those eyes the seed of fear, "Be happy I gave you the water."

I said nothing. I waited. I knew Terry had one more thing to say, and I let him. "So," he said, "I need to know, Jack, I need to let others know – just a few others – will you go back to Utopia for us – for you?"

"I," I began, and then did what seemed to come naturally, unscripted, like an image from a dream; I pictured a giant faucet in my mind – crude, yes, even remedial for a guy in urine-caked pants, maybe – and I turned that faucet on.

"I want to know where my belongings are," I said.

Terry looked at the goon sitting next to me and nodded. The goon then reached into his pocket and pulled out a zip-lock bag. In it was my chewed-up red straw. Nothing else.

"You travel light for a girl," said the goon.

In my mind's eye the liquid from that giant tap came rushing out, cascading, falling through space to awash, to make clean and pure what it needed to cleanse, transcend; to breed new life.

In the van, my muscles clenched and contracted and I broke the tie binding my arms, leapt across the space at Goon One and knocked him clean unconscious with one thwack from my own head. I glanced at Terry, just long enough to finish my sentence, to tell him what he already knew, but maybe, just maybe to throw him off a little bit with my third-grade psychology. "I," I had begun, "am going to go see my daughter," and I turned away from him and burst out the back doors of the moving van.

At least, that's what I had hoped for. The doors wouldn't budge, much as the adrenaline working through me should have allowed. A bit dazed, I spun back around, hunched over in the van, and saw Goon Two looking at me in the rearview mirror and now brandishing a gun.

"No!" yelled Terry.

Okay, I thought, *a little trust-building there.*

I ran forward to the seats as Goon Two, ignoring Terry, tried to aim at me while driving. I reached him and grappled with his arm and the gun went off. He'd managed to get it halfway around to point at me, and so had shot Terry inside. Shot Terry in the side of the face.

The van now lurched and sidewinded along the road. It was a country road – it looked like we were still in Vermont. I hit Goon Two in the face with my free hand. It was a blow that, while it couldn't bust through the locked back doors of the van, knocked the driver right out.

Terry screamed in my ear. The scream sounded like something was flapping in it. Like his cheek maybe. I yanked the unconscious goon from the driver's side, pulling him through the gap between the two bucket seats. In the movies you see it all the time – the guy takes out the driver of a moving vehicle and deftly slips into the seat himself to take over the driving – the vehicle may have only swerved a little in the process and even managed to maintain consistent speed. This wasn't a movie. This was my fucked-up life, more a dream than anything else after all.

In this dream, the van went off of the road and flipped. Not being tethered in, I was tossed about like a coin in a spin-dryer. I knocked into both walls, the ceiling and the floor several times, it seemed, and I bumped into both goons more than once, and when the van finally came to a rest, the dream stopped, and there was nothing but the sound of wind, and the picture of black, and the sound of howler monkeys in the *cedro* trees, and something moving through the night, sleek and powerful and silent with glowing eyes.

*

There was one window in the room and I could see the thing passing by it. I could hear its guttural purr, and even smell its musk. It was a panther. Not a jaguar, but *pantera*, as Wild Dick had promised. It appeared to be on guard duty.

Dust motes swirled in the fading, diffused light by the back window, the window overlooking the neighboring jungle. The humidity was a presence in the room, and seemed to have crushed Julianne down to where she sat in the corner, the whites of her eyes luminescent.

It was a room with no furniture. The gritty floorboards creaked in most places. I had yet to sit down, but was slowly pacing, feeling the fear tiptoe in as the fog of alcohol rolled back. Soon the fear would be as cloying a presence in the room as the heat and humidity. Perhaps Julianne knew this. Perhaps she knew that I was of no use, that I could not help her, that soon I was going to be more afraid than she was, a useless paranoid wreck on the floor myself, waiting for someone to come and rescue me.

No, I thought. It felt like the word had been whispered by an actual voice in the room, and I actually turned around to see if someone was behind me.

I looked and saw that there were two doors – the one we had been ushered into the room through, and one directly opposite from it. Both doors were on the front, windowless side of the room. There was a hallway there; I'd seen it as Wild Dick's thin henchman had pushed us through the room outside of this one, a slender corridor bearing windows. The place was almost structured like a hotel; contiguous rooms off from a narrow hallway with doors linking them, likely locked.

I paced to that door then and tried it and found it was indeed locked. The knob resisted a turn. The door itself was made of a dark hardwood. The walls of the room were a kind of clay. I remembered something from the days the Brandis brothers were laying plans to build their own ranch. They'd been discussing the building materials available in Costa Rica. There was no use of drywall here, for instance. There were no softwoods. The climate in the Latin American country was too humid, too moist for any such materials. What was employed instead were some of the indigenous hardwoods, stucco, clay. The room Julianne and I were in might as well have been a cave of stone. And in our cave, the only likely exit, the bustable glass window, was being patrolled by a giant, wild cat, slinking past occasionally. We were trapped.

The fear threatened to poison my thoughts again. It was just a crack in the dam, this fear, one spout foretelling the greater flood.

"What do they want with us?" Julianne asked the question through what sounded like the end of silent tears – she was congested, her voice wet.

"I don't know," I said. It was the stock answer. But, I really didn't. I had an idea. I had an idea that it was still a part of Wild Dick's crazy revenge. I had an idea it had something to do with vengeance, but also with extortion. Wild Dick was perhaps looking to ransom me to the Brandis brothers. Wild Dick had the package.

I found myself looking at the other door again, the one likely leading to another room like ours. I walked toward it without another thought or word and found myself knocking.

"What're you doing?" Julianne sat up straight in the corner. Her tone had changed from one of resignation to alarm.

"Hello?" I knocked again. I could feel Julianne's fright wafting over to me and, strangely, my own fear temporarily displaced. "Hello?" I knocked once more and then took a step away from the door. I kicked it, and Julianne gasped. She may have caught a scream in her throat, I thought, and was glad she had.

With the kick, I was done. I turned to her and my mouth opened to console her when I heard, "Who are you?" The voice came from the other side of the door, so muffled by the hardwood and clay barrier between myself and it that had I already been speaking to soothe Julianne I likely would not have heard it.

I quickly turned and pressed myself back against the door. With a strained whisper I asked. "Mr. Blair? Is that you?"

I jumped back when I heard the scratching sound, but it hadn't come from the door. Immediately I turned and faced the window at the back of the room and saw it. Julianne turned and saw it too, and this time she did scream, and she backpedaled away from that end of our chamber on her feet and palm heels.

Yellow eyes watched us there, the claws that had scratched the glass sliding down now and out of sight, leaving a streaky residue. The beast's breath created condensation on its end of the window. I thought it might bust through then and devour us, regardless of its post – it was a wild thing, after all, whether or not it had some semblance of training – when the door on the other side, the one we'd come in through, swung open.

The thin man with the bushy moustache entered with his *pistola* out in front of him. He took only two steps, and stopped. Julianne and I both had looked in his direction when the door'd flown open, but were instantly drawn back to the window. The thin man must've followed our gaze, for he took one step in that direction, scowled deeply and said "*mueva!*"

The beast dropped out of sight.

"*Sea callado,*" said the thin man, "*Callese y no mueva.* If you make sound, *yo le dolore*; I'm going to hurt you." He looked at me, and pointed the gun at Julianne. "*Yo la dolere ella,*" he said, and I realized that his free hand was massaging himself in the groin. He then retreated from the room, the sweaty, skeletal man of our nightmare.

After the door snicked shut and he was gone, I went to Julianne. I was trembling as I held her, but I couldn't stop it. I said, "I'm sorry this has been such a bad date," and she hitched once with either a laugh or a sob, or a combination of both. And then she was silent.

As we stood there, from behind me, the voice came again, heavily muffled. "Yes," the voice said, "it's me."

I waited, and was still. Julianne may not have heard – her head was buried in my chest. Even if she had, she wouldn't have known, I thought.

"Get me out of here," said Calvin Blair (if it *was* him) from the room next to ours. "I swear to God I'll make it worth your while. I'll make you rich," he said.

My thoughts raced. Not of riches, but of something else. I thought about the conversation I'd had with Lincoln that morning – *Monday morning, eight a.m.*, he'd told me. That was the time I was supposed to meet with Baradez at Blair's estate. But Blair was here – where was Baradez? Attempting a rescue? Dead? It was now Saturday night. Still holding Julianne I turned and looked at the door to the next room. My eyes seemed to penetrate into it, and my mind continued to churn.

Julianne pulled away from me then. "I need to lie down," she said. As she moved from our embrace I could smell the perfume she'd put on that morning now commingling with a light, somehow aluminum aroma of sweat and fright, like rain dripping from steel eaves. She got slowly to a seated position, and then lay down on the wooden slats. The light from the window washed over her, and I could see the tracks the tears had made through the dirt on her face, and thought of the panther's claws. She rolled onto her side, drawing her legs up, slightly fetal, and brought a loosely curled fist up under her chin. The fingers where white, smooth, delicate. I realized again that I was in love with her.

I turned to the door to Blair's room and leaned into it. I said, "Okay" in less of a strained whisper than before. There was no response. I stepped to the side of the door, turned, put my back against the wall and slid down onto my butt. I'd seen the move in dozens of movies at the Grand Army Plaza theater, and had always felt skeptical about it. *People don't do that,* I'd always thought, and realized I just had.

I saw my father then – a flash in the dying light of the room, his black curly hair and pained dark eyes with that swipe of purple fatigue beneath. He looked away in that vision-instant and it took me a moment longer to realize where he'd looked. Out the window.

Okay, I thought, *just for a couple of hours of rest.* And then what? I was going to smash through the window where a wild panther awaited to tear my throat out, somehow evade the beast, get round to Wild Dick's truck, if it was still parked in front, and retrieve the package from the truck bed, even if it was still there? Then what – luck-out with the keys still in the ignition and rattle off to Moravia? Or San Jose? I had no idea where I was. And what about Julianne?

"Jack," she said, startling me.

"Yeah?"

"Would you come here?"

I crawled over to her on my hands and knees, realizing that I ached, realizing how badly I wanted a drink. I didn't know how much longer I could keep the dam from cracking open.

"Lay here with me please," she said.

I did. I took the same shape as she, and put an arm tentatively around her. She didn't grab onto it. "I'm sorry you met me," I said. As the light continued to fade in the room I waited and hoped she would say that she wasn't, but she was silent. After the darkness was complete, I felt that she was sleeping, and lay awake, tired as I'd suddenly become, my words hanging in the air, suddenly more stark and important to me than anything else.

I had no idea what time it was when I awoke. Julianne was not beside me any longer. That was the first thing I noticed. The second was that my head hurt. My stomach was queasy, as though it had been swabbed out with a woolen cloth, leaving a residue behind. And I felt an ache in my bladder and realized I had to pee. I forgot about it when Julianne spoke.

"It's almost morning," she said. I turned – and a shard pierced my temple and outside corner of my eye as I did – and saw her standing by the window. There was, indeed, faint light glowing outside of our room. It looked almost the same as it did just before I'd laid down next to Julianne, telling myself I was only going to rest briefly, and I wondered – insensibly, I later realized – if maybe Julianne was confused and we had only dozed for a few minutes.

The light did look different. I slowly got to my feet, trying not to remember having to pee, to feel or acknowledge it, and again something stole the attention away from it.

There were voices outside of the window. I walked toward Julianne, whose body language suggested she already knew this; she'd already been listening.

"…don't want to have kids," someone was saying. "they want to fuck and have big stud fuck them. So, you can either talk about it, or you can be big stud who fucks them."

I turned and raised my eyebrows at Julianne.

The same speaker outside of our room continued to talk, and I pressed myself as close to the window as I could, smooshing my nose into the glass and looking left and right. I could see no one. "If a girl says she's not with anybody, or that she's single, means there's a guy who she's fucking here and there, and another guy she goes out on nice dates with here and there." There was a pause. I thought I caught what could have been a shoulder, and arm, just inside the angle of my vision. "She's only single because hasn't found rich guy who can fuck her right!" The speaker then laughed a gravelly laugh. Was there a back porch, I wondered? Was this some guard shooting the shit at the start of the a.m. shift? Why was he speaking English?

Beside and behind me, Julianne made a noise and shook her head slowly from side to side.

"What?" I asked. I was straining, hoping to hear something, anything, that could help get us out of there.

"Men being pigs," said Julianne. "What else is new."

"We don't know there's more than one guy. He could be talking on the phone."

Before Julianne could respond, I heard a distinctly separate voice. "I've been up for two hours and already I want to kill myself – is that normal?" And again the not-so-jolly chuckle from the original speaker I'd heard. Was this just Wild Dick out there with his thin man assistant? It didn't sound like them, not exactly, but, then, there was a wall occluding the sound. Before I realized what I was doing, I tapped the glass with my fingernail. I heard Julianne breathe in quickly. The laughter outside stopped at once. Maybe, I thought, I was still a little drunk after all.

Within seconds I saw the rustling of the layered *cedro* leaves and heard the shuffle-grit of steps coming toward the window and then a hulking, greasy-dark form appeared. The window was dirty and smeared and distorted the man on the other side of it. "What?" He spat at me. He was fat, far bigger than Wild Dick, with a five o'clock shadow that seemed to cover his fat chin and neck like a bib at a barber shop. His eyes shone in on me in the marshaling light, one eye blurred by window smear, the other clear and glinting with malice. "What the fuck do you want, *pinche gringo?*"

"I have to go to the bathroom," I said.

The unmistakable disgust and hatred in his features morphed into the mechanics producing that gurgling laughter, and he grinned through the smudged window at me. "So go," he said, "*pinche maricon.*"

"Okay, sir," I said, "thank you. Sorry to bother you."

The way he was smiling, as though hooks had speared into the heavy, loose flesh of his face and pulled up, making him grin like a puppet, now folded back down into that face, the face of a man who had nothing to lose. "You tap on the glass again, I'm going to come in there and rape you." And he disappeared.

I continued to slowly back away, as if he may appear any moment. I was thinking as I retreated that my hangover could have been responsible for making this man more hideous than he was. That I might not have understood his accented words accurately. Then Julianne said, not with humor, but with a tremulous matter-of-factness, "I prefer the panther."

I turned to her, thought of something conciliatory to say, and could come up with nothing. I found myself sitting back down on the floor. I needed to think.

Panther at night, rapist guards by day. It seemed ridiculous, actually, that anyone, even someone as much a lunatic as Wild Dick would put a panther in a sole-sentinel position, so likely there were other guards at night as well, and the panther hung around because Wild Dick tossed it generous hunks of raw meat. And maybe, just maybe, Wild Dick had once lured the great cat out of the jungle and into the cleared front of the house, cajoling it to the porch where the stuffed jaguar sat, dead-eyed and motionless, and the panther sniffed around, and looked at Wild Dick, and had understood.

"Hey," said the voice on the other side of the door – a voice, now in the growing light of day and utter realism that made my skin crawl. The idea that a powerful, multi-millionaire like Calvin Blair was sitting in a dim, humid room, likely dirty, and beaten like we were, was an unpleasant thought. The night before it had been almost a comfort, and now it was the

opposite. It meant that Wild Dick and his men were in some deep, deep shit.
It meant that Blair was. It meant that we were too. "You still over there?"

"Yeah," I strong-whispered back, "we're still here."

"Those guys used to work for me," said Blair.

"Way to pick them," I said, pacing near the door.

"You thought of a way out of here yet?"

"I'm working on it," I said. Though I had never met Blair in person, I
was growing to like him less and less. "I'm working on it."

But yeah, I thought, *we're still here.*

Still here, I thought, *still alive. I'm coming for you, baby girl.*

There was something on top of me. A weight pinning me down.
Something sticky on my face, between my eyelids. I could hear dripping.
Things were dark.

I realized I must've been out cold for a few – minutes? Hours?
Unlikely hours. Someone would have been here by now. Lots of someones.
I wouldn't be here if it had been a few hours. No. Minutes, only. Even
seconds, maybe. Dreams could happen in seconds, dreams that seemed to
go on for days transpired in a few shifts of your eyeballs beneath the lids.

Sticky. Something was trying to glue my eyes together. *Blood.* My
blood? I couldn't tell. I couldn't take inventory of myself, not like this.

I shoved. The weight – soft and heavy and wet – started to give but
then fell back and I caught a glimpse of daylight. That did it for me. There

was a body between myself and freedom. My hands were free. Somehow I'd twisted and strained and snapped those bonds, but I barely remembered it.

I shoved again. The weight came off of me and I heaved it to the side. Still it tumbled back, pinning me even harder, squashing my chest.

My bearings slowly came around as I struggled to regain my breath. I realized my back was against the passenger side door – the van had come to a rest on its right side, on its passenger side. I couldn't get the weight – the *body* – off of me because the bucket seat's back was to my left now. I had to get the weight up and *over* that seatback.

I took in a nauseating, painful breath, as much air as I could squeeze in, and gave it everything I could, pushing up, left, and over, and the weight finally gave way. As some of the outside light reached me now, I could see the hand of the body that'd been on top of me, draped over the on-it's-side back of the passenger seat, and I swatted it away. I didn't want to know who it was. But I had to. Were they all dead?

I started to get up and winced and fell back and nearly cried out when a lancing pain tore through my chest as I'd attempted to curl up into a sitting position. *Broken ribs.* I'd never had broken ribs before, but I knew that's what it was. A couple of them even. I hated the thought of broken bones more than the pain. The idea that something was *wrong* on my insides, that there were splinters of things floating around in me, it was an obsessive-compulsive's nightmare – a mess you couldn't clean.

I needed to get up. I needed to see who was dead, who wasn't, who maybe was already gone. Most importantly, I needed to get the hell out of the van and get going. Where had we been when the wreck had happened?

I thought back, and felt we had been socked in by country on all sides. That was good. Still.

I sat up again, grunting as the pain ripped through my chest like barbed wire encircling my torso, being cinched tight. I gritted my teeth, squinted my eyes closed, grunted once more, and sat up. I lifted up my head and looked directly upward at the window of the driver's side there, partially obscured by another obstacle. Goon Two, the van's driver, hanging in his seatbelt. *Seatbelts save lives,* I thought, *click-it, or ticket.* This guy clicked it, I thought, and bought his ticket.

It made me wonder if anything else was broken in me; I'd been tossed about like a lotto ball. There could be internal bleeding. I might not have felt anything too terrible so far because of the adrenaline still coursing through me (*which you can control now don't forget what happened*) but before I started climbing around like a monkey I decided to do a quick systems check.

I rolled my shoulders, and my ribs flared with pain again. I moved the rest of my arms, bending my wrists, rotating my forearms, hinging my elbows. All okay. Sore, bruised, possibly cuts, lacerations, but not broken. I reached up then at the thought of blood and wiped the stickiness from my eyes.

Come on. Go. Was I in shock? I was in shock. That's why I was taking so fucking long. I-

"Hello?" It was a voice from outside of the van, sounding a little ways off, but not far. A man's voice. I thought I could hear an engine rumbling as well.

Mueva, you son of a bitch. No more time. If my legs had any cracked parts, or my insides something squished, than I'd find out soon the hard way.

I started clambering to a squatting position, my right hand searching for purchase along the dashboard, my fingers finding a hold that might have been a coin bin or an ashtray slot, my left using the back of the bucket seat. I managed to swivel my legs underneath me in a kind of cramped gymnast's move. Now the suspended body of Goon Two was inches from my nose as I looked up. I was seeing the back of his neck and his right shoulder. It was a small grace not have to see any glassy, dead eyes.

"Hello? Is anybody in there? Is everybody alright?" Closer now. An older man's voice, a little papery around the edges.

Should I call out? I couldn't decide. I needed to get old goonsy-numero-two out of his sling, though. That was my only way out, past him, or –

I turned and peered through the darkness of the van's main hull and to the small window which had already been opaque. It was broken now, dimple-cracked, distorted and impossible to see out of. There was no wedge of light to indicate that the rear doors had been wrenched ajar during our tumble. They could be pressured shut by the crumpled steel of the van's framework. I could spend time navigating and getting back there and wind up trapped.

I started to work on Goon Two's seatbelt and immediately he started to shift; the dead weight shifted and started sinking down towards me. A second later his head slipped back and over the edge of the seat and the belt caught him under his neck so that his face now suddenly hung in front of me, crushed on one side where he'd taken the reinforced windshield in the face.

I felt the urge to throw up rifle through me, and my ribcage flared red-white in protest. Instead I started clawing at Goon Two, grabbing his clothes

and body and where I could to wrangle him free of the seatbelt and down
and past me and he started to fall faster, limp hands brushing my face (I
could feel the knob of one of his knuckles graze my nose) and alongside of
me, yanking him down, simultaneously climbing past him.

"Helloooo?"

"Yes!" I suddenly yelled. "Yes! Hello! I'm here!" I started to crawl
out of the smashed-open driver's-side window, and stopped. Slowly,
gingerly I dropped back into the overturned cab, settling my weight onto
Guard Two's body now, a role-reversal, and peered into the back of the van,
my eyes now more accustomed to its darkness. The baggie was there
perched on a seat armrest; it was within reach and I stretched for it, my
busted ribs on fire. I stuffed the baggie with the straw into my pants pocket
and withdrew into the cab again.

Once out of the van, popping out like a man from a sewer, I thought, I
that I was about twenty yards from the road, which was upslope. We'd
tumbled down, down, where the trees sank away from the road. Standing on
the road's shoulder, hands on his knees, was the man who'd been calling. A
little ways away was his red pick-up truck.

"Help," I said. And he started down. "No, no," I said. "Get in the
truck, keep it running, turn it back on, whatever." And before I got the rest
of the way out I took the gun, the one I'd pulled out of Goon Two's holster
as he oozed past me to slump against the passenger door where I had been
two minutes ago, and held it out in front of me.

"For real," I said.

*

"Where we goin'?" Said the old-timer. He remembered me from driving by as I'd fought with the deputies. His eyes had widened as I'd climbed up the embankment to the road as he recognized me, and then they had flicked to the van, then back to me, putting together whatever story he needed to. He'd just stood there and waited for me and once I'd managed to climb up onto the asphalt, had even helped me to my feet. I put him in his late seventies.

Maybe his *operating system is shot*, I'd thought as we'd pulled away from the shoulder, watching the wreck of a van disappear quickly from the sideview mirror. *Maybe all of our operating systems have to go.* I also had thought that the van, where it lay, was easy to pass over if you were driving along with your focus on the road or on something else. Old-timers like this took it all in. *Wishful thinking.* Maybe.

Now we shivered along at 45 miles per hour in his pick-up. "We're going to see someone very special to me," I said. "Now, if we can just take on a little more speed."

"You're the boss, boss," he said, and I heard the sirens in the background.

"Shit," I said.

"What?" The old-timer looked over at me, his face framed in lily white hair, tucked under a battered blue cap, his equally blue eyes filled with genuine question, even concern, it seemed.

I listened. I listened hard. I heard the truck's little four cylinder engine purring along, like a kid's bicycle with playing cards in the spokes. But I didn't hear any sirens.

My ribs flared with pain, as if arguing, and I grimaced, and gritted my teeth.

"You need a doctor," the old-timer said.

"No. I'll get all fixed up where I'm going. You know Jamaica?"

"Yah mon," said the old-timer, now facing the road again, and it made me laugh, even though it wasn't funny. The laugh ripped through my chest. "What's your name?" I asked, choking. I realized it was almost a whisper. My left arm draped my ribcage, as if it could protect the bones from anymore damage. My right arm, my hand, was plunged into the reddish leather bench seat, pushing down to try and keep my ribs afloat somehow. The steel of the gun was cool against my skin, just to the right of my tailbone.

"My name's Murphy," he said, "Don Murphy, but you can call me Jake."

"Jake," I said, not bothering to ask why. I watched the road stretch out and undulate in front of us. The banks of woods on either side were giving way to open country once again. I kept glancing in the sideview mirror, and straining to hear the road behind us over the sounds of the truck and our conversation, waiting for those inevitable sirens.

Wondering if I would be listening to them the rest of my life, real or imagined.

*

THE PROPERTIES

When I awoke I was instantly paranoid and on the defensive – I hadn't realized that I'd fallen asleep. I swung my hand around to the back of my waist, not aware of exactly why, only the inarguable need to check there for something important. In a second, I found it, and my fingers closed around the grip of a hand gun. Thing was, that little investigation cost me more than I ever would have expected – it was as though my entire chest, upper back, diaphragm, and stomach were torched all at once by a heat so intense it was at once hot and frost-bite cold. I cried out from the surprise and rancid pain, and proceeded to throw up – this time no false alarm, this time for real.

Luckily the window next to me was down – I faintly recalled now, as my business came up and out of me – how I had rolled it down for the fresh air blowing in, and I had put my head back, just for a moment, as random, tumbling, dream and nightmare thoughts had blustered in with the open air. As I upchucked I managed to keep my eyes open, slitted, but open, and I saw that what quickly projected out and then boomeranged back by the wind, was red in color.

When it was over I slumped back on the bench seat of the pick-up's cab, mindful this time of all the tender spots, and sighed. I could feel the person beside me – *Don "Jake" Murphy*, it came back to me – looking over.

"I know you don't want to hear it," said Jake.

"I don't. No doctors."

"Medical attention at least. Now, b'fore you object, I wanna tellya. I was on my way anyway to see this person. He's a vet. Deals mainly with cattle. But a broken bone's a broken bone, I figure. He could fix you up. He's fixed up people before."

"The garden," I said.

"What's that?"

With the shock of pain upon waking, the disorientation, the vomiting, I was suddenly swooning. It wasn't pleasant. It felt like I'd taken a drug I didn't want in the first place and was suddenly trapped inside of it, like slipped a mickey. Back home we used called it "surprise birthday." My tongue felt fat in my cotton mouth. I was parched. I hadn't had something to drink since the rec room at the county jail.

I thought of Terry Hackford. Was he still alive? I'd never seen who I had to roll off of me in the van. I'd never checked for a third body altogether. I'd just gotten out. I'd-

"You're white as a sheet," said Jake.

"She's at the garden," I said. I felt a spit-bubble form and pop on my lip after my sentence. I wanted to throw up again, but was afraid of what would come out. There certainly wasn't anything else in my stomach. I'd been refused any food while locked up, and it wasn't like Terry had brought me a sandwich. If it'd been meretricious of ole Terr or not, at least I would've been fucking fed. I was going to pass out soon.

"And she'll take care of you," said Jake, "I know. But, son. Bondville, Jamaica – they're another hour away. You won't even make it to her, less we stop. Not with that stuff coming out of your nose."

I didn't want to, but I did it. I looked in the sideview mirror. I was utterly pale, as Jake had suggested. My usual light brown complexion, the

Italian from my gramma and father, was blotchy and pallid. My eyes looked
like they'd retreated into my skull. And there was more blood coming out of
my nose.

"Okay," I said, watching the strange, haunted version of myself work
its jaw and lips in the truckdoor's mirror. "I'll go. Where is it?"

"It's right here," said Jake, "just in time."

And he turned off onto a dirt road, a long driveway leading past an
acre of corn, to a large red barn with white trim and a big door with a white
X on it, and a little white house with a screened-in porch. There were grey
chickens clucking and the smell of cowshit hung low. I heard a screen door
open and bang shut and clopping foots down the three steps to the driveway.
Dirt dust sworled about us, and Jake got out of the pick-up.

"Dr. Madison," I heard Jake say, "I've got something for you."

My eyes flew open at the name. I wanted to get out of the truck all at
once, but I found I couldn't move.

An hour away – dear God I'm only an hour away. Please. Please.

I was made of lead. Even if I could get the door open I wouldn't have
been able to swing my legs out. Wouldn't have been able to even get out of
the cab, much less run. I saw myself, though, running through that corn,
blackbirds stirred and flying away and cawing irritably.

It could be a coincidence, I thought. *What are the odds? There have
to be plenty of those – Madisons. Could even be some distant relative.*

I heard the scuffing of steps coming round the front of the truck and
over to me. The dust was settling and there was a sketch of a person in the
haze.

It was not the portly veterinarian I would have liked to have imagined, bespectacled with rimless glasses, jovial and red-faced and used to probing cow parts with his chubby fingers. No.

My head rolled to the right and my chin dropped to my chest. What was happening to me? Did I have some terrible internal injuries? Was I losing blood internally at such a rate that I was dying right here? I didn't even think I could talk anymore. All I could do was watch helplessly as a pair of dusted black boots stepped into my field of vision. I could see the bottom half of blue jeans. I rolled my eyes up and could only see as far north as the waist of this person at my door, this person who could do anything to me for all the state I was in, utterly helpless, unable to move. I could see the belt. It was a black belt with what looked like some sort of Celtic knot for a silver buckle. There was a zero in the center of it, or an "O".

A hand came through the window and slipped under my chin, lifting my head up so that I may look into the eyes of the hand's owner – Dr. Cameron Madison.

He smiled, but then his smile faded and he shook his head slightly back and forth, looking me over now with his squinted eyes. "Three-five," he said. "You're a mess."

*

"What goes up must come down, Jack. We can do some amazing things, yes we can – and we continue to progress, continue to do more and more amazing, wonderful things, but we can't break the laws of the universe, it seems."

Cameron was pacing the room. Though garbed in country boy gear with his boots, jeans, white button-down workshirt, he walked like a professor addressing a class. It reminded me of his lecture at the commune, at Utopia. I had been under duress then too, drugged by something he had given me. Was I drugged now? It seemed that, either way, Dr. Cameron Madison only really felt comfortable with a "captive" audience. I felt like telling him that, but I seemed to still be having a problem getting my mouth to move.

"Though what we do," Cameron was saying, "some people think we *are* breaking the laws of the universe – mother nature's laws, God's laws. I always felt that God didn't have any laws. I always felt that we are both the creator and the created of God. Man has laws. Not nature. Not God. Even physics, Jack, thermodynamics, yes? You're familiar? Energy can neither be created nor destroyed? Bodies in motion? A body in motion will remain in motion unless acted on by another body? I am that body, Jack, acting on you. Har de har. And here I am, spewing the same rhetoric and telling you 'what goes up must come down.' Because, Jack, I am limited. 'A man's got to know his limitations' – Clint Eastwood. It has been driven – into – my – brain" – he smacked a fist into an open palm with each emphatic word – "since I was a child. Yours too. So, we have to let the science show. We have to let the science speak. We can *dream*, Jack, we can *think* metaphysically, and think telekinetics, and think pyrokinesis, but we can only *show* with science – that's all people will believe, but you have to get them to believe to change the paradigm."

I somehow found the ability to talk again, a little. "What."

Cameron stopped pacing. He looked out the screen door, perhaps to see where that traitorous old man was, that white haired Judas. *Judas, not Jake,* I thought, *you old fucker.* Cameron looked back at me. That was how I thought of him, how I thought of him at first, and even after. Not as Dr. Madison. As Cameron. The glorified college boy. First Madison Avenue Punk, now cowboy.

"What goes up must come down." He dropped to a squat in front of me, in the middle of this modest living room with the two adjacent couches, the one end table and matching coffee table, both a plain brown, the white, yellow-flowered curtains framing the picture window overlooking the dirt dooryard, the corn. "Reprogenetics, Jack. *Re*-programming genetics. Not just swapping out gene for gene. No, no, no. They've busted that over and over again; London, Prague, the fucking Swiss. No. This is not about just getting new parts. This is about creating in the human being an ability to *repair itself*, to reprogram itself. This is about a baby, born with CF, starving, throwing up, given our help, able to *repair itself*, able to take those defective genes and *reverse mutate* them, Jack. So that an unviable human can make itself viable. That's what I'm talking about, Jack. That we can all go back to utopia. That we can all go back to the garden." He stood up.

The garden, I thought. My speech was coming round rapidly. "You r also talking-ga about patents, camrn. You're talking about…" I had to swallow, my throat was still dry, I wondered why I had been given nothing, why I had been left in disrepair. "About a *drug*." I finished.

Cameron had turned again, presumably to gaze out over the corn, or over his envisioned empire of perfect people, people who'd come into the world as they were, errant, defective, doomed, and how he, the king, had saved them. Made them whole again. With his miracle drug. Now he wheeled on me slightly, looking a bit perturbed, but otherwise maintaining his politicking stance.

"Yes, Jack. A drug. The cure has to be delivered somehow."

"So that's how you did me?" I licked my lips. They were cracked.

"You gave me a drug? You didn't get in there and monkey around?"

"Yes, Jack, we had some 'monkeying around' to do. The drug is not finished yet, obviously. And you are an example of that, of a work in progress."

"And you want to take me back in," I could barely swallow, but I did, "and do more work on me." Why the hell wouldn't anyone *get me a drink*??

"In a way," said Cameron. "Yes, there is more to be done."

He fell silent and looked at me as though I were a car he was going to remodel. He brought a hand to his mouth and ran a finger over his lips. That did it for me.

"Can I," I said, "please," I escalated, "have a drink of fucking water."

"No," he said immediately, dropping his hand and his eyes flicking off to a place just beside me. "Dehydration helps to slow the process. Terry was wrong to give you anything. Don't you see what happened? You were able to do what you did once you'd hydrated."

I felt my strength returning, regardless. I was getting somewhere. "You said, 'what goes up must come down,' you said that twice. What did you mean?"

"I mean that there are consequences." He still had that ponderous look on his face and wasn't quite making eye contact with me, and then he did. "Right now," he said.

"Did I…crash?" I asked. Almost feeling the strength to sit up, but making a quick decision to stay prone instead. "Like, did I – just now – did I have a kind of hangover?"

"Mmmm," said Cameron, and he turned around and walked over to the window, bringing his hand to his mouth again, stroking his bottom lip from side to side. "I think you're asking the wrong questions now, Jack."

"I did, didn't I." I couldn't help myself. "This surge of adrenaline I had – I *summoned* – it has a consequence. I go potato-sack afterwards. And…" and *water is the key to both the strength and salvation*, I finished inside my head. *Who would have thought? Water.*

"I think that's enough for now," said Cameron, turning back around. His eyes widened. I had sat up, my legs off of the couch. I was going to spring, and he knew. I had just enough. I could take him out and then get to the kitchen and have all the water I w-

Cameron had bent to the end table at the end of the couch I was on. There was a click, and the firearm was in my face. I reached behind me – mindful, slowly, already knowing.

I found myself standing. Cameron's eyes squinted again, and he stiffened his gun-wielding arm, sort of jabbing the thing at me.

"Sit down."

"What? You're going to kill me? You're going to kill your prize p–"

The gun went off. It seemed a lot of guns were going off lately. I found myself back on the couch, smelling the acrid smoke pealing from the barrel of the gun, smelling something else – the singe of cloth and flesh.

"No," Cameron said, "not kill you, just shoot you."

The image of me running through the corn, scattering the blackbirds, free under the taut blue sky, began to fade.

I began to fade.

Still, I thought: *water*.

"I'm so thirsty," said Julianne.

I was sitting across from her, my head lowered, thinking, when she spoke. I looked up at her, hearing in her voice that Julianne was starting to lose her cool.

"I mean, what're they going to do with us? Are they going to feed us? Give us water? Why are we in here? Huh? Why?"

"Julianne…"

She was standing – at least she wasn't right near the window – and she looked as though she were about to start pacing. Or hopping up and down. "Why am *I* here? Because I met *you*?"

I closed my eyes, expecting her to take that road further, to finally spit blame on me, all over me, which I deserved. I'd just been trying to get laid. Or, well, I'd been trying to fall in love. To fall infatuated, anyway. I was as addicted to infatuation as I was to boozing it up. Mercifully, she didn't take it any further than that. "Who's going to pay ransom for me? Who's going to pay? It's not like they know my family, or anything, or who I am. Do they? Do you think someone has called my family, in *Pelham*?" Her eyes

widened in the dim room and she looked at me, though she wasn't actually
looking at me. Then she did start pacing, just a couple of steps back and
forth, side to side, and ran a hand through her wet, dark hair. "I don't know
I don't know I don't know," she chanted, and then stopped. "Are they going
to let us go to the fucking *bathroom??*"

"Julianne," I said, as diplomatically as I could muster, "we don't want
them to come back in here. We–"

"We don't? Oh, we *don't?* Maybe we *do.* Maybe we want them to
come back in there so we can kick the living shit out of them and *get out of
here.*" Her last three words were loud, a growl, and I squinted my eyes shut,
expecting an immediate, punishing blow to come from anywhere. When
none came, and I opened my eyes, I saw that Julianne was now sitting,
sitting directly across from me, her forearms balanced in her knees, her head
to the side, looking toward the one window. "Sorry," she said.

I looked at the door to the next room. Blair had said nothing since
he'd asked if we were still in the room next to him. He'd fallen silent after
I'd affirmed that we were. Maybe he was just listening. Maybe he was right
on the other side of that door. Maybe –

I got to my feet. I could feel my heart rate increase as I stood. The
room seemed to lighten a little, as if my pupils had dilated. I crossed the
room diagonally and came to a stop in front of the door. *What the
hell...what if...* I took the doorknob in my hand and started to turn it.

Locked. Not even a quarter-turn leeway. Of course it was locked.
But there was *some* leeway. The doorknob wasn't entirely immovable, it
had given that ten or so degrees. Likely it was a mortise lock, with a key
needed for the bolt on the other side. A passage lock would have been

preferable. A passage lock could be gotten around easily enough; I'd picked my fair share.

I took a step back from the door. I looked over at Julianne. She was still looking out the window, or, at least looking in that direction. I still felt enlivened. I wasn't discouraged by the locked door.

I turned and looked beyond Julianne and through the window and into the lush greenery. The Costa Rican jungle. The jungle in Costa Rica was typically dense. You couldn't see into it the way you could see into some jungles, some forests. Here it was thick, piled upon, in some places so dense that the green never stopped, that it was wall to wall. Here, however, outside this window, there was some room to see in.

I walked toward the window. I looked into the jungle, not worried that the panther might leap up at any second and show those killer's eyes, or that the fat man would-be-rapist would return to leer in at us again with his smudged eye and giant spread of chin and neck. I looked through the dirty opacity, I looked into the jungle, I walked right up to the window and looked through it and into the green, past the trees and vines and in.

I stood there like that for I don't know how long.

"Julianne," I said, "what do you have on you?"

"What?"

"Anything? Do you have anything on you? Did they leave you with anything on your person?"

"They didn't get this," she said right away. I heard her rustling around and then she stood up and walked up behind me. She held the object out. I looked over. Lipstick. A copperish cylinder of red lipstick. Or whatever special hue it was – something other than "red" I was sure. I took the lipstick from her. "They didn't check that little pocket. You know that little one, inside the bigger one?" I looked at her. Her hair was hanging in her face but I could see that she was smiling as she looked down and fingered the small right inner pocket of her jeans. She had pulled up her shirt above her waist with her left hand to expose the pocket and I could see the curve of her hipbone. "Is that all you have?"

"Uh-huh," she said. She let her shirt drop and then reached around behind her and slid her hand into her right back pocket. My eyes flicked up and I watched her bite her lip on one side as she did this. She was looking away, out the window, up at the ceiling, and then she looked at me. She smiled. She pulled whatever it was from her pocket and, still keeping eye contact with me – those hazel eyes flecked with green, and tiny dots of yellow, now illumined by the window – and I noticed that the tear-tracks were still faintly there on her face, a smudge of dirt or grease from that long ago truck ride, near the back of her cheekbone, in front of her ear. I could see it because she had tucked her black hair behind her ear – and when had she the time to do that? Between handing me the lipstick and lifting up her shirt and the front pocket and the back, and I pictured something I'd seen at the Brooklyn Museum, in the Indian exhibit, that one goddess with the many arms – Shiva? Was that it? – and all of that jewelry.

I looked away and at what she was holding. It was a folded up piece of paper. I looked at her again and she gestured for me to take it, jerking her hand at me. I took it and unfolded it. It was a page of homework, or, no, perhaps a quiz, and it had been graded, and there was a name up in the left-hand corner, Arnez, Guillermo. Guillermo had gotten a C on his quiz. *Not stellar, Guillermo.*

The paper was well creased, getting ragged. I had a feeling there was more to it and turned it over. There was indeed.

On the back was a sketch of a woman. It was, honestly, quite good – I felt a surge of jealousy and had to admit to myself that it wasn't just a sketch of a "woman," but that it was unmistakably a sketch of Julianne. My jealousy was that of any other man – or boy's – love of her, and of this artistic expression of it. Clearly she had been flattered; she had stuffed it into her back pocket. It had been there since I'd met her. The whole time I had felt like I was someone she could connect to, the first person here she'd met that was from her neck of the woods, that could make her feel a little more at home, and she'd had this *other* connection, this kid who was drawing pictures of her in class – good pictures – and giving them to her.

I blinked and folded up the paper and realized I had just been totally, utterly thrown off track. What was the point of that? Why had I even asked her for this damned thing?

And then, yes, I remembered, and I began to write the message I had somehow known I was going to write even before knowing if I had the means to do so.

"I'm going to have to ruin this sketch," I said.

When I had finished my brief scrawl, I brought it to the door – the other door, the one where the thin man had brought us into the room – and Julianne called out to me in a whisper. "You're not going to let me see it?"

"No," I said, and quickly slipped the paper under the door. I would have liked to have tortured her more – and, given enough time, I would have eventually even let her see it, thus giving up the trick like I always seemed to do. Luckily, time was not with me to ruin myself. Not that Julianne would have understood the content of the message anyway. I had only consulted with her on one word, "trade," for its Spanish translation.

"Trade what?" Julianne now asked. I was still feeling that sting, that bitterness. I was starting to know myself. I knew that even in a life or death situation like this, something that required all of my focus and attention to get out of, I would have easily gotten lost playing the little bit of leverage I now had until, again, I inevitably lost it. I wouldn't stop playing until I lost it. Like the last time in Atlantic City, no matter how you had tried to pull me off, old pal, I just wouldn't stop playing Blackjack until I'd lost everything, remember? It seemed to be the only way I could...I didn't even know. I thought maybe it was called entropy. That a nice visual illustration of whatever "it" was would have been a guy constantly dumping his airplane into the sand. Get up, start over, take off and...kamikaze into the dirt! Like a *pichiago*. Like an addict.

"You just got jealous," said Julianne.

Oh God, I thought, *here we go. Game time. Here come the roles and the rules, baby*. "Of what? Your red lipstick? I'll put some on if you don't think I can handle it." I tossed the stick over to her anyway, somewhat surprised when she snatched it deftly out of the air. She didn't say anything, just looked at me as she slipped it back into her "little pocket."

Then she did ask, "come on, whaddit say?"

"I shouldn't tell you."

"Oh come on. You're jealous of some 14 year-old kid learning English in my class who has a crush."

"And can sketch."

"You can't sketch?"

I shrugged, thinking instantly of my father, thinking of the huge black portfolio he'd sometimes come up the stairs with. Thinking of my own little secret, my own portfolio, stashed just weeks before coming to Costa Rica, almost a year to the day after…after the day I'd begun my own work, I supposed one could earmark it. I'll tell you where that portfolio is, I promise, I'll tell you in a little while.

"So, what," said Julianne, and she put the hand on her hip after sliding the tube of lipstick home. "You are going to torment me by not telling me what you wrote with my Autumn Blaze lipstick?" *I knew it*, I thought, *not just "red," no way.* "For revenge? I'm sorry but I didn't ask the kid to draw a picture of me."

"Yeah, but you kept it."

"Yeah, I did. I thought it was nice. Someone was paying attention to me. I'm invisible here, you know. Oh yeah, yeah, every fucking stuccolayer in town looks at me and whistles and calls me *"poco caballo"* and wants to stick their little prick in me. Yes, I am aware. And the women, lots of them, not the rich white women who just ignore me, but the locals, the wives of those stuccolayers, they just look at me like I'm an alien. And I *know* these are all good people. I know that they are gracious and hardworking and…I don't know. I don't know."

"Julianne," I said softly, having figured something during her rant, "I think we're getting delirious."

"Fuck *YES* we're getting delirious," she said, actually stomping one foot. "We haven't been fed, we've had no water, I've had to PEE like a goddamn *caballo* and *you're acting like A FUCKING CHILD!!*"

The key struck the knob in the door behind us. It was sooner than I'd thought. Well, it had forked in my mind – I couldn't have been sure whether they would have immediately taken the bait or would come in first asking questions. Maybe both, but, they were definitely coming in. I could only hope someone else was doing the other thing, someone else was doing what I needed them to do.

The lock was disengaged, the tumblers turned and I spun around. It was now or never. The door swung open. It wasn't the thin man, and for some reason I was emboldened by that. It wasn't the fat rapist either. It was an unfamiliar guy, about my size, but with a *Kalashnikov* slung over his shoulder. He held the note in his hand and was looking at it as he stepped in, a little too dopey, a little too asleep-on-his-feet, and just perfect for me.

He looked from the note to me, and then to the Julianne. He licked his lips and looked back at the note. He was now thinking so hard that his forehead dimpled above both of his thick wiry eyebrows.

"Why did he look at me like that?" Julianne asked me. "Huh? What does that note say?" She stepped forward quickly then – she was like a cat herself – and she reached out for the note. The guy with the AK 47 yanked his hand back away from her. "*Que dice?*" Julianne shouted at him. "*Que dice?*"

The guard stood there, looking at her. He was older than we were, maybe as old as Wild Dick. There was a scar on his jaw, on the left side. He wore his sideburns long. He glanced at me and he jerked his head toward the door.

The moment had come.

"Wait!" Julianne yelled after me. "Wait – what are you doing?! Don't leave me in here with him! Wait!"

I didn't look at her. I just focused on the carbine slung over the guard's bare shoulder (he wore a sleeveless t-shirt) and then at the door, and out the door, where I stepped into a room that was a vestibule. The door to our holding room closed behind me, sealing her in, and I heard Julianne screaming, and cursing at me.

There were two more guards sitting at a table in the antechamber. They both stood when I entered the room. It was a nice room, considering. There were lanterns on the wall, flickering, encased in iron sconces. The walls were the same hard red clay, reinforced with rebar and concrete, no doubt. The wooden floor creaked, but I knew beneath it was more concrete, clay, mortar. The place was a fortress, ahead of its time. The doors out of the vestibule were locked with two deadbolts. Beyond the guards who had stood up from the table was a corridor, lit with more of the oil lamps. I pointed in that direction and raised my eyebrows. *"Bano?"*

The guards studied me. Behind me, Julianne screamed again, muffled by the hard slab of door between us now. Their eyes flicked there, and then back to mine, both of them, in unison. They acted and looked like twins, and I was reminded of the Brandis brothers. One of them nodded at me and the other jerked his head toward the hallway.

I made my way as calmly as I could, though I wanted to sprint. Once in the bathroom I could barely piss. My bladder felt as hard as a stone. Finally, it came. Even through the heavy doors and clay and concrete I could hear Julianne.

Hold on, I thought. I just needed that little bit of time, that time to lull suspicion.

Finished relieving myself, I walked back out of the bathroom, down the cave-like corridor flickering with light and shadow like a dungeon, and into the antechamber. Both of the twin guards were still standing, both of their eyes fixed on the door to my cell, both of the AKs in their grips.

I had no idea what I was doing. I stopped just alongside of one of the twins, my heart triphammering in my chest, my blood rushing in my ears, and I reached out and grabbed his gun.

It was as I'd hoped – transfixed on the goings-on in the next room, his grip was lax. I wrenched the weapon free easily enough and went to hit him in the face with the butt of it, only I missed. I caught him in the ear instead of the nose or jaw. He cried out – also something I hadn't wanted, as the other twin got the gun fire-ready and turned it on me. I swung the back of the AK at him and this time connected solidly with the side of his face. His gun went off, riddling the clay over my shoulder, punching holes in the double front doors.

I had no time now. The second twin was on the ground, his hand on the side of his face where I'd bashed him, but the first had recovered. His ear bleeding, I saw, he went for his weapon in my hands and tried to get it back. We struggled. In the midst of it I headbutted him. It was the first time I'd ever headbutted anybody, I'd only seen Victor do it. I have to tell you – it's effective. The first twin let go instantly and staggered back, his hands flying up to his face, the backs of his legs hitting the table where he spilled over. Now both men were on the floor, and the door to my cell, Julianne's cell, flew open.

The guard with the sideburns and scar stood there, his eyes wide, his gun coming up at me. His pants were unbuckled. I had no idea how to fire an AK 47. There was a slide on it, and I thought that maybe you cocked it there, but, I wasn't thinking, you know? In a situation like that you do what you do, what you can; you go with what you know. All I wanted was not to get shot. Self-preservation. I was terrified.

So, I rushed him. I dropped the gun and both of my hands were out in front of me, seeking. I think my eyes were closed. I made contact, my left hand purchasing a face, a finger slipping into one wide nostril, the other had closing around his neck. The gun came up the rest of the way and the tip of the barrel caught me under the ribs, right in the solar plexus. I gasped, and I shoved.

Lucky for me, the same techniques worked here, it turned out, in Central America, that did on smashmouths in good ole Brooklyn, US of A. I took the long step with my right leg and hooked my foot around the man's ankle, and we toppled back into the cell-room ass over tea kettle and his gun clattered away. I continued to squeeze on his face, feeling his wet lip working under my pinky finger, my middle still jammed in his nostril, two more hanging onto his eye sockets, my thumb pressing under his cheekbone. He was making gagging noises as I strangled him, that thumb, that right hand thumb pressing down on the carotid artery so that the blood flow to his brain would be impeded, and that it would backflow into his lungs. But, I let go. I grabbed up the gun. This time I thought I'd use it after all. He started to sit up and I smashed him in the forehead with the butt of it. His head wrapped hard on the floor and he was out cold.

Julianne was on the floor in the center of the room. Her pants had been removed and thrown aside and she was in her underwear. Pink underwear. Both of her arms were over her body, crossed over her breasts, her hands hooked into claws, and she was shaking. I opened my mouth. I wanted to tell her that it was a plan, that I knew I could distract them with her, gain the upper hand, make a move. It was supposed to be quiet, stealthy, and then we were to escape. I wanted to tell her I never meant to actually trade her for a trip to the bathroom, but I didn't have the time to say a single word.

The front door burst open. I spun and half hid behind the doorway to our room and took my chance with the gun, bringing the slide back until it clicked and fired. The trigger on the AK stopped partway, reminding me of the doorknob between the rooms. I looked down, for just a split second, wondering about a safety. The two men who'd entered wasted no time getting to me, reaching me, knocking me on my back so that all the breath exploded out of me. They trained their guns on me. The thought flashed: *Why am I still alive?*

That was when Julianne came running, screaming and batshit-crazy. The man closest to her swung around and I was sure – in fact, I could swear to this day that somehow it even happened then and yet we managed to skip back, just a moment in time so that it didn't happen – Julianne was blown away, but she wasn't, and she hit into him before the gun went off and he dominoed into the other man, tripping over the one who had first come into our room so that there was a pile now, the two men on top of the sideburns guard with his belt undone.

There was a pounding on the other door. Calvin Blair.

I scrambled to my feet. I found the safety on the AK, another sliding lever along the left side, and pulled it back and stripped the two men of their weapons – one with the another AK and one with a rifle I didn't recognize. I handed the two firearms to Julianne, flipped the AK around and went to work knocking them out.

The first one went out the same way as the sideburns guy – the backend of the rifle to his head and down he went. The second didn't work out the same. He screamed and reached up and tried to get the gun away from me, grabbing at it. I wrenched it away and hit him again. I was sweating, and my grip was slick, and I lost the gun.

He rolled and went after it and got it. I leapt onto him and fought for it. He was bleeding from a gash along his hairline. He looked at me with giant eyes. Then he looked over my shoulder.

The twins were up and about again, I knew it. I headbutted the guy on the ground with me, and saw a white explosion behind my eyes. It hurt like a bitch, an instant migraine, and when I looked I saw that he still wasn't out. And the twins were coming; I was toast, we were finished.

Julianne fired. I looked up and saw her and her face behind the flashing and she looked like a maniac. She mowed down the twins before they even got all the way to our door.

The guy beneath me stopped struggling. His eyes, still luminous and now pleading, his hands held up in front of him, those eyes fluttered back in his head and his arms stiffened out, and his head fell back against the wooden floor. Out. "Finally," I said.

I looked at Julianne. I turned and saw the note on the floor. Julianne turned and looked there too. I bent and picked it up. "Come on," I said, stuffing the paper into my front pocket. She stayed where she was, her chest heaving, looking at me with what was nothing less than murderous rage.

"Julianne," I said, "we have to go, right now."

One gunman with a blasted nose was cursing and starting to get up, trying to roll a body off of him. It was all so confusing, I tell you. It was all so hot. I flipped the gun around and jabbed the business end in his direction. "Get down," I said. My whole body was vibrating, trembling, sweating so much, and I could feel how slippery the gun still was, how tenuous my grip on it. The man looked at me, his eyes blazing hate, and slumped to a sitting position against the door frame. The other man, the second man, was holding his head and dragging himself into the antechamber. It sounded like he was crying. Sideburns was still out cold. And the twins were dead.

I turned back around to face her. "Now," I said, "Please."

She just kept on looking at me. I had no idea who she was. I felt like someone else myself. Our chance encounter from the day before, the Coronas, our amatory banter in the Brandis ranch, my effortless fall into love.

"It worked," I said. "Come on, it worked." Still she remained where she was, in her panties and t-shirt, holding a rifle, hair plastered to her forehead. Without thinking I said, *"Nunca je visto los ojos..."* – I licked my lips, shut my eyes, then looked directly at her – "...*los ojos tan bonitas como los tuyos."*

Julianne walked toward me. I winced, ready for the blow. She brushed past me, and out through the door. I followed.

We moved through the vestibule. The oil lamps licked and flickered.

Onto the porch. The stuffed jaguar on our right.

And, miracle of all miracles, the pick-up truck was there in the dusty circular driveway.

*

I was in between worlds. I was floating, I can remember floating. Not the kind where I was up above my body or anything, but really floating. In a kind of womb. In the black. Black suffused with red, as though there was a membrane between myself and the light.

"What religion are you?" It was a disembodied voice, and it was muffled. Perhaps it was somewhere on the other side of the membrane, or perhaps it was in here with me.

"I don't know," I said. I had been dreaming. Dreaming of running through corn, dreaming of escape. And then there was jungle, I was peering into the jungle, I was running through it, and it was a group of scarlet macaws that scattered at my intrusion, not blackbirds, and there was a woman with me. Julianne. For some reason my mind kept wandering back to Costa Rica. There was a connection there. Between Costa Rica and here, now. I'd almost gotten it.

"Where am I?"

"You're safe."

Though I had no body here in this red-filtered blackness, I could feel pressure where my shoulder would be and where my ribs would be.

"So," said the voice, "you don't know."

I thought. "I guess I'm half 'fuck-me'," I said, "and half 'fuck-you.'"

"Funny," said the voice. "But tell me, really."

An image of my gramma, diminutive yet plump, sitting on her rose-embroidered couch in her Park Slope apartment, arose and floated in the darkness before quickly dissolving away. "Half Catholic."

"And the rest?"

"I dunno," I said, suddenly wishing I was back home, suddenly feeling the childish urge to be with my gramma, the woman there for me while my parents fought, when it had gotten bad. Before the end of it, and after it. "It's a mixed bag," I said.

I heard the disembodied voice make a sound like "hmm." Then it said, "you know, that's not very solid. A person has to make choices. There is nothing to fear from someone who hasn't made choices. A person who has made a choice and will serve it and guard it with their very life, now *that* is a person to reckon with. Open your eyes, Jack."

I did, and the darkness rolled back. I looked up at Cameron who was finishing up operating on me. I looked around. Was I still in the country house? For a minute I'd thought I was back in that cell, back in that ransom hotel eight years before. I wished I was. Not because I preferred one situation to the other, but, so I could have done things differently. So the worst hadn't happened like it had. I was, I realized, a different person then. Or, perhaps more importantly, I was different now.

Cameron was wrapping my shoulder in a white bandage. I looked down and saw that there was already one around my ribs, a big, thick bandage that went from my navel up to beneath my armpits. I also saw that I was in different clothes. Slacks, a button-up shirt, wingtips. "You *undressed* me?"

"You were in piss-soaked clothes, Jack. Covered in blood and...God knows what else. Can't have the prodigal son looking like that."

"My bag," I said, "the little plastic bag. Where is it?"

Cameron pulled something out of his back pocket and, smiling, dangled it in front of me.

"This thing?"

I tried to grab at it, just a reflex, and my shoulder flared with pain so unbelievable that I thought I was going to pass out again. I remained still, out of breath. I watched as Cameron returned the bag with my straw into his back pocket.

"Now," Cameron said, "you are going to need to rest for some time. You've had quite an ordeal." He kept smiling, and I realized, maybe not for the first time, but with the most conviction, that Dr. Cameron Madison was crazy.

And here I had questioned my own sanity for so many years.

"Where's the old man?" I asked. "Jake?"

"Why?"

"Because I would like to bash his head in."

Cameron *tsked* and shook his head. "We're going to have to do something about that anger," he said. He stepped back, finished with the bandage, and admired his work, looking me over. He nodded once to himself, turned to his right and grabbed something out of my field of vision. Then he brought it to his lips, a glass of water, and drank from it greedily. I heard it land on the table as he set the glass back down, emptied of its contents.

"What was the point of shooting me?"

Then he looked at me. "Things will be a lot friendlier if you cooperate," he said.

"Friendly," I said, licking my dry lips. "I could've sworn I heard that sentiment not too long ago." I cleared my dry throat. "Didn't work out too well for that guy, the friendliness, as I recall."

Cameron laughed. "You're cool, Jack. I can see why they offered you."

It was as though Cameron had casually tossed a little dart into my brain. Literally, there was a flare of pain in my temple, the same side as my bulleted shoulder. "Who offered me?"

"Oh, Jack," Cameron said, "you make such a big mystery out of things. It's all right there, right in front of your face. But," he said, running that finger over his lips again, "I guess with your ailments, your self-absorption, your addictions, that comes with the territory. You're near-sighted. We can fix that."

I ignored his attempt at insults. "Why did you ask me what religion I was?"

Cameron looked at me as though I were someone who had been seated at the board-meeting the entire morning and hadn't learned one single fucking thing. "Because, Jack," he said, dropping his hand to his side, "this has gone on long enough. We're going to have to bury you. You know, and we want to send you off right."

Julianne and I stood on the porch looking over the dooryard and circular dirt driveway. I could hear her breathing, loud in the stillness after our terrorizing fight with the three guards. In the distance I could hear the babbling screech of howler monkeys and stilted song of the *aricaris*. The jungle was behind us, but also across from us, forty or fifty yards away and on the other side of the truck. It was, really, all around us.

"Oh God I have to *goooo*," said Julianne. I knew what she meant. My bladder had felt like a throbbing hot brick in my groin for the past many hours. I was even wondering if, had I not given myself the opportunity at last, would I have been able to go at all, or would I have permanently gunked up the works? Maybe there were leaks springing inside Julianne now. Was that possible?

"Go. Quick."

Julianne looked at me. I still saw and felt that murderous urge, that utter mistrust in her, but she had become somewhat human again, somewhat recognizable in the past few moments since we'd stepped outside. Then she slung the rifle over her shoulder, pulled her pink panties down and squatted on the front porch of Wild Dick's ranch. And went.

I looked to the right where the dirt driveway sloped down, cutting a narrow swath through the jungle which tumbled closer to the road as it descended. I had no idea how far it was to the next road going in that direction. To the left, the road ascended and wound up and behind the ranch house and out of sight. Since the driveway in front of us was circular, with its own little patch of jungle a cultivated oval in the center – the *planter de la centro* – there was no telling which way we'd arrived the afternoon before. The truck was pointed one way, toward the driveway to the right, stretching down and away, but that meant nothing.

It didn't matter anyway if there were no keys in the pick-up. "Come on," I said when she'd finished and redressed her underwear, sticking my hand out in front of her, "let's go." When she didn't take my hand right away, I turned and looked at her. Never before and never since had I seen a woman as beautiful, as terrified, as angry as the one I saw standing there on Wild Dick's porch, all of 23, a foreigner, a fellow New Yorker, a kid, really, who taught other kids English. She looked to me from the truck, the driveway, and finally took my hand.

We started quickly, taking the three steps off of the porch in a leap, running toward the center of the driveway, and around, almost ten yards from the pick-up truck and possible freedom when I noticed movement in the little jungle in the roundabout focal, in the place where we were vulnerable from all sides. Movement that could only mean one thing.

As I remembered this, I also understood it had been suppressed memory. I had, in years since, reflected on my time in Costa Rica as an innocent time, as a time-well-spent, even as fun. That's the thing with memory, I now figured, is that it's not a bear-trap; we injected it with the positive attitude we lacked in the present, we forgot the horror and disbelieved it ever even existed. What I had done, what I had *chosen* to do, regardless of the circumstances, I wish to this day I could *un*choose. I never should have left her in there with the man with the scarred jaw. I never should have done any of it. I should have died if I'd had to, if it had meant staying with Julianne, protecting her. But, I hadn't. And I had to live with it, so I'd suppressed it. Until Cameron Madison, years later, would excavate it from my depths with his witchdoctory.

Yet, in that moment, I knew Cameron's statement wasn't a mortal threat; they were not going to actually kill me. Why would I go on pretending like they were when you know that I am here to write about it, at this time, in this place? I respect you more than that, old *palomino*. No, Cameron meant to kill me in every other way. Social Security, Birth Certificate – un-create me as a *persona non grata*, make me fully the property of the Utopia Corporation. At least that's what I figured at the time – it made the most sense.

Maybe he should have done it up, though, the real thing. Maybe he should have.

The movement in the bushes was exactly what I'd feared it would be, and the great black cat leapt out of the miniature jungle in the middle of the driveway with no roar, no sound, only the glint of teeth and inhumanity of its eyes.

I slammed into Julianne and we both toppled over, the beast soaring above us. It landed perfectly on its feet, twisted its body around in a U-shape and snapped, catching one of Julianne's arms flailing above her head. I couldn't – having never seen a cat bigger than the fat orange one that'd hung out on my stoop one summer when I was a teenager – believe the size of the thing. It was bigger than any dog I'd ever encountered, the size of the tigers I'd seen at the Bronx Zoo, blacker than the unconscious.

Julianne screamed, the sound another first for me, an utterance like I had never heard; pure primal fear. Mortal fear. The sound of ancient reptilian birds, carnivorous and haunted. I rolled away as the panther dragged Julianne back towards the porch, and I saw that her arm had disappeared into the cat's mouth up to the elbow.

The AK 47 was still slung over my back – it had dug into my shoulder blade with a hot pinch as we'd fallen over. On my stomach I slung it round in front of me and took aim on the panther. It was no good. The giant black cat was pulling Julianne to the porch and shaking its head from side to side. In the midst of the horror I thought of something that made the vomit rise to the back of my throat – the thing was following some sort of training. Julianne continued to scream, and her eyes caught me, just once, and they were finally completely unrecognizable as her own, they were only the eyes of purest terror, and my own terror recognized them.

I stood, looking for a better shot, wondering why no one else had appeared, no other guards, no other rapist maniacs, nor Wild Dick himself. I swung the barrel of the AK 47 down to hip level and started advancing on the panther. It had almost brought Julianne back to the porch steps when I saw my chance and fired.

In my defense, I still really had no idea how to fire such a weapon, and, in that moment, the terms "semi-automatic" and "automatic" were nowhere near my thinking. When I squeezed the trigger the gun came to life, spraying bullets at both of them, biting into the giant cat (I could see its silvery-black and coarse hair ducktail with the impacts.) Two or more rounds caught Julianne before my finger released the trigger and I had any idea what had happened. The panther loosed its jaw-grip and leapt away, not opting for the porch where its jaguar cousin sat frozen in purgatory, but lateral to it and away. The AK 47 fell away from my grip and landed with a puff and a clatter on the dirt driveway.

Julianne was shaking all over, her chin pointing to the sky, head tilted back, as though she were still watching the beast drag her, or perhaps looking back into the porch we'd sprung from as a better sanctuary, as a place to return to. Blossoms of blood spread out along her white, thin-materialed top, one above and one below her left breast. I walked to her, and she began to shake even more violently, and then the muscles in her neck gave and she was looking directly up at the sky, then at me, as I knelt over her. Her arm had been eviscerated from elbow to hand, barely hanging on by the bone. I didn't know what to do for her, what to say.

"Julianne," was all I could come up with. Her eyes found me. And I remember that, finally, those hazel eyes were at once startled and wise, as if all of this had happened to her before, and she was only incredulous that she was here to live it again, that it actually *had* happened again.

"Where's my mom?" She asked.

"I don't know," I told her. I saw by the dark spot between her legs that she had wet herself, even after her perfect desecration of the porch. I looked up and away from her, the tears stinging and threatening, the guilt over me like a stench, mincing my guts away to shreds, filling my heart with hot blood. I felt like I could explode. I turned my attention to the front door, ajar. I could see the leg of one of the felled guards. Those *mono* monkeys screeched in the trees, no doubt agitated and excited by the commotion. A spectrum of birds were chirping, cawing and chorusing, and insects hummed and buzzed continuously, yet it seemed very still, very thick, very quiet. When I looked back down at Julianne, she was dead.

I stood up, now shaking so badly myself that I thought my legs would not work. Then I heard the growl of the panther around the far corner of the ranch, and that got me moving.

I turned, took a few steps, picked up the gun and somehow managed to start jogging around the *planter de la centro* and to the pick-up truck.

It was not the same pick-up truck after all. My eyes had deceived me; my hope and delirium had deceived me. It was a different truck, bigger, faded orange, and I found that the door was unlocked. I got in and shut the door behind me, fingers groping the wheel chuck for the ignition, for keys, when the panther leapt up onto the roof and started snarling and swiping at the windshield.

There were no keys. I checked above the visor. In the ashtray, filled with *cigarillo* butts. I could now feel all of the heat draining from me, as though somehow I had popped open a spigot and the life was pouring out of me like water onto sloppy mud. The thing on the hood was beautiful, awful, and it meant to kill me, it meant to bite into my soft stomach and yank out my entrails with its teeth, somehow avenging the untimely death of its cousin, somehow avenging even its hatred of Wild Dick.

My eyes closed without my permission. My lips began reciting a prayer my gramma had taught me as a small boy, "the Lord's Prayer." The panther left the roof. A moment later and it had jumped into the truck bed and was slamming its paw against the rear windshield.

It could crack, I thought, *the window could be smashed and the panther could get in.*

I was helpless. In my frantic entry of the truck I had even left the rifle in the dirt outside the cab. It would only be a matter of time before the panther got in or someone else showed up and...that would be it.

I first sensed the others that had already arrived in a way that I could not, and can still not explain, only that it could have been simply that the panther's attention was diverted. It stopped banging away at the back windshield and jumped from the truck bed. I wrenched my neck around to see where it had gone. It was a black streak, running up the driveway to the north, and then stopping all at once, its feet a blur of black and pluming dirt, and the horses then appeared, coppery and shining with long black manes, looking nearly identical to one another.

The panther leapt up at one, and I could see the ivory white of its teeth, the blood red of its gums even from my distance. It was going for one horse's neck, but missed. I could hear the snap of its jaw. My own bladder went again with the sound of that snarl and snap. The horses continued on, galloping toward the truck, and the panther followed. They seemed to either be unaware of it or unafraid, at that moment, until the panther sprang again, catching another horse, slightly lagging, by the tail. The horse nickered and reared back, and I saw, with some horror, the cat climbing up on to its back, using tooth and claw to get itself there.

Without thinking I opened the door. I ignored the rifle. One unfettered horse neared as I climbed into the back of the truck. As it passed I did a little leaping of my own, falling sideways across its bowed back, grabbing fistfuls of its hair to keep from sliding off of the other side of its belly and onto my head.

I stayed on. The horse neither noticed nor was pained by my handholds in its flesh, my kicking feet. I maneuvered my body sideways and then swung my left leg over the horse. I wrapped my arms around its neck, my face buried into its mane. Only then did the horse seem to care that I was on its back and it stopped, reared up once, landed, and then kicked out with its feet. It was trying to buck me off.

I could hear the panther behind us, but dared not look. It sounded, though, like the beast had left the other horse and was now coming after us.

The horse must've sensed this too, because it ceased to attempt to rid itself of an unwanted passenger and began to run again, faster than before.

Can a horse outrun a panther? For some reason the idea struck me as some nutty riddle, or some code phrase used in campy espionage. *I don't know*, would come the answer, *can a pig outstink a skunk?* My mind was obviously in shock at this time, for all I can remember is having this ludicrous idea, and then being nowhere in my head but in that moment, of only moving with the horse, willing it to outrun the monster on our tail.

I wouldn't think of Julianne again for hours, not until the horse came to a rest along the river where I met a man named Alejandro. I wouldn't think of how I left Calvin Blair behind, had killed a woman who had only committed the crime of having some noontime Coronas with me, and had made a terrible enemy of Wild Dick.

I wouldn't think of the Brandis Brothers, and how I must've failed them, until some time later when the man named Baradez at last tracked me down, unconscious in a bar. A few days later he put me on a plane back to the States. In-flight I threw down one trembling cocktail after another and got so stinking drunk again that JFK security had to haul my limp self off the plane and carry me to the waiting car.

I was now in another vehicle. It appeared to be a kid of private ambulance. Cameron sat beside me in the back – I was on a gurney. I could only imagine that the driver was my good friend Don "Jake" Murphy.

"This area is interesting," said Cameron. He was looking out the back window, and swaying with the movement of the vehicle and the road. I found myself wondering if biochemist Dr. Cameron Madison was on his own self-prescribed cocktail of drugs, and I figured it was more than likely. "It's a mixture of biomes," he went on. "It's part coniferous forest and part temperate deciduous forest." His eyes returned to me. "It's a great place to grow things. Very fertile. I can't wait to get back to my greenhouses."

"You're taking me back." I said. It wasn't really a question, and it made me cough, my throat was so dry. To my surprise, Cameron handed me a cup of water. I looked at him with suspicion. "You'll be okay with that little bit for now," he said. I looked down at my body and saw the tube in my wrist and vaguely understood. If I was going to be in Cameron's custody, I was going to be in his control. Whatever water did for me – somehow alerted my hypothalamus, my adrenal glands to my semi-voluntary control – Cameron was intercepting. To him, I was little more than an observable experiment.

My body rocked back and forth on the gurney with the movement of the vehicle and some water slopped onto my chin. Cameron dabbed it up with a white sterile pad as tenderly as a mother would her baby's spit-up. "There," he even said, and took the empty cup from me. I felt like I could drink a gallon. I also wondered, with all of the peeing I'd done while virtually dehydrated, if a cup of water was going to turn me into a fire hose.

I closed my eyes.

"Where were you just now," Cameron asked, "do you remember? You were dreaming."

"Costa Rica," I said without hesitation. It was clear to me that the best plan of action was now receptivity and passivity. It was clear to me that the Brandis brothers had sold me. I never would have believed it possible before, but the exhuming of my Costa Rican debacle put things into a greater perspective, a realist's point of view. The Brandis brothers had sold me to the Utopia Corporation. I had fucked up their plan to recapture Calvin Blair – which, as I now, after eight long years, finally fathomed – likely involved my collateral death in the first place. I had been expendable.

"Costa Rica," said Cameron. I kept my eyes closed, but could envision his face, plastered with a superficial look of sympathetic bliss. "Mmm," he said, "beautiful place, too, I hear. And getting more popular all of the time."

"Smarter too," I said, and cleared my throat. "The building codes they have now are incredible. Everything double and triple fortified. Homes are built like castles. Hurricane-proof."

"Very, very smart," Cameron agreed, and I pictured him nodding. I pictured myself springing out of the gurney and tearing into his neck with my teeth, like the panther had the horse. "Very smart," he went on, "because it's all going to happen. It's all going to get worse. We're still on the collision course with mother nature."

I opened my eyes. My body felt completely limp, but I could feel everything. *Mild sedative,* I figured, *painkiller. And whatever synthetic Utopia drug to block my new ... tendency. And other things.* Cameron had other things planned for me, his living experiment. It was one thing I was sure of. "You?" I asked, "a sky-is-falling kind of guy?"

He rubbed a finger past his lips and nodded conversationally, filled with bullshit humility. "Oh yeah," he said, "oh yeah. A storm is a very simple thing, Jack Aiello. Jack Landi. Whatever you liked to be called – I think I'm still going to call you by my favorite name, 0035. Sounds kind of spy-ish, doesn't it? A storm is nature's way of righting an imbalance. The greater the imbalances, the greater the storms. So, it's a good time to put your hard-hat on, if you know what I mean. And, well, after mother nature does her job, there will be a new people. And that's all I need to say about that."

He smiled wanly at me and looked back out the window.

I looked there too, suddenly acutely aware that I was headed north again, and that miles were growing between myself and my daughter.

Again I imagined myself launching off of the gurney, smashing Cameron's head through that back window for a better view, snapping the neck of the traitorous Jake Murphy and turning this vehicle around.

But I remained lying there for now. For now.

I watched the trees roll back and away through the small window as we drove back to Utopia.

BOOK 3

War Of The Naturalists

THE TWO CAMPS

"The jellyfish are consuming the oceans," said the guy next to me.

In the giant, army-style Quonset hut, there were fifty or sixty white-lined cots which had arrived, been set up and dressed in the short time since I'd been there. The Quonset hut was enormous, the ceiling some fifty feet at the peak of the tube-like architecture, maybe three hundred feet long, like a giant soup can buried half in the earth.

The guy next to me was the only other one in the barracks besides me, but I had a feeling there were going to be more occupants soon. For now, we were alone. The only soldiers in the huge room stood at the double door entrance, far out of earshot. Still, we spoke in low voices.

"Oh yeah? The jellies are taking over?" My shoulder throbbed. My ribs ached. My back felt knotted, gnarled. They were the kind of medicated pains that you forgot about until you moved and they burned through your whole body, front to back, top to bottom, bringing to mind, for some reason, the term "flash fire," though I didn't really know what a flash fire was.

"They look like aliens," said the guy, laying on his back, looking up at the sloping, cambered roof, a dull silver-grey. "We're over fishing the tuna, swordfish – all of the jellyfish's natural predators. So they're flourishing. Plus," he said, rolling over to look at me, "all of the carbon dioxide we produce seeps into the ocean, making it more acidic."

He looked familiar to me, this kid. I tried to sort through all of the people I had met in the past couple of weeks. I fought my way through the pain killers and whatever cocktail Cameron Madison had me on. "The jellyfish like that, I guess."

He didn't seem to know what to say. His eyes rolled away from me and his body followed so that he was back looking straight up at the curved ceiling. He'd told me that his name was Jared. I put Jared at about 23, 24 years old. He was solidly built, athletic-looking. I watched him lay there, and I heard the roar of a crowd, and saw a basketball arcing through the air, and I remembered.

"You play for UVM," I said. "Number forty-three, right?"

"Yeah," he said, "point guard."

I sat up, carefully, mindful of the many pains, this time, so that I was propped up on my elbow, leaning on my good side. "How did you get here?"

He shook his head side to side on the pillow, still looking up at the ceiling. There was an apsis there, a kind of skylight, and it shone down on him so that he glowed. "I don't know," he said, "I had a twenty-two point game, went out afterwards, chicks, a little Remy…and I just woke up here."

I thought of the morning I'd awakened along the shores of Lake Champlain. "Let me ask you something," I said, and this time I tried to sit up straighter without thinking, and the pain tore through me and I cried out.

"You okay?"

"Yeah. Did you…well, did you sign up for this?"

It was his turn to sit up on his elbow and he looked at me, full of indignation. "Look, my game was fine. I wasn't on scholarship. I didn't ask anyone to turn me into the fucking bionic basketball player, okay? I did

protein shakes, glutamine, okay, some anadrol. The shit's easier to get at my
school than weed. Alright? Everybody does them."

Steroids, I thought. *Adrenaline*, I thought, *cortisol*.

"For real," I said. "And…you didn't come to these people? You
didn't ask them to…juice up your game?"

"No, man," Jared said. He hit the side of his bed with a fisted hand.
"Look, steroids are lipids, okay? Fat! They're naturally occurring. You've
got to be careful of the oxidation levels, whatever you do, yeah, yeah-yeah.
Oxidation, free radicals, you know, that's what destroys your cells, that's
what kills you." Then he was calming down, and he looked at his hand, and
his hand was shaking.

Quietly, I asked him, "Did you research that kind of thing, or did…the
doctors here…" I didn't know how to finish.

His eyes flicked up to mine. I saw that they were a dark brown, and
laced red. Jared reminded me a lot of myself. The parts of me that were
changing, that I knew now to be false, to be useless. All the anger, all of the
blame. I offered: "They gave me some pain killers, and Dr. Madison has me
on something that…I don't know. Inhibits me. But he also said he was
going to do something about my, uh, 'near-sightedness,' I guess. 'I can fix
that,' he said. Did he say anything like that to you?"

"I don't know, I've never had any problem with my vision," said
Jared, and rolled over onto his back and let a long breath out.

I opened my mouth, but shut it, and let him be. I watched him breathe
and we were silent for a moment. I looked at the other beds. I imagined
them filling up. Cases like me, like Jared, filling up the room. People who
had been manipulated, unwittingly experimented on – lied to. Filled with
drugs. Talking about things of which they'd had little or no previous idea

about. What was the point? Knowledge was supposed to be dangerous by those who wanted to control you. What did Cameron, or any of his kind, have to gain by having his subjects see so clearly, to know things we otherwise wouldn't know?

And I thought of the soldiers present during a meeting I'd had in a place much like the one I was in now. I thought of Private Ramirez, Private John Hackford.

"Hitler," Jared suddenly spoke, staring up at the ceiling, at that light, his hands now clasped behind his head.

"What do you mean?" But I thought I might already know.

He rolled over to face me again, propping his head up with his arm once more. He was wearing the same thing I was – a kind of white two-piece linen fatigues, like something I imagined mental patients might wear. Velcro pants instead of drawstring. A cotton v-neck as soft as a baby's ass. Cameron had paraded me in wearing the makeshift suit he'd provided, only to have me strip down, shower in a bathroom with dozens of spigots, and put on the new get-up. "It's about a pure race," Jared said, "a perfect race."

This struck a deep chord. "You don't think they're – I dunno – searching for immortality?"

Jared sniffed and looked down at the edge of his bed, at his sheets, and started plucking at folds there with his other hand. I caught a whiff of soap and body odor wafting from him. The rest of the room smelled sterile, if only slightly like aluminum, which, if anything, smelled like rainwater in a jar to me, and made me think of Julianne. "Not with one body," he said, red-ringed eyes coming back to mine. "Not by keeping one body going the whole way," he said. "I don't think so. I think…" and he rolled onto his back again.

"What?" Unlike the blasts of pain from my ribs via careless movements, my shoulder was now a reawakened, steady throb of pain that seemed to draw energy from my head, my heart, my groin, like a black hole in my body. I was starting to fog over from the pain, and considered calling out for someone, anyone, for more painkillers. But I didn't.

Jared said: "Genes have...memory, right? I mean, that's how we evolve. Right?" He turned his head to look over at me briefly, and then redirected his eyes to the Quonset ceiling.

"I don't know that we really understand how things evolve," I said, thinking of Maya, of what she had said in our jail cell together. And I thought of Cameron Madison, the night of the storm, the first time I had been here, in that stale, false little home that'd been an eerie version of an amusement park prop. A stage.

"Some things," I said slowly, tasting the words, "are irreducibly complex. What I mean is, they need all their little parts to function, or they become useless. Like a go-cart. Take away the wheels, you're not going anywhere." Jared rolled over again on his side to face me and I continued, "Take away the seat, you've got nothing to sit on..."

"Or the motor, nothing to run it."

"Right, exactly, you got the hang of it. So, think of what these guys do. They're biochemists. So they deal with the very, very small parts of things. The proteins – even smaller than the genes – the proteins that do the things the genes tell them." I watched his eyes and it seemed I still had his attention and understanding. "So, for something to evolve, all of these little things have to evolve. It's a team...a bunch of players making up the team..."

I blinked and shook my head from side to side, wincing at the pain. I was losing myself. "What I mean is, some things that evolved, well, unless they evolved overnight, all the little proteins and enzymes mutating at once, they could have left a creature very vulnerable to something – say a claw was evolved, or something. Well, while the claw was taking hundreds, thousands of years to evolve, the animal would have been vulnerable to attack and could have gone extinct. Or, wait; let's say an animal evolved a defense mechanism like some sort of crazy acid spit. You know, there would be times when there could only be the acid in the mouth, and not the protective skin of the gland–"

"And the thing's mouth would have burnt up with acid," said Jared. His eyes had a dreamy quality. I suddenly pictured Jared in a tiny apartment with *The Anarchist's Cookbook* in front of his face, basketball game on the television forgotten, bearing that same expression in his eyes.

"Exactly. Anyway, Darwinian evolution is challenging, because Darwin didn't have biochemistry."

Jared nodded. "But, what about memory? Genes having memory?"

I felt a sudden wave of nausea and vertigo come over me and slumped back.

"You okay?"

I nodded on my back, my head on my pillow. I licked my waxy lips.

"Let's say they do," I said. "What were you thinking?"

"Well," he said, throwing a furtive glance at the soldiers guarding the entrance, breathing somewhat strongly (I could hear the whistle of his breath in his nostrils while I had been sermonizing), "I think what they're doing is planning on not creating one body to be immortal, but, you know, create like a super-race."

I forgot about my nausea and my pain.

"A super-race they can maintain by administering their drug to. Immortality would be a cure, and any good drug company knows that cured people don't need prescriptions."

I had sat up in the bed again without even realizing it, pain forgotten.

I asked, "But if the genetic memory is there, won't each generation get better and better – I mean, closer and closer to perfection – and not need the drug anymore?"

"Yes," said Jared, seeming pleased with himself in a way that made me suddenly love the kid – and feel a pang of nostalgia and guilt for Peter, who I'd left behind in Newport Center Hospital more than a week ago. "Exactly. Because the plan for them to have the people taking the gene-mutating drugs is only the first part of the plan."

I thought of terrorism. I thought of Homeland Security. Liberties lost. I thought of the major, monolithic pharmaceutical companies, and Cameron talking about them being declivitous; patents expiring, jobs lost, billions of dollars disappearing. I thought about Exxon patenting and owning a living organism. I thought of being called a product. I thought of Jared's Hitler analogy, of Maya's derision of Darwinism – and how it took hundreds of thousands of years for evolution. Until now. Until man and machine were becoming one. How our toying with artificial intelligences, computers, sophisticated robotics, quantum theories, the A-bomb, fusion, how it all went together. I was beginning to see how it all fit together, like I was dreaming awake. How we were our own machines, and how there were faulty machines that could be perfected. Faulty machines that would otherwise be discarded, ignored, swallowed up and digested and passed through the bowels of the system. People nobody would miss, or more, really, people nobody would care were gone. Drug-abusing athletes. Gay activists. Addicts. Drunks. Hacks, like me.

The double doors to the hut banged open. Cameron Madison marched in, a white lab coat flaring out behind him like a cape. Behind him were two more of the soldier-types, like Hackford and Ramirez had been, like the on-duty guards, decked out in dark blue camouflage fatigues. And they had the next white-garbed prisoner in their grip.

The pain in my chest flash-fired again as I tried to get up off of my cot. I doubled over and hit the floor, my arms wrapped around myself, shaking, shaking like Julianne had been.

Their captive, bleeding from one nostril and purpled around one eye, was Maya.

A white Hummer limousine pulls up outside of the Quonset barracks. That's the next thing I remember.

But I'm dreaming. This time, I'm really dreaming. I know this because all of the sudden I am aware of a cessation of the pressure on my chest and throb in my shoulder. And I realize that to see or to know that the white Hummer limousine was pulling up I'd have to be outside. Floating, in fact.

I felt the pressure on my chest intensify and the image of the white Hummer in the steely grey drizzle of twilight outside of the Quonset hut was vaporizing away into thin air; what was replacing it was a blackness that wasn't quite black, but the headboard of sleep. Nothing.

"Are you going to behave, Mr. Aiello? Number three-five, are you going to behave?"

My eyes fluttered open and the considerable brightness of the barracks flooded in. The figure standing over me was blurry, but I could make out a helmet, and a gun. There was a soldier on top of me, his knee on my chest.

"Don't," I heard myself faintly, painfully whisper, "Chest...hurts..."

"As long as you behave," said a familiar voice, a voice I was growing to associate with my old camp counselor back long ago during those three summers my folks insisted I get out of Brooklyn. He was this guy who wore too tight jogger shorts and his socks up to his knees and just had this nasal, condescending voice. Cameron Madison was starting to sound like this guy to my memory cells. "As long as you cooperate," he said.

Cameron Madison. The day he'd picked me up – bailed me out of jail. Driving that silly hybrid car with his wrap-around shades on, that start of a pointy tattoo visible above the collar of his J-crew dress shirt. The punky badass. The self-aggrandized mad doctor – bringer of the Change, the answer.

"Okay," I coughed. "Just get...the fuck....OFF."

For a moment longer the pressure remained and the hulking silhouette of the soldier loomed. Then I saw in my peripheral vision Cameron give a short nod of his head and the pressure was gone and the guard slipped from my sight. Instantly I began whooping for breath, which was a mistake, because each greedy intake of air seared my lungs like an electric fire. Like a million tiny wires running through the soft lining, the alveoli each flaring a singeing orange as the breath came in, griddling the pink meat of my lungs so that I expected to exhale smoke. I rolled over on my side, faint with the pain again, unable to stop coughing despite how much it hurt.

My eyes squinted shut, I opened them. I saw that Jared was no longer in the bed beside me. I suddenly had a thought – *Maya* – and I found that I was able to get off of my side, twist around and even sit up. My coughing stopped.

There she was, about a dozen beds down on the other side, a doctor in a white coat and a soldier next to my bed as well. I quickly glanced toward the other end of the barracks – nothing, no Jared – and then turned back in the Maya direction. I could see half of her face through the space between the soldier's arm and his torso. It looked like her cheek was streaked with crying. I felt my body surge with adrenaline. I could also see that beneath her own white liniments was a bandage around her shoulder. I had a stinging memory of having shot her. Maybe in a dream.

"Jaaaack," said Cameron. "No no. Focus, Jack. That won't help you."

"What is she doing here," I said.

Cameron sat down on the bed across from me and clicked a pen. He had a clipboard with him and he looked at it over the rim of his Armani framed glasses.

"She's always been a subject, Jack. Just like you. We used her to help bring you in, that's all."

"So it is bullshit. I never came to you. I never asked for your help."

"No, three-five, we're not the Mayo clinic. We're not Betty Ford. This is not a panacea, not a healing retreat. This is what I was trying to tell you before…before you got so impatient with me. You were given to us, three-five. For science. This is science."

"This is government," I said. I glared at Cameron, who didn't look at me back. He had raised his eyebrows a little, but he kept on scribbling.

I spat between his feet, satisfied, regardless of how it ripped at my lungs, to see that what came out was blood. "I'm getting sick of these little chats with you, Cammy."

Now his eyes flicked up to meet mine – those royal blue eyes. He would have made an excellent bad Superman, I thought, and felt a twinge of déjà vu at the thought. "Good," he said, "the feeling is mutual." He looked back down at his clipboard and began scribbling something. "This will be our final conversation, anyway."

I blinked at him. Things were running together in my mind like paint. Like too many colors. Hadn't he just told me, sometime in the past 36 hours, that he needed me? Or did this just mean that he, that Cameron, was going to be leaving this...project. Or at least moving to some other aspect of it?

"What about the white limousine?" I asked. It just came out of me, like gas.

His eyes flicked up again, peering over the clipboard, peering over the black rim of his squarish glasses. For some reason, I thought of Daniel.

"What do you know about that?"

"Is it outside right now?"

He cocked his head a couple of degrees and stuck the pen in his mouth. I hated that he chewed on his pen. I hated *him*. I hated Cameron and realized I'd hated him from the first moment I saw him. Back then it had been sheer jealousy. Jealousy and humiliation. Jealousy that he might be that asshole guy with the perfect woman I had just met – the perfect woman in the fuck-you-up-for-life-be-careful-she's-a-witch way, not the marrying kind, you know what I mean. And I had been humiliated that he was my rescuer, that I was in over my head, up the creek with – you get the fuckin' idea. And I...I had just gotten a feeling about him right off. You just know it when you know it. *This guy's a prick – with a capital (but small) "P".*

"No," said Cameron the Prick, "it's not outside right now." He regarded me further like an amusement, like an oddity, like some trinket in an antique shop he couldn't quite figure out but didn't really give two shits about either. No, he regarded me like material in a Petri dish. Or like a malfunctioning toaster. I hated him more than ever. I wanted to kill him. I tried to calm down. This was what he wanted.

"Interesting development, though," he said. "Very interesting." He scribbled something else down. He then clicked his pen a couple of times and said, "When was your last drink, Jack?"

The question sounded like something you'd hear your first day walking into out-patient rehab, precisely what Cameron was attesting he *wasn't* running; I hadn't expected it, and it came like a punch to the gut. At the same time, for the life of me (it was my turn to quizzically cock my head at an angle) I couldn't seem to remember when exactly it had been. Which was strange. The thing a recovering drunk *always* remembers, above all else, is how many days, hell hours, *minutes* it's been since he's had his last drink. That's what I'd always heard. That's how I'd always figured it. That's what I'd always expected because, like I said, on some level I'd always known I'd be that guy chewing the hell out of the red straw and drinking watered-down Cokes.

"Get me my straw and I'll tell you."

"Your straw," said Cameron. He crossed his legs, leaned forward with an elbow on his top knee and tapped the pen to his lower lip. "You like that straw."

"It's my cross-addiction," I said. The bandying was affording me time to formulate some other things. I looked over at Maya again, now lying down, now maybe sedated.

"Okay," said Cameron. He said it in such a chipper way, the prick. He reached into his inner labcoat pocket and pulled it out, baggie and all. He tossed it to the ground in front of me. I quickly undid the zip lock and took the straw out, sniffed it, determined it was okay (it didn't smell like much other than old plastic) and popped it into my mouth.

"All better?"

I nodded. I talked around the straw. "I think it was...a week ago? No. Two weeks ago. At least two weeks ago. Maybe three. Whichever day it was your mom was blowing me."

"That's fine, fine," said the prick doctor, scribbling something.

"And what was that drink?"

Again, total blank. I had nothing. I had a vague idea that I had already given up liquor at an earlier date. At one time my friend – again, we'll call him "Marcel Moresco" – had drawn out the equation to me that vodka equaled me with a bloody mouth multiplied by someone else with a broken nose, as in $v = (bm)(bn)$, or "vee equals boom boom." I'd joked about it, shitfaced at the time on boxed wine with Marcel on the stoop, who, as usual, wasn't drinking at all, but just clicking away at his laptop. I'd cut out the vodka sometime after that. And that was when I was still in Brooklyn. One of the smashmouths. A guy who loaded truck and sometimes spied on people who were selling fake wallets and sometimes, occasionally, took a bat to someone's legs at the Brandis brothers' request. I always took Marcel with me, though. He had the poundage. I just liked to swing the bat. Except with George Klembeck. I'd known something was wrong that time. I'd-

"Three-five? Jack?" Cameron was waving the pen in front of my face. "Stay with me here, guy."

"A beer," I said. "Maybe some vodka." I remembered suddenly rolling around with Peter on the stinking shag carpet of his apartment the night before my job interview in Burlington. I remember how the filth of the place had seemed charming in the drunken gloss of the night, and how the next day I'd realized I was actually two doors down from H-E-double toothpicks, as my gramma would say.

"Beer, vodka," said Cameron, "okay, sounds good." He wrote and then paused. He then scribbled some more, and then he looked at me. He really examined me with his eyes. And he was thinking too, putting something together.

"Do you remember Terry Hackford?"

Terry Hackford, I thought, *is this a trick question?* Cameron had to know that Terry had sprung me from the County Jail. Cameron seemed to know everything else, or at least acted as thought he did. Unsure of how to respond, but going on a hunch, I said, "You mean the soldier I crippled the last time I was here?"

"That was Hackford's brother, John." Cameron continued to really eyeball me. I felt like asking him if he was considering having my babies, but, I didn't. Instead, I asked him, "*Was*? He didn't die because of me, did he?"

Cameron laughed a startling belly-laugh that sounded faker than a department store Santa Claus in White Plains. "No," said Cameron. "But, he dutifully resigned shortly thereafter. He's fine. You don't remember his brother, Terry? Come on, three-five. Tell the truth. Don't make me have to shoot you up with sodium amytal again."

It was odd to me. Very odd. It seemed to make all the sense in the world that Cameron would know about my affiliation with Terry Hackford. Hackford had seemed to know all about Cameron, for one, spouting off about how he was playing God, his delusions of grandeur. I thought of the stray bullet, one possibly meant for me, tearing into Terry's face.

I was really starting to wonder about Terry. To wonder if I had misjudged him. If I had misjudged and then killed him.

Cameron was watching me. I hadn't spoken for a few moments. Likely I had already given myself away.

"Yes," I said, "I remember him."

"That's the spirit," said Cameron. "'Honesty is the first book in the chapter of wisdom,'" he said. I must've looked at him funny because he said, "Thomas Jefferson."

"So," I said, "what about him?"

Cameron looked at me like he was confused. Then the expression dropped and he said, "Oh! Nothing. Nothing for now. Just going down the list."

I looked over at Maya. Still sleeping. Or, drugged.

I thought back to the few first nights in Burlington, back when I thought I was actually here to find out what happened to the Brandis brothers' disappeared – and likely dead – nephew, Phil. Back then I had suspected that, for some reason, I had been sent on a bit of a wild goose chase, but I didn't have a reason. Thirty-six or so hours with Dr. Cameron Madison had changed that, had jogged my memory; I'd seen into the past, lifted what I had so carefully, thoroughly covered.

Offered, Cameron had said back at the veterinarian's place – if that's what it had been. Yes, I had been offered. The Brothers had decided to get rid of me, for years waiting for just the right way, the right time, the perfect payola after I had fucked their Costa Rican operation, likely costing them a lot of time. And money. Blair hadn't only been into internet gambling, no. Here was a guy who'd flourished in everything he'd touched – and everything he *did* touch, including buying into biotechnology, and all sorts of biochemistry patents. You could do that, I'd learned – and why not? If you could patent a living thing, and if you could own it, then you could sell it too. After all, if you were a corporation, and your legal obligation was to make money for your shareholders, what money was there in stagnant ownership? You *sold*. You traded up. You made money. So, you could patent a living thing, you could own a living thing, you could sell a living thing. Blair had sold – thanks to the Brandis muscle. The Brothers were the ultimate fence. And they had brought the product to the Utopia Corporation. Somebody else had patented the technology, not these guys, not Cameron's crew. They had just bought it, and they were the ones crazy enough to start implementing it – a crazy gene mutator, an insane notion of a drug that mutated the genes – each drug prescribed specifically to that individual, tempting them with its promise to heal them of whatever ailment, from addiction to breast cancer to only-child-syndrome. They would take the drug and they would feel better and their genes would be reprogrammed into perfection; while they walked, talked, shopped, ate, shit and slept, they were being "worked on" by a drug. Reprogenetics. Not by God or by natural selection, but by the Utopia Corporation, by Dr. Cameron (prick) Madison. And when they propagated they would pass off the learned genes, the new genes to their children, and the children would have the better trait –

But – wait. When would they be allowed to propagate? Wouldn't that be major? Wouldn't it be that after they had spawned, propagated, copulated, conceived, really, that they would be useless to the Utopia Corporation? What would be the point of giving them any more of the drug, of them getting any "better?" Once they'd had offspring, they would be virtually worthless, expendable…

Was the Utopia Corporation going to attempt to orchestrate breeding as well? Were they going to manipulate when and where and how many kids each one of their subjects had? And when did the offspring – even legally, actually, legally was the horror of it, though I still couldn't quite fathom just *how* it could be permitted – when was the offspring the property of the Utopia Corporation? Would they be extracting zygotes – *embryos* even – right from the uterus of one of their subjects, or would they wait until the child was born to rip it out of the arms of its mother? Like Jared, UVM point guard number forty-three, had just said, what was going on now was only the first step.

And so, it all finally fit. Utopia didn't have the power to control such things.

Corporations were powerful, some of them so influential they *were* the government, but people didn't knowingly vote for corporations. (At least, not in Vermont.) They voted for politicians. They voted for representatives. They believed in government, and did what the government told them, lest they go to prison, lest they disappear off the face of the earth.

The Pharmaceutical Industry. A billion-dollar industry. Rivaling Big Oil. Possibly surpassing Big Oil, what with the war and global warming and all of the uproar. We'd turned and attacked oil, for real. We'd stuck up for ourselves and reclaimed our independence and openly thwarted foreign oil and dependency on fossil fuels – at least, we were getting there. But, drugs. Drugs were a different story.

I saw that Cameron Madison was staring at me. And I saw that he was smiling.

"Fascinating effect, wouldn't you say?"

I didn't know what he was talking about. But then, I did.

"It's a sort of neural disinhibitor. Don't you wish you'd had one of those while studying for university finals?"

"I didn't finish college," I said. It sounded weak and stupid, but anything to separate myself from this man across from me was worth it right now.

"That's right," he said, nodding, "you dropped out of divinity school. Imagine, three-five, *imagine* having that *focus*, imagine having that *clarity*. You, you see," and Cameron tapped a finger to his temple, "you have all of the clues, all of the data up here. People experience so much, we take in so many things. You can walk into a crime scene and take one look around and have all the evidence you'll ever need but never solve the crime."

I opened my mouth, but he waved his pen like a windshield wiper in front of his face.

"Don't take it personally. It's because of how unique you are. You, three-five, you suffer from mental confusion, like so many people do."

I saw people lined up around the corner at the drug store. Mom and Dad wanting to ensure their child's health, longevity and happiness. I saw numbers on their skins, bar codes implanted, shining silver. I saw tanks in the streets. I saw war.

"But you," said Cameron, "you're a little different."

I couldn't resist; I heard it come out of me: "How?"

Cameron tapped the pen against his lips, and smiled. He didn't answer.

"Why do this," I asked, "why give me – whatever you gave me – so that I could see this?"

"I didn't put anything in you that you didn't already have, three-five, like I told you. I just helped you get there a little quicker."

"Like you're going to be helping lots of people 'get there a little quicker'."

"*Think* of it. Think of the productivity, three-five. There are people now who say that the world won't be around in fifty years. That we've fucked it irrevocably. Think of the *dispassion* that creates. Think of the chaos! Think of a world where people figure they had nothing to lose. It's scary, isn't it?"

"It's scary for those in power. For those who gain from our control, our dependencies, the little worker ants."

"Ah, ah, liberal bullshit. Think bigger than your little life, three-five. The bigger picture. Think of the economy. Think of a downward sloping economy. Entropy. *Poof.* Dust. Think of the suffering, the lives lost, the confusion. Now, if we had healthy, *smart* people who could figure things out, who could shape the new world, wouldn't that be a good thing? People go on and on about their freedoms, three-five. Freedom this and freedom that. Everyone wants their freedom. To do what? To stay trapped.

Trapped in their houses, by their televisions, by their fear. Clickety-clacking to each other on the internet, afraid to go out and *live*."

Cameron tossed the clipboard onto the ground and stood up. He put his hands on his hips and started pacing in a circle. I wondered if these people he was talking about looked a lot like what he saw in the mirror each morning in his little fake house on the commune.

"Like I said, three-five, this is our last conversation, so we're going to have to cut to the quick. There are big things in store for you, three-five, *big* things. You should be grateful."

"But it's not my *choice*," I said. "That's the freedom these 'people' are talking about, Cameron."

Cameron stopped pacing and just looked at me, and his grin returned. It was a Cheshire cat grin, a horrible thing to watch. It was like witnessing black ink spill slowly across a table, or poison ivy growing up and into a child's window.

I closed my eyes in the face of it. I saw a blankness. A blank screen. I saw:

Operating System Not Found

And a blinking cursor beneath it.

I typed: "The Utopia Corporation purchases the patent to this revolutionary gene mutation technology from a fence. That fence is the Brandis brothers, who bought it from Calvin Blair. Or, stole it really. Kidnapped him and ransomed him for it, thanks to a crazy Latino named Wild Dick."

I opened my eyes.

Cameron kept smiling at me. The smile said, *go on.* And I did. In my brain. Whatever drug Cameron had given me was working like a champ. Like a running-back on cocaine. On cocaine, but perfectly sane. Sane.

The Brandis brothers.

Calvin Blair – playboy, entrepreneur.

Where did Blair get the patent from? I still didn't know who had originally developed the technology, or why. Scientists at a University? Like UVM? MIT? A privately funded group? But funded by whom? And what did Terry Hackford have to do with it? He seemed to be trying to stop it all, using Maya to infiltrate, trying to bring it down somehow. A crusade against God-playing. Against a New World Order. Or was there something else? Why did my mind seem to snag there, that I was missing something, one final, crucial thing? I had the equation. V equaled BM times BN. What was missing?

And my mind seemed to pounce, only in a different direction, for just now – just how *did* one move something, some sort of product, like gene mutating technology? Not something from the loading dock that you just shipped off in a crate. Not something that you just sent over the computer. Or wrote down on a cocktail napkin and slid across the bar. I mean, there were formulas and stuff, real equations and shit, but, really, how did you move something like –

Baradez.

It was just a name. A contact for the Brandis brothers. Some guy who'd found me drunk in a small village outside of *Siquirres.* Crying into my tequila about Julianne. Then I'd blacked out there for a while, and he put me on a plane home.

I thought of waking up on the banks of Lake Champlain. My eyes opened again. Madison was grinning positively ear-to-ear.

"Getting there?"

I glanced past him to look at Maya once more. She was still lying on her back and I couldn't see her face. There was a doctor beside her now, doing something to her.

And where was Jared?

"Focus, Jack. I can see you drifting again. What I gave you is something like Ritalin, only much more powerful. You have to be careful, because if you go off too far in one direction, start bouncing around on tangents, you might never come back. We might never find you again."

"So focus me," I said, looking into the flat blue of his eyes behind the reflective lenses. "Ground me."

"Well," he said, "we'll have to go backwards a little. Just a little, before we can go forward one final time. But, I think you already got the important part. I could see you working it out."

"About the patent," I said, "about the technology."

"Yes," he said.

"And how it was sold," I said, "how it was moved from Blair through the Brandis brothers to you and your corporation."

"Exactly."

I blinked once, I remember that. For some reason I thought of Les, the guy in the cemetery with me and Peter.

"Me," I said to the grand prick Dr. Cameron Madison. "The way the technology was moved was…through me. I'm it."

And Cameron Madison grinned so wide I thought his face could shatter.

*

I never had an off switch. I'd never been able to stop myself, to shut myself
off. I would go to the clubs in Manhattan – the one in the old church on
Sixth and 14th was my favorite – and I would just go and go and go. I
would feel tired, but I wouldn't stop. I couldn't stop. I would feel drunk,
but I wouldn't stop. I would be seeing pig faces and angels and the stained
glass windows would melt into the face of Christ, but I couldn't stop.

Horus. He was a guy in Egypt in 3000 BC. He was born on
December the 25th, so the story goes. Of a virgin. His birth attended by
three kings. It all has to do with astrology. The constellation Virgo. The
Virgin. Virgin technology.

It's the sun. It's always been the sun. Heliolatry, the first religion.
Worship of the sun. Now we call it the sun and science says it's a star but
we still don't know what a sun or star is. They're just names. It's no
wonder they're worshipped.

Marcel had a kid. A little boy. Marcel was fat, sorry, but, yeah. And
for some reason fat people seem to make good parents. They're so cozy
with their kids. Whip-thin people running around bug-eyed and neurotic
from the gym to the Starbucks, they're no good as parents. When you see on
TV the nice family in Nebraska who made the news because of how many
kids they foster, like, little darling African kids and Asian kids and retarded
kids, they're huge people. Literally.

Marcel's kid was sitting on his lap one day, one night – one of the few
nights I can remember with Marcel when he wasn't out on the stoop,
smoking his menthols and drinking Diet Cokes – that we were inside
together. We were watching TV. His little boy, almost three at the time,

Jocelyn (which I always thought was a girl's name, but never dared to say, and not just because of how big Marcel was – I'd knocked guys out his size before – but because Marcel was very much like family to me at the time, and that's what family often does together – watches TV, because they're too fucked up to tell one another how much they love each other, how much love bursts forth from them), well, Jocelyn would ask about everything on the TV. We were watching some Discovery Channel thing. (Marcel's wife, Angela, was always out, and always looking like she was sleepy, or bored, or fucked up, or had just gotten fucked. She was skinny. Marcel was the source-parent, I thought of him.) Anyway, Jocelyn would point at the TV say "What's that?" And Marcel would say, "That's a tiger sleeping." And Jocelyn would say, "Tiger sleeping? What's that mean?" And Marcel would offer some explanation about sleep, and sip his Diet Coke, and shift Jocelyn around on his big, reclined belly, and I would be thinking, what a smart kid. What the hell does "a tiger sleeping" mean? What does "sleep" mean? We call it sleep – so what? We have no fucking idea what it's about. So, you get my drift. Gravity, dark matter, parallel dimensions, we don't know.

Attis was another guy. From Greece. 1200 BC, I think. Same deal with Attis. He was born on December 25th to a virgin and blah blah blah.

Mithra, in Persia, about the same time.

Krishna, in India, 900BC. Horus had been betrayed by Typhon, I think. They all performed miracles. Most, if not all (I wasn't there, personally) had, like, 12 disciples. They were killed, maybe crucified, and dead three days.

Dionysus, In 500 BC Greece, was called "the King of Kings."

They were baptized, to some extent or another. They were
prophesized. They were oraculated and then ostracized. They taught and
spread the word around age twelve.

Twelve. It all has to do with astrology. With the earth spinning.
With the sun's "death" – the sun at its lowest in these places around the 25th
of December. The constellation Virgo in the sky. The 12 signs of the
Zodiac.

Anyway, I know all this. I knew all this then – I went to school for it.
I knew it, but it didn't matter. It was like Maya had said – why did one have
to preclude the other? I mean, just because Jesus Christ isn't anything new,
like, in, the whole legacy of those before him, so what? When I'd be all
revved-up and wadded-out and couldn't stop and I'd be at the club that was
the old church, I'd see him in the stained glass, and I'd fall down – I did this
at least once, anyway – and start to cry. So what? What does it mean? That
I was secretly in love with the sun and stultified by the darkness of night,
only to attempt to overcome it by dance, drug and drink? That I knew there
was something evil in me, something "dark," and I wished for some "light"
to set it free? That Jesus Christ really did die on the cross for my sins? I
didn't know. I didn't know and don't know what you know, old friend, or
what's happened to you, but I saw him in that club, I saw him that one late
night, his face in the glass, and then I saw him everywhere, and everyone in
the place was dressed in those old robes and shit, and the next day, riding
back to Brooklyn in the cab I took from Moe's apartment near Union Square
(remember Moe with his damned Chihuahuas?). I looked out of the back
window as we drove and everything was so silent, even the noise was silent,
and so *one*, man, the silence was all this *one fucking sound*, and nothing was
different from anything else, only variant, and every face I saw, man…I

started to cry in the back of that cab. They were all the same faces – only variant – they were all the face of God.

Maybe that's what they had been trying to do. Maybe the people I eventually found out were the original engineers behind the whole technology, maybe they were trying for something good, right? I know, I know, "best intentions" and all, but, I want to think so. I want to believe so. I want to believe that what they were trying to do was something *co-creative* with the divine, something divinely inspired, anyway, and not for money, not for control, not bad things. Not for evil. That's the way it's got be looked at.

At least for me.

I blame my gramma, God bless her, with those nylons falling down her legs as she rocked in her chair and spoke to me, my little-big Italian gramma, with all of the scars of the years on her heart, and the belief in Christ there, inside that scarred heart, and me, the rogue. The bastard I was.

But, like I said. I've never had an off switch. And that was often a problem, I guess. I'd stay out late nights talking to bums, deliberately ignoring the smashmouths and talking to the bums. I'd get their story and then get their truth. And we'd laugh. We'd have a good time.

These guys that come up to you with their stories; they're hurting.

*

Les...why was I thinking of that old coot? Les with the flat face and horsy teeth. Why would Les pop into my mind at a time – in a place – like this?

Because of what he told me.

What? I almost said aloud. What did he tell me?

But then I remembered. We had been in the cemetery, trimming the shrubbery, scraping lichen from the stones, raking the windblown detritus. Me and Peter. And Les. Les had told us about the thing he'd heard, the commune. It was Les who had tipped us in that direction.

"Nothing is ever really what it seems," said Cameron Madison, tapping the syringe with his fingernail.

I was now in restraints.

"These plans," I said, and licked my lips. It felt like there was some sort of waxy chalk there, on my lips, stuff I pictured to look bluish-white. "These plans you say you have in store for me..."

Cameron brought the needle to my arm. He poked around and found a vein.

"Not to worry," he said. I stared at him. Anyone, I thought, who looked like some punk-hiphop hybrid like Cameron did, and then talked like some stuffy professor of philosophy in a tweed coat didn't deserve much time on the planet, as far as I was concerned. That and the fact I doubted Cameron Madison's love of and desire to protect humanity's best interests, if you can blame me.

I tensed and jerked my arm away from the needle. I strained against the straps across my chest and arms and legs.

"Now three-five," said the grand prick. "We've been over this."

All this time I'd been wondering, worrying – yes – I'd been worrying, call me human – that I was a liability to these people, that I was a threat and a nuisance. That I was operating outside of their system and that was dangerous. Yet, they'd just given me the keys to the kingdom. I thought: *thank you Les, you flat-headed homely old fuckstick. Thank you, truly.*

"Have we?" I locked eyes with Cameron, who glanced up from where he was trying to stick that needle in my jittering arm. "Then how come you got me strapped down here like you do to your mom?"

"You did the mom joke already. Hold still," said Cameron.

He looked back at my arm, trying to puncture it. I looked over his head. There was a soldier standing inside of the room with us, next to the door. The whole place was made of sheet metal. We were still in the barracks, tucked away in one of a couple of cubicles within the tube-like structure. There was a chance I could still get to Maya. And Jared.

"I can't let you do what you're going to do to me, Cameron. Maybe not just yet."

Cameron stopped moving. So did I – I stopped arching my back and pulling away from him as best I could and relaxed for a moment.

"What are you talking about?"

"You're a real manipulator, Cameron, but I guess that's stating the obvious." My eyes flicked to the soldier at the door. I wondered, weirdly, in that moment, how much he cared, or didn't care, or knew, or didn't know, about what was going on here. I thought of Mike, the FPR guy. It seemed as though all sorts of folks from my recent past were springing up to say hello; a phantoms' reunion. And I felt a pang of something like remorse, in some chamber of my heart; so much I'd missed in my life, all that was right there in the present, missed because I was barreling through for the future, looking over my shoulder for the pursuing demons, tucking into the run at the onrushing train – speeding toward it to get the whole damned thing over with.

My mother, singing, sitting by the window in Fort Greene. Her red hair.

My father, his tall, hunched posture, tight black hair (that he was always scratching, for some reason, and my gramma would swat his hand away from his head) with his wide eyes in the stairwell, where he sometimes hid. That runnel of blood coming out of his nose that had signaled the beginning of the end.

My mother, her voice lingering like a ghost in the apartment long after she'd disappeared.

"It's like you're banking on me to be stupid, Cameron. And I can't blame you too much – I haven't been the best example of a sleuth. But buttering me up – diverting me with the superthink magic of your drugs, here – that's almost painful. That's just mean. You prick son of a bitch."

Cameron's face – wherein I had seen, and cherished, a moment of fear when I'd first began my little sermon – now remolded to its detached, arrogant pate once again, and he looked back at my arm. "Jack. You know I don't think you're stupid."

"Sometimes," I said, feeling the cold tip of the needle prick my skin, "yeah. Sometimes I'm the guy – lots of us are – that looks into the fridge going 'where's the milk?' I admit it."

Cameron laughed – he *actually* laughed this time, like a through-his-nose kind of laugh, and I saw his shoulders hitch once with that snorfle-laugh, and felt the needle leave my skin, and I made my move. I knew it was the last chance, the last time I was going to be making such a move in our little dance – one of those things you just felt intuitively, you just knew, without any reason other than maybe because it'd all happened before, or that it was all a sphere, not a contiguous line, but circular, spherical, and at any given moment you could touch another moment, no matter what the time, or the place, you could touch it. I sort of touched my ending then, and knew that this was the last time I was going to escape, the last time I was going to be "given" the chance to run. I knew it, because I knew what I was going to do.

And I knew that time was truly running out. Cameron hadn't come right out and said it – it would have potentially been humiliating to him, to admit any sort of subordination on his part – but guys like Cameron, though they might have been be top in their fields, they might've been be top in their own minds, wielding their powers of science something like mad children with sparkling fireworks; there was always someone behind them, because they always needed money. There was always someone behind them, behind the curtain, in the dark, pulling the lever back on the cash machine.

In this case, I knew who that was. I knew who *they* were. And I knew how to get them. Part of them, anyhow. It was all I had to work with; I hoped it would be enough.

The straps came off easily, insofar as restraints go, anyway. I was sure, though, that if Cameron had managed to stick me that whatever was in that syringe was meant to ensure that the backlash effect the gene mutation drugs had on me – the ridiculous rage-driven strength I seemed to be allowed when I dosed myself with a good deluge of adrenaline – that I wouldn't have been able to. He was about to counter the effect, I was pretty sure. Just an armchair-mad-scientist myself, but I was learning quickly now.

The straps popped as every muscle in my body hardened to a kind of vibrating rock, and one of the brown belts actually slapped Cameron's head, and he cried out. The soldier was moving right away (I silently applauded him, I don't know why – maybe it was Marcel's constant campaign of *Support the Troops* that had been driven into my skull – no matter what the war, support the troops), but I was going to take care of him first anyway.

I sprang from the gurney and the soldier's gun swung down and took aim on me.

I was sure he had orders not to shoot me. That was the game now – that's what it always had been, back when I was first here sitting across from the desk of five of the mad doctor fucks – that's how I'd escaped. I was product. And not only that, I was *prototype*. I was the patent, the thing, the impetus by which all others like me would be made, codified, cultivated.

Still, the business end of that gun swung down as the soldier took a step forward and I saw his finger – through the trigger loop – snap the safety off and then come back to rest on the trigger. I was there, though, and I swatted the barrel out of the way with my left forearm and with my right arm extended, palm out, headed through the line, I hit him square in the chest.

With the step or two he'd taken towards me as he'd brought the gun down to firing position, the soldier had moved in front of the door. Now he smashed right out through it as I rammed into him and his firearm, knocked loose from his grip, hit the ground.

The gun went off. The sound of it was spectacularly loud, echoing in the cavernous sheet metal of the building. It spun on the cold hard, sleek floor, spraying its deadly spit.

In the meantime, I stopped myself from falling through the door after the soldier, catching the door jamb with the hand that had deflected the rifle barrel's aim, and spun back around in time to see Cameron, holding his head where the belt had smacked him, still holding the needle with his other hand, that white smock on, the clipboard resting on the concrete floor, just standing there, with those bright red roses of blood on his white, starched pant legs, and then he slumped to the ground.

There would be more armed soldiers here any second. I walked across the room to Cameron. He was gripping one leg around the shin with both of his hands and gritting his teeth.

"Fuck," he said. "It's the tibial artery, it's a major artery, we need to pinch off the flow of blood, slow the bleeding."

I stood there, looking down at him. He was in a fetal position of a kind, lying there. I didn't have much time. Cameron opened his squinted-shut eyes and looked up at me.

"No," he said. "No. You'll just be a monster, Jack. That's all you'll be. What would your father think?"

My decision to do what came next was quick, sudden, in the span of a few breaths as I stood looking down at him. I knew it could be a deal breaker, but they'd pin the shooting on me anyway. Cameron was chief guy on this. It was his baby, regardless of who'd begun it. If I did this I could go back to the "other side", back to where I'd thought I'd been anyway; naïve enough to believe that Les telling Peter and me about the commune was a lucky break, that I was some sort of independent, free-roaming variable, that I was autonomous, and, if anything, that I was beholden to the Brandis brothers for a job, nothing more.

His mouth was still open, Cameron's was, ready to spew more propaganda, more coercion, more priggish, prickish Cameron crap. But, in the end, I think I did it out of mercy.

As I turned and bent and picked up the soldier's rifle – and this is completely true, I'm telling you – my whole being left the present for a moment and I was in Brooklyn again, on Prospect Ave, hitting George Klembeck in the mouth under the moon near the purple trees, Victor and Ryan egging me on.

I came to and was standing over Cameron. Blood was pooling all around and under him. He couldn't walk; I couldn't take him hostage. But, I didn't need to. His eyes fluttered and he glared at me. I saw incomprehension there, anger, and a childlike frustration. Some other kid at the beach was messing with his sand castle.

But, like my father had said to me once, you do most of the work and then something else gets in there and takes you the rest of the way, or doesn't. That's how you know when something is meant to be.

Support the troops, I thought, *no matter what the war.*

"Don't," said Cameron. He held his hand up, palm out.

I vowed never to kill again. I pulled the trigger.

I left the room and I walked down the corridor between other cubicles like it. I had the rifle, but I carried it so that it pointed to the side.

I heard the footfalls of many boots before I got to the end of the corridor and stood at the edge of the main room with all of the cots. Soldiers were there, a phalanx of them dropping to one knee and taking aim, others coming in from the outside, stopping in various places to take firing position. I heard many firearms cock, and felt the beads all over me, like leeches on the skin.

"Don't!" The doctor – I recognized him now, Dr. Pembrose, came run-shuffling out between me and the soldiers, waving his arms. I could tell he was afraid of getting shot himself, and I give the son of a bitch credit for what he did. He put himself between me and them, only a few feet away, his arms out like that, his palms facing them, and he yelled, "don't shoot! That's an order!"

I wondered if he had the kind of authority to back up a command like that, and I found I wasn't overly concerned. The soldiers would have been briefed. If there was one thing a soldier knew it was his target, and he knew whether he had authorization or not. He may not have understood the war, or knew when he was going to go home, but he knew when he could fire, and he knew when he couldn't. I'd gambled, and this time I'd hit for 21.

I took a couple of steps forward and slid my hand over the good doctor's shoulder, and leaned forward to speak into his ear.

"Tell me where he is," I said.

"Who?"

I watched the soldiers. I looked and saw Maya, sedated or not, sitting up and looking at me. There were three new inmates as well, and another doctor, the red-haired Moritz, she presided over one of them. That one, lying there, he might have been Daniel, but I didn't have the time to find out.

"You know who," I said.

"He's not here," said Pembrose.

"Yes he *isssss*," I hissed into his ear. "Now walk."

I pushed forward and spurred Pembrose to move. I didn't point the gun at him, I just kept him going, my arm slung over his chest like that, my hand over his heart. I glanced at Maya once more as we moved through the soldiers. I smiled at her, and she smiled back. It was a sad, worried smile, but it would do.

"I need a radio," I said to the soldiers, and I looked down at one of them, still on his knee, following me with the sights of his rifle. "Give me your radio," I said. He looked at the soldier next to him, then looked down and removed the radio from his belt. He slid it across the floor to me.

"Pick it up," I said to Pembrose. He squatted and I went down with him, just in case, just to keep close. He picked it up and held it up over his shoulder, to hand it to me.

"Hold onto it for now, doc," I said. I urged him forward again, and turned us, so that we backed away, and out of the barracks, and back into freedom.

Or, at least, choice.

Sometime later, it started to rain. I noticed I still had a restraining belt wrapped around my left thigh. I decided to leave it on.

I kicked through the leaves. I'd been expecting, at least, to hear an alarm – a siren, like an air raid *waaaaaaa* – but there was nothing. The building I escaped from had been near the edge of the clearing where the Utopia commune squatted, one of the last buildings before the woods were reclaimed. As the rain pattered down on those colorful early-autumn leaves, and the day grew thick and grey around me, I had ducked into those woods.

I was compelled to see my daughter. It had been long enough. I had to see her, touch her, hold her – she needed to know her father. I had no illusions of becoming her *daddy*, that time had come and gone; the water was spoiled. Now, well, now let's just say I had even more reason to get to her.

As I pushed through the branches and walked over rotted trees and around the stones I thought of who, if anyone, could have talked about my daughter, who had known. Who had I told about her? Marcel. He was the only one. He could have been leaned on by the Brandis brothers – he was my good friend, but he had Jocelyn, a kid of his own. But one of the Brothers' muscle-guys, Grey Frank, he could have been standing there in Marcel's living room with that tiny little jackknife he always carried around, the thing stuck up one of Jocelyn's nostrils, just a little, while Marcel, on his knees, fat face slick with sweat and tears, could have talked – all this while I'd been taking a piss somewhere, or sleeping, or in one of these drug-induced, gene mutator side effect narco-fugues. It was likely. Hell, it was more than likely. Don't think I didn't consider that; don't think I didn't worry about Marcel's own pain, about that beautiful little boy of his. And as I pushed through the thickness of the forest, the rust-colored, dead ferns soaking my ankles, the evergreens – the small spruces, firs (I was learning) – caressing my arms, wetting and welcoming – I realized that if they knew about my daughter, about Katherine, that I could be walking into a trap – going from one cage to the next. I did. I knew somebody could be there right now in Bondville, there in Katherine's house waiting for me, reading magazines and drinking pop while my daughter asked kid-innocent questions and Katherine paced and worried until the heavy said "siddown" real authoritatively and my daughter started to cry.

I was thirsty. I had been moving through the woods for a good hour. I had heard no siren, no hounds at my heels. The silence wasn't discomforting, though it would have been otherwise; I knew they had other recourse than to chase after me through the sogging woods.

I was soaked, but my skin wasn't drinking. I took a maple leaf and made a cup out of it. I shook a branch or three of a man-height spruce and glistening drops pattered into the leaf, forming a little puddle. I drank from it.

I got moving again.

Night was going to be falling soon and I had nothing to put on over the lightweight, white in-patient clothing from Utopia – now besmeared green and brown in streaky places and soaking wet. It was apt to get cold soon, and I would be cold. I was no survivalist; I was a kid from brick and mortar. Drinking rainwater from a leaf was about as Daniel Boone as I got.

I'd seen some litter along the way – a faded, dented Budweiser can, a trio of Labatt Blue bottles that'd reminded me of three drunken bums leaning together for support – a ripped open bag of Wise potato chips, it too faded, now containing pine needles and leaves instead – and I had been somewhat encouraged. But I had learned a few things during my time here in the Green Mountain State. It wasn't like Prospect Park, where, yeah, you found beer bottles (and sometimes other things) tossed apathetically into the underbrush. There was still litter here in these Vermont woods – obviously

– but that didn't mean Wellhouse Drive was only a few hundred feet away, like it did in the park. What I mean is, these Vermonters took their littering seriously – they'd go miles deep into the wild to do it.

It was like that with any place, though. Well, I was a New Yorker, so you'd know that, statistically, I would have never been anywhere else, and aside from Costa Rica and Jersey, and you'd be correct – New Yorkers typically harbored an emotion somewhere between fear and loathing for the rest of the world (unless it was Long Island) – but I could intuit, and, what's more, I'd heard stories, I'd read the news. Most places, sure, come on, purported to be this perfect place. If they wanted the tourism draw, especially. And you'd get to these places and, yeah, on the surface, they'd be pretty sparkling-bells-tinkling. But you'd only have to peek under the tablecloth, just step one foot off of the beaten path – say, the railroad tracks just outside an otherwise pristine little mountain village – to see the folly. Human pigs. Or the crime just behind the pearly-toothed smile of things. Or the depression. The Goth kids cutting themselves and getting tattoos on their privates and on their faces – Christ, their tongues; I'd heard of it. It wasn't just the suburbs. People always picked on the suburbs, where looks were supposed to be everything and behind closed doors everyone was a drugged-out closet psychopath. I'm not saying wasn't true. Living in the suburbs was the closest thing to living in a petting zoo, my friend Coma told me. (We called him Coma on account of how thin and pale he was, and how much drugs he did.) You were both the ogler of the animals and the animal ogled, he'd said, and you did things like animals in captivity did. You masturbated. You formed homosexual pair-bonds. You coveted what the other animals had. This was what Coma told me, anyway. He was a pretty far-out-there kid for a suburbanite – one of the only Westchester kids who could come around my neighborhood, all ganglia and freckles on pale pink skin he was, and not get the shit kicked out of him, just get roasted pretty good by the neighborhood kids.

The wind started to kick through the trees as I walked, weaving my ways as best I could to avoid heavy brambles and tangles and stick to a hardwood path. My shirt was torn in a couple of places. It felt like the temperature was dropping a degree a minute, and it was definitely getting darker. I wasn't scared, not of having to fend for myself out here in the night, but that I might eventually have to sleep, and if I did, I could be vulnerable. My shoulder ached constantly, and my ribs felt like hot, shifting ropes; the last of the pain killers were wearing off. I suddenly craved a cigarette, and realized, like the drinking, I couldn't quite remember the last time I'd partaken.

It was getting cold and dark, and I was hungry and thirsty and in pain. If I didn't get somewhere soon, I'd have to camp it out here in the sticks where I'd be vulnerable to capture, not to mention pneumonia. My father had pneumonia – that's what got him in the end, did you know that? Some freaking rare kind, something like "walking pneumonia", which just sounded as horrible to me as it was, making me think of some sort of zombie, some kind of creature, spindly and thin, thinner than ole Coma, lurching slowly and stiffly around, killing whatever smelled it, whatever breathed it in.

I saw lights. Or thought I did. I stopped. Some old farm house? It had been there for a minute, I was sure, a yellowish light not too far away through the trees, like a lamppost at the end of a ranch house driveway, or a lantern in a cottage window. I stretched up onto my tiptoes, leaning from side to side, peering, and then lowered myself down, slowly, into a squat. Nothing. It must have b-

Then a noise. The snap of a twig. What else? The shush of pine boughs over clothing. Not a farmhouse, then, or a cottage. A person. Someone with a flashlight.

I remained where I was, still, though my body did what it had been doing ever since that night in the UVM lab room with Maya – it clicked on, like a boiler gunning to life in the basement when someone upstairs dialed-up the thermostat. Only I wasn't dialing up any thermostat when it happened. Madison said I could do it voluntarily, but it certainly didn't feel that way; it still felt like I had little-to-no control over it. And maybe that was why the other drugs. Maybe that was how Cameron had been perfecting me. He'd been the optimist, sure – it was *his* baby, after all – telling me that I could turn it on or off at will (*or had I been telling* myself *that? Things could get easily convoluted with this whole mutation thing,* haha) while all the while he was still working on me – a living experiment. Giving me the drugs that were the prototypes to spring on the public. Drugs acting as the enzymes needed to catalyze the mutating genes, and to stabilize them. Drugs to turn the subjects, from generation to generation, into the perfect, flawless beings. The true children of Utopia. Back to the Garden, if you will, back to a sinless existence.

There was another noise. Closer. It was amazing how in the gloaming of the forest, and the quiet of it – the half-asleep drizzle of the rain, the occasional chittering of a squirrel – how in the immense quiet there was so much clarity about the body, about thoughts. I was reminded of my first time in the woods, so recent yet so long ago. In Brooklyn you didn't have to think, if you didn't want to. There was a distraction around every corner. But now, now I could feel my body – I can't emphasize it enough – I could *feel* my blood rushing, actually sense and picture and hear the tumbling of it

through the canals of my veins, right down to the molecular level, these little
red blood cells all tumbling along, purposeful, self-sacrificing. Little
warriors. I thought of my first trip into the woods with Peter, ages ago.

A chorus in my ears, the blood, the adrenaline, the endorphins. Like
the cicadas in the trees. Not so much the high-whine of tinnitus, but more a
concert hum – all of the strings getting in tune with one another, singing out
like that, making that perfect *one* noise that was so captivating, that had
spellbound me like the orchestral music my father sometimes played on the
turntable. The music in my ears was that harmony. I was entirely unafraid.
I felt more curious than anything – more than likely whoever they were,
they'd seen me, and they'd shut the light off once I'd been spotted. But how
did they expect to creep in on me without my hearing? Maybe they figured it
didn't matter; there was nowhere for me to go.

I felt a sudden twinge of regret for Cameron Madison. I had to admit
it. I had him to thank, in a way, for how I felt right now. A knee-jittering,
nervous wreck of a livewire I'd been just a few weeks ago. A bumbling
idiot. Now I felt like one of Coma's animals, only I wasn't in a zoo, I was
free.

Still, squatting there in that last second or so, I had another one of
those crisp, clear, shapely feelings – a feeling that was more like a living
presence than a thought – I was going to pay for Cameron's death. I'd
already known it, known it when I'd been standing over him with the
soldier's rifle (one that now was in better hands than mine) but the feeling
now was something like a response to that premature enlightenment. Maybe
it was my gramma's influence, her fear of sin – and of *killing* being chief
among them, go figure – but you could concur if you were a Buddhist, a

Taoist, a Hindu, a secular humanist; shit came back around and bit you in the old padded seat, did it not?

I sprang, then. This was the other thing that I've told you about that'd been happening: I just did things, things where instinct seemed to eclipse – or outpace – any sort of intellectual planning, any rational deduction. Pain once again forgotten, I leapt up onto the birch tree in front of me and scrambled and caught the small but tensile branches in my grip and hauled my body up, got my feet onto the branches and continued to climb like this.

The light flipped back on – I'd known it would. Closer, very close. It had been the size of a glint in an iris to me moments ago, and now it was as big as the moon over the Manhattan cityscape.

"Hey! Hey, it's me!"

I stopped climbing. I thought I might recognize the voice. In fact, from as far away as we were from one another, I thought I might even be able to detect the odor.

"Peter?"

"Yeah! Yeah. Hey – what're you doing?"

I had to think for a moment. My body was still thrumming, but it had topped-out at the sound of Peter's voice and now things were decelerating. "Climbing this tree," I said.

"Well, come on down!"

His voice was a whispered holler. He moved through the woods less carefully now, things scraping and cracking. I maneuvered back down the tree – admittedly a little *more* carefully then I had climbed it. I could feel myself scowling in the near-dark. I could almost make Peter's figure out behind the halo of flashlight. "How the hell did you find me?" I suddenly felt the hairs rise on the nape of my neck. The fluids in me threatened to surge again. For now, it was a kind of readiness-equilibrium. Hypervigilance, you might say; this could be a fucking trap. I could have just given myself over to yet another crafted move executed by our friendly Utopia Corporation neo-Nazi-types.

"On the radio," said Peter, holding up a dinosaur of a two-way radio in his hand. He was positively loping now. And, then, boom, he tripped and fell face down, not twenty feet from me. My suspicion, my alert, vanished. This was Peter. Dreadlocks and all, Peter. A bit stinky, Peter. Maybe-his-elevator-didn't-go-all-the-way-to-the-top-floor, Peter. At any rate, a guy who, for some reason I felt, wasn't apt to betray me, no matter what they threw at him. Not even for the 30 pieces of silver from Sanhedrin. Then again, Judas had thought that Jesus would get a "fair trial." I thought of Watson, and Crick, and beating them into the dirt beneath rows upon rows of corn.

I shook the thought as I freed myself the rest of the way from the tree. Peter had been contacted in the way I had planned. My wariness was warranted, I allowed myself – but, if we didn't have the faith to follow through with what we ourselves had initiated – what good were we? What good was anybody?

Peter got to his feet, as I got to mine, the pains already starting to return. I felt a smile try to push my cheeks back, and fought it, lips quivering a little. Peter had leaves sticking out of his hair. My first disciple looked something like Pan getting up from a late day nap after a little too much dram.

"Hey, it's good to see you, man," he said. Peter resumed walking and threw his bare arms around me. He was wearing a cut-off t-shirt, bright red, it must've been, though in the dusk it appeared purple, with a picture of Che

Guevara on the front of it. The aroma coming from Peter's pits wafted freely with the hug.

I pushed Peter off of me. "Good to see you to man. I didn't expect to, but it's good. Who sprung you from the hospital?"

"Wendy," said Peter, his eyes excitedly wide and white in the dripping, dimming forest. "She's sort of the head chick of the Naturalist party. After I got sewn up at the hospital–" and he stopped, looking me up and down. I searched for a hint of blame in Peter's eyes, and he said, "Holy shit! Are you shot too?"

I nodded, touching my shoulder.

"Holy shit," he said again, "that's kind of awesome." His eyes returned to mine, and I saw no blame in them, only kinship and excitation. "Yeah, so, she came and explained to me that she knew who you were, and that she wanted to help and shit, and…she gave me a job, man! I'm a perimeter scout."

"That's great, Peter. Those your bottles and chips I saw a ways back? He looked confused.

"Never mind," I said. "It's good to see you."

He started to open his mouth again, no doubt to jabber on more about his adventures, his new job, when he looked me over again. "We need to get you to the camp; you look like shit, man." So classy, this kid. I wondered if he'd ever, in his life, washed before dinner. I loved him.

"Here," Peter said, and handed me the flashlight. I kept it on, but pointed at the ground. Peter reached into his pants pocket, I saw, and pulled out a cell phone. He flipped it open and started punching numbers that sounded alien in the now-dark. The phone glowed. I gaped at it. "You get service out here?"

"Yeah," Peter said, "they just put up a tower not too long ago." He put the phone to his ear.

"Wendy," he said, "yeah, I got him. Okay. I'll meet you there." Peter talked like a kid talking to a buddy on the other end of a tin-can-and-string phone. He snapped the cell shut. I could still see the whites of his eyes, faintly glowing. "They're going to war," he said. "I mean, it's crazy. They're going to try and take down Utopia."

I didn't say anything.

"Jack?"

I realized I was staring at the ellipse of light thrown by the flashlight. It illuminated a rotted log, moss covered, and there was a slug there, glistening. I moved the light away from it, still keeping it down.

"Okay," I said. "Let's go."

I could feel Peter's grin in the dark forest. He reached for the flashlight. I hesitated, and in that moment, a whole other life bloomed and stretched out before me. Another path. At the beginning of that world, I said, "I'm sorry Peter, I do love you man, and am glad you came for me," and then hit him with the flashlight – a decently heavy *Maglite* – and knocked him out. I then fished around in his pockets, got the cell phone, and ran. I called the last number Peter had dialed as I ran. "Wendy," I panted, as I bulled through the trees and bushes, "this is X. I have incapacitated Peter." I described to Wendy where he was, so that they could locate him. I told her that if anyone tried to follow me, I would kill. I would kill anyone in my way.

"Here," is what I actually said. Because it wouldn't be right. Now was the time to continue and play ball. To go with the flow. I'd stopped running that day on the Honda Shadow, I could stop running now. I could follow through with the grander scheme.

I could do that, I thought. I could.

Peter turned and loped off into the blackness, his light bobbing in front of him. I followed.

"Wendy" was not as I'd pictured. Why do we do things like that, I wondered, standing there in front of her for the first time – why do we form images of things we've never seen? On what basis? Admittedly, yeah, I thought of a red-headed girl with Pollyanna pigtails. Thanks to you, fast-food-corporate America. But Wendy didn't look that way at all. She was heavier, for one, brunette and dark-eyed for another.

"Hello, Jack," she said, taking my hand, not to shake it, but just to hold it for a moment, "I'm Wendy." She glanced at Peter, standing there next to me, looking like a proud boy scout receiving a merit badge. Wendy had a British accent. I could smell a flower-like scent from her, one of those flower-patchouli smells, something like fauna kept in a closet, plants kept under a special light in closed-corridors. "Glad you could make it," she said.

"Thank you," I said. "I just need to make one phone call."

*

I couldn't remember the last time I'd eaten. That seemed to have become a theme with me. I told Wendy this – about being hungry, not about my personal themes – and she seemed happy to oblige. I sat down to a one hundred percent vegan meal. I was so hungry I didn't care. Yeah, I'd pictured a big, hefty, juicy burger, fat dripping, pink inside, loaded with gooey, heart-stopping cheese, but the avocado sandwich with sprouts and soy-cheese-product was perfectly acceptable. It took me four bites to finish, and I was offered more food. Some kind of small nuts. Carrots. Multi-grain bread and non-dairy butter. Whole wheat pasta and organic tomato sauce. I ate it all with the same gusto as though it were fried chicken and cornbread from the corner of Fort Greene Place and Atlantic Avenue.

I was in a room like a greenhouse. Surrounding us, flora and fauna of all manner, tufting from pots, dangling in garlands from the latticework, sprouting from long banks of greenery. I was seated at the head of a table that was long enough to make me feel like royalty. Wendy sat on my right, and various Naturalists sat around, eating, watching me while I ate. There was a young blonde with a cluster of freckles high on each cheek and sprinkled atop her upper breasts who more appropriately fit the Pollyanna picture. There were women and then there were men, each dressed in slightly variant versions of Farmer in the Dell clothing: overalls, checkered shirts, sandals on their feet. There were persons of African American descent, Asian descent, Caucasian, Middle Eastern. The person supplying the food, a skinny, short man with a beard that seemed to start just below his eyes and disappear into his flannel shirt, looked as though he'd stepped right off of the boat. Irish, maybe. Or German. He could have been a homeless guy you saw around my neighborhood back home, back when I was a kid and my neighborhood still had homeless characters around, but he looked clean and he looked healthy enough. Just skinny.

I thought of the old man who had picked me up on route 4 after the debacle with Terry Hackford – Don "Jake" Murphy. The sweet old man who was a lying bastard working for Madison. The raggedy old stinker who had gotten me back into all of this when I had been so close. When I had been free. Or at least entertaining the notion of being free. Before I'd finally been dragged back in, this time with no escape hatch. This time with commitment I'd neither asked for not wanted, but I had had no choice but to take on. Take up the mantle, so to speak. I'd had no choice – had I? But then, I thought, we always have a choice.

"Everything okay?" Wendy asked. With the lilting accent it sounded like "*ow-kai?*"

I nodded, full of mouth. The cook – or, whatever you call them when it's a vegan ordeal – just looked in my general direction, those eyes sparkling but not seemingly fixed on any one thing. Maybe a lack of meat in the diet helps you maintain a natural high, I wondered. Or the guy was stoned.

I sipped from my chalice – that's what it was, really, one of those cups you'd see Vikings drinking from, or Biblical men in robes, hanging there suspended forever on a wall in the Brooklyn Museum – and a lovely sauvignon blanc slid down and into my stomach. It was non-alcoholic. And I only knew what sauvignon blanc was thanks to Daniel. If Victor or Ryan or Grey Frank ever caught wind I knew what the fuck a sauvignon blanc was…well, you know what they'd do, old friend. I'd never hear the end of it.

"You're in a lot of trouble," said Wendy. I stopped in mid chew, wondering why she'd chosen to say that, why now, and then resumed eating. One thing about vegan food – it was easier to chew. Maybe there was something to the idea that we humans, with our flat teeth and side-to-side chewing motions were really supposed to be herbivorous after all. Still, hadn't we developed the technology that allowed us to make meat soft enough to chew and digest? We might not have had sharp teeth and crushing up-and-down jaw motion abilities, but then, we weren't ripping through hide, fat and gristle there in the killing field. We ground the shit up. We stewed it. We sliced it. We used our brains to get around our flat teeth, low-acid stomachs and veggie-ready intestines. We outsmarted meat, that's what we did.

I wondered where my mind was going – if I maybe was coming down from Cameron's wonder drug, his Ritalin-esque focus aid. I thought of an ad, suddenly, a slogan rippling on a banner against an azure sky: *"Ritalin: God's Little Pill."*

"What do you mean?" I asked Wendy. I felt that I was smiling a little. I wanted to check the bottle to see if there was some .5 percent of booze in the wine.

"I mean…" She said, and gave the cook a look that told him to leave, please. She then came around from the other end of the table and stroked some viney plant nearest her. Behind her were yellow blooms I thought Daniel would call Forsythia. "I mean that you've killed Cameron Madison."

I raised my eyebrows at her over the lip of my wine glass. She looked over at me. "That was an accident," I said.

"Really?" She tilted her head at me. It was my impression that, though hospitable and cordial, Wendy had yet to make up her mind about me. And, then, to my own measure – how hospitable had she been thus far? It could have been the trickery of her British accent, that false sense of propriety and civility that came with the subdued, florid vowels and marching consonants. A person could forgive a lot through the skin of that accent. As in, "cheerio, and now we're going to have to cut off the other testicle, then," and, lying under the scalpel you're thinking, *what a nice people*. And the meal – the meal wasn't necessarily something in my *honor*, was it? It seemed we were all eating, that it was dinner time in general.

I set the glass down. I wiped my mouth with the flesh-colored napkin on my lap (odd choice for vegan hospitality, I thought) and was suddenly plenty full. I looked over the table for water, found the pitcher and poured myself a glass.

"Yeah," I said, "really an accident. As I was escaping, Madison was shot by a stray bullet from one of the soldiers."

"And that was what killed him?"

I took a sip of the water, relishing it, feeling the hairs on the nape of my neck standing like quills. "No," I said.

"No," she echoed.

I could feel the blood moving through me, if that's what it was. I glanced at some nearby plants. Ones that looked to me like some form of cactus. I thought of a plant in the desert with no rainwater for days on end getting its first drink in a thunderous deluge at long last, and how that plant must feel, its body hydrating, filling up, returning to life.

I said, "What do you care? He's your enemy."

"Well," said Wendy, "there are enemies, and then there are enemies."

"Sort of a 'he needs to exist in order for you to exist' kind of thing?"

"Jack," said Wendy, "we're very pleased with what you
have…brought to the table," Wendy said, and smiled. She had a fantastic
smile. I finished drinking my glass of water and pushed back from the table.
The others were watching, watching my every move as they pretended to be
tucked into their twig-and-root meals. The blonde with the braided hair, the
older man in canvasy overalls with the beard and bushy eyebrows. *He's a
writer*, I thought, *working on a book about the Naturalists.*

Wendy leaned over to me. I could smell that canned flower smell
again. It was an odor that reminded me of the first time I entered into
Cameron Madison's "house," the small, two bedroom place that'd made me
feel like I was inside a prop house at a theme park. A place where plastic
things lived. A place you didn't want to be inside of. Not because of the
smell, not exactly, and not because of the plastic people, not exactly that
either, but because of the unshakeable feeling that you were inside of a
chamber, and that the chamber was a portal of some kind. That it was a
place where the air was unmoving, where nothing was organic, where
nothing *lived* , nothing *breathed* and this was the exact kind of place that
was an arrival spot. It was where something could manifest. Something you
never wanted to see with your two eyes. And then you realized in the
stillness that the residue of this thing, the residue of this other, alien place,
this outworld, as you stood there in the antechamber – it was soon to be
everywhere. Smothering everything. Waiting for the return.

"You're really riding the bloody bronco with these drugs," said
Wendy. She leaned down and her lips were a few inches from my ear. "A
real cowboy." She pushed herself back, stood up from the table and walked
around behind me. I continued to blot my mouth with the flesh-colored
napkin. I couldn't seem to stop doing it. Blot, blot. Left side, right side.

"Lucius Brandis is coming after you himself," she said.

I put the napkin down.

"That's our intel. That's why there were no sirens, no fuss, not so much as a fart in the hay over your escape." It sounded like *faht in the hi*. "It was all determined very quickly, very efficiently. As much as a commodity as you may be–" she turned around to face me and leaned forward again and I could see the tops of her breasts spilling towards me, gleeful to fall free from the green tanktop she had on – "and you *are* a commodity, Jack. Zero-zero-three-five. Ex. You are very special. You are one of a kind." She stood back up. She started walking backwards. "But the call was made; take you out." She made a little gun with her thumb and forefinger and pointed it at me, the imaginary hammer coming down as she winked her left eye and clucked her tongue once. A pop-gun. "Bang." I thought of meeting Maya for the first time in the clearing near Utopia's grounds. I thought of the fake gun.

"Who made the call?" I watched Wendy closely. Her face, that was, not those dangling boobs, much as I wanted to.

"The man in charge of Utopia's operation here in the park." Wendy said, walking backwards. "Phil Brandis."

I did my best to fake surprise. "Brandis is alive?"

"Of course he is. He's been running things for almost two years now. You hardly ever see him. He flies in, flies out." Wendy made a little plane with her hand stiffened, palm down, indicating take off and landing.

"Who is your intel? I hope it's not Peter."

Wendy laughed. "No, it's not Peter." *Petah.* "He's a very nice bloke, though."

"Yeah, he's a good *bloke*. And you trust every one here, Wendy?"

She raised an eyebrow at me and then waved an arm to indicate the table of Naturalists in front of me. "Unlike Utopia," she said, "everyone is here of their own free will. Everyone wants to be here. They've chosen this life." I looked at the blonde with pigtails, a sprout sticking out of her mouth. She quietly sucked it in. I looked at the big black guy next to her, arms the size of fire hydrants. An Asian man, he too with a beard, his long and thin and white from the chin. "This is our life," said Wendy.

She looked back at me and scowled. "You really don't trust anyone, do you?"

"Yeah," I said, "I do."

Ever since I'd fucked up in Costa Rica, the Brandis brothers had been looking for a way to get rid of me, I knew that now. But, always resourceful, always efficient, the Brothers had sought to get some use out of me too, to turn their coin. A useful way to destroy somebody. That was a Brandis brothers' specialty. Why not give me over as a guinea pig for cutting edge gene-mutation research and development? Why not – when they had "x" amount of dollars invested in it – more money, anyway, than they had wanted to invest, when they had originally just wanted to take everything from Calvin Blair Latin-style? Kidnapping and ransoming. Only Jack Landi, smitten in two minutes by an American girl in the TOEFL program, went ahead and blew it.

"Do you understand what happened?" I winced at Wendy's question, as if struck. I picked the napkin back up and started to knead it, like dough.

"Meaning?"

"At the beginning. In Central America. Do you…know?"

I swallowed. I looked at Wendy. She explained.

Finally, recently, the technology had become human-ready. It had taken eight years to further develop for human subjects to be completely viable from my trip to Costa Rica. The package that had arrived in Moravia, ensconced in some earlier means of transporting the technology, maybe test tubes, maybe shaving kits, maybe chocolate *bon-bons* – I'd never gotten a chance to look inside, and Wendy didn't know. Baradez had been instructed to inject me, and the stuff had been inside me all of this time; I was a carrier. It was latent, just part of an equation, needing a catalyst.

"Like the biologist's joke," said Wendy, "'I wish I was an enzyme so I could unzip your genes."

"Funny," I said. "So – what? What is the catalyst? What does it take to activate the mutations?"

Wendy shrugged, and I felt cold. I felt like I had many times lately, like I already knew the answer to something. I thought of my baby daughter. I asked, "Sex?"

Wendy tilted her head to one side. "That's part of it," she said. "Like anything else, you can pass this on to offspring. Once the recombinant genes are there – the coding moves on to the next generation. But, just getting heated up, just the release of certain hormones, that can trigger things, but that's sort of piecemeal. *Madison* had ways to get things going good. Like you know, like what really started when you woke up on the side of the lake that morning."

"You were watching?"

"We've always been watching." She winked. "And Phil Brandis never disappeared. That was just smoke for him to slip into obscurity. And an excuse to get you up here."

But I had wanted to come up here, hadn't I? I wanted to get away from the city, to clean out, sober up. It had been my decision, hadn't it?

Despite these questions, and despite the cold awl that had bore into me as I imagined my daughter carrying the same thing that was in me, I had to stay on track. "That was *him*," I said, taking pains not to grab up the fork again and skewer myself in the eye with it for show. Wendy's left eyebrow raised. "That was Brandis. The helicopter," I said, "first day I set foot in the commune. Madison greeted someone who came in a helicopter. Phil Brandis," I said. "A man I'd only ever seen from a couple of small pictures in the Brothers' office."

Wendy nodded, looking thoughtful, almost sympathetic. She seemed to study her nails for a moment. Then she looked back at me. I realized her eyes were greenish. Or maybe they were just reflecting so much of the room. "I'm sorry, Jack."

I shrugged. I put the napkin on the table in front of me again and stood up. I didn't feel like sitting at that table anymore.

Some time had passed. I don't honestly know how long I stood there, digesting my meal, digesting all of the information, and still keeping up my ruse. A minute? Ten? I finally broke the tension with one last question.

"Who created the biotech, Wendy? I mean who originally developed it?" This was, honestly, something I still didn't know. Or, if I knew it, I wasn't allowing it to come to the surface, but keeping it locked away somewhere in my mind, because right away I thought of Terry Hackford, averse to the whole ordeal as he may have become.

The rest of the Naturalists at the table had finished eating and were seated more casually, some with their hands folded, some legs crossed. The man with the beard – the one who reminded me of a writer – spoke up. "Christian Scientists," he said. I looked over at him. I also glanced at Wendy for a reaction, but she appeared okay with his testimony.

"Why? I mean, just to see?"

He seemed to ponder this, looking at his plate, and then looked back at me. I saw that his eyes were brown. He reminded me a little of my father, if, that was, my father were still here. Then the bearded writer-man shrugged. "The waning power of conservatism," he said, "wrong-thinking people."

I grabbed the back of my chair where I stood and leaned into the table. "You mean to tell me this all started to get votes?"

Again, he shrugged. "Rampant liberalism, you know. 'God is dead.' All of that sort of thing."

I surveyed the group of them that sat around the table. Not exactly your socially, fiscally conservative types, I thought. Socialists. *Naturalists.*

"I don't understand," I said. It was honest.

The big-muscled black guy spoke up. "Hitler failed," said the big man, "because we opposed him, ultimately. We won the war. But who is going to defeat the United States of America? Nobody. Nobody but the States themselves, from within. With everything turning towards global warming activism and the threat of a new paradigm – a world with no suburban way of life, of green technologies – it was just too much. More than half of registered republicans voted democrat in the last election. How do you fix that? Wait for the pendulum to swing back the other way again? What if this time there was no inertia? What if things actually *changed*? It scared too many people."

"But this began years ago," I said. "The biotech science, I mean." The words sounded foreign coming out of my own mouth.

"Sure," said the big-muscled man with the professorial voice. He shrugged and said, "but at that time it was Bill and Hillary Clinton." He smiled a broad, white smile. The full Flatbush cemetery, my gramma used to say. "Maybe the republicans paid Monica Lewinsky to, you know." Some of the Naturalists chuckled.

"We can protect you," said Wendy, standing next to me. I turned and found my gaze slipping to the curves of her beneath the tank top again. I pulled my eyes up and found her face. "Jack, listen. We can help you."

I stood motionless, feeling unreality creep up and around me, once more unsure of things. I had made a pact with myself there, back at Utopia, and decided what to do and now things were in motion. Given this new information, though, this penultimate piece of the puzzle, what was the right thing to do? If I proceeded, I could be contributing to what the prophets of the world had been saying for the last century – that absolute power corrupted absolutely, and those who had lost the upper hand would do anything to get it back and rule again. People genetically engineered to keep the system going the way those powers saw fit. Voting the way those powers wanted, continuing to live their lives in a way that enriched the rich and finally evaporated the middle class. Living in a way that would ride the juggernaut right into oblivion – right to the end of the world. But if I didn't, if I changed my course now, the people that I had come to care about – at

long last, people that actually had come to matter to me more than myself –
they would be lost.

I put one hand out in front of Wendy. Not to stop her, not to say,
"don't come any closer," but because my hand just came up like that. "I'll
handle Lucius Brandis," I said, again without really thinking, just having it
spill out of my mouth. I almost grabbed the water pitcher from the table and
tucked it under my arm. I realized distantly I had to whiz.

You'll be alright, kleinnes, I heard Lincoln say in my head, *just do
what comes natural,* and then I heard a broken, cackling laughter, the kind of
laughter that sounded like rocks breaking away from a hillside and tumbling.
Lincoln. The Boxer. Fort Dix. Been through two wars and a stroke, but
with a mind still harder than a brick shithouse in a Costa Rican hurricane.

"Listen," she said again, and Wendy did stop, some two feet away
from me. I saw her eyes flick back and forth, looking from my right to my
left. I searched those eyes for falsity. There had just been so damned much
of it lately, and now it had to come from me.

And for some reason I thought of Daniel again.

"We can help you – but we need your help, too. If you just go off and
face Brandis alone…"

She trailed off and looked away. *We'll never hear from you again,
because you'll be a stain on the pavement of some backwoods country road.
Like route 4, maybe.*

"…You'll be denying us a chance to succeed here."

I could feel myself bristling. This was what I expected, but it
engendered anger just the same. I was sick of betrayal and double-crosses. I
was sick of hidden agendas. Sick of lies. And yet, here I was, playing a role
now myself; I too was living a secret, and I had to be careful. It was time.

"I know what you want," I said.

"Oh?"

"You think I'm some sort of peace offering. A sacrificial lamb." I swept my own arm over the table. "You fatten me up for the kill, yeah? You sit me down to eat your chicken feed and tell me you can protect me, when you just want to keep me here because you've already called the Brandis brothers, or – if you haven't, your mole has" and I swept my narrowed gaze emphatically over those at the table, "and you just want me to stay so you can strike your deal with them." It pained me to see the genuine hurt on Wendy's face, the look of a person so drastically misunderstood, but I had to do it. If I was going to leave here for now, for the time being, and do what I needed to do first, I couldn't have them knowing what I'd done.

I then turned and started for the door, more garlands framing it.

"Jack, that's not true and you know it," said Wendy. I stopped moving. "We want what you want. We want people to remain free, as you want freedom. You've been trapped for so long, Jack. The Brandis brothers don't care about what this is. To them, it's just another job. You're just an instrument. But to us, Jack…Jack, you're family."

"Then I have to get going," I said, still facing the door. I closed my eyes tightly and forced myself to say nothing more. I heard Wendy start towards me again.

"You are too hard on yourself," she said. "You've done a lot of good, you just can't see it yet."

It felt good, hearing that, and of course part of me wanted to turn and tell her everything. It was hard to go it alone, harder than anything else. To know something and not be able to share it – to have to use people in order to get what you needed. I didn't want it anymore. I was through. After this, I was through. It was a comforting feeling, a bit like coming home.

"We are going to move against Utopia soon," she said. "Very soon. But," and I heard her footsteps stop, "I'm not going to stop you from leaving. That's not what we're about."

Again I imagined the cook reemerging, that beard on his face like a pelt, now a rifle jutting from his white-garbed arm, but dismissed it. Those were the old tapes playing. Things had changed. I was on a different path now, and I knew it; it felt like the entire universe had shifted and oriented around it.

"Thank you for supper," was all I could think to say, and I pushed out of the door and into the night without looking back.

I didn't say goodbye to Peter. I didn't say goodbye to anyone; I hadn't really even met the brunt of them yet. I was soon gone from the Naturalists, those fifty or sixty folk nestled into that clearing, and I was swallowed by the woods again.

I stuck fairly close to the access road – nothing more than a couple of ruts and an overgrown median – *tres natural* – but chose not to walk there. The woods were still relatively sparse, and only occasionally did I encounter the kind of bramble that tore at my clothes, some that I had to circumnavigate (Marcel had taught me that word) and the going was relatively easy. I was confident now that I had a belly full of food, though

vegan-shmeegan, and that I'd come across...well, what? Resistance, I
supposed. Opposition to the Utopia Corporation. It felt good. It felt like
balance at work, like good and evil hacking it out like always, for old time's
sake. Of course, in this case, I had to admit the ambiguity of what was good
and what was evil. Cameron Madison, yes, a bit on the darker side of things.
Call it overamplified ego. But the science there, the means to cure the
infirm, to relieve undue suffering – was that evil? I had suffered for years,
coming in and out of bouts of drunkenness, drug abuse and depression –
sometimes so bad I did find myself on the Brooklyn Bridge, looking down.
And now...well, I've said all of this before.

Regardless, the fight wasn't my fight, was it? I was just a guy who'd
been duped into it. Besides, I didn't even know the Naturalists' agenda. Not
really. Nothing I could testify to. I had caught a glimpse of a tuft or hair
under Wendy's arm when she'd play-shooted me with her finger, but aside
from a little Women's Lib, what did I know about the Naturalist's politics? I
mean, when you got into something like that – and when you were actually
calling yourself the "Naturalists," you were really asking for it. What
defined natural? How far did you go? Were you allowed aspirin?
Contraceptives? Plastic utensils of any kind? Could you watch TV?

Yeah, you could get pretty radical with that shit. What they stood for,
I rationalized, squinting to see through a blob of forest tangle, was probably
okay, though, and probably for the right reasons to want to stop Utopia.
Because it wasn't a *real* utopia, now, was it? It wasn't a *natural* utopia.
There was something I'd read in school, by a guy named Mircea Eliade –
The Myth of Eternal Return; we couldn't go back to the archaic. What was
going on at Utopia wasn't naturally occurring in humans – or, it was, but at a
far slower rate of evolution. Madison and his gang, they were looking to

speed that up. Madison had his own reasons – save the human race – and, if I were to believe the bearded man from the table, the underpinning agenda was the ultimate fascistic control of the United States of America's people. Such was probably where the Naturalists had their beef. No pun intended. And you couldn't blame them.

I made it through another swath of underbrush, ducked under a branch or three, wound through the rain-slicked bark of a cluster of beech trees, and realized I could see a road. I could see what available light was in the sky – glimpses of the moon, the stars, or maybe even a streetlight, reflecting off of the wet asphalt. It had stopped raining and the clouds were breaking apart, I'd seen upon leaving the Naturalists' clearing, but everything would likely be wet until morning, until the Sun.

After a short while I was on the road. Instinctively I turned left – what I thought was south, what my internal compass told me was south. I was hoping for a road sign. I was hoping I didn't look too much like a freak in my dirty white and torn liniments, visible bandages soaked and drooping, so as to not catch a ride; I looked like a mummy.

I raked fingers through my wet hair and waked the shoulder. My feet made wet, slapping noises and I consciously tried to be quieter. I could smell the oils in the road, the wetness and fermentation in the forest. The air was still. All was quiet. I brushed at my face, hoping to remove any bits of forest, leaves, cobwebs.

Suddenly I was laughing. It just bubbled up and out of me. Unchallenged. Before, I realized, bending into the fit of it, there had been something to stop me, something to cause me to suppress. It wasn't wild, macabre laughter. It wasn't insane laughter. It was belly-shucking laughter, truly from the gut, the kind of laughter of jolly old Saint Nick, maybe. And I understood it, as it flowed out of me, and as my laugh echoed in the forest on either side of me, it was a *true* laugh. Not at anything funny. Not from humor. But from something else, from some place else. Finally, capriciously as it had come, it subsided. A rollicking bout of laughter I never would have uttered, or had heard uttered, on my long ago home streets. I settled myself, and got to walking. I started thinking of things I was going to need.

I would need, for one, a few bottles of water.

I would need, for another, things to go a certain way with one of the Brothers. With the aged fighter. The one who called me *kleinnes*. And so I thought about these things as I walked.

After some time, headlights appeared behind me. The first car to come along since I'd been on the road and, my thumb out, miraculously, the car pulled over.

I was suspicious, but I'd heard that country folk still picked up hitchers, even in the dark. I jogged up to the car, came along it on the passenger side, and dipped my head down so the driver could see my face, and hopefully discern my good intentions. The driver had to lean across a bench seat – the vehicle looked to me like a Volkswagen, or something, a smallish, station-wagony kind of thing – and roll down the window.

"Howdy," I said. I was getting good at the lingo too.

"Howdy," said the driver. It was dark, but he looked to be a guy about my age. That seemed to make sense. If it was a little old lady pulling me over I'd have to either pull her face-mask off or recon the backseat for the Brandis thug looking to put a fiber around my neck when I got in the front seat.

"Where you headed?" said the driver.

I felt myself starting to offer the truth. Indeed it had become an urge, a need. Another car appeared, then, making me uneasy. It shooshed by us on the other side, headed the other way. I couldn't see inside of it. I looked back to the driver. "Bondville," I said.

"Cool," he said. "Going home to Rutland. I can get you close."

"Great," I said, but my body wasn't moving. *Don't freeze, man, you'll freak this guy out.* The spell broke and I lifted the door latch and got in. I pulled the door shut behind me with a tremendous *thunk.* "Nice ride," I said.

Grinning, the driver said, "thanks." He stuck a hand out. "Marshall," he said.

"Marshall," I reported back. "Jack Gainesville."

We shook, and then we pulled away.

As we quickly put distance between ourselves and the patch of road where I'd come out of the woods, I felt a kind of sadness. It wasn't remorse, or regret, or anything depressing – for once. It had something to do with that laughing bit I'd had. How it had been the first time, ever, really – I'm telling you old pal, the first time I'd ever felt really alive in my life, really natural, really free.

And how I knew somehow it would never come again.

THE GARDEN

I had fallen asleep. I'd slipped away sometime around four a.m. Marshall told me later, when we made a stop for gas.

Marshall Cohen was his full name. He wore a well-groomed beard and glasses. He was an assistant professor. He told me this early into the ride, during the somewhat nervous small talk two strangers levied when suddenly confined together. He worked at Johnson State University. Marshall only got home on the weekends. And that's why he was driving through the night – to get to his home, five hours from his work – and see his two children. As we were having one of those first chitchats, I was marveling at Marshall. He and I were the same age. Only a month a part, we'd found out sometime around three a.m., and here he was, this guy, holding down this real job with a wife and two kids.

Marshall said he only had to do this for about two years – this kind of ridiculous commute – and then he could move his whole family up to the Johnson State area. In fact, he said, the plan was to live in some of the private quarters owned by the school. Since he was gone so much of the time now, he said, his wife had no choice but to stay with the little ones. And that was how he, and she – Kristine – had wanted it. They were three-years-old and one-year-old, their kids. A boy and a girl.

As we shared stories (mine, of course, fabrications, or, at least, very uninformative bits of general information, despite my newly acquired need for truth-telling) I couldn't help but compare myself to Marshall. Again, almost exactly the same age. And here I was, single, caught up in this ridiculous mess, barely able to take care of myself half of the time, and there was Marshall, with his nicely trimmed reddish-brown beard, his black glasses, his somehow dressy flannel shirt on, with a devoted wife, mother to his children, and those two little bubbies themselves, living on a piece of goodly land outside of Rutland.

"It's not so bad," he told me, "to be away. I mean, I know nothing is a substitute for the real thing, for real contact – *nobody* knows that better than me – but there is the internet, the cell phone…Kristine and I talk three, sometimes four or five times a day. I see pictures almost daily. And she has a webcam and I have a webcam so we can, you know, see each other, and, it's good, I mean…"

And through his somewhat bumbling charm I could see that Marshall was honestly happy. He was one of those guys, I judged, who was just meant to be happy. He probably smoked a joint or two on the weekends, one with the wife, in the basement, both of them giggling. He drank beer from local microbreweries – and God knew in Vermont there were plenty of them – micro everything in Vermont – and when he did, he had two, two and a half, tops. He'd leave a beer half-full on the counter or end table and go to bed, or get back to whatever he was doing. He was probably a vegetarian, but I didn't ask. Or, if he ate meat, it was slow-food; it was from a local farm. And he wore mole-hair sweaters and merino wool shirts without sneezing. And he didn't get irritated – hardly ever. But if you pushed him – I mean, if you really *pushed* Marshall Cohen, I figured, and it was for the right reasons – he'd snap on you. He was the guy that "snaps" maybe three

times in his life. Not like the guy sitting next to him in the orangey-dark of
the car, still rubbing out the stains.

Everything in Marshall's life was twos and threes. Two kids.
Counting wifey, three loved ones. Two beers; three, tops. Two joints,
maybe, over a week. Two or three times in his life he'll ever hit a guy in
anger, and it would be real, justifiable, righteous anger. Two or three.

"It can get tough, though, you know? I mean, with all of that tight
little ass around."

I sort of jerked. I had been close to dozing. That wouldn't serve
etiquette too well, though, to nod off while the guy that picked you up in the
middle of a rain-slicked night in the middle of nowhere was talking to you.
It broke the hitchhiker code. It-

What was he saying? He glanced over at me in the dark and I could
see a glint in his eyes as he raised and lowered his brow. "You know what I
mean?"

And just like that, just like the thousand times before it, when I
thought I had everything all figured out, or someone all catalogued, the
inevitable always happened and life revealed itself.

"Yeah," I said. It was a cursory "yeah," but I also could understand.
In fact, my mind started working again, leaping off in a whole new direction,
bounding after a whole new ball of thread. I saw Marshall Cohen as a cute
19 year-old co-ed might see him. I saw him sitting at his desk, studiously
exploring a term paper with his fingers, glasses on, the nice beard, a hemp
sweater covering his shirt and tie, with the tie just exposed about the rim of
the collar, that little cutie co-ed just standing there, toeing one heel of one
foot with the other, biting her lower lip as she watched Mr. Cohen, him
unawares. She thought of him in class, and how smart he was, and how cute

he was, and how she often lost track of what he was saying. How she was sort of jealous of his family, his wife, but attracted to him because he had them, because she knew he loved them, and that made him a beautiful man. And 19 year-old co-eds loved beautiful men, especially when they, from suburban Massachusetts, also pictured him splitting wood in the sweat-slicked torso buff, and putting on drives in the depths of autumn woods, he invariably the leader of the hunt, cueing the others with silent and esoteric signals.

Did he ever tap any of that ass, I wondered? Was this a stranger's way of seeking some sort of contrition…angling towards a confession here in the ditch hours of the night?

"Yeah," he said, and sort of sat back and leaned back into his chair, and into the driving, and fell silent, and that was that.

We talked more, but no longer of personal things, but of politics and the environment. Marshall was a very smart guy, I concluded, and, yes, dedicated to his family, but also human. Also a man. And, in the company of another man, which permitted locker room talk. We rambled on, and soon I passed out, after all.

When awoke around five a.m. at the gas station, we were almost to Rutland. Marshall had gotten out and the shutting of the door had awakened me. I got out, stretched slowly, feeling that sluggishness – though not as severe as the total impotence from before, upon arriving at the faux veterinarian's place. I'd had a dream, and the residue of it was on me like sweat from a run. Marshall was pumping gas. He looked at me, smiled, then looked at the pump and shook his head.

"Jesus," he said. "Climbing again. They say it's going to be bad by Christmas. Maybe not as bad as it's been, but, bad." I wondered why he didn't own a hybrid, or something, like a Prius. Instead he had this rattletrap VW.

I apologized profusely for having fallen asleep on him, for having not kept his company.

"Oh no, man, no sweat. When you gotta go, you gotta go."

The sentiment stirred my bladder awake. I jogged to the bathroom, inhaling the night air deeply. It was sweet, though interlaced with the whiff of gas and asphalt, and the promise of a city nearby, even a Vermont city.

In the bathroom, at the urinal, I wondered if we were being followed, and thought to check things on the way back to the car.

In the stall next to me was the scrape of feet, and then a flush. I urinated, and the dream I'd just had while asleep in Marshall's VW came back in a wave, like the tremors and nausea of a post-operative sickness. It was a familiar dream; I'd dreamt something like it once before.

The fire. The effigy. The giant bear. Mike, the FPR guy, sitting in the white Subaru, watching, drinking. Drinking out of a coffee mug with the image of a barn, a ranch-style country house and a red sleigh sitting in the snow encircling it. A vivid dream; the firelight reflected and dancing in Mike's eyes.

They were jumping and leaping around the fire – children – children dancing around this tower of flames out there in the nowhere, with the canopy of stars, little kids buzzing about. Me, watching, floating, there but not really there, almost omniscient, I saw something amid the kids, and heard it moving. It was a spider, and it was long and thick. Its body was the size of a large pear, its legs each two feet long, black and red like some jungle snake's scales might be. As it skittered beneath and through the lower limbs of the oblivious, dancing children, I could hear it. Over the sound of the drums, the sounds of the kids' laughter and shouts and the massive crackle of the fire – in fact, by its sound making all of these other noises seem paltry, muffled, inconsequential – I could hear its legs knocking against one another, sounding like rods of bamboo clacking hollowly.

The fire fed on the giant, carved statue of the bear. The effigy. I wondered – seeking to detect even in my dreams, it seemed – what the bear represented. Was it the symbol of the Naturalists?

The children jumped and hooted and danced. I dream-thought to note what they were wearing, and by that notion either invented or discovered their wardrobe. They were wearing those white linen fatigues; Velcro straps for their own safety, billowing around their spindly bodies, each of them no older than eight years, no younger than four.

Four to Eight.

I found myself recalling a dream within a dream. In that memory something was knocking from the other side of a wall next to me. A wall of my cell. Something, over there, stuffed into too-small shoes, knocking. Some sort of hideous accident, locked away. Children filing into barracks, smartly stopping in front of and about-facing into their meat-locker cells.

I drifted back to Mike, the FPR guy, in his state-issue vehicle, now a Jeep Cherokee. No, I didn't drift, really, I was just suddenly there, an awareness outside of his window. A ghost. Nobody. Just an X of a signature, if even that. Mike sipped from his mug and I could smell the whiskey in it; even in the dream the booze was odorous. He watched the children, blank-faced, slurping. And then I was there beside him, watching myself from outside of the Jeep as I sat next to him, and I leaned over to him, and I whispered.

I told Mike that you were complicit in dreams, like you might surf a wave, but you didn't control the temper of the ocean. You went with what it told you. I saw myself lean back into the seat again, and look out of the front windshield.

Now the children were gone, and the fire snapped and sparked on, but dying out some, and the bear was charred away to just a shape there in the thick of the bluish-orange, a hulking shape like that which had knocked on the other side of the wall while I'd sat in my cell.

I could still hear the bamboo-stalk clacking of the spider's legs, but I couldn't see the spider. Now the sound, though, was more like hardwood trees knocking together in the forest night. A lonely sound, receding into the woods where things were cold and alone and unknown. I couldn't see the spider, but knew it was there, and that's when my daughter appeared in front of the bonfire, her hair blowing as if by the winds of the blaze, standing in the white get-up. A shadow passed over her, and I cried out.

That was when I'd awakened at the gas station.

I shook off at the urinal, zipped up and flushed it. At the same time the stall door opened and shut. I heard the steps behind me. I pretended, for a moment, to still be peeing. The man walked passed me and to the sink, where he turned on the faucet. I then stepped away and started for the door, looking at the chipped, green, grouted tiles of the wall. When I reached the door I opened it and stepped, and as I stepped I looked back and saw the

man at the sink. I saw his reflection, a man with an eye patch, rubbing his
hands together under the water, looking up at me. I left.

The gas station was outside of Rutland – south of it, Marshall told me – in
the small village of Pierces Corners, two miles from Marshall's home.

"You sure you don't want to stop in?" Marshall asked, still with the
spigot pouring into the gas tank. I looked, in a little bit of shock, in a way
only a New Yorker can, or a Brooklyn truck monkey – one who never drove
and only loaded, that is – at the price of gas. It seemed high even to me.

I could scarcely believe Marshall's offer. But, then, I was getting
somewhat accustomed to the selfless kindness of so many whom I'd
encountered here in the Gay Mountain State. Daniel, with his endless
mothering, his indefatigable ear. Peter, like a loyal dog since the day he'd
left his job and followed me off to his own hospitalization. Even Maya, in
her own way (and just to think of her, especially in the small, cold hours of
the morning at an unfamiliar gas station in the seeming middle of nowhere,
was pinching, like iced tongs squeezing the heart) had been kind, had tried to
be of use, of service for something she'd thought was right.

How could you have left her there?

I pushed the thought away. I had made my decision. Things were in
motion. Maya would be okay, she was a survivor.

"That's nice of you to offer, Marsh–"

"You know," he said, squeezing the last from the spigot to make a rounded number at the pump, "get a shower, get a hot meal, maybe even get a sleep if you want to. You were really knocked out there," he said, and smiled, "operating system down."

I shuddered inside when he said that.

But he hadn't said exactly it, no. Operating system *down*, he'd said. Not *gone*. Not unfound. Marshall was just using some assistant-professor-geek humor. He could have no idea what it had felt like there for a while – must've been when the drugs were first kicking in, or when, maybe, some actual *mutation* had been taking place within my genes, my proteins – and still felt like that at times. Like I was a wiped hard drive. I didn't know much about computers – never even owned one, if you can believe it – but I know why Banjul kept all of those papers filed everywhere in that crummy office at the loading dock. He'd had a computer crash on him once, a hard drive go blank as a head-trauma victim. After it'd happened he swore off computers forever – cursing in his Indian way, making Hindi references and bringing down his own Middle Eastern version of hellfire on electronic intelligences everywhere.

How was I going to go and sit at this man's table? Move within the walls of his normal, cozy, perfect life

(it can get tough with all of that tight little ass around)

or, at least, near-perfect life? How could I breathe there, given who I was, given whom I had finally *come* to know who I was, at long last?

And that's why you can do it.

The voice in my head was right. It was – maybe for the first time, likely for the last – possible for me to spend a moment as a part of someone's real life, the kind lived by people who made the world go 'round, living by the rules, by routine, with some measure of actual joy in their life, some experience of real tragedy.

Just a quick meal. Just a clean up.

"How far do you put us from Bondville about now?" I asked.

"Oh," said Marshall, replacing the spigot in the pump's holster and rocking back on his heels slightly, "we're about thirty miles north of there. Take about 45 minutes down 7 and over, or down 155 into 100. You know, I could j–"

"Marshall, no way." It actually made me laugh. "You've got to be kidding." I waved my hand in the air like a clown might. "You drive all through the night to get to your family...Jesus, man."

Marshall looked like he had no idea what I was talking about. If only he knew the extent to the selfishness I had grown up around. Not Brooklynites, no, I'm not indicting my people for anything like that, because, by and large, we're all pretty helpful around my streets, but my mother's family. The Debutantes. Never have I known a more self-serving, self-absorbed, *selfish-cunt* lot as they who lived in Greenwich, Connecticut. Without money, they could do nothing. Marshall shrugged, palms up, and walked around the front of the car with a *well, there's no helping you* look on his face, and got back in. At once he turned the engine on and rubbed his hands together and blew on them. He cranked the heat. I noticed he had a scarf on. I hadn't seen it before. I'd thought only New Yorkers wore scarves – at least, certainly not country boys like Marshall. Well, maybe because he was in academics.

You're an asshole.

I thought of Marcel, wearing his own scarf on occasion, sitting on the stoop with his laptop and Diet Coke, and something clicked:

Marcel.

Marshall.

Marcel and Marshall.

I could see my breath, I could see Marshall's breath. We just sat there and breathed and let the car warm back up. We'd only been here for five minutes but the cold air outside had drained the warmth of the car like a cat stealing a sleeping child's breath.

I realized he was still waiting for my answer to his invitation.

Marcel and Marshall...

I realized I might be going crazy still. Perhaps I was detoxing from Cameron's drugs. Why hadn't I thought to take anything with me? My own stash?

Because I didn't need it, dammit, that was why. I had to get out of this shit altogether.

But what was going to happen with the...side effects? *You'll be a monster, Jack, that's all you'll be,* Cameron had said under the gun. *What would your father think?* But instead of my father, I pictured the thing coming out of the meat locker. I thought of how I'd wanted to rip out Crick's throat with my teeth. Unchecked, what was I capable of? Would I want my daughter to see me like that, her father, a twisted experiment purposely incomplete to honor the pharmaceutical end of the deal "they" had rendered? They – the Brandis brothers; fences, Calvin Blair; the trade and... the third party. There always was. Checks and balances. A triumvirate. That way two groups could always team up and overpower the other. Or one would try to get away with it all. I thought of the guy in the bathroom

with the eye patch and shivered again. Marshall – God bless the guy –
reached over to turn up the heat even though the VWs thermostat was
already dialed to its max.

"Okay," I said, "to your place."

Marshall broke into a wide grin.

I thought of Marcel, and his kid Jocelyn. "What's that, Jackie?" "It's
a tiger sleeping." "Tiger sleeping? What's that mean?" "I don't know,
kid."

I don't know.

He dropped the shifter into drive and said, "glad to hear it." It was
five-fifteen in the morning. There was the faintest light beginning to paint
the eastern sky. There were no mountains in that direction, but the land
rolled a little, like the back of a horse, grazing. The light there was just a
bluer shade of black.

We got going, and pulled out of the gas station.

If it was a trap, it seemed too obvious. If it wasn't, I was going to get
a nice meal, clean up, and get hiking.

Or, there could be that third possibility. Something else going on I
hadn't quite put my finger on yet.

Always a third. Always.

A triumvirate.

The magic number was three.

*

We pulled off from a country road onto a long, country driveway, with a squat house and what looked like a maple tree and a field all around. The woods that bordered the field were about a hundred yards back from the house. Marshall pointed.

"In there," he said, "is the Appalachian Trail."

"Wow," I said. I had no idea what the fuck the Appalachian Trail was. "That's amazing."

"Yeah," he said.

I took a guess. "So…you own a piece of it?"

"No, no," he said, his forehead wrinkling, and we bumped down the road, closer to the squat house, with its four front-facing windows and door with small tessellated portico, "state owns that. My property ends right at the foot of the woods there." His hand drifted across the windshield.

"Jesus," I said.

He shrugged. "It's a nice plot."

Marshall, of course, had no idea what I was going through. He probably believed all people were born good. He probably went to church.

We arrived at the house. In the slowly brightening morning it looked a dark red. Both of the downstairs windows were lit with soft light, giving the house sleepy eyes. There were flat fieldstones for a walkway to the portico. There was a two-stall garage to the side of the house, attached to it, between it and the tree – I saw a tire-swing dangling there now that we were close enough – and Marshall stopped short of going inside of the garage. "Door rattles and wakes the kids," he explained to me, actually whispering. "I'll bring it in later."

He took a moment to study me in the dark, as if he'd just realized he was about to let a stranger into his home, a hitchhiker no less, who'd been vague about his comings and goings and even vaguer about his present, let him into where his soft wife was, his soft, sleeping children, warm and vulnerable, drooling in their beds.

"You ready?" is all he said. He sounded to me almost like a coach, or a therapist might, helping to make a big decision. He even seemed to hold his breath for me.

I thought again of a trap.

But what? Were they waiting inside? Where were the vehicles? There was nothing but open country around us. Had they snuck down the "Appalachian Trail" on foot, like so many Native Americans may have before them? Would a helicopter descend after I'd passed out from eating too many doped-up waffles the secretly witchy wife had prepared?

Seriously, though, as much as my mind could work rationally at the moment, here was a struggling family man. Sure he seemed honest and kind and genuine, but what would it take – in dollars and cents – to simply get him to pick up the fugitive, woo him home with promises of home-baked apple pie and warm showers and detain him there, just long enough for the dark cavalry to arrive? A couple thousand bucks? More? The promise of house payments made for a year? Life?

And then I looked down at myself, and thought that perhaps I had been a bigger fool than I had even thought possible.

I was still wearing my mental-patient outfit, after all. The one the kids in my dream were galloping around in. The once with Velcro. Now muddied and soiled and ripped in places with my crusty bandages showing.

What could this man – of reasonable intelligence, working at a university – be thinking? What had I even told him? I couldn't quite remember.

He started to look at me less like a therapist-coach and with a bit more wariness. I realized a couple too many moments of silence had passed and it was growing awkward for even a guy like Marshall.

"Aren't you…" *worried about me*? I thought to ask, but I backed up and changed direction a little. "Aren't you afraid your wife, your kids…" I looked down and spread my arms to indicate my appearance.

Marshall's knitting brow smoothed again and that high-school-yearbook smile dawned on his face. Then he lowered his head, where it sort of bobbed. "Whatever trouble you're in, Jack," he said, "I know you're a good guy. They'll know it too. You're not nuts, you just need to get cleaned up." He looked back up and sort of squinted at me. The day had grown even lighter since we'd arrived. I wondered when his kids awakened. What sounds they made when they bounded down the stairs for breakfast. If he and his wife were allowed to fart in front of one another.

"You're about my size, too," he said, and nodded once to himself. Then he looked me in the eyes and said, "You want to look good for her."

It took me by surprise. "What's that?" *What's that?* – coming out as *wassat?* – was some of the country dialect I'd picked up. Again I backpedaled and tried a different path. "What do you mean?"

Marshall then looked almost embarrassed, like a man caught peeping into someone's journal, or reading one of their emails over their shoulders. He folded his fingers together. For some reason it made me think of the priest at St. Johns, back way back when I used to go to church with gramma. "In your sleep," he said, "you were talking about your daughter." He looked back at me. "You do have a daughter, yeah?"

I nodded, still a little shocked. I realized my nod was the first truthful communication I'd offered this man since he'd picked me up other than my destination, at last. Where I was going and who I was going to – the only truths I'd really told.

"Well," he said then, in an all-decided and all's-well tone of voice, "we need to get you right to go see her."

And he got out of the car. And he shut the door quietly behind him, and so did I, and he leaned across the roof of the car saying, "I take it it's been a long time."

I jiggled my head up and down. My tongue felt useless.

He nodded once in that Marshall way. A curt, "got-it" nod. One that some people probably liked, and handed out tenure for. A no-bullshit – "okay, I understand, moving on" – sign of affirmation.

He opened the back door to the vehicle and got out his suitcase. Then he shut that door and said, "let's go," and turned and walked down the fieldstone path.

In the air, wafting in from a nearby dairy farm, the slightly tangy fetor of cow manure, and the smell of hayseed. There had been no stars I'd noticed so far that night, but as I looked up at the spreading blue, I saw some there shining. And for the first time in a long time that I could remember, I said *thank you* to someone, or to something.

*

By the time I got through Kristine's delicious, ample version of a Ranch Breakfast – eggs, rye toast, sausage, bacon, oranges (sliced into wheels and split along one side of the rind for easy feeding) and strawberries, I knew sleep was inevitable.

I wanted to get going right away, had told myself I would – just the meal, plenty of thanks, and back on the road – but I knew it was ridiculous. I could pass out alongside the asphalt at this point. Here at least there was shelter, and, if I continued to believe it, anonymity.

The kids weren't up yet. Marshall and Kristine spoke in practiced whispers, finishing each other sentences, seeming to have lapsed back into a familiar relationship and routine only thirty seconds after the first kiss Marshall planted on her when we'd walked in the door. I learned that the Cohens traditionally enjoyed a quiet breakfast together (Kristine wolfed down the same ranch breakfast we men did) on Marshall's first day back, before the kids were roused. "They can be a real handful at mealtimes," Kristine said at one point, butterknifing through a sausage, careful not to scrape the plate and make too much ruckus.

"Marty is still in that early three year-old '*no* to everything' phase," she explained, forking a fingernail-sized piece of sausage into her mouth. She was oddly attractive, I found, not usually my type but for some reason intriguing. She wasn't really what I had pictured as Marshall's wife, either. I'd expected her to be more diminutive, perhaps. More willowy, more girly. Instead, Kristine looked as though, given the right setting, she could whoop her pencil-pushing husband in an arm-wrestling match. "And Caitlyn, you know, I'm still feeding her." She indicated her boob with a dip of her fork in the air and a tilt of her head. "Plus she eats some soft solids." Marshall was chewing away and nodding here and there with his bird-like Marshall nod, his eyeglass lenses flashing in the overhead light. Outside, despite the autumn morning chill, I could hear birds chirping. Far away, I heard a dog barking intermittently, as though challenged by the receding shadows of night, the advancement of the sun and lightening day.

Not that Kristine was unfeminine looking, I thought. Her high cheek bones and slim wedge of a nose with their flared nostrils actually called up an image of Katherine Glaston. Maybe it was just the way she was dressed that threw me – what looked like work pants, maybe Carhartts or Dickies, and a Henley shirt on – but even that was strangely attractive. She still wore long hair, and it was very pretty, dirt-blonde, tied back into a high pony tail with hardly any frays, lustrous in the morning light, wavy even.

I realized the drowsiness then, more than before, at the point I took what would be my last bite and imagined what it would be to take her upstairs and slip into Kristine Cohen before I slipped off to sleep. It was the kind of out-of-my-control daydream, covetous, ungrateful, that a person was likely to have when on the brink of unconsciousness.

Marshall wagged his fork at me and was sucking at his teeth. "You look like something I've seen before."

That sort of perked me up, ambiguous though it was. Hypervigilance, a constant state of alert didn't disregard ambiguous potential threats. No sir.

"Many a student up all night partying before the mid-term," he said, and grinned. "Jack, go hit the sack."

I looked at Kristine and opened my mouth to say thank you for breakfast when she said "use the day bed, downstairs, end of the hall there. It's in Marshall's office. But he won't be needing that today."

Kristine stood up and came around the table and actually hooked me under the shoulders, lifting me out of the chair. I mean, I stood up as well, but I was again envisioning her slamming down Marshall's arm in a match, or pinning him to the bed, she on top, maybe taking his hands and pinning them down to, as she thrusted…

And I blinked out of that and started walking, feeling suddenly seven years old. Marshall said, "good night," with one hand in the air and the other picking up his glass of milk, then he was gone.

"Bathroom's on the right, right here," she said. Indeed, the bathroom was just past the kitchen. And then was the back room, Marshall's office, and the day bed. "Sometimes Marshall takes a cat nap or two while grading papers, or working on his book. Did he mention he was a writer?"

As Kristine pulled down the covers on the bed and turned me to sit down, I shook my head no. I took my shoes off, gently brushing her aside from doing so. She smelled like the citrus she'd recently sliced up, like the oranges, and there was also something powdery, and the scent of some simple shampoo in her hair, like *Prell* or *Head & Shoulders*.

"What? I'm surprised. It's usually the first thing he'll tell somebody. He's writing a book about the area, about the Appalachian Trail…" I nodded and lay down and she pulled the covers over me. She put her hands on her hips. "…and some of the communes up around his area," she went on. I swam back from the blackness a little, struggling against the undertow.

"Nhh?" I said. "Really?"

"Yes," she said. "Marshall is really fascinated by this whole state. He's not a local like me. He's a transplant."

"From…?"

"Oh, he's a Brooklyn boy. Surprised he didn't tell you that, either." She was looking around the office, now she looked down at me. "We'll get you some clothes after you get up and shower. You look about Marshall's size."

I opened my mouth to protest, even started to get up, to tell her I was too dirty to be in her bed, how could I have even laid down, but she shook her head right away. I saw, for some reason, maybe from the angle, that she had full lips. Her breasts shook with the motion of her head. "No. Go to sleep."

I could hardly argue. The blackness felt like it was pulling at the backs of my eyes, the back of my head, my body already being sucked into the bed, into the beyond, like snow melting, or sand washing away into the tide that pulled at it.

Kristine said one more thing, but I didn't even hear what it was, and then she was gone, and so was I.

Just for an hour, was my last thought.

*

When I awoke, it was dark, and I was disoriented. Where was I? Back in the barracks? I thought I heard someone talking, and it sounded like Daniel.

I tried to move, but couldn't. I tried to speak but found my throat was closed up.

Something moved in the room beside me. I thought of a jellyfish. I thought of an octopus, or a cuttlefish. All three terrified me. The first had no brain, the others more brains-to-body than any other creatures. Swimming about like that in the deep, deep. What business did this giant, brainless, alien thing, this jellyfish have, and this hugely brained, freakish creature with suckers and a beak – what business did they have? What was the cuttlefish doing down there? Where had it come from? What was it thinking? This thing, a floating head in the depths with those sad, alien eyes, pushing itself around amid the currents with its beard of tentacles. What business?

What business do you *have? They're just creatures.*

Just *creatures,* I thought. *Just.* Who ever came up with the word "creatures" obviously didn't share one bone, one cell – one *gene* with me.

Movement again. Just a shadow. Near what might have been a door.

Terry Hackford, I thought. But no. Terry was dead. Dead and buried or just dead. He might have gotten away from our wreck – I had – but he likely would have made it only as far as I had gotten, and *he* was the true liability, the true threat to Utopia.

Terry had been purportedly looking to protect my interests. The first human-guinea-pig-rights arbitrator. It was funny. It was bullshit. He was affiliated with the very people who'd created the whole mess in the first place, the Christian Scientists. That was, if I were to go on what the bearded man at the Naturalist's table had said. And it was tough to go on what anybody said these days. And so Terry, if he stood for what he'd claimed he did, it made a kind of sense – as soon as there was some new strain in the human species, some offshoot in the culture, some aberration, some new thistle in the reeds, there was someone who was willing to step in and stand up for them. People were always looking for a cause.

Movement a third time. Still, those voices. Daniel...

No, it wasn't Daniel. *Marcel*? Well, Marcel had that kind of lisp thing, but not a lisp – more like a sucking thing that happened on either side of his mouth when he talked. So that an "s" had an extra sound to it, like "esch". But, of course, it wasn't Marcel-

Marshall. Right. And the shadow slipped away, and then I saw there was indeed a doorway there, and I heard, "Marty?" A woman's voice. The one who smelled like oranges and powder – I could still detect it in the air. Still, as I came around, I heard it. I heard the humming, and I knew – I was positive – if for only a moment I knew that it was my mother standing there by my bed, back for me after all of these long years.

I could move again. The spell of abeyance was gone. I sat up, and my head pounded for a second. My lips were dry. "Thirsty," I said, testing my voice. It was rust-hinged at best. I felt weak. Numb in places. Instead of feeling rested I felt like I could sleep for another year. How long had I been out?

Footsteps, coming toward me. Down a short hall, I thought. Past a bathroom...

"Jack?"

The woman. In the doorway. A taller shadow. Not a jellyfish or an octopus. Not my mother. My head throbbed dully.

I should say something. For some reason I'd forgotten how to speak. A feeling of unreality washed over me, and not for the first time; a feeling of total alienness. I could be anywhere – where was I? Nothing was familiar. Panic started to course through me with hot tentacles. Thin filament tentacles by the hundreds. Thousands. Like sharp veins. I could feel the blood rising in my head, increasing the pressure, a giant brain pulsing. Mental confusion.

The room filled with light and I shrank from it. Then I realized it wasn't so bright, it was a desk lamp. A writer's desk lamp – or a banker's lamp, whatever it was. Green shade. Dangle beads of a short gold pull-chain. A smooth trough in its base to rest pens or pencils.

"Sorry," she said, and I looked at her.

The panic drained from me almost at once, like a drain unplugged, an eddy of soiled fluid. "Could I get a glass of water?"

"Of course," she said.

"Thank you – so much," I said. I was sitting up in the day bed, my legs swung off to the side. My Velcro shoes were there, and so I put them on. She was back very soon – Kristine, that was her name – holding a tall glass with water that winked from the desk lamp's light. She stood a few feet from where I now stood, close enough to hold out the glass and I could take it. I drank greedily from it. I looked around the room. In the throw of the lamp's light I could see books, but not quite make out the titles on the spines. There was a picture right above the desk and its centered lamp that was of Marshall and Kristine on horseback – he on what looked like a chestnut colored horse, she on a roan. They both smiled broadly. Another

framed picture lower and to the right was of the four of them, the family
Cohen, around the table, smiling. It might have been Thanksgiving. There
were other pictures, there were other things to notice, observe, other Marshal
Cohen doodads and artifacts; things that were pieces of information, clues,
but I didn't want to know anymore, I didn't want to see. Instead, water
running down and into and through me, I stepped forward, now in that place
where I seemed to have no control and total control at the same time.

My step drew me closer to Kristine, my glass empty. She opened her
mouth, maybe to ask if I wanted more, probably to, and I saw again how full
and perfect her lips were.

I lifted my hand to her face. She winced and looked at it and moved
back perhaps an inch or two without stepping, and then seemed to settle
back into place. My fingertips touched her, just behind the curve of her jaw
and along her neck, and my thumb brushed a light trail across her
cheekbone, towards her lips, stopping just short of the corner of her mouth.

He's cheating on you, I thought to say, *with one of his students.*
Nasipi. Exchange student from Cape Town. He told me while I was
unconscious. He told me he had to tell someone. Even a sleeping stranger.
But I wasn't asleep. Not really.

Instead I took my hand away. Kristine's eyes glistened in the
duskiness of the room.

"Thank you," is what I said.

"You're welcome." She blinked. Something was gone; over. She
stepped back and looked me up and down with her eyes, like she'd done
while feeding me and shooing me off to bed.

"So let's get you those fresh clothes. I'll start the shower for you."
And she slipped from the room.

I walked out, past the bathroom where I heard the squeak of bathtub knobs being adjusted, and the falling of water on porcelain.

Water, I mused, and felt a smile on my mouth and thought, not for the first time either, *who ever would have thought the answer would've been water?*

I heard someone yell and my smile vanished. Three more steps and I could see into the living room. I hugged the wall and peered in, my heart beating faster again.

Marshall was wrestling with his three year-old son. Marshall was down on all fours, glasses, I could see, removed and perched on a nearby end table, and the kid was just running into the side of him, little arms up in the air, belly-butting the side of Marshall's ribs, rebounding and going again while Marshall waxed threatened and pained. The little girl, I saw, was in a high chair in the neighboring kitchen, pacifier in grinning mouth, bouncing there and making dribbling noises with her arms up like her brother's, her legs kicking. With many of the lights in the place turned on now, I could see that it was one big room, really, the living room and the kitchen, one big family room. Nothing fancy. Two small couches and a stuffed chair and two end tables in the living room. No television, I noticed. Where the kitchen linoleum met the brownish indoor-outdoor carpet of the living room was the small dining room table, the kind that could have extra leaves added for company. The baby girl sat beside it in her high chair. Past the table was the kitchen-kitchen, an L-shaped section of cabinets, stove, sink (no microwave) and an island with the pots hanging above it.

"Hey," said Marshall, and the boy stopped at once, and looked where his daddy looked and fell silent, suddenly taking to chewing on his shirt sleeve and looking at the floor three feet in front of him.

I know how you feel, kid, I thought. The little girl, though, kept on dribbling and bouncing. Tiny bubbles popped around one side of her pacifier.

"Hey," I said. I suddenly felt completely awkward, water or no water. Not panicked, no, just awkward. I was in the middle of a Kodak moment. A whole series of them.

"What time is it?"

"Uhmmm," Marshall lifted up a hand – a hoof, or a paw, to Marty – and looked at his watch. I saw that it was a calculator watch. "Six-thirty," he said.

"A.m. or p.m.?"

He smiled for a second, then realized I was serious. "P.m.," he said. "We're going to have dinner in a minute if you w–"

"No, no, no," I said. I was no longer hugging the wall, but I didn't come into the room. "I've overstayed my welcome as it is."

"Oh no, you–"

"I will take you up on that quick shower." I rubbed at my stubbled jaw. "Thank you," I said. I stopped and looked at both kids. The girl was cooing merrily. The little boy Marty now managed to look up at me from under his lowered brow. "You have a beautiful family," I said. I retreated before Marshall could say or do anything else nice, and turned and nearly ran into Kristine.

She offered a short squeal. We did one of those quick side-to-side, I'll-pass-this-way-but-you're-thinking-that-was-the-way-to-go to impasses, but finally got around one another.

Then I was in the shower and shaved and done and redressed with what Kristine laid out for me on the lidded toilet – a pair of blue jeans, a tan and gold and dark brown checker-flannel shirt, a pair of black socks.

I stood in the doorway as they sat around the table, thanking them again. Marshall insisted on seeing me out the door. I looked at both of the kids and then at Kristine, and she held my gaze until moments before I was through the door when Marty spit some potatoes out of his mouth and she tried to catch them. Then I was gone, and she was gone for me.

In the driveway I batted away Marshall's offer to at least drive me back to the gas station.

"What happened to my old clothes?"

Marshall looked me up and down, admiring, I guess, how I looked in his wardrobe. "Kristine didn't think you'd want them. She'll burn them later." He then opened his mouth before I could ask him the next question, and he actually swatted his forehead with the heel of his palm. "Jesus," he said, "I almost forgot – she took out your pockets – sorry, she didn't mean anything. Hold on." He disappeared back inside before I could say anything else, before I could tell him that it was okay that Kristine looked through my stuff, because there was only the one thing. Marshall returned, empty handed. "Oh, I guess there was nothing. Just some trash."

"Little red straw," I said.

"Yeah a lit–" His eyes widened some, but he didn't slap his forehead again. I liked Marshall. I was smiling when he went inside one more time and still smiling when he returned with my bent, chewed red straw. He looked at it for a moment, then at me, then held it out in front of him. "Quit smoking?"

"Yeah," I said, "that too."

He offered me his University business card and told me to look him
up. He told me good luck with my daughter and everything, and then I
walked away, past the single maple tree, down the long country driveway.

I felt like a new man.

The stars were out but it was a warmer night. I heard the door shut
behind me to the Cohen home. I walked.

As I walked I marveled. Things I had never expected to be traps were
gaping pitfalls. Things I feared and mistrusted were of no threat. I decided
then, once and for all and conclusively, that my sleuthing days were over.
They had never been too real to begin with – let's face it – but to me they
had been. Naïvely, they had been. Drunkenly, they had been. Illusions.
Dreams. Jellyfish.

I was done.

At the end of the road I turned left. I knew that way was south.

Whatever was waiting for me in Bondville, I was ready.

Where's my mom?

The cab let me off in front of Katherine's single storey ranch-house. I
thought of Costa Rica.

I had taken a cab from downtown Bondville – and I describe it as
"downtown" but loosely. I had been first dropped there by a guy named
Wilford (there were actually such real guys named Wilford in Vermont) who
had a bright grey beard and matching grey eyes hooded beneath the bill of a

cap that read "Woodmeiser" on the front. We'd stopped at the hardware
store – Bickford Lumber – and I'd called a cab from the payphone across the
street, in front of a deserted-looking post office. That was downtown.

When I stepped out of the cab it was nighttime again, and a figure was
sitting on the porch. I sat up and a light came on. I saw Katherine standing
there, and I walked up the lawn. The night held a perfume, that scent of
farms I was becoming familiar with, and something else, something arable,
like wind through cornhusks, whickering like thin canvas sleeves. *Where's
my mom?*

I stopped at the bottom of the porch and looked up at Katherine. I had
the damned red straw in my mouth, and I took it out and jammed it in my
jeans pocket – Marshall's jeans. I was nervous, but it was a different kind of
nervous. It wasn't the quaking fear beneath the Brooklyn bravado, and it
wasn't the paranoia and other-dimensional mental anguish of being a drunk
and a drug addict. It felt normal. It felt like what normal people felt, I
imagined; a little bundle of butterflies, a slight increase in the heart rate, a
dash of social angst.

Then I looked at Katherine, really saw her, and not just looked at her
while I thought about myself and she scowled down at me and I realized I
was scowling too. I broke into a smile.

She asked, "You tired?"

"Actually I've been sleeping all day."

That was how we spoke for the first time after years had come and
gone.

We went inside and made pleasantries and drank some kind of tea.
The house was dark and quiet. A cat stirred somewhere that I only heard
and didn't see. I wanted to ask about Leah right away, but I knew it wasn't

the right time. When Katherine went to bed I lay awake on the downstairs couch listening to a clock softly tocking away the minutes until I snuck to the porch where I could see the first tips of dawn, for the second day in a row. Sitting there I heard, but didn't see, a rooster crowing.

Around seven a.m. I heard footsteps upstairs – the unmistakable footfalls of a morning-enthused child. I sat on the couch and folded the blankets I'd been given and rubbed my eyes.

Katherine came down the stairs first and asked me how I'd slept. I told her fine. She smiled and went into the kitchen to make coffee. I looked up the stairs and Katherine said from the other room, "she'll be down." I heard the girl turn on a faucet that must've been in an upstairs bathroom. Then the sound of water rushing down through the pipes in the wall. I stood and walked to the doorway at the foot of the stairs and looked into the kitchen. "Is she taking a bath?"

Katherine shrugged and pressed on a coffee grinder. The sound was shocking in the quiet. Then she took out an instrument I'd only seen in one or two places before – a coffee press. I stood there and watched the entire operation, fascinated.

Katherine wasn't what I'd expected. It wasn't that she looked bad or anything in her dark jeans and blouse and sandals, but that she looked false to me, somehow, maybe in the way – and I guess "surreal" would be a better word – that a celebrity might look to you upon meeting them – maybe meeting them in the morning before coffee or waffles or the hair and make-up team got to them.

The water stopped upstairs and Katherine brought me a cup of coffee and wordlessly walked to the front of the house and opened the door and went out onto the porch. I followed.

We sat together on a bench-swing with an old seatpad that had faded blue and orange stripes with an afghan thrown over the whole thing. After a few moments of watching the sun climb higher in the sky and clouds from the north coming in and gradually shouldering together, we heard the footsteps coming down the stairs. I looked at Katherine and I must've looked scared, the way she smiled at me.

I stood and walked down onto the lawn, I don't know why. Katherine stood up too. I just took a few steps and then turned around. Maybe I knew I wanted this to be as good as it could, to last as long as it could.

Leah, my daughter (Leah Glaston, I found out a little later amid less-than-pleasant circumstances, and not Leah Aiello, which would have been unusual for a number of reasons), came out onto the porch with a red bow in her hair. It was the kind of bow you'd expect to see in a Grimm Fairy tale or Hallmark card commercial. (I didn't know why my brain cross-referenced those two…maybe some residual glitching from Dr. Cameron Madison's "neural disinhibitor" drug, but I didn't care.) A mass of blonde hair seemed piled above her oval face, bobbing like cotton or silk, tied up with the bow. She walked toward her mother's legs, her eyes large, almond-round, dark brown.

"Leah," said Katherine Glaston to the little girl, my daughter, "this is Jack."

Something twanged inside of me, like a guitar string that has unexpectedly snapped. For some reason I had been just naturally anticipating *this is your **daddy***. But what could I expect? This was the first time I'd ever laid eyes on my daughter, and she was three years-old. I hadn't been there at her birth. I had never signed a paternity statement. I had never sent her a Christmas present or talked to her on the phone. The only thing we had between us was the dark-haired woman standing on the porch with the slight rinds of morning fatigue under her eyes, visible even from where I was, and two phone conversations we'd ever had since Leah had been conceived.

On the porch, where they stood, I now saw a silver moose that hung from a rafter with five or six chimes dangling beneath. A low wind blew – and that's how it felt, *low*, like it only ruffled past my jeans and through the lower part of my shirt – and the chimes tinkled. From the corner of my eye I caught a glimpse of a rooster walking, strutting in that head-jabbing way, albeit casually.

"Can you say 'Hi, Jack?'"

Leah was curled around her mother's leg in a way that made me think of a Koala hugging a tree from some pictures I'd seen in Marcel's collection of *National Geographic*. "Hi, Jack," came a tiny, muffled voice. It sounded like a voice you expect a cartoon character to have. Unbelievably cute.

"Hi," I said, and waved, and felt like a complete idiot. For some reason that's how I felt from head to toe in that first couple of moments – like a complete idiot. Like my life was ridiculous. That I'd missed out on everything. That I missed out on reality. Something seemed to spring loose inside me again. It was like I was a machine with the gears and coils starting to come loose.

Machine. Marshall. Marcel.

She hadn't even called me by my real name, my daughter. She didn't even know it. She would never know it.

I dropped my hand. I was still standing on the lawn. I started looking around, not knowing what else to do. There were four posts to the porch in front of Katherine's house. No screen, but I didn't see why a screen couldn't be applied. I heard it got really buggy in Vermont in the springtime. Of course I'd also heard that bugs were disappearing.

My legs felt like liquid lead. I could smell something in the air again I could only recognize as shit. But I'm sure there were better words for it, *farm*ier words, like "scat" or "dung" or something. It wasn't manure – I knew that smell by now. It was probably chicken crap. I thought I could hear the foul clucking somewhere behind the house and the low wind.

It was suddenly hard for me to meet Katherine's eyes, but I did, and then I looked away and around me where I was standing, and saw a couple of small stone statues that looked like little buddhas or gnomes. There was a whitestone walkway that bent like a rainbow the rest of the way to the porch; I was just off to the side of it.

"How are you, Leah?" I said.

"Good," said Leah, and seemed to come unglued a little. She was tucked into a little pair of earthy-green overalls, an orange shirt underneath, the color of a very late day sun. The chimes tinkled again, and I felt a shiver run down my back. A storm was coming.

Were they here? Were they just on the other side of that front door, listening? It was absurd; I'd already spent the night. Still, they *had* to know about Katherine. The Brandis brothers knew anything they wanted to, didn't they? Again, all they would've had to have done was put the lean on Marcel. He had a kid. He'd have to talk. He'd have to mention Katherine.

And again – what about Marshall? What if they'd picked up my trail and it brought them to him? What if they were stringing him up right now while his duct-taped wife and kids looked on with virgin terror?

Marshall, I'm sorry, man.

(Machine Marshall Marcel)

I stepped onto the first stair. There were three stairs to the porch. Green tread. White riser. Everything in threes.

Me, Katherine, Leah.

The Utopia Corporation, the Naturalists…the scientists.

Three disciples, Daniel, Peter, Jared.

Three women, Julianne, Maya, Katherine.

Machine. Marshall. Marcel.

Three.

I took the second step. Leah seemed to shrink back. Her mother gave her an encouraging pat on the shoulder. She said to me, "anyway, how was your trip up? I never asked you."

My trip up. Right. From Brooklyn.

"Good," I said. It was like I was arriving for the first time. And I was. I think Katherine had planned it that way. I glanced down at the orangey-sherberty colored workboots Marshall Cohen had lent me. *Herman Survivors* they were called. I guess they could pass for street wear, only they were too scuffed and worn. I wondered what Katherine thought of my appearance now in broad daylight. I just let the conversation keep going. "I've been up in the area for a little while," I said, wincing a little, bracing for the pain I might see on her face. There was none I could detect. I listened to the wind for a moment longer, listened to see if I could hear anything, but it was only the muffled cluckery of the chickens. So I knelt in front of my daughter, my eyes leaving Katherine's, sliding down and away from her.

Leah didn't shrink back anymore. She had her thumb in her mouth, though. Had it been there the whole time? And she was fiddling with her bow with the other hand. "I like your bow," I said. I noticed it wasn't really red, but the same color as her dark orange shirt. Only the bow was made of a silken kind of stuff, so that it gave off different shades. "It reminds me of my red straw."

"A red straw?" She said it around her thumb, and it sounded like *a wed stwah?*

"Yeah," I said, "I chew on it." I wrinkled my nose and I think I even winked, like I was some ace with the kiddies, like I'd been doing this for years. I don't know why, it just happened, like the feeling-like-an-idiot part. Leah, though, she smiled behind her thumb. Here brown eyes sparkled. I stood back up. I looked Katherine right in the eyes. She seemed to hold that sort of fatigue there, but there was something else. Our history, maybe. Our brief time, the memory of it in there, the concerted nerves of those memories lighting up like certain city-street-lit highways and shining out through her eyes. I looked there and I tried to see if there was any compromise she might give away, any danger.

"Let me see the *stwah*."

"Leah," Katherine said, and put a hand on her daughter's shoulder. "Ask nicely."

Leah said, "may I see it, *puh-leeze*."

"Sure," I said. Still on my knees, I straightened my body some and reached into my pocket. I made a face, rolling my eyes up and sticking out my tongue with comedic flourish. It had the desired effect, and my daughter giggled. I pulled it free with equal flourish and held it in front of her nose, right in between the both of us. "There it is," I said.

"Eww," she said, making a face.

"I know. Eww."

Then her expression changed and she said, "can I see it?"

"Of course," I said, and she reached out and took it, and her small hand touched mine. *My daughter.*

Straw in hand, I was forgotten. Her mother was forgotten. Leah turned, this new prize in hand, this new mystery, and walked away on the porch. I was sure, having had some experience with Jocelyn, that the attention on the straw would be fleeting, and then there would be a new adventure. With Leah down at the other end of the porch, wielding the straw like a wand and talking to herself, I stood, brushing off my knees. I realized I was still very sore. My bandages and most of my bruises and scrapes were hidden beneath Marshall's wardrobe, but I couldn't conceal the grimace when I stood. Katherine started to open her mouth, perhaps to say something about this, but I spoke first.

"I know it sounds a little weird – I've already spent the night – but is anybody here? Anybody else besides us?"

Katherine blinked. I watched closely. There may have been something, a trace of guile, but it went too quick and she spoke. She said, "I have a restraining order against my last boyfriend. So no, no one's here."

Now it was my turn to skip a beat, to be caught a little off-guard. "A restraining order?" I looked behind me, down the porch at Leah, feeling my skin tighten around my eyes, my ribs close in a little around my chest, and back to Katherine who was already shaking her head *no* in a dismissive, *don't worry* kind of way. "No, he never touched either of us. Just called all of the time. Would show up late and sit on the porch and cry. Creepy stuff."

I thought about this, and decided it was okay. I looked into her again. I had never been able to look at people this way, I was thinking, just distantly. "But there's no...other sorts of people here?"

"You mean like lawyers? Jack, what are you talking about? It's just us. Some of my family was here last weekend, but that's it. Oh, Leah had a play date on Monday with her friend Jayden."

Jayden, I thought, and fought the urge to roll my eyes. I thought of Peter, and someone's girlfriend who had been named Sierra. I thought of entropy. I thought of biochemistry.

The feeling of coming apart on the inside had abated. I still felt a little like throwing up, and I realized right away that no matter how harmless Katherine might paint it to be, the image of some guy sitting on their porch in the dark, crying, was going to stay with me.

A lot of things would stay with me, most things, right up until the end. Right up until the final *operating system not found.*

Katherine ducked her head at me, catching me in that thought. "Come on back inside," she said, and turned toward the door.

"Leah, we're going inside. You coming?"

I looked and saw Leah at the end of the porch, poking her head out of the railing spindles there, watching the rooster. I saw that the red straw, indeed forgotten, left on the warping floorboards.

"In a minute, momma," she said.

We went in.

*

There was a back porch to the house as well. And beyond it, the garden.

The real garden, I thought, not even quite understanding my own meaning. Madison's garden had been real enough, it had just been some perfunctory sort of cover. And the Naturalists' garden had been real too, though more a greenhouse than a garden, per se.

We went through the house, Leah still at the forefront of my thoughts, but now I had the mind to look things over. The floors were a darkish hardwood. There were, what looked to me, like plugs in the wood. I was no flooring expert. Katherine saw me looking down. "It's against the wood grain on purpose," she said, "I did it. I like the look." I had no idea what she was talking about.

A grandfather clocked tocked softly back and forth. The sound of it was the company I'd kept the previous night. The gold pendulum winked as it swung. The cat – orange – leapt from the post of the stairway banister and quickly padded up the stairs and zipped out of sight. "That's Pasha," said Katherine. "She's a snoot."

It smelled vaguely of patchouli in the room, but more of some other implacable fragrance, something I couldn't quite put my finger on. It was as if there was almost a hint of men's aftershave in the air.

This front room, in the daylight, was like a living room that didn't look too lived-in. *Perhaps up the stairs*, I thought, *Leah has her own bedroom and there are coloring books and crayons and stuffed animals and dolls lying about. And Katherine has her bedroom down the hall, and in that bedroom she entertains men who are not her daughter's father.*

There were two pictures hanging between the end of the stairs and the door out of the room that lead further into the house. Each picture was of a woman, black and white. One looked slightly older than the other – the pictures, I mean, whereas each woman looked to be in her seventies or eighties.

"My two Ruths," Katherine explained. "Ruth Stout and Ruth Spring. Organic gardeners. Aren't they beautiful?" I didn't know if she meant the pictures or the women in them. I suddenly felt the old confusion start to sneak back in. I shivered involuntarily.

"What?" said Katherine. We stopped walking. The door banged open behind us, and I jumped and turned, ready. Leah came dashing in, yelped a bright and curt "hi!" and kept going into the next room. I settled and saw Katherine looking at me with that same scowl I'd seen on her face when I'd walked up to the porch from the cab. She then turned away from me and back to the pictures on the wall. "She's from Connecticut," Katherine said, pointing at the woman in the slightly more worn looking picture, "and she's from Indian Lake, in the Adirondacks." Katherine kissed her first and second finger on the tips and placed them on the wall in between the two framed photographs. Her hand and arm slide to the side of her and she moved, somehow willowy, into the next room.

I wondered what she must be thinking, me showing up at night instead of the morning I'd said I'd be there (I'd called from the Naturalists' compound, having used Peter's cell phone and then been careful to erase the number from the dialed calls log.) I wondered what she must be thinking about the way I was behaving. I also wondered at what I found different about her, physically, that was, and this something that, despite all else, was nagging at me.

I walked into the kitchen. "This is the room that's *lived* in," I said, unaware that I was going to speak. Leah was kneeling on a stool with a red vinyl top to it, like something you'd find in a fifties diner, something salvaged. She was getting into some crackers that sat on a very busy counter space.

To my immediate right was the countertop, where Katherine had made the coffee, the sink, cupboards high and low. To the left was a tall piece of cabinetry, something someone might call a pantry. I could hear the Allman Brothers playing, and I forced the sound-memory away. Hanging above the cabinet – pantry – was a jumble of gleaming chrome ladles, whisks, spatulas, the gamut. And piled all around it were crates, apple boxes, stuffed canvas bags, hemp bags, some clothes – seven or eight dresses, like the one Katherine had on, resting atop some more bags and crates on their hangers, laying in a way that made me think of a drowning victim hauled up onto shore, loose and sodden and able to bend in strange, upsetting ways.

I thought of the one body I'd seen, when I was fourteen, hauled from the East River when it was dragged after a little girl went missing in Battery Park. A tourist's daughter. But it wasn't her they'd found, it was some guy who was a suspected Mafioso. It was what had made me want to get into spying and all that. It had also made me throw up, which should have been, yeah, my first clue about the inanity of my career aspirations.

There was no woodblock in this kitchen but the table in front and to the left of me – occupying most of the floor space in the otherwise reasonably sized room – was so rudimentary it looked like something you'd call a block. Unfinished wood, rough-hewn legs, it was a squat, massive chunk of a table. Like something an apprentice carpenter would build cutting his teeth. Yet somehow it fit, and someone it looked to be purposely the way it was.

Wouldn't that be nice, I thought, and saw Cameron Madison coming at me with that dripping needle. I then thought of Katherine's physical stature again, and an ice-cold feeling closed in on me, making my wounds ache and throb. I suddenly wondered if they'd gotten to her, if she too had been manipulated by the doctors, if more people had than I'd originally thought back at the barracks. If the bearded man was truly right; if the entire state, maybe even the east coast had already been infiltrated, *infected*, really, like a plague. Because that's what it was. A plague.

I must've worn my thoughts on the exterior because Katherine put a cool hand on my forearm. The skin of her palms and fingers was paper-dry, taut. On the large elemental table was more of everything. Harvest. The boxes were full of corn, zucchini, green beans, potatoes, spinach, and more. Now I understood the earthen smell I'd registered in the front room. It was the smell of reap. It was the real smell of a real garden.

"The soil was so rich, so friable this season," said Katherine, inhaling deep in through her nostrils. Then she looked from the table to our daughter. "Come on, honey. Let's go show Jack the garden."

I shook away the feeling. I concentrated on where I was, concentrating on soaking it all up, storing it all away. The house, then, was simple enough from what I'd seen, a little cluttered, and just the right size. There was another room off the kitchen, perhaps a den or a study or something like that. Above me were the two bedrooms, maybe even a spare room as well, and the bath.

Leah hopped down off from the stool, still crunching some crackers. She had two in her small right hand. They were octagonal.

Katherine lead us out onto the back porch – a veritable flea market, it was filled with so much stuff (but all *good* stuff, I thought, all stuff I would like to pore over for hours, stand there and go through it all while my daughter skipped and played nearby and Katherine drifted along in the rows of our garden).

But I *could* have that, I *could* do that, couldn't I? I still had a choice, didn't I? I could make a stand. I could stop what I'd set in motion. It might put them at risk, but it would be worth it. It would be worth it.

The screen door squeaked appropriately and Katherine bobbed down the stairs (four this time, four, not three) and Leah followed more carefully, taking them with each with two steps, holding her crackers up in the air like she was trying to keep them out of harm's way, as though she were wading deeper into a mud hole.

The garden sprawled out in front of me. Long and rectangular, going on for what looked like a football field's length until its end border. Hemlocks and hardwood trees bordering the garden to my right. To my left and beyond the far end, field. Field that went on until it rolled down and out of sight.

It felt like I was standing on the edge of paradise.

The garden was mostly harvested, though. Instead of a bright bouquet of vegetation it was husks and witherings and a deep, dark brown of soil, and pumpkins. Leah, once free of the stairs, raced to those pumpkins. Katherine stood on the edge of the dug earth and turned and smiled at me. Then her head cocked slightly and an expression something like compassion came over her, something I'd never known on her face. I realized I was crying. At the same time, I heard thunder rumble in the distance.

Katherine came over to me and hugged me. And I knew at last what it was about her body that was different. Her breasts were softer. They had been firm when we'd had our fling, and now, after breast-feeding, they had softened. That was all. No experimentation. No gene manipulation. No conspiracy. Just nature. Motherhood. "It's a lot, I know," she said in my ear. "You're doing great."

I snuffled back the tears and wiped at my eyes, the bridge of my crooked nose, pulling away, but she held on to me.

"I know," she said, "I know."

And that did it, and it opened up the gates, and I cried. I wanted to cry forever. I wanted to tell her all that had happened. All that had gone on since I'd seen her last. The drugs, the drinking, the great fall I had in Brooklyn. I wanted to tell her about George Klembeck, about what we'd done to him. I wanted to tell her about Julianne, how I'd tried…how I'd tried but I'd failed. How she'd lain there, dying, asking me where her mother was. I wanted to tell her about my father, about what he'd looked like in the end, and how I hated him for dying, and how he was a stranger, and always had been. I wanted to tell her about the beatings and the killings; everything I'd done, and tell her I was beginning to understand it now, I was beginning to see, I was starting to know the emptiness. I wanted to explain my visions to her, and that I knew that they weren't just my visions, that it was all such a thing, a huge thing I couldn't get my mind around but felt I know longer had to, and that the less I tried the more I saw, the more was revealed, and that it was amazing, and that it was beautiful. And I wanted to tell her about how I'd always been thinking of her. Thinking about Leah. That Leah had become my guiding light, or that, possibly, a guiding light had been shining *through* her. I wanted to tell her that, most of all, I finally felt home. I was here. I was home.

"I..." I began

"I know," she soothed.

"I...I just want to stay here," I said. I couldn't help it. It fell out of me.

"I know," she said, and held me tight. Despite myself, I could feel an erection gently forming. I tried to pull away again, get a hold of myself. I didn't want Leah to see me like this. I didn't-

"I know," Katherine breathed in my ear, squeezing me around my shoulders, "they told me everything."

Daydreaming. There's a difference between daydreaming and over-imagination. Daydreaming, for me, I realized at some point after Katherine Glaston whispered into my ear that "she knew" for the fifth time, daydreaming was *under* imagination. Daydreaming was sort of like the ebb and flow of the ocean's current while the nightmare – the hurricane, the *over* imagination, raged above. I had been floating beneath the surface, caught in the undertow.

Terry Hackford sat across from me. We were in the room with the Grandfather clock swinging, the cat now back on the endpost of the banister, watching, pausing to clean its face with a whetted paw. The air was scented

with Terry's aftershave. I should have known. Ice-pick me in the nose
holes, I should have known.

"It's your choice, Jack," said Terry. He had a huge scar running down
one side of his face. It went from the temple next to his left eye and
connected with the left corner of his mouth, dipping, at one point, so that it
reminded me a little of the symbol for "ohms" I had seen once on some box
or other I was loading onto a truck. It wasn't really even a scar; a scar
would be premature. It *would* be a scar; there were still stitches in his face.
How long had it been since we'd flipped the van? A couple of days? A
couple of weeks? I had lost all sense of time. I thought of the man in the
bathroom outside of Rutland, looking at me in the mirror. The eye patch.

"My choice?" I spat the words out. I looked at Katherine, who
seemed to shrink back from what she saw in my eyes. "When did I ever
have a choice?"

Terry leaned forward and crossed his hands over one knee. He was
standing with one leg up on a hassock. I was sitting in the winged-back
chair I suspected was some family heirloom of the Glastons'; it was thick
with must. Every move I made caused a plume of dust; motes danced in the
streaming, late-morning light of the living room. I wasn't tied up or
anything, Terry had insisted I sit down. He had two others with him, and of
course I recognized them right away; Watson and Crick. Crick's nose was
bandaged, and he was looking at me with nothing but pure malice. I could
tell he wanted to kill me – if he weren't such a good Christian and all.

Above the stitched wound running almost the length of Terry
Hackford's face, the eye was bruised around the outside, and red with blood
on the inside. The bruise was dark blueberry-blue and purple and yellow
with tentacles. Like a squashed octopus, maybe. And Terry stood a little

funny, favoring his left leg. Not trying to strike some war hero-regal pose, no, but treating that one leg gingerly. If I had to, Terry would be easy to get through. Crick looked like he might be the type to still come after me even with a severed head. Watson merely looked tired.

"You," said Terry, leaning forward but not putting weight on that left leg, "have always had a choice."

"I've been a puppet," I said. It shot right out of my mouth. I was growing furious, and if I was directing my frustration at Terry, my hostility at Terry like one might a therapist or a priest, scapegoating them into a bit of a punching bag, making their face the face of the enemy, contorted with wounds though it already might be, I didn't care. "I've been played since day one," I said, turning to glower at Katherine. Leah was in the kitchen, set-up at the big block table with a coloring book and crayons. At least that was a little mercy, not having her in here to see this. *A monster*, I heard Cameron say, *that's all you'll be.*

"There is no question you've been manipulated, Jack," said Terry, in both that friendly, understanding voice and at once tempered with its own anger and frustration. At least Cameron Madison, in his grand prickness, had been up-front, I thought. He'd been an arrogant asshole and he'd talked like one. He'd wanted to dominate the world and wasn't afraid to show it, or tell about it. But Terry Hackford with all of his college-buddy / confidant / counselor bullshit was something else. It was sickening. And I always found myself the thirstiest around him, like a sixth sense, like I knew something bad was coming. The room fell into shadow as one of the marshalling storm clouds moving in over the house blocked the sun. The dust motes disappeared, covered in illusion again.

"Do you remember our talk?"

Terry and I had talked a number of times, but for some reason I knew which talk he meant. Not the first time we'd met, but the second.

"Yeah, you told me you were sorry for hitting me."

"And I was," Terry said, bobbing his head, wrinkling his forehead just enough to convey sincerity. And I remembered something. I had hated Terry Hackford from the first moment I'd met him. From the way the attractive bartender had responded to him, his jockish nature, that reddish crew-cut and square jaw, the way the other guys seemed to follow him, and especially, most of all, that following morning when I'd come across him in downtown Burlington – no, when he'd purposely bumped into me, *that* was the real story – how he seemed to have no hangover whatsoever. How he'd apologized and tried to be my friend.

"You remember I said that some hangovers could make you see and think things that weren't real."

I did remember. I remembered Terry saying that and then, as I sat there in that musty chair with the cat licking its paw over my shoulder and Katherine looking at me with what appeared a mixture of fear and sadness, I realized that I'd gotten myself all wrong. I didn't really hate Terry Hackford, I didn't really resent him. At least, not anymore. It wasn't Terry I wanted to be. It was Marshall Cohen. Chalk this moment of clarity up to the last remaining peptide of Dr. Madison's wonder drug? Maybe. Or maybe it was just that obvious.

"Yeah," I said, "I remember."

"But what is real? We talked about that. How maybe, probably, there is some reality that, well, is sort of outside of us, but also a part of us, we are a part of." He'd taken his hands in the middle of the sentence away from his

knee and waved little circles in the air with his palms to help illustrate
"reality."

He went on, "You said reality was subjective. And I said that reality
was *collective*." Terry took his foot from the hassock and started walking
over to me. The limp was obvious, and he didn't seem to try and hide it.
Crick took a step closer as Terry walked. If he was canine he would've been
growling at me. "And I told you that it was about conscience. That if you
had a clear conscience," and here Terry tapped his temple just like the late
Dr. Madison had been fond of doing, "you're going to be okay."

I looked up at Terry, my muscles tightening. But I wasn't as
perturbed as I had first been. Something was different. "And I asked you if
you were just covering for a dirty conscience…"

"And I said 'I wish'."

He stopped a couple of paces from me. "Do you know why I said
that, Jack?"

"It sounded snappy."

"No. Because it's true. Part of me wishes I could do whatever I want
and say whatever I want to people and just scrub clean afterwards, but I
can't. I've never been made that way. You, you're sitting there, looking at
me, judging me, telling yourself how dishonest I am. You're telling yourself
you don't like me because of how I am and can do what you aren't and wish
you could. Am I hitting close to the mark? But that's not it. The reason
you don't like me, Jack, is *because* I am honest, Jack, *because* I have a clear
conscience. Don't you want that too?"

My mouth was dry. I wanted that water now, but I was waiting.
"Terry," I said, "if this is where you start telling me that through Christ all

my problems will be solved..." I jerked a thumb over my shoulder. "You might as well convince me to pray to the two Ruths."

Terry glanced over my shoulder and, whether he got my reference or not, dismissed it. He made motions with his hands, palm down, like an ump calling an out at Fenway. "Jack, you've got it all wrong. What – you're going by what the Naturalists told you? That Christian Fundamentalists got some scientists together to harness the power of gene splicing and genetic manipulation in order to get votes for their favorite political leaders? That's bass-ackwards, Jack. Politicians want the religious right on their side to influence voters, not the other way around."

"Terry..." I began. My head was starting to hurt. Like I was hungover, which was impossible. I had just slept too much.

"Listen," said Terry, "why does someone have to be either an evolutionist *or* a creationist?"

I thought of my first meeting with Maya, jailbird-style. I heard her voice saying, *On the molecular level, we're all machines.*

"People are so primitive," Terry said. He looked less frustrated now than exhausted himself. He shook his head and his left hand floated up to his cheek, where he might have touched his wound, I thought, if he didn't become aware at it at the last second and drop the hand away, acting ashamed of himself for reasons I couldn't grasp. "You stick two people in a room together and given enough time they'll have each taken their side on everything. A bunch of people, and all you have are in-groups and out-groups. You're in, and everyone in your group is in, and the rest of the world is out. It's ridiculous. Let's *expand.*"

"Yeah," said Katherine, "and then you would have the 'non-expanders'. There will always be conflict."

Terry looked at her, as if to respond, and I broke in. "I'm tired of this, Terry. I've listened to Cameron, I don't need to hear you. It's pissing me off. Terry. What do you want?"

Terry took a limping step or two backwards and half-turned toward Katherine. "I got here yesterday," he said, "and met Miss Glaston. She agreed to work with me. To work with *you*." This seemed to be some marker phrase, some key, because now Katherine stepped forward, wringing her hands, chewing her lip a little, her face changing from that composite of fear and pity to something that appeared more consolidated. Her long dark-brown hair, pin straight, shined beneath the light of the room's incandescent chandelier. "Jack," she said, "I've given this a lot of thought." She stopped walking towards me. She hadn't been looking at me, but looking at the red-wine colored carpet. Behind her, in the corner she'd been in, were two tall sets of book shelves. I remembered thinking of browsing through them, learning about biochemistry and gene therapy. And I thought of Kristine Cohen, and Marshall's writing den.

"I've given it *a lot* of thought – not just now, since…this, but since Leah was born – and…" now Katherine looked at me, and her hazel eyes seemed to shiver with tears, "…and if you want to, I'd like for you to be here. I'd like for you to...be with us."

I looked at Katherine, I looked at her very closely. Her eyes stayed on mine. The tears brimmed, but did not spill. Then I looked to Terry.

"And you're okay with this?"

Terry shrugged. It didn't seem like a dismissive gesture, but more one of resignation at the fates handed out by the gods. "It's your choice, like I said."

"And what's the other choice?"

At last I thought of my dream, and Mike the FPR guy, sipping his spiked coffee, looking out at the huge bonfire that licked and snapped at the black sky.

Terry had turned away and was limping slowly back to the couch when he stopped at the question. Now he slowly rotated back around to face me, his head lowered a little, that jagged, dipped line running down his face where it had been ripped open by one of his own goon's bullets. He looked at me, and I could see something. I could see that the posturing was done, that the I'll-save-you shtick was dropped, that the Terry Hackford bravado had not a chink but a hole in the armor, and now something was looking at me from out of that hole. I realized I had been ungrateful. As soon as I saw that essence revealed, that truth, that inevitability, I wished the old Terry was there instead. I wished to be back when I didn't know a fucking thing except that I needed to get sober and find out if a guy named Phil Brandis was dead. Back when the greatest mystery was whether or not my gay roommate Daniel was sneaking around at night and sticking it into women instead. I didn't want to see what I saw there in Terry, looking out at me, because it was the onrushing train; the one I didn't want to hurry the hell up so much anymore. What I saw there was grim reality.

"The other choice is to come with me, to join me, and end Utopia."

Still, it hit me like a blast of wind, as though all the doors and windows had blown open. And I realized that they had, that Katherine's front door had blown open, that the cat had leapt from the banister and disappeared, that Leah had yelled out something, that I heard papers blowing around somewhere, and then saw Katherine chasing after them, even Watson trying to help – I saw one in the air, it looked like a sheet of music – and in the midst of the maelstrom I looked at Terry again and saw that the commotion hadn't bothered him in the least; he was still looking at me levelly, plainly, the face of reality and, of course, I realized I knew what was coming next.

Though they were twins, they were nowhere near identical. Though he slouched to the right a little, his shoulder there lower than the other (which made me wonder if that had more to do with the stroke he'd suffered at five years before or all of the right hooks he'd thrown at the New York Athletic Club,) Lincoln Brandis was taller than his brother Lucius. It was true he had become a sort of sidekick to his twin, making the phone calls (*"you'll be alright,* kleinnes,") making the coffee, taking the mail slowly to the corner of 7th street and Fleming, but it didn't seem to diminish him in the slightest. If anything, the humility of it made Lincoln Brandis even more regal. And while this brother Lucius preferred the black suits and shining slivery grey shirts, and wore his hair slicked and bluish-black, Lincoln was furnished in plaid pants and handmade sweaters that complimented his tightly wound, reddish-grey curls.

Thus it was Lucius who looked sorely out of place as he stood in between the driver's side door to the black Bentley and the car itself, drawing his firearm – I knew what it was, I'd seen it before, a silver Browning .45 – and looking around at everything from behind his black Aviator sunglasses, no doubt marveling, incredulous even, at what he was seeing. Space. Open country. No doubt smelling things with that somehow aquiline nose of his – apples, sod, *manure*. Not that Lucius Brandis would even know what manure was. As far as I knew he hadn't ever left the city save for the occasional trip to Westchester, to Jersey.

Lincoln got out next, from the passenger side, standing slowly, unfurling with some unease. I could believe that the two of them had made this trip; I just couldn't believe that Lucius was *driving*. I suddenly felt, believe it or not, guilty. (See, one of Lucius's tactics to get me to do what he needed was to guilt me into it, to make me feel grateful for everything he did for me and exploitative of him at the same time – some of the other boys in his employ would even call him *Mussolini*, but always behind his back and well out of earshot.) Lincoln was different than his brother here too. Lincoln got people to do things by encouraging them. *Just be there, just do what comes natural*, I heard him say in a long ago conversation.

We were, all six of us, that is, myself, Terry, Watson, Crick, and then Katherine and Leah, standing on the front porch, watching with unique yet similar disbeliefs as these two men debarked their sleek, black, city-folk car and started up the sloping front yard to the foot of the house. The wind blew fiercely around them, tousling Lucius's perfect hair so that coarse, shining clumps of it stuck out in ducktails. He pressed the hair back into place with the heel of one his smooth, paper-pushing palms. The other hand gripped the Browning.

As soon as Katherine saw the gun her eyes widened and she bent and put two shielding, protective arms around Leah and ushered her back inside. I would have done the same, though I was frozen where I stood, for the moment. I realized then that what I had seen in Terry's eyes, the thing looking out of him and through him – and at me – had been death.

Terry leaned toward me and whispered out of the side of his mouth. "Now's a good a time as any to choose."

As he said this Watson and Crick brought out their own weapons – each pulled a Glock from holsters strapped beneath their suit jackets – and one of them, Watson, said, "that's far enough." I looked at Crick out of the corner of my eye – easy to spot him with the gleaming white bandage, the bruise-flares, like wings, beneath his eyes. He was chewing on something – gum, though I hadn't seen him pop any such thing in his mouth.

Lucius and Lincoln did stop walking. I saw Lucius's shoulders come up in a *What? What did I do?* kind of gesture. He let the gun barrel to his Browning swing down and point at the earth, pivoting on the finger he had hooked in the trigger loop.

"Drop the gun," said Watson. I was impressed, distantly, by the level quality of his voice, by some intonation that suggested he'd done this a hundred times before, and nothing was going to go any differently today – he was going to get what he wanted as always. I wondered where Terry had originally found these guys. Were they recruits, or were they volunteers? Had they been altar boys somewhere? Were they soldiers? How many more like them were there? And I realized I didn't mind having them around so much anymore. They who had been my captors were now my protectors.

For some reason I found Lincoln's eyes just as he found mine. Even from some fifty or sixty feet away I could see the bloodshot in them, the yellow tint to the white surrounding the grey irises. I could see the folds in the skin over those eyes, and the way one particular wrinkle ran up one side of his forehead but not the other, and the skin around one eye drooped lower than the other – the same side as his shoulder. I looked down to his mouth, which curved down a bit to that same side. But still, Lincoln Brandis did not

look crippled. Terry Hackford, with his gimp, with his marred, once-
handsome face, seemed more crippled than Lincoln Brandis. There was
something surrounding Lincoln, something coming off of him, like a
pheromone, an aura that exuded strength – the kind of strength that a river
has, or a lake carved from glacial ice.

Lincoln didn't need a gun.

"I said drop it," Watson said to Lucius in that "let's get going, you old
hayfork" tone of voice. And Lucius shrugged again and let his Browning
plop onto Katherine Glaston's spongy front lawn.

But something was wrong.

Watson started forward then, started to walk toward the stairs,
ostensibly to go down and frisk and detain the two Brandis brothers.

You have no idea who you are dealing with, I thought at him, and
Terry leaned to me again and said.

"So?"

And I said, "Tell them to get back. We all need to get inside the
house, *now*."

Terry frowned at me and Crick snapped his gum and started to follow
Watson who was now descending the three front porch steps, his wingtip
shoe about to squish into Katherine's sod-lawn, the way Lucius Brandis had
squished, and I saw Lincoln's eyes again. I didn't like what I saw in them
because I saw remorse.

"Stop them," I said, but it was too late. Of course it was. We'd never
stood a chance. Lucius Brandis was no fool. He was a showman. He knew
how to focus attention, and how to divert it. He knew how to get what he
wanted from people. He knew he'd make a spectacle of himself just driving
right up to the house like that in an oil-black Bentley, getting out in broad

daylight with his black suit and winking silver wristwatch and Browning .45 automatic handgun.

No sooner had Crick stepped onto the front lawn behind Watson, the prepared attack came from both sides, where more Brandis brothers' men had been hiding. While I had been standing there staring at the whirlwind of flying papers, losing my mind once and for all, and before hearing the car engine and the door opening that had brought us all to the porch to see, the Brandis's men had arrived and positioned themselves at either side of the house and out of sight. As Watson and Crick funneled off of the porch, and onto the lawn, they were mown down.

I saw pink and flesh-white spray and a piece from the side of Crick's head disappeared. Both men were jostled about like puppets for a terribly long moment, held in the air by the ammunition tearing into them before crumpling into a heap at the bottom of those three porch steps. The Brandis men were using submachine guns. I yelled out something incoherent. I had just gotten to like Watson and Crick; even though Crick looked like he'd sooner I was dead, I'd liked him.

The firing stopped and my ears were ringing and the Brandis men revealed themselves, one stepping out of those hemlocks to Terry's and my left, the other just appearing from around the corner of the porch. The firing stopped but there was still some noise in the air, something that for one heart-palpitating second I thought was a siren – for the first time in probably my entire life I would have been happy to see police – but I soon realized it wasn't.

It was Leah, crying. Crying a high-pitched little girl cry. A scared cry.

I felt my bladder surge, to flop and seem to roll over in my gut like some eyeless, gossamer, living thing, and I felt something higher up from my stomach, something behind my ears and under the back of my jaw, something like a hot syrup come downing from the base of my skull and sluicing the nape of my neck and oozing into my shoulders and arms and back and everywhere, down to my toes.

I said I'd never kill again. I realized it was stupid to make promises to yourself you knew you couldn't keep. You only let yourself down, and what was the point of that?

"Leah!" I called out. The crying stopped. Lucius, bending to pick his gun back up, turned his head to look at me. The men – four of them all together, trotted over from either side of Lucius and Lincoln and gathered around them, weapons trained on Terry and me.

"Leah, honey," I continued, my voice loud but even, "get daddy a glass of water, honey. Can you do that?"

All of them – that was except for Terry's two eviscerated goons in the heap there – were watching me. I looked at each one of their faces, coming back to Lincoln last. Something seemed to flash and swim in those grey eyes of his. Something that reminded me of my bladder flopping around in my gut, like some mindless fish.

"Okay!" It was a muffled voice, a distinctly little girl voice, the sound of someone snuffling back tears and freshly eager-to-please. Then Katherine. "Jack! Jack? She's not going out there!"

I ignored that for a moment. I said to Terry out of the corner of my mouth but loud enough that the men on the lawn were likely to hear, "okay, I choose. I am going to go with them. I need to protect Katherine and Leah." Then, straight out of my mouth, leaning forward only slightly, realizing that my hands were laced together atop my head, Terry's too, though I didn't remember either of us doing it, I said to the group of them (but really, to Lucius): "I'll come quietly. I just need a glass of water. Please don't hurt the women. They have nothing to do with anything. That's the deal."

Lucius reholstered his weapon. He countenanced something completely different now. He'd been playacting before, affecting the dimwit mobster out of his element, the hack baddy who was all thumbs and impulse, mugging for us as he got out of the car and walked toward the porch. That had been a practiced act. This was the real Lucius now, the one who, I knew, couldn't stand that I was offering any kind of terms, that I was demanding anything, that I was even talking. He looked up at me with nothing but pure enmity. Any pretense of fatherhood he may have once shown me, to get me to do his bidding, was gone forever. The true Lucius Brandis had no need for me breathing; me, personally, that was; I was only alive because of what was inside of me. I could be tortured, though, without a doubt. Torture was the protocol here, no problem. Torture for anything and everything I knew that might be valuable to him, said tortures performed by Lucius and likely one or more of the men beside him, Lincoln standing in the background, watching out of his sloping face, out of those grey eyes, there to fetch a towel or a bucket of water or tinsnips for my lips, earlobes, nipples, to hand to Lucius for the cutting.

"Leah!" It was Katherine, muffled, inside, close to panicked. "Honey! No!"

The door behind me opened, just a little. I saw the men on the lawn stiffen. I saw another flash in Lincoln's grey eyes as he stood there, slumped like an old tree, but not weak, not sick, because he had it inside him. And he knew what was happening. Somehow, inside his hand-made sweater and plaid pants, this man who had never used a cell phone, a laptop or an iPod, somehow he knew what was happening.

I held up my hand, palm out, non-threatening, a white flag. *Peace.* They watched me, these men, and all but Lincoln seemed too dumbstruck to really know what to do, and Lucius's hate was temporarily supplanted with this bewilderment, even this amusement.

Now I was the showman. On my stage. On the porch. The little hand reached out with a glass about three-quarters full of water. No doubt her mother had taught her to not fill a glass to the brim, for it was likely to slop and spill. *You're a good mother, Katherine,* I thought at her, *oddball though you might be, kissing pictures of women named Ruth, you've raised our daughter well.* The glass was a *Speedy Gonzalez* glass. It was clear, with orange and reddish decals. It read "Speedy Snaps Up The Cheese!" and depicted *Speedy* happily evading a mousetrap and dashing away with a big piece of Camembert or Swiss.

I took the glass of water. I saw my daughter's little oval face there in the crack of the doorway, and then Katherine was there, above her, pain and fear in her eyes, and I looked back to Leah and she smiled and I mouthed "thank you" and took the glass to my lips, turning around so they could all see how harmless it all was, and Katherine pulled Leah away and the door snicked shut and the water then come to my mouth and I tilted my head back and drank. I saw Terry watching me out of the side of my eye. The water was cool and good and slightly metallic.

Marshall. Marcel. Machine.

I drank the water.

*

EFFIGY

My mother, humming. Rocking there by the window. She would look like she was content, but she wasn't. She would hum, and the humming was pleasant, and she would smile. And then one day she was no longer in her eyes. She was gone. I remember that day very clearly. I was twelve. I came in from school with my backpack wearing my shirt and tie and blazer and I had already secretly stashed a painting of mine in the stairway. (My father would later find it, but never say anything to anyone but me, even given the nature of the painting, the nature of the image, that giant fire and the people burning.) She asked me how school was and I set my bag down and the white curtains flapped at the window. The rocking chair where she sat was by the window she wanted to fly out of. She had her back to me as she fixed me something to eat. I didn't realize then how young she was. When she did finally turn and come to me at the table where I'd sat down she handed me the sandwich and said "there" and smiled and looked at me as she said "there," just for a second, I saw her eyes, and I saw that she was gone. It was a body standing there, it was my mother, the flesh of her, but she was gone. She left my father and me three weeks later.

At my father's funeral, when I was sixteen, I thought I heard my mother humming. But, of course, she never came. One morning, just before dawn, in the "gullet of night," Marcel used to call it, I was coming down from ecstasy and heroin and a fifth of vodka and laying in Battery Park feeling the most insurmountable despair I have ever felt and I thought I heard my mother singing, but of course she wasn't there.

I never saw her again, I never saw her since. You might say this is my epistle for her. My father already knows everything. I believe he sees life through me.

As I stood on the porch I felt the water flowing down and into me, like I had felt that fast, slick electric ooze that came before it. The adrenaline, or something like it, had been released upon my command, and now the water would feed my muscles, my glands, even my nerves – for water feeds everything: man, animal, plant, cosmos. The only reason Space is called space is because there is no water there. Water is both energy and matter. Water transcends even entropy, because water is already chaos and sameness.

My cells suckling the liquid, my glands soaking it up like sponges, my muscles drinking through the fibers. It was like working out, or stretching; yoga. The wriggling fish in my gut quieted and stilled. I set the glass slowly down on the porch now that I had drained it of its contents, holding my other hand up and out, sort of warding the men off, sort of that white flag, sort of just some universal gesture that says, "wait – for whatever reason, just wait. Everything – wait." And it did. And they did. They waited. Most likely out of some curiosity. And all was still, and all was silent, for a moment, except I thought I heard on the breeze my mother singing, but of course she wasn't there.

*

"Lucius," I said, "I found him."

"Come down here," said Lucius, and he used the business end of the gun to point from me to the ground at his feet. His voice was no-nonsense. There was that accent to it that seemed to bleed in some times. It reminded me, like it always had, of some Austrian or German *capo* at an internment camp. It was something that came out in his voice when he was at his most strict, his most unforgiving, so that "come down here," sounded like *kum dun heah.*

Terry looked at me, wide-eyed and questioning. I blinked at him once with both eyes. I'm not quite sure why. I left him there on the porch and went to Lucius Brandis and his men in their black suits.

"I found him," I said, walking to the edge of the porch, my hands out at my sides, palms out, fingers splayed. I started down the stairs. At the bottom, I had to walk around the pile of Watson and Crick bodies.

"Stop," said one of the Brandis men. I was about twenty feet away from the group of them. "Turn around," the same man said. I did. I rotated 360 degrees, my arms out, knowing the drill. I looked at Terry as I turned. He still had his hands on his head. He looked genuinely afraid.

Good thing about your clean conscience, I thought, but pushed it away. I still didn't know Terry's whole story; it was no longer fitting to judge him. It probably did no good to judge at all. I looked at the windows of the front of the house. The curtains were drawn in each of them. I saw no tiny oval face or hovering mother's face looking out at me. That was good.

I finished the rotation and kept my arms up and out. "I found Phil," I said to Lucius, looking him right in his green eyes. He had eyes that made me think of a giant cat. Like a panther.

He scowled at me. The change was a welcome one to his stone-face of complete disgust.

"I thought you may be involved." *I tot you may be invulffed.* "That's why we come here. You've always been a coward, so we knew you wouldn't have the balls to return to them."

For some reason I glanced over at Lincoln. Maybe I just wanted to read his eyes again, see what he was thinking. My glance caused Lucius to look over at Lincoln as well. Then he looked back at me, back at Lincoln, back at me. I almost laughed, but I didn't. That my whole body felt like it was burning helped to staunch the case of giggles. That my whole body felt like fires were licking through the channels of my veins, howling down the tunnels of my nerves, flapping and flailing and raging in the caverns and bowls and all pumping blood and oxygen kept me from breaking into a fit of it. That I was going to have to kill again after all, and at my daughter's house stayed my tittering. What was the point of promising yourself something you couldn't ever follow through on? It just made you feel guilty. And that was no good. And that, too, kept me from laughing.

I knew why the brothers were here, of course. I hadn't expected them to come to Katherine Glaston's house, that part I'll admit. But that they'd made the trip was exactly what I'd wanted. "I *mean*, Lucius," I said, "I *found* him. That was the whole reason you sent me up here, wasn't it? That was the reason for all of this?"

I watched Lucius thinking. I enjoyed that he didn't know what to say, but it was no longer funny. Nothing was. I helped Lucius through it, Good

Samaritan that I was. "I'm sorry, Lucius," I said, "I've finished my report. I don't work for you anymore. I'm out. I'm free."

Now his expression changed again. He was a handsome man once, no doubt. Now – and this seems crazy, maybe, but I've told you how my senses are extremely keen in these moments – I could've sworn I saw foundation make-up on his face. And that wasn't funny either. In fact, something about that was the complete opposite of funny.

The expression though, on that made-up visage, on that fake face, changed to what I'd hoped it would. He was dismissing me. He was going to "call my bluff." I glanced at Lincoln again, but furtively. Whether he knew what I was doing or not, I decided it didn't matter.

I took a step toward Lucius. One of the men closest to him racked a shotgun.

"I do this of my own free will," I said.

"I was suffering from what Dr. Madison called allostatic load. Sounds kind of porno, I know."

I sat in the backseat. Lincoln was driving this time. Lucius sat next to him in the passenger's seat. Once again I was flanked by two backseat goons. The one on the left of me smelled like menthol and was chanking on what had to be a cough drop. The one to the right of me seemed like he could fall asleep any minute, and I noticed him watching the scenery go by with the lack of recognition of someone kidnapped by aliens and observing the terrain of a strange planet.

Lucius was looking straight ahead, not saying anything, but I could feel him seething. It was a feeling like there was heat coming off him, the kind of heat that would make you throw up if you got too close to it. I swallowed and continued.

"So," I said, "I had the symptoms. Suppressed appetite, tingling, often numb hands and feet, heart palpitations. My mind was constantly perceiving danger. I was drinking to help get myself through all of that, but the flipside of drinking made it worse. Dr. Madison fixed it. He altered genes – at first I thought there was some addict-alcoholic gene he was going to wipe out," (I laughed for effect) "but it's a group of genes, with grey area, more or less responsible for as acting as a network that perpetuated the allostatic load. The conditions of modern living – those aren't genetic, but we do create the conditions as beings, so there is a relationship there – am I boring you, Lucius?"

He said nothing. I met eyes with Lincoln in the rearview mirror.

"Anyway," I said, sighing, as though I agreed with Lucius as to how boring and tedious it all was, "Madison induced mutation and also fixed me up with this handy ability to control my noradrenalin, or norepinephrine. Basically, I have voluntary control over a little thing called my amygdala. It's pretty dope," I said. I shrugged. My arms rubbed up against the goons on either side of me. I knew that I could shove both of them out of the doors of the moving vehicle. I could basically flex, just wing my arms out a little to either side and send the boys flying through the rear doors. But Lucius was as fast as a striking cobra – I knew from the few cracks on the jaw I'd gotten from him when I was sixteen and first started working for the brothers

– and he had a gun, and I didn't think I was capable of preventing, or surviving, that kind of attack just yet. Could be, but I wasn't certain.

No, I would continue with the plan, such as it was.

"Turn right up here," I told Lincoln. Then I said, "You ever hear of the locus coeruleus?" I looked first from one goon (almost asleep) to the next goon (suckling that cough drop like a newborn a teat) and then to Lincoln's eyes in the rearview mirror. He was watching the road, but he then looked up and at me. "I know," I said, "sounds like a constellation. Or a Mexican football team or something, I don't know. It's this warehouse of hormones in the brain stem." I leaned forward and managed to tap the back of my neck, around where I imagined my 'brainstem' would be. As I did I thought of Cameron Madison, tapping his temple, Terry his. "Stores hormones. And it stores norepinephrine. Know what that does?"

"Shut up." It was Lucius. His voice sounded like sharp stones to me. Maybe I had kinesthesia too; I'd learned over the weeks that I was borderline everything.

I went right on, ignoring Lucius. "What that does is causes you to be able to act quickly, to think super clearly. Problem is, guys, it sort of hinders your ability to make long term, long-range plans. So you sort of run on instinct, you know, you don't have to think, and everything is crystal clear. For the moment."

I wasn't surprised when Lincoln spoke. I'd been waiting for him, in fact. Even with all of the blows he'd taken to the head and even after his stroke, Lincoln Brandis was still the smart Brother. Oxford, Dublin, Paris Universities – he hadn't just boxed there. Lucius, on the other hand, had never finished high school.

"So you're telling us you haven't the ability to manipulate us, to trick us? I don't believe it, *kleinnes*."

Just be there. Just do what comes natural. You'll be alright, kleinnes.

I sat back. I had still been leaning forward from tapping at the back of my neck. The goon to my left shifted irritably, pushing his shoulder into me.

"Maybe," I said.

It was enough for Lucius who spun around, the Browning no longer in his lap but in my face.

When it came, I was ready. I leaned forward, and I let loose a tremendous yell. I leaned so that the end of Lucius's Browning was pressed against my forehead. I pushed into it. "Come on!" I yelled. "Come on!" I yelled that over and over, as the goons on either side of me struggled to get their weapons out and figure out what to do with the situation. Right at the time I heard the first weapon cock – the goon on my left, the one with the cough drop was faster – I shoved both of my arms out to the sides, palms out. Both rear doors of the Bentley exploded as the goons were thrust out of the vehicle where they smacked, rolling and tumbling and scraping, onto the asphalt. As soon as they were gone I grabbed the end of the Browning and ripped it from Lucius's hand. In only a couple of seconds I had now reversed the situation – the gun was in my grip, my finger in the trigger loop – and Lincoln had just begun to apply the brakes and slow the Bentley down.

I pressed the gun into Lucius's eye, still yelling something. I can't remember what I was yelling, only that when Lincoln brought the Bentley to a stop along the shoulder, I finally started making some sense.

"It's one thing that you would use me, Lucius, get me killed if it need be, *but you didn't have to involve her!*"

"Who? Who are you talking about?" Even though I had the gun on him, even though I had slammed both goons out the back of the car by extending my arms, wrenching steel and shattering glass and sending two two-hundred-pound men pavement-surfing, Lucius was not afraid. His words were a hiss through his barred teeth. His eyes were hard and seemed to vibrate in his skull. The pupils, I remember thinking distinctly, were like the shells of black spiders, balled up to play dead only a moment before springing.

"*Julianne*," I said, "*JULIANNE!*"

No reaction from Lucius, only those clenched teeth. "It's not my fault," he hissed, "if you had a whore with you when Richard got there."

I felt like smashing him. I felt like tearing those eyes out with my fingertips. I felt like yelling inanities; "He prefers to be called *Wild DICK!*" But I didn't. Instead, I looked sideways at Lincoln, sitting there, looking straight ahead, that one eye drooping, his breathing measured, calm.

We were like that, the three of us, for a little while. What broke our spell was the sound of one of the gunmen, one of the goons, calling for help further back along the road, a voice fading in and out with the gusts of wind that shook the stopped car.

I sat back then, spreading my legs, letting the gun dangle there in my crotch. My heart was thunderous; my whole chest felt like it was beating. My arms and legs felt like oak. My genitals were stones. I could smell ozone in the air – that smell of no-smell, that odor of a different kind of air, a burnished smell, something toxically clean. A bromide.

"Yeah," I said, "you have a point. She didn't have to be there. She wasn't supposed to be. I brought her there. It was my fault. Her death was my fault."

Neither of the Brothers said anything. I was starting to have the feeling, an awakening, really, something one comes 'round to after an outburst – the other people involved and the gravity of them, their presence, the ear-ringing reality returning to one's perspective at last. They were tolerating me because I had the gun. I was valuable, but not invaluable. I could be replaced, after all. Any lost time could be made up for. The science, perhaps, was even already ahead of what I contained in the infrastructure of my very being. I could be antiquated. It would still behoove all parties to keep me alive, yes. And that the Brothers wanted off the hook I had them on, wanted resolution, that was something. But nothing, I knew, after spending half of my life with these men, *nothing* was ever good enough to checkmate them. Checkmate didn't exist for them; they would kill your king soon as look at you.

"But I have you both to thank," I said, careful to include Lincoln as I cut my eyes back and forth between them. "If Baradez hadn't pumped me up with the junk before shipping me back from Costa Rica, I wouldn't be the miracle you see before you today." I saw Lucius's mouth open, just a little, at this reveal. In Lincoln, the lines in his face seemed to deepen; a trick of the morning's light through the trees along the road.

I heard something then, a dragging sound, a scratching beneath the wind. Like a branch along the pavement. I turned in time to see the cough drop goon appear in the space where one of the rear doors had been. I had time to see that half of his face had been grated away by the road, his eye wrecked, and that one shoulder and arm were exposed; one hand entirely blood and pulp, and then his gun came in and something flashed across my field of vision and all was black.

*

For a while I thought the sound of the fire was only in my dream. But when I opened my eyes I saw that it was real. I saw smoke drifting up toward a canopy of stars where a zephyr of wind tore away into the starred sky. Then: Wendy's upside-down face. Her hair was blowing around, a strand of it caught in her mouth.

She smoothed back my hair and placed something warm on my forehead. It stung, and I winced.

"That's a nice gash," she said. She pulled the hair out from between her lips. "You're a bloody mess again. After we fixed you all up."

"Am I dreaming? I can never tell anymore."

"No. But you're lucky, I'll tell you that. Peter found the group of you. You weren't too far from the camp – the last country route anyway – but he was out scouting." She rolled her eyes, and smiled. "He came across Lucius arguing with his brother outside of the car, off the road. Shouting about someone who'd knocked you out; they had no one to give them directions."

I laughed. I laughed and I noticed that, for once, miraculously, I didn't hurt anywhere. Not even my head. I put my finger tips there, to my temple, probing around. I felt numb. "Did you give me something? Where are the Brandis goons? Gone?" I imagined Lucius putting them out of their misery, dragging them off the road into the woods.

Wendy smiled an upside-down smile. It took me a moment, but I realized I was lying down in the back seat of the car, and the door was open and Wendy was standing there over my head.

"There were just the two Brandis brothers."

"Where are they?"

"They're eating."

I heard the fire give a couple of pistol-cracks and then a billow of smoke obscured the dark night's mouth of stars for a moment. "Jack," said Wendy, smoothing back my hair, and in my mind I saw her as she'd been in the greenhouse, making the little gun with her thumb and forefinger and pointing it at me.

"I know," I said. I got myself sitting, Wendy helped me. I looked at her. I wondered what her mouth would taste like. "What did they offer you?"

She raised her eyebrows. Then scowled. "What?"

"Before, at dinner the other night, I was putting it on, yeah. But they *did* offer you something for me. I want to know what. Was it a threat? 'Give him to us and we won't hurt you?' Or did they actually offer you something? Money? Soy? What?"

"Jack. Please."

I jerked my head around her; I craned my neck to look up over her shoulder. "You got a terminally sick kid around here somewhere? Needs a crucial operation the Brothers offered to hook you up with?"

She said nothing, only looked at me disapprovingly. Then she did say, "Jack, you know better."

"Do I?"

We were both silent then, the wind stirring around us, blowing bits of colored leaves and pine needles and dirt. I looked away and saw the fire. There were huge rocks around it, and it was far away from any trees or detritus. It purled from side to side in wild, impetuous lurches. It fluttered like a hundred tattered flags.

"Okay," I said to Wendy, "okay. Help me the rest of the way up."
She helped me stand up and get out of the ruined Bentley. On my feet in
front of her then, I watched her large hazel eyes watch me.

"I know," she said. I thought of Katherine. *I know. They told me
everything.* Then Wendy said, "I mean, don't they believe in anything?"

"No. They're from Brooklyn."

She smiled again, briefly, then scowled. I noticed that with Wendy
she was always either doing one or the other – smiling or scowling – and she
seemed to have no in-between. "Is that better?" She must've meant
standing. She had the cloth in her hand. "Yes," I said, and grunted and
leaned forward and stretched to touch my toes, something I don't think I'd
ever done before then.

The earth was cool to the touch of my fingers. I smelled dirt and
some wet leaves and gasoline. And I could smell the fire, permeating it all.
Three or more people – Naturalists, no doubt – were stoking the fire, I saw.
It was already about six or seven feet high and waving turgidly about. I saw
a small figure, a child, dash between two teepees. All around were the
humps of the Quonset huts, the pilings of the teepees, the low curves of the
three greenhouses. My eye was drawn back to the fire.

"Are you sure that fire is safe? In this wind?"

"Storm's supposed to blow over," said Wendy.

No it's not, I thought.

I had dreamt it.

*

I thought of women. I thought of Maya. I thought of Julianne. I thought of Wendy. Of Kristine. And I thought of Katherine. And Leah. Of course, Leah.

I thought of friends. Daniel. Peter. Jared.

I thought of the players. Terry Hackford. The Brandis brothers. Watson and Crick and Wild Dick. And, of course, Dr. Cameron Madison, who I'd killed.

And I thought of the many mysteries. The medical mysteries, yes. And the others. The threes. *Marshall, Marcel, Machine.*

I remembered: "Operating System Not Found," and I saw the bodies tumble through space as the van rolled off the road and into the gulch which would become the death-place of two men and the scene of one of my many escapes.

I thought of being manipulated, being puppeteered, being property, being sold, being bought, being experimented with, experimented on. I still wondered how real my choices had been. How could I distill what was a real choice? Were there any real choices?

It seemed all so connected.

And I thought of Leah. Leah, springing off of the counter with an octagonal shaped cracker in her hand, brown hair flowing as she raced down the back porch steps and into the garden. Where the pumpkins were.

Leah.

And I saw the fire again, only this time it wasn't a dream, or a memory, or a memory of a dream, this time it was in front of me. I had no more confusion. That didn't mean I had all of the answers, no. I just had no more questions.

It was time to meet with Terry, for the last time. And then we would meet with the Brandis brothers. One last sit-down. They would want to see Phil, alive or dead. I was banking on it.

So before I did anything else, I walked away from the fire, away from the clearing, to where the edging of woods inlet a small, rutted road, over to where Mike the FPR guy was sitting in his state-commissioned vehicle, a Jeep Cherokee, his face glowing in the distant firelight, drinking his coffee and dram.

I got in the passenger side, though I was no longer a passenger.

I was still dressed in Marshall Cohen's clothes. I thought of his wife, who had graciously fed me. I shut the door.

The interior of the smallish Jeep was warm. I realized how bitter the night chill had been becoming outside.

"How's it going, Mike?"

Mike took a sip from his tin cup and looked out at the fire through the front windshield. I looked there too. I saw some small shapes – kids – running around in the dusk and firelight. I thought of a giant, wooden bear. I thought of a giant man, a baby, really, a giant baby with torn clothes. *Whump whump whump* in the cell next to me. *Thud thud thud* of the chopper and Madison running over to it, ducking the way humans do around those huge spinning blades, his hair flattened to his skull, running over to meet the man in those aviator sunglasses that was Phil Brandis.

"How are you, Jack."

"I'm good," I said.

Mike looked over at me for a second. His head didn't turn so much as his eyeballs rolled. I could see the fire dancing in them. Mike was a big guy. He had one of those coats on with the big fluffy hoods. He took another sip from his tin cup. I could smell the booze in it, like a cleaning product fart in the air.

"Uh-huh," he said. And his eyes rolled back and he looked out at the fire again. "You still think they're going to go for this?" He asked. He didn't sound concerned. It sounded more like an obligatory question. Like chit-chat. We were shielded by the woods, tucked into the trees, but the wind still buffeted the sides of the vehicle and whistled through the evergreens. Leaves scrabbled at the roof.

"They have no choice," I said. "Lincoln – the one in plaid – he suspects something. I know he does. He's the smart one. But all Lucius can think of is his money. And without Phil behind Utopia, these Naturalists will compromise everything."

"What's to stop them from killing us all after they have him?" Mike's eyes rolled over to me again. I wondered if he was stoned; the eyes looked red and glossy. Maybe it was just the fire. Maybe he was drunk.

"Me," I said, and swallowed, and realized I was thirsty again. The air inside Mike's FPR Jeep was stale and dry. I could smell the booze in his coffee, a bit of B.O. and something that might've been animal pelt. What did I know about animal pelts? I was from somewhere else. Somewhere far away.

I thought of the Brandis goon in the car ride here, watching the scenery go past with what felt to me like mounting anxiety. Like someone on a trip to the moon, getting farther and farther away from Earth by the second.

"You?" said Mike.

I told Mike about what Terry Hackford had proposed to me in the hour or so we'd had before the Brothers had shown up. How, Terry (though a surprise) would work in to our scheme. I told Mike, and he drank his spiked coffee thoughtfully, scowling out at the commune and the fire, and then, finally, nodding. I told Mike not because it was an essential part of the plan, for him to know any of this, any of the details; the "after,"

(*operatingsystemnotfound*)

but because I liked Mike. For some reason the oversized woodhick had grown on me. Sitting there in his dark green, shiny jacket with the big furry collar and the patch that said "Forest, Parks and Recreation," I had developed a soft spot for the lug. Him and his hard coffee. Looking too big inside this little Jeep. Glaring out the window at the fire.

"Mike," I said.

"Mmm." Sip.

"Listen, I have one other favor to ask you."

"Mmm."

For some reason, before I could place my request, I thought of Calvin Blair. Calvin, who'd been shanghaied by the Brandis brothers. Extorted. And I had been set up. Wild Dick had been on their side. It had been staged and I was a pawn and all of it had been about money – money was what was at stake for the Brandis clan. Money meant power. If money came from the dog races, great. From shipping and receiving, fine. From experimental technologies – *patented* technologies dealing with biochemistry, the human genome, control over the frigging amygdala, fine, great, why not. And I remembered again that I was someone's property. I was the property of the

Utopia Corporation. The Brandis brothers were the primary stockholders, so I was really, then, property to them. How fitting it all was. Or would be.

But this wasn't kidnapping – well, kidnapping Phil Brandis was kidnapping – sure, sure, eye for an eye, stick that in your smashmouths, Brothers – this was something else.

"I need you to do something for me."

I could've asked Peter instead. We'd formed some sort of bond, yeah, alright, but Peter was still Peter. He was still B.O. and knuckleheaded ideas and wandering around in the woods with his dreadlocks bobbing. He was still a boy. I could've asked Daniel – and in addition to having to get back to Burlington in order to do so, that was too complicated. First, Daniel had some kind of unwitting part in all of this experimentation, and I wanted to stay away from that. I'd ask Marshall Cohen, but he had his own family.

Mike was perfect. Flawed, yes. But it felt right.

I said, "Check in on my daughter from time to time."

Katherine would never ask for support. She'd asked me to stay, yes, but I didn't think she'd meant it. And she had support – financial anyway – from her family. She was independent enough, and Leah had it good. But still, there was something here I just felt was right. Something for Leah from me. Just…I didn't quite know *exactly*, but just…a guy around was all. Just a guy here and there that could, just, be a *guy* around Leah. And who knew. He was about Katherine's age. And he was big enough to ward off any freaks that might decide to sit on her porch crying all night after she'd stopped screwing them. Yeah. Mike was a good candidate. I found myself smiling.

"Her name is Leah. Her mother, Katherine. I'll give you their address later, just before it's done." He wasn't looking at me, he was still looking at the bonfire. The small shapes of little people were still leaping around. I wondered where the parents were at the moment. It was only kids, it seemed. "Would you do that for me, Mike?"

He took a sip, and it was apparently the last. The tin cup was actually the top to a thermos-type container, and he screwed it back on. I saw a tear of brownish liquid running down the side of it. *Guy stuff*, I thought. I smiled wider.

Mike then wiped his mouth with his jacket sleeve and the back of his hand.

"Sure," he said.

"Thank you."

He didn't respond to this verbally, just a short, barely perceptible nod. Then he shifted, and he shifted so abruptly I jumped. He didn't notice. He reached around his waist and took a revolver from his holster. I remembered the gun. Mike popped open the chamber and started loading bullets into it. The leather seat squeaked under him and he grunted here and there. He spun the chamber and slapped it back in. Then he looked at me, this time turning his whole head and not just shifting his eyes.

"You ready?"

I took a deep breath. I needed one more good, tall glass of water, but otherwise, I was ready. I felt the old nerves jangle up inside of me for a moment, and panic threatened, but it was a very distant panic, like the rumble of a storm that has since moved off, growling over the earth and slipping further away, looking for fresh victims.

I was free. Free of drink, free of passivity, free of fear.

Almost. Almost there.

I thought of a song that I hadn't heard in years, one that Marcel used to play. Marcel was a damned eccentric, I thought. An original. The song was "I'm Your Captain," by Grand Funk Railroad. Why an overweight half Latino, half Italiano living in Prospect Heights listened to three white country boys was beyond me. But I remembered the end of the song, and the group's chanting lyric, or mantra, *"I'm getting closer to my home...I'm getting closer to my home..."*

I knew what they meant. And it wasn't a place in Bondville with two porches and a garden out back and a grandfather clock clucking and apple boxes everywhere. For some, yes. For certain lives. For certain Marshall Cohens and Marcel Morescos it was. For Marshall and Marcel, they were home.

I was Me. I was Machine. Property of something bigger, able to do what I could to ensure some measure of peace.

"Okay," I said, getting out of the Jeep. The air was even colder than I'd remembered, almost taking my breath away. The wind howled and whipped. I waited for Mike's lead – it was only right; he'd done so much of the legwork. He walked around to the back of the Jeep and popped the hatch. I kept watch on the clearing, until then, after the hatch door hissed up and open, I looked in.

Phil Brandis was lying there hog-tied and duct-taped over the mouth. His eyes fluttered and he then opened them wide and saw me. I waved at him. "I'm your captain," I sang in a hushed voice, "I'm your captain...return me my ship." Mike didn't even bat an eyelash.

*

I could go back if I wanted to.

I could go back if I wanted to.

That was the thing. That was the thing I was thinking as I walked to the greenhouse flanked by Terry Hackford and Mike the FPR guy, Wendy leading the way.

I had seen Peter, but only briefly. He'd looked confused, poor kid, and sort of half-waved, and let his jaw drop a little, like he was going to say something – either hi or goodbye, I could tell he didn't know which – and he had a shovel he was leaning on and he was dirty; I could see that even in the twilight. It reminded me of cleaning the gravestone with him and old Les. This was the last time I saw Peter. Or, well, it was the last time I knew Peter.

Wendy turned to look back at me, her jet black, shiny and somehow *pointy* long hair flipping over her shoulder. She looked at me, and she knew. Wendy knew what was going to happen. She was one of the ones who was sharp enough to read herself into the case. And she wasn't upset I'd used her, either; she didn't seem to be offended that I'd feigned offense and disrupted what should have been the dinner of my *entre* into the Naturalists. I no longer was making my mind up about Wendy. She was solid. And, like I said, she already seemed to know anyway, as though she had just been waiting for the cue to drop her own act and proceed with what her intuition had been telling her all along. Wendy knew, but she didn't give me that *be strong* look, I have to thank her for that. Maybe that was because Wendy was strong herself. Or, she was heartless and just didn't care. But I didn't think so. She was too plump to not care. Girls with nice full figures like

Wendy's, they cared. They cared because they ate good foods, the right foods, because they took care of themselves. Not that skinny girls couldn't care...

My mind was wandering away from what was important, spinning into those silly generalizations and cloudy vagaries, now completely detoxed from Dr. Cameron's wonder drug, his *uber*think serum. Wendy looked at me with her brown-almost-black eyes shining in the night, her face lit from the side by the popping, cracking, rippling bonfire, and there was just a stillness in her look – it almost felt like an emptiness to me. I remember it so clearly because it was one of the last moments. The last real moments, I mean, where I still felt like – well part of me did – that none of this was really happening, none of this was really real, that the screen was going to suddenly tauten and then ripple upward and the trees and fire and the whole fucking neo-hippie-yet-conservative compound and all of those dancing kiddies would disappear and it would just be me, left in my apartment in Brooklyn, the one I lived in after gramma finally passed, the last one I lived in before my trip up here, the last place I dwelled where I was fully, completely, blissfully inside my delusion.

Wendy continued forward, turning her head back to see ahead, that hair whipping again, that sharp contrast to her otherwise softness – that sharp hair and those empty eyes. But they hadn't been empty. They had been full of something else. They had been full of...*reality*. Something like that. Like what I'd seen shining through Terry at Katherine's house, yeah, but not just death. It was so hard to place, so hard to define – it was hard to understand then, when it happened, and it still is now as I write this, as I get to write all this down. It wasn't emptiness. It was fullness, almost completeness. I regretted then, in that moment, that I hadn't gotten a chance to know Wendy further – that out of all of them, from Maya to Katherine to Kristine – hell, even to Daniel – that I hadn't gotten to know them better, all of them, but especially Wendy, that Wendy could have been the one. Funny how that happens, funny how you spend all this time after the treasure and when you finally find it, you're dying.

"What do you think?" Wendy spoke to me in a whisper. Shadows moved around us. Silhouettes in the firelight. Murmuring voices, cracks of laughter.

"About?"

"All of this."

We were in step with each other now. I shrugged. I said, "I see war. I see revolution."

"Who wouldn't want to be cured of all their ails? Even if it meant...being owned?"

She was speaking rhetorically, I felt. And I was quiet. She pressed me, "but what do you *see*, Jack? Are we going to win this war?"

I couldn't help her then. I didn't have an answer. Maybe I still don't.

Terry, coming up on my left, was looking over my shoulder at the big fire. At the dancing kiddies. I looked there too and could see now that there were adults there after all, one in particular running after a little figure who was screeching with delight. The adult-sized figure was hunched over and running with comma-shaped arms in that *I'm-gonna-get-you* posture. Only now I did see a couple of adults talking, one of them with an armload of wood and the other apparently telling him not to put any more on. *Good idea*, I thought.

Mike drew up along side of Terry now, walking with his head down, the hulk of him. I had my own goons now.

I looked down at the bottle of water Wendy had given me – not spring water, no – Wendy was well-informed, she'd told me, that the bottling process of spring water, the chemicals in the new plastic and what have you – could be deadly. I thought of Costa Rica. But this, this was a bottle of water from a well right here on the compound. I lifted it to my lips and took a sip. It tasted good – sweet, almost. I never thought whenever I had heard or read about someone tasting water that was sweet that it was actually true. But it was.

Wendy opened the door to the greenhouse. I heard Terry, who was looking ahead again, suck in a breath. Not a big one, but I heard it. I remembered again when he has been the guy counseling me on the bench near the chess players that day, that day so long and so long and so long ago. Mike made a sound too, but it was more a suppressed hiccup than anything else.

I realized the smile was still on my face, and felt a tendril of water slip down the corner of my mouth, and the door opened and I saw the Brandis brothers sitting there, waiting for us.

And I thought, *There's no going back.*

Lincoln Brandis looked up at me with those steely grey eyes, the skin around them sort of sagging. That skin, sloping down and away toward his temples, that old-man-skin made his eyes seem even harder, like ore. I imagined one of his long ago opponents in the ring seeing those eyes, rethinking the stick and move to go into dentistry or horticulture as a career instead. Those eyes, I thought, were what had done most of the fighting.

Lucius Brandis sat with a rifle across his lap. His Browning hung from his Docker's clutch strapped around his now exposed shining grey dress shirt, the accompanying suit jacket since removed. His gelid blue eyes seemed to look everywhere and nowhere at once. They were the eyes of years of mistrust and paranoia and hate. Lucius looked very uncomfortable amid the begonias and turnips and sage and avocados that surrounded him.

One of the Naturalist members had set the room up with four chairs facing four chairs, with a couple of apple boxes upside down and stacked for a sort of conference table. I thought of Katherine. More, I thought of Leah, and her octagonal-shaped cracker, the curve of her little bow lips, the red bow in her hair. I wondered if my old red straw was still sitting there on the porch, or if the wind had blown it away or if, maybe, she had taken it inside up to her room and put it somewhere special and safe.

The way the chairs were arranged, I was reminded of a long ago meeting, back when I was someone else. In Utopia, back when I was locked in a cell next to something that pounded *whump whump whump.*

Lincoln and Lucius sat flanked by their surviving two goons. I wondered, though, where the other two were, if they were really dead and dragged away like I've figured, or if they were still alive and gruesomely patrolling the area; that they were out there in the night lurking behind the dancing children, in the shadows beyond the bonfire, both road-wrecks, bleeding and disfigured and insane. Wind rattled the greenhouse panes, and then, as I thought might happen, the first big fat drops of rain started smacking into the special UV glass. At the same time, someone outside, a girl, screamed.

Everyone in the room who was already seated stood. The rest of us turned towards the door. A Naturalist member – *the greenhouse keeper*, I thought, a short man with a bald pate atop his head – went scrambling by.

Wendy held her arms out in a *sit down it's cool* gesture and we three, Terry, Mike and I, took the chairs opposite all of us watching the Brothers, and then Wendy sat down last. Now I felt like I was back home at one of those few seminars Banjul Banajab had made us truck monkeys and drivers attend, and there had been a hot power-business-woman with a phone or a microphone or something attached to her ear and sticking out in front of her mouth. She'd told us how important we all were to the business and client. *We* were shipping and *we* were handling – *we* were the ones that were the beating hearts, the strong backs behind those two little words *shipping and handling* every time a customer ordered from Amazon or Crate & Barrel! Us!

I thought of my father sneaking around with his bleeding nose and his coughs and his terrible, holy paintings tucked up into the crotch of his armpit and hidden in the stairs above our little shitty Fort Greene apartment. My mother and her power. Her power to leave us. Her power to help kill my father.

There was more commotion outside. Shouting. The rain was smattering the roof in those big pearly drops like snot-comets from the sky.

"Is everything alright out there?" It was Lincoln. I thought he sounded genuinely concerned, and I wished he didn't.

"It's okay," said Wendy. "Not a good night for the fire after all, maybe. They'll see to it."

What would I have done should my mother have shown up in that moment? That moment, right there, sitting across from the Brandis brothers, holding on to my every wit, gritting my teeth to face my fate? Would I have relented? Finally receded from the deal upon seeing her face, hearing her hum a tune? What if she had come drifting into the room? What if she told them all she wanted to take me back, that she was sorry, so sorry, that she was so sorry she had left me, her baby, her baby boy and she held me to her breasts and rocked me and hummed and sang to me? Would this meeting adjourn? Would the Naturalists disband? Would everybody, shoulders sloped, head dropped, sluggishly walk away from all of this, like people caught by their parents at a party, or coming down from some drug, or waking up from some ridiculous notion or scheme or revolution? How many revolutions had risen and faded away over the face of human history?

"Then, gentlemen," Wendy said, startling me a little, "should we begin?"

"The fuck is this place?" Lucius, elegant as he dressed, slick as he looked, was never one for table manners.

"This is one of our greenhouses," Wendy answered, nonplussed. She crossed her legs primly. "I thought it a suitable place to meet," said Wendy, with no trace of defensiveness or deference. Wendy, the Neutral Naturalist.

Lucius just snorted. "Let's get on with it," he said. "Where is my nephew? Is he alive, or dead?"

"He's alive," I said.

"Alive or dead," Lucius said, not surprising to me, "I want my nephew. You know this." Lucius looked right at me. His eyes still had that unfocused quality, but he looked at me. The eyes looked unfocused because he was also looking at what he hated, and what he hated was a shapeshifter, a hovering poison, a quicksilver mirror. "I hired him to find my nephew," Lucius said, speaking to Terry and to Wendy, "and now he tells me he has

kidnapped my nephew." Lucius pointed a finger at me. It was a straight
finger, as Lucius did not suffer the knobbed, twisted arthritis his brother
Lincoln did. "I get a call; I get a phone call that Philip has been kidnapped.
That I must come and meet with him in order for him to be released. I didn't
think he would show," said Lucius, and snorted, looking at me. I wondered,
a little, why he was going on like this and it occurred to me then that the
human in Lucius Brandis – the organism (like the fake house where the
otherworld waited) – that could be vulnerable, like anything else. "I figured
he would try and play house."

"You misled and used him," said Terry, sounding much like a defense
lawyer to me – I'd heard a few speak on my behalf over the years.

Lucius snorted again. "He belongs to me, to us. We can do with him
what we like. We own him. I could kill you all right now and take Jack
with me back home and be protected to the full extent of the law."

"You couldn't," said Wendy, "but your corporation would shield you,
yes. Utopia would shield you."

Lucius ignored her. He suddenly sneered at a plant next to him, and
brushed away at it brusquely. I thought to myself that there were two sides
to Lucius, from what I remembered – petulant and angry, and then, the other
Lucius, the one that had never seemed human to me, the one that had always
seemed puppeted by something else. He looked back at Terry now, and me.

"I could kill everyone in this whole fucking place," Lucius said, and I
realized that that other thing, the one that could get into him and use him,
was near.

He stood up. He had a firm grip on the rifle. I saw out of the corner
of my eye Mike's hand move to the butt of his own firearm. Outside, there

was another scream. Even over the wind and rain I could hear the crackle of flames. The fire had spread.

Wendy drew a breath beside me. I knew she was thinking of the children. That would be the only thing that might make her lose her cool.

"What do you *WANT*?!" Lucius bellowed. "Didn't you know this was coming? This is what the whole deal had been about? He–" Lucius pointed the rifle at me "-lures us here with my nephew as bait? We negotiate with you to shut down Utopia–"

Wendy cut him off. "–To stop the experimentation on unwitting subjects in Burlington and in the North Kingdom. That's what we asked. Those were the t–"

"Like you're going to stop there." He glared at her, and Wendy, not to her discredit, flinched. Lucius raked her up and down with his eyes. "I know you," he hissed. His tongue came out and swabbed at his lower lip. I looked at Lincoln. His head was down, his hands folded in his lap. "We agreed in order to get Phillip's body back so he doesn't make any local newspapers that spill into national newspapers. Uh?" He jabbed the gun in the air at her, his accent thick, his face blood red. "You give to us Phil, we leave the area. Do you think I'm that stupid? That you just go away? No. I'm not. In time, you'll come back. Asking for something else. Fucking with my business. You slippery *cunt*."

Now the sky opened up. I saw, looking up, that it had taken no time for the stars to disappear as the clouds had rolled in, covering all. The rain pummeled, like the rain had pummeled back when I was in that cell. Outside, there were more shouts and screams. I looked at Wendy. I felt how badly she wanted to go out there.

I looked at Lucius, where he stood, seething, and I got to my own feet.

"Stop," I said. I saw Lincoln look up. "There's one more thing, Lucius. You have to let Maya Burns and a young guy named Jared go free. You will have Phil back, alive, I promise. And, no, Wendy probably won't stop. Or the Naturalists. Or Terry and his Jesus Team. They won't stop because, to you, it's just business. To them, it's *life*, and there's nothing more important." I took a quick breath. "You old motherless immigrant."

Lucius's face was blank, unreadable. I expected more remonstrations, I expected more of his spewing hatred, but that's not exactly what I got. Instead, I finally, and utterly, knew that I was no longer dreaming. That I wasn't going to wake up. Have you ever had a dream of dying, old pal? I know you have. I know we all have. It's as inevitable as cutting a tooth or laying down the motorcycle. You dream that you are dying, or going to die, or are already gone, and you are filled with something more than dread, something well beyond reason or rational reduction. It is, really, an otherworldly feeling. But then you wake. You wake and you are grateful and, I suppose, such is the purpose of the dream. But, like I said, I was not dreaming. I was fully awake. I was fully present as Lucius Brandis set his gun down on the earthen floor of the greenhouse and came at me, his hands out, going for my throat. I was completely in-the-moment, you might say, as we toppled over, him on top of me. Wendy cried out. Mike got out of his chair, brandishing his handgun, the goons then training their firearms on Mike. It was total, complete, bittersweet reality as Lucius pinned me, crushing my head into the dirt, gripping my neck with such ferocity I thought the finger nails would sink right in. His teeth barred, a spindle of drool hanging from his lower lip, his eyes wide and inhuman, his face infused with blood, he was the beast, he was the panther, he was the *other*, having broken through our little game of life. The Other was now here in

the room with us, something I would never want to see again and never wish
on anybody, so help me God.

I got Lucius off of me. What I did was I bend my knees and shoved
upward with my legs and pushed to the side with both of my hands. When
his grip came loose, I felt something in my neck go, something that felt cold,
and felt as though it had been exposed, and knew then with such certainty
how frail we humans were, how the molecules of our bodies were only that,
molecules, and that the right beast could rip through our flesh like butter.

And so I was on top of Lucius then, now looking down at him, and I
knew I could crush his skull, and I knew Wendy was still shouting, and that
Mike and the goons were still shouting, and that Terry was watching,
helpless, as I dipped my head down, bit into Lucius Brandis's neck, and tore.

I stood up. I looked down and watched him.

His mouth opened to say something; his mouth worked and his eyes
rolled and he held his hands against his own neck and throat now, feeling
around. The goons approached and cocked their weapons and pointed them
at me as I turned, and both of them stopped, and they looked at me, and I
could feel the blood running down my own neck, and around my mouth.
Beneath me, Lucius Brandis spurted from the neck and tried to speak and
died. I looked at Lincoln, his only brother. Phil was the nephew of their
sister, dead of complications from the birth of her elusive son. I looked at
Lincoln and the goons stood still and they looked at him too. Wendy had a
hand over her mouth. I could see that any chance I may have ever had with
her was infinitely wiped out. As with any chance I had ever had at living
life in general. I was a faulty machine. Born to self-destruct.

The rain beat and drummed and the wind howled but somehow
Lincoln's words we all heard; they were the loudest, a quiet man though
he'd become.

"It's a deal, *kleinnes*," is what he said.

I turned to Wendy, and I looked toward the door. "Go," I said to her.
Her eyes searched me. She then took her hand from her mouth, swallowed,
and took a handkerchief from a nearby shelf and handed it to me. Finally
she stood and hurried out. The door flew open behind her, immediately after
she'd closed it behind her, and sheets of rain swept in. Terry rose and sealed
it closed again. It took a moment before I realized what the handkerchief
was for. Then I began to blot at the blood – Lucius's blood – around my
mouth and chin, as I had blotted with the napkin during my last supper with
the Naturalists some time before.

"Where is she going?!" Bellowed a goon. "And who is *he*?" The
goon seemed suddenly unsure of everything, now pointing his gun at Terry.

"That's my friend Terry," I said. "Make the call please, and my other
friend Mike here will return with Phil." Mike still stood with his gun out at
hip level, like a cowboy. He looked at me.

I stood a few feet away from Lincoln. The rain was now omnipresent.
The wind shook the greenhouse.

"Jack," said Lincoln, trapping me with those granite grey eyes, those
somehow compassionate eyes, *mein kleinnes* – those eyes showing you
compassion as he beat your face in with fists, back in a long ago time before
those fists had become gnarled and knobbed with arthritis. He had that
slight slur to his speech, but still spoke with more wisdom and authority than
a dozen imperial Luciuses. "While you may have done this, while you have
killed my brother, while you may have Phillip – if you know that he is not

worth our corporation, then why barter with it? You must have something else to offer. We do, of course, have a responsibility to our shareholders, and to modern medicine."

And, I tell you, I swear to my sweet gramma in her rocking chair who might've said, "you-a gonna wear dat?" to Lincoln, in his plaid pants and homemade sweater, that the old boxer winked at me.

Stick, move. Move, counter move. I'd just ripped someone's neck out with my teeth, and the world of business went on.

"Lincoln? Lincoln? What? You're going to–" The speaking-goon was antsy, like a child. Confused. Lincoln cut him off, saying, "Be quiet, Mickey."

And so I threw my final punch. No longer would it have to be explained what had been done to me, exactly, what I had been endowed with – maybe it would have to be proven for others to sign off on it, but it would work, because they could run tests, they always had their tests, because I was Dr. Cameron Madison's prime creation. I was his golden goose. And, "because," I said, wiping the blood from my mouth, then holding the cloth to my bleeding neck, "I'll give myself up to you. You can have me, and all I hold inside of me. I'm yours."

The rest of the night we worked at batting out the fires. The rain took care of most of it, but not completely in time. Four of the nearest teepees had been snagged by the windblown blaze, and burned to the ground. Only the few other structures, a couple of yurts in the distant perimeter of the clearing, the greenhouse, and a round, living-roof home (serving as a kind of headquarters and post office) were untouched. More teepees were singed and a wooden cabin was still smoking. Mike called in other FPR rangers who came and caught the blaze from spreading too far into the woods. By the time the rain and firefighters had saturated all, damage was significant. There was talk of disbanding for a time, of rebuilding somewhere else.

Terry Hackford. Terry and I had had a nice discussion indeed. Terry was working on gutting the Utopia operation from the inside out – he already had a counter team (of whom Watson, Crick and Maya Burns had been chief members) working on sabotaging all of the science and research that fed the Corporation. It made sense, change coming from the inside, not the out. This seemed fitting to me.

I was basically in custody – again. I left the Quonset hut the following morning with two Brandis goons flanking me. They paraded me out into the dreary, rain-soaked morning so that remaining Naturalists stopped their clean-up work and looked over at me, adults and children alike. I didn't see Peter anywhere. The song surfaced in my head again, *I'm getting closer to my home...* and this time I realized that it was actually playing, that somewhere someone had a boombox or something and the Mark Farner-penned opus was pealing away, reverberating in the trees. I thought of Costa Rica, and the elegant pantry-cabinet with all of the liquor and the stereo with speakers going all through the house and the Allman Brothers singing "Whipping Post." And Julianne.

You rest now, Julianne.

Wendy's eyes were different then, and as one of the goons (*ex-cop,* I thought) tucked my head into the back of the Brandis brother's Bentley, I could see that Wendy's eyes were wet, and that she was straining to hold back emotion, which was, as you know, pretty unlike Wendy. It was surprising to me considering what I'd done in front of her. Her hands were black to the elbows with soot, and her face was smudged with it, her eyeliner run into black tears. She didn't say anything, and I'm kind of glad that she didn't, and thankful to her for that. I don't know why. Just that if she had said something then this would sort of end up like some cheesy romance story, which you know it's not. Or, at least, it hasn't been, has it?

The one goon there, the one who had been looking out of the window on the way up to the Naturalist commune like he was observing planet Mars – the one Lincoln had called "Mickey" – was babbling excitedly into a cell phone, telling someone named Danatisha that he was coming home. Lincoln glanced over at him with a look that would have most men pissing down their legs and Mickey snapped the phone shut, lost his smile and got into the other side of the backseat beside me. The goon who had stuffed me in, I didn't know his name yet (*ex-cop*), got in after me into the driver's seat.

Lucius's body was to be retrieved by members of Utopia and tended to and shipped home appropriately. I envisioned the funeral, and Lincoln's eulogy, which would be terse, heartfelt, and completely untrue.

All tucked in, I watched as the old fellow got in the front, ostensibly doing so with a bit of discomfort, maybe even pain. Lincoln then had a word with Wendy after rolling his automatic window down.

I looked around outside of the car. The goon driver had left his door open while preparing something – a map. The dismal morning was like a twilight, and with the car's dome light on I could see as much of the reflection of the Bentley's interior and as the vague shapes outside. I saw a vehicle pull up and two people get out. It could have been Maya and Jared.

Likely it was. They stood together looking on with the rest of the Naturalists. Then the goon shut the door and the overhead light went out, at first dimming, and then gone. The vague shapes closest to the car became Terry and Mike. I had been able to see my own reflection and little else – me, there in the backseat of the Brandis brothers' car, on his way back home at long last. And then, along with the dome light, I faded and was gone and Terry and Mike remained.

Lincoln was done talking to Wendy, his window droning back up; I couldn't see her. I didn't want to. If I saw her I knew I might suddenly cave. There was that last bit left. I knew it. Better, I figured, that I looked on the ugly mugs of Terry and Mike last. They kind of reminded me now, you know, of Ryan and Victor from the good old days, the days of stomping on George Klembeck until his skull cracked. But, these guys were better. At least, well, as messed-up as it was to think like it given the circumstances, these days were better.

Terry held up a hand. Mike reached into his jacket and produced a flask. I smiled. I waved back and Mickey, next to me, looked over and frowned, then turned to the window and lifted his own hand and waved like he was a fairy, mocking us. It made me smile harder, I don't know why. I thought of Daniel, and I thought the whole thing would've had him in stitches. He had that kind of humor.

The car pulled away. Terry Hackford and Mike the FPR guy and Wendy – the lead coordinator of the Naturalists – were gone. As were Maya and Jared, if, that was, it *had* been them standing there , and I hoped it had.

The Utopists in charge of Lucius's body had been given explicit directions to pick up Phil Brandis from Mike, where the nephew of those notorious Brooklyn fences still lay, no doubt resting comfortably, in the back of Mike's Jeep.

And then I was driven away.

I got a new doctor. That was what happened next, and, really, last. It was like Dr. Cameron Madison was reanimated. Sort of. Maybe it was just a ghost of the grand prick I saw in the new doc's face.

This was in Long Island City, Queens, like I mentioned. This is where I am now.

Long Island City, Queens, is a place I'd been quite a few times before. This is where stuff was held when someone went to jail. There are buildings full of evidence lockers, big warehouses of them. Sometimes I think about the little busts I made, back when I was a snoop, and wonder if any of those fake watches are here in one of these buildings, near where I am. Near where I grew up, near where my father died.

This is also the place where the Brandis brothers had the new labs set up for Utopia. There was a whole other operation running here, but I can't talk about that too much. That's part of the deal. I trust now, though, in Terry – *In Terry We Trust* – and that's been a help getting me through these last few days. Plus, I'm still sober. So, there's that.

The final deal, anyway, was this. Or, really, the one small stipulation on my end; I wanted to write all of this shit down. I had to. I was afraid that if it was all still in there when they…did the thing, – *operating system not found* – that my head would blow-up or something. For real.

I don't know. My stipulation was reasonable, I think. Just to write all of this down and give it to one person. One person that I knew wouldn't feel endangered, wouldn't feel compromised by knowing any of this. Because, really, what have I told you, anyway? All these names could be faked. All of the places rearranged.

And so Marcel, old pal, by the way, all of my paintings are hidden under your stoop, where we used to sit. Not *under* the stoop, not exactly, you big boob, but in the laundry room right below there, in the basement. You'll know where to look. Take care of yourself, and Jocelyn.

So, this about wraps it up.

I really don't know what else to say.

I mean, I guess you've figured it out. Or, figured out your own version. I was a pretty good trade, I think. For what I've learned to do, for what I was given. I am a monster. A ticking time-bomb. You can't have someone like me walking around free. That's for other people. That's for the Peters and the Daniels of this world. That's for my daughter, Leah.

I think of this now, this missive, or story, or journal I wrote down (what's a missive, anyway?) as like a warm-up. A way of cleaning house, of getting ready for the big demolition. The big sweep.

That's something my gramma would do, I think. She'd clean the whole house so it looked nice before the wrecking ball came through.

God bless you, gramma.

I love you.

*

-tjb

February 5, 2006-
May 12, 2009
Lake Placid / Vermontville, NY

the end.

www.ingramcontent.com/pod-product-compliance
Lightning Source LLC
Chambersburg PA
CBHW031141050726
47495CB00018B/284